MW00657581

Hidden Shadows

Linda Lucretia Shuler

To Randy,
With much appreciation for your financial wizardry,
Linda

Twilight Times Books
Kingsport Tennessee

Hidden Shadows

This is a work of fiction. All concepts, characters and events portrayed in this book are used fictitiously and any resemblance to real people or events is purely coincidental.

Copyright © 2015 Linda Lucretia Shuler

All rights reserved. No part of this book may be reproduced, stored in a retrieval system or transmitted in any form by any means electronic, mechanical, photo-copying, recording or otherwise, except brief extracts for the purpose of review, without the permission of the publisher and copyright owner.

Twilight Times Books
P O Box 3340
Kingsport TN 37664
http://twilighttimesbooks.com/

First Edition, December 2015

ISBN: 978-1-60619-009-8

Library of Congress Control Number: 2015948424

Cover art by Brad Fraunfelter

Credits
"Lady stranger wearing a smile." Lyrics © 2015 Linda Lucretia Shuler
"Girl, you're for me, girl." Lyrics © 2015 Linda Lucretia Shuler
"Ain't it grand." Lyrics © 2015 Linda Lucretia Shuler
"I wish I were a little fish." Lyrics © 2015 Linda Lay Shuler
"Ice queen, ice queen." Lyrics © 2015 Linda Lucretia Shuler
"My sweetheart evermore." Lyrics © 2015 Linda Lucretia Shuler
"Until we meet again." Lyrics © 2015 Linda Lucretia Shuler
"This here ol' house." Lyrics © 2015 Linda Lucretia Shuler

Printed in the United States of America.

For
Linda Lay Shuler
Mother, Mentor, Friend

Sing to me in the shadows
Come to me in evening quiet
While my heart awaits the dawn
And the sun upon the fields

Mountain Waltz

Summer, 1996

DEATH WAITED TO DANCE FOR HER THROUGH THE EYE OF THE CAMERA. IT WOULD be a slow dance, graceful as a waltz against a slate blue sky.

She gazed at the view framed in the lens, unaware of danger: Colorado mountains rising all around, glowing pink and purple in the morning sun. Her husband Thomas grinning on the precipice of a sheer cliff, the canyon wide and deep behind him. A golden eagle hovering above, drifting silent in the winds, wings outspread like a dark angel descending.

All she had to do was press her finger, one small click, and the photo would be taken. Yet she hesitated, wanting this moment to last.

Thomas grew restless, waved at her to hurry, pulled a cap from his jeans pocket and rammed it on his head. "Going to take all day?" he teased. "C'mon, Cassie girl. Everybody's waiting."

The air smelled of fecund earth and crushed leaves and coffee warming over a campfire. Cassie glanced toward the scattered tents and the handful of friends who had traveled with them. No one seemed in a hurry. After a long week of roughing it, they likely welcomed the last few hours of leisure before heading separate ways, as did she.

There was something magical about this mountain, this breeze warm upon her skin, the shifting colors and glowing sky, the soaring eagle. And Thomas, standing like a young oak that had sprouted from the rock, a natural part of the elements with wildness in his blood.

The camera was an old Nikon with a bulky zoom, and hung from a strap around her neck. "On the count of three," she warned Thomas. "One, two..."

She snapped the photo, the sound swallowed by the eagle's cry. The bird dived into the canyon, the shadow of its great wings sweeping across the precipice. Cassie saw it through the camera's eye, saw Thomas and his startled response, his head jerking upward, his foot stepping back, the rocks beneath crumbling away.

Time and motion slowed as if in a dream.

Thomas stretched out his arms as though he, too, were about to lift from the ground and fly. Then he seemed to float backward, softly slipping from the cliff edge. His cap lifted away, light as a fallen leaf carried by the wind.

He looked directly at her, mouth agape as if wanting to speak, and dropped from sight.

Cassie ran toward the empty space where he once stood, the camera whacking her chest, seeing everything, seeing nothing, a scream ripping her throat. Her red hiking boots flashed forward and back as her feet propelled her on and on. Red boots, red as blood, red as the fear roaring in her heart.

She teetered on the precipice. There, far below, sprawled face upward on a jagged outcropping as though sleeping in the sun, was Thomas, still as the stone he lay upon. Wind touched his wheat-gold hair, lifted the hem of his shirt, tasted the blood spreading from the back of his head like the bloom of an exotic flower. Ruby tendrils reached for the edge and dripped into the canyon depths.

"Thomas!" Her cry echoed among the mountains, *Thomas! Thomas! Thomas!* "I'm coming down!" *Coming down! Coming down! Coming down!*

She stumbled along the rim in a frantic search for access. The mountains yawned as if cloven with a knife, the sides shimmering, the floor sinking into shadows. Afraid of tumbling into the vast emptiness, she dropped to her knees and crawled along the precipice, pebbles and debris raining down from her scrabbling hands.

God help me!

A root thrust a gnarled arm from the wall some ten feet below. If she could somehow manage to get to it, then to the narrow shelf below that, and then…

How far down had Thomas fallen? Her mind couldn't calculate. He looked so small from where she knelt, so *abandoned*, like an unwanted doll.

Oh, God! Oh, God!

She lay flat, the rock-strewn earth digging into her stomach and legs, and stuck her feet over the lip. She could feel the tug of the wind as she inched downward, fingers grabbing at the dirt, her boots seeking a hold. Grit caked her teeth. She was sobbing, unaware of the sound, thinking somewhere in the deep recesses of her mind that she heard the anguished cries of a wounded animal.

Then she was airborne, lifted by a half-dozen hands and hauled onto level ground. She struggled against the arms that held her fast, the clamor of voices, the contorted faces. They dragged her to safety, the precipice receding through her tears.

She couldn't breathe. Her body shook and turned cold. They laid her on a sleeping bag and wrapped her in blankets, constraining her like a mummy while the sun slid across the sky and the eagle returned to its flight, wings glittering.

Thomas. Her lips formed his name. She looked up and imagined it was he who soared across the blue, gliding in the winds as if his spirit had risen free and now gazed down upon her. The bird dropped closer and closer still, transforming into metal and roaring as it dipped into the canyon and disappeared. Dust whirled in torrents from the blast of its wings.

She tore the blankets aside and lurched upright, clinging to the hands she had once fought. She had no sense of minutes or hours, only of an icy numbness that settled into her bones.

Whap-whap-whap! Propellers rose from the abyss, lifting the helicopter, lifting the basket that swung from its belly and carried her love. Even from this distance she could see the gold of his hair, the silken texture. The helicopter hovered like a giant prehistoric bird, then began its journey. She stumbled after it, the shadow slithering along the rugged mountain, until it vanished into the horizon.

The Ghosts Are Singing

Summer, 1999

THREE YEARS HAD PASSED SINCE DEATH DANCED ON THE COLORADO MOUNTAIN — one thousand eighty-odd long days shadowed by grief.

Cassie drove with the window down, squinting into the glare as miles slowly passed and the Texas sun blazed hot in the noon sky. Gnarled oak, honey mesquite and cedar crowded for room in the rocky Hill Country soil, crawled up outcroppings and plateaus, and butted against prickly pear cactus, purple-stemmed grass, and the occasional cow or goat. Willow City Loop, the road was called. An odd name, since there was no city. Just a couple of buildings missed in the blink of an eye. And the loop straggled with dozens of turnoffs, gravel-tossed and rutted and often identical, rambling to pastures or buildings unseen from the road. Fortunately, the one she sought was marked by boulders tumbled in disarray like the ruins of an ancient castle, setting it apart from the rest.

She longed to be thirteen again, worry-free and anticipating the summer ahead in her grandmother's home among the hills. But here she was, old enough to be mother to the girl she barely remembered, driving under that same sun toward the same home, now holding only echoes of long-ago days.

I'm still not ready for this.

The renovated Thunderbird jounced across cattle guards, through gray-weathered wooden gates, and past split-rail cedar fences. Little had changed since she was a girl traveling this dusty road in her grandmother's creaking Studebaker. She could almost smell the bitter scent of torn leather and hear the rattling complaints uttered by the car they had christened Methuselah since it seemed destined to live forever. Mimi would drive it like a madwoman, stomping on the gas and grinding the clutch as if in a battle of human against machine.

Oh, Mimi, how I miss you!

Thoughts of her beloved grandmother often came unbidden, and with them the memory of Mimi's hands clutching hers for the last time.

"Promise me!" Mimi had sighed, pale and shrunken amid the rumpled bed sheets. "Promise!"

"I'd like to, but..."

"Live there one year, that's all I ask. You'll make the right decision after that."

"But how?" Something clattered in the hall beyond the door, followed by a spurt of laughter. Cassie paused, startled. Gaiety seemed out of place in this dreary nursing home. She squeezed Mimi's fingers, surprised at how spindly her bones had become. "Thomas and I just opened a boutique, remember? *Spirit of the Southwest.* I may be an old lady before I have time to spare."

"Go when you can. The land will wait."

Cassie nodded, "All right, I promise," loving this worn-out old woman who bore little resemblance to the vibrant soul she remembered. When had her grandmother withered into a husk? She leaned in close, her breath stirring wisps of the silver-streaked hair. "Why me? Why not Mother?"

"She can't… hear them."

"Hear what?"

Mimi closed her eyes, her voice a mere shadow. "The ghosts are singing."

"There are no ghosts here," Cassie said gently. "Just me."

"They sing for you," Mimi murmured, and said no more. She never opened her eyes again, nor spoke.

Had someone told Cassie that in only a half dozen years from that moment she'd fulfill the vow made at her grandmother's bedside, she'd have laughed in disbelief.

But now there was nothing to hold her back. Nothing and no one.

There, finally! The marker she was looking for: a jumble of boulders under an arching mesquite, a wooden plank nailed to the trunk. A sun-bleached arrow pointed toward the hill beyond with the words, *Spring Creek.* She turned and winced. Gravel pinged and splattered under her treasured Thunderbird and exploded from the wheels as she bounced along rutted dirt hard as concrete, winding upward until Willow City Loop became a ribbon curling far below.

She didn't see the armadillo until it was too late. It froze in the middle of the road, mesmerized by the oncoming monster. Cassie yelped and swerved, bumped over jagged rocks, crashed through prickly pear, then nose-dived into a shallow ravine. The motor sputtered and died.

She sat with hands clenching the wheel and foot pressing the brake. After a moment, she opened the door, almost afraid to look. Briars scratched her bare ankles as she walked up the incline and down again, bracing her hand against the car, eyes sweeping every inch of metal and chrome. Other than tilting thirty degrees and settling on the rim of a flat rear tire, the Thunderbird seemed miraculously untouched, a fine layer of dust powdering the pastel yellow finish.

"Now what?" She groaned. No way could she change a tire at this crazy angle. There wasn't a soul around to help, nor a house in view. Just the armadillo lumbering along unscathed and a couple of distant goats.

She pulled a scrap of paper from her pocket. On it she had written the name *Justin Grumm,* followed by his telephone number. Although Mr. Grumm was the caretaker of Mimi's property and had exchanged letters with Cassie about the estate, she had yet to meet him in person. He and his wife lived about a half mile ahead in a white cottage on cinder blocks that had been there ever since Cassie could remember, the time-warped porch supported by pillars hacked from mesquite. Mr. Grumm had been delighted to hear from her several weeks ago. "Excellent!" he declared after Cassie explained that she was planning to move into Mimi's home and would need a key. She had liked his voice, warmed by the trace of a German accent.

"Good lord, you're going to live there a year before putting it up for sale? Why bother?" her mother had asked from somewhere in Paris with husband number four or five, Pierre something. Tuff, or Taft. Maybe Tift. In the longrun it wouldn't matter since Lillian seemed intent upon changing husbands along with the seasons. "Mama's dead, God rest her soul, and won't know one way or another. Just clean the place up, throw away all that junk, and put it on the market. You could be in and out of there in a couple of weeks."

"I promised..."

"Promises don't count when the ears that heard them are buried six feet under."

"How can you say such an awful thing?"

"You're throwing a year of your life away! Let the past stay in the past and get on with living. Why isolate yourself in the sticks? What are you running from?"

Cassie couldn't answer, then or now. Maybe she *was* running. Maybe she just wanted some peace. Maybe she didn't know where else to go.

Maybe she was hoping to pull the raveled threads of her life together.

She had tossed luggage in the trunk and back seat, topped helter-skelter with odd items. Her potted rosebush sat alone in the front, belted and secured, crimson blossoms glowing. Long buried amid its roots were two treasures, one already turned to ash and the other rendered so by time. The rose and its roots had traveled with her from one city apartment to another, and now would be experiencing a much different life in the country – as would she.

Telling herself to hurry and *do* something, she reached into the car for her cell phone, pausing with a start when she caught her reflection in the side-view mirror: raven hair windblown, cheeks flushed, eyes murky as coffee brewed too long in the pot. Tiny wrinkles creased the corners. "Crow's feet tapping at my door," she groused. She'd be forty-five soon. Forty-five! Where had the time gone?

She dialed the phone and was met with silence. Disgusted, she flung it onto the dashboard; it skittered off, bounced against the gear shift, and plopped to the floor. No cell, no call to Mr. Grumm, no rescue. She would have to walk.

The rosebush presented a problem; she couldn't risk leaving it in the blistering heat of a locked car. She hoisted the heavy clay pot into her arms, struggled up the road toward a wild black cherry tree, and dragged it the last few yards into the shade. "Take care, my loves," she said. "I'll be back soon."

One more trek to the car for her purse and keys, and she was on her way. The sky gleamed colorless, with a scattering of clouds to break the bleached monotony. Blackbirds spiraled overhead, satin feathers glinting. Cassie imagined what they saw from their avian drafts, looking down – a lone woman, soft summer skirt brushing her legs as she trudged uphill along a rock-strewn roadway. A bare wind breathed upon her face as the earth fell away behind her, and when she looked over her shoulder she could see an eruption of vegetation-furred plateaus on the horizon, their tops so flat and defined it looked as though God had skimmed them with a buzz saw, while up ahead the hills leaped from the earth rounded and full.

The dry air tasted like scorched weeds. Her feet moved on, their beaded sandals soon swallowed by dust. "Idiotic," she grumbled. Why hadn't she worn something more practical, such as… what? Her hiking boots came to mind, red with black laces wide as ribbons, boxed somewhere among her other belongings stored in Houston. Although she had worn the boots only briefly, she was loath to do so again and equally loath to throw them away. So she hid them from sight and from the memories they evoked.

Those memories tugged at her now, pulling her heart along with them.

She had met Thomas Brighton at an outdoor music festival in Colorado. Tall and blond and wide-shouldered, he sat on the sun-warmed Vail slope, eyes closed while the sound of fiddles shimmered among the aspen. As she approached, his eyes opened, vivid blue, and she felt as though she had come face to face with a Viking from ages past somehow hurled into the present. He smiled and motioned for her to join him, offering his hand. She settled next to him, trusting the inner voice that whispered, "Yes."

Ten years later, while celebrating their wedding anniversary among those very same mountains, it all came to an abrupt, horrifying end.

She buried his ashes in the roots of the rosebush he had planted beneath the bedroom window. When she could stand to live there no longer, when phantoms prowled among the darkened corners and empty rooms, she dug up the bush, put it in a clay pot with as much of the dirt and ashes as it could contain, and left. The roses were the only constant in her life as the years passed, the one thing she treasured above all else, protecting the dust of her youth.

Stop thinking about it! she scolded herself. That was another time, another world, another self. "Don't dwell on sadness," Mimi had often told her. "Lift your eyes to the heavens and your spirit will follow." As much as she loved her grandmother, Cassie knew from experience that the only thing you got from looking upward was a stiff neck.

I'm like a dog with a chewed-up bone, gnawing on old grief.

A train whistle shrieked faintly across the miles. She turned and looked back at the slope she had climbed, the massive stretch of sky. A splotch of yellow marked the presence of her car below, tipped and waiting on three solid wheels. The whistle echoed once again, as if lonely and weeping for something lost.

She shook the dust from her sandals and continued onward, one step following another, the air glistening with heat mirages. Her mind quieted and she fell into an easy rhythm, feet moving steadily, arms swinging. It was almost a surprise when she saw the caretaker's cottage standing as she remembered – except for one thing.

Or many things. Perched on the fence and crowding the yard were multitudes of angels in all sizes and shapes, constructed out of metal scrap – wings of rusty tractor seats, halos of wagon wheels, billowing skirts of chicken wire, trumpets and harps from shovels or hoes, scissors or hedge clippers. Mobiles of angel forks and spoons dangled from the porch overhang, and several angelic giants with bodies made of barrel hoops appeared ready to launch themselves from the rooftop.

She walked up the steps onto the porch and peered through the screen door. The room beyond, bright with splatters of blues and yellows, resonated with the sound of clocks. "Hello?" she called over the barrage of tick-tocks. A fat white cat, face round as a stuffed pillow, appeared from inside and looked up at her with cobalt eyes. "Hi," Cassie said. "Is your mommy or daddy home?" She knocked on the door, the frame rattling under her knuckles.

"*Ja*, I'm coming!" A woman approached, almost a perfect match to the cat – small and plump and silver-haired, with lively hazel eyes magnified behind thick, gold-framed glasses. She smiled at Cassie through the screen.

"Mrs. Grumm? I'm Cassie Brighton, and I..."

"Mrs. Brighton, *gut, gut!* Justin has been expecting you." She opened the door, its hinges protesting, and glanced at the road. "Where's your car?"

"Somewhere at the bottom of the hill. I drove into a ditch and got a flat tire. So I walked."

"In this heat? Oh, my dear girl, sit down this minute. Let me get you something to drink." She led Cassie toward an overstuffed chair draped with a floral shawl and scurried away.

Before Cassie could protest, Mrs. Grumm had gone and the chair beckoned. She sank into it and rested her feet on a needlepoint stool, the shredded fabric testament to its daily use. A replica of the cat smiled at her through the worn threading along with the name, *Strudel*. "How did you rate your own portrait?" she asked as the cat brushed against her legs. Perhaps thinking this an invitation, Strudel leaped upon the arm of the chair and stretched its head toward her lips as if wanting a kiss. Cassie had never been fond of cats but didn't protest when it curled into her lap and began to purr. "Like a miniature lawn mower," she murmured, and closed her eyes.

Bong! Tweetle-too! Cuckoo-cuckoo!

Cassie jolted out of her chair, tumbling a disgruntled cat to the floor. From every room in the house clocks clanged, sang, or rang the hour. There must have been two dozen – no, surely more. Cassie spun around, delighted. A tall grandfather clock with a huge round head atop a narrow body chimed in a stately fashion, a minuscule sailing ship tick-tick-whistled, and an intricately carved village with costumed folk danced around a well and tinkled "Edelweiss," each telling her it was four o'clock in the afternoon.

"Are you rested?" This spoken behind her, the voice deep and obviously amused.

Cassie turned to face an impossibly tall man, all bones and joints, with a toothy smile spread in a wrinkle-grooved face.

"Yes, thank you, but I... was I... Did I fall asleep?"

"Thoroughly. Snoring is healthy, by the way. Clears the lungs."

"I'm so sorry, I..." Cassie stammered.

"Justin!" Mrs. Grumm scolded. "Enough teasing." She smiled at Cassie. "Pay no mind to this old man. You napped very lady-like. Now come, I have something for you."

Justin ran a hand through his fluff of sparse hair as Cassie, pulled along by Mrs. Grumm, entered the kitchen. It was a cheerful place, decorated with crisp white curtains and a blue tablecloth. A pottery jar filled with sunflowers graced the windowsill.

Cassie soon found herself sitting at the table, enjoying a glass of iced tea garnished with mint. "Delicious. It's been years since I tasted fresh mint."

"It came from my mother's garden long ago, in Villach. Every spring it sprouts up more, like weeds."

"Can't kill the stuff." Justin pulled out a chair and sat at an angle, long legs half under the table and half out.

Mrs. Grumm opened the refrigerator and reached for an ice tray. "You want to give her the key, or do you expect her to kick the door down?"

"Stop fussing, *Schatzi*. I didn't forget."

"You left it in the freezer, next to the ice cream."

"Well, hand it over then." Justin grinned at Cassie. "That house will be happy to see you. It's been empty too long."

"Cold as the devil." Mrs. Grumm wiped the key with a dishtowel and laid it beside Cassie's plate. "Sometimes this man of mine is so forgetful I wonder he can find his own head,"

Forged from iron and tipped by an ornate heart bound in vines, the key was longer than Cassie's hand. "How beautiful!" she exclaimed. "I wonder how old it is."

Justin shrugged. "As far as I can figure, the olden part of your house – the one in the back that the rest was added onto – was built sometime in the mid 1800's. So close to a hundred sixty years, give or take a few."

"I didn't expect a key like this."

"You've not seen it before?"

Cassie shook her head. "Mimi never locked her doors. She said the spirits in the woods would watch over things. I gave up trying to talk sense into her head."

"Now don't you worry about bad spooks. Only good ones fly around over there."

"There you go again, giving the girl a hard time." Mrs. Grumm patted Cassie's shoulder. "We're surely happy to meet you at last."

Justin nodded. "What took you so long?"

"Well, I..." Cassie floundered. How could she tell them? *What* could she tell them? Her troubles were hers alone: the emptiness that faced her, the dreams that plagued her.

"Justin, enough for today. Let the girl tell us all about herself later, when she's rested."

"All right, all right. I know I'm a nosy buzzard."

Relieved, Cassie nibbled on a ginger snap. "These are wonderful."

"Berta isn't too bad with the sweets. Except for her *grebbel*."

"So you're complaining about my doughnuts now?" Berta smacked him with the dishtowel. "You ate three this morning, silly old fool."

"Had to force down each bite. Pure torture."

Cassie watched the Grumms grinning at one another and something twisted inside – a longing, a regret. She drained her glass and set it aside. "Thanks for your hospitality, but I really must be going. Do you know who I could call to upright my car and fix the flat? Is there a gas station nearby?"

"I reckon so, if by 'nearby' you mean within twenty miles or thereabouts," Justin said with a chuckle. "Guy's Auto is closer in, but he doesn't work on Thursdays. Today is Thursday, isn't it?"

"Yesterday was Wednesday and tomorrow's Friday," Berta said, "so unless the world has turned upside down, yes."

"That settles that, then."

Cassie's heart plummeted. "Surely there's someone around who could help. I'd hate to leave my car and everything in it until tomorrow."

"Guy may not work on Thursdays, but this man does." Justin stood and adjusted the pants at his narrow waist. "Come on, then. Let's get the job done."

"Stay and have dinner with us afterward," Berta said. "There's not enough in your refrigerator for a good meal tonight – just eggs and such. We didn't know what you might need."

"How kind of you. I didn't expect anything at all."

"Drive straight here once the tire is fixed and I should have something nice and hot for you both."

"Oh, but I couldn't. I mean I shouldn't. I have too much to do. You've both been so lovely to me, but I haven't been to the house yet and..." Several clocks chimed the quarter hour. "And it's already four-fifteen."

"It doesn't get dark until after eight. Please, we'd love to have you." Berta nudged Justin. "Isn't that right?"

"Right as blueberry pie – which we'll have a good portion of tonight, fresh-made."

Cassie was tempted, but she still had a long day ahead of her, a car to upright and a tire to change, luggage to unload, a house to inspect. "May I have a rain check?"

"Of course! How about tomorrow at lunch?"

"That sounds delightful."

"Good! I'll see you at noon. Fix that car good, Justin. And try not getting your shirt dirty. I just washed it."

"Stop fussing, *Schatzi*. You've scrubbed this shirt so much there's hardly a thread left." He leaned to Cassie and muttered, "Berta goes into fits when she sees dirt anywhere except on the ground, and even then it better be clean dirt."

The roses, secured once again in the passenger seat, filled the car with their heady scent as Cassie followed Justin's blue pickup truck. A sign with red and white letters was painted neatly on its door: *Grumm Clockworks* and below, *J. Grumm, Master Clocksmith*. They parted at the cottage; Justin stuck his long-boned arm out the truck window and waved as Cassie passed by. She continued along the high-rising hill before turning into a rough weed-choked drive. Following its wanderings, she arrived at a wooden gate so old the earth had swallowed part of the supporting frame. Scattered posts leaned into each other, vague remnants of the proud fence that might have been built by her great-great grandfather.

She had always been curious as a child about her ancestors, but Lillian refused to speak about them, saying, "They're all dead and gone. Let them stay there." Mimi, who normally talked a blue streak, remained strangely mute – with a single exception. One evening, while the two of them were swapping tales on the porch swing, Mimi let slip that their ancestors had come from Germany long years ago, sailing over a troublesome sea then traveling in an ox cart along the Guadalupe River and upland until they arrived at this very place. "Someday I'll tell more," she had promised.

But the day never came.

Cassie got out of the car and pushed the gate. It opened easily enough, although the bottom edge dragged along the ground. The hinges made a low creaking sound, a three-syllable whine, as if saying, *come on innnnnn.* She gripped the dry wood, suddenly transported to the past, a girl in shorts with her hair in a ponytail opening the gate so Mimi could drive through. Turning, she half-expected to see a ghostly Studebaker swimming in the heat behind her.

She returned to the car and sat, looking through the windshield at the hills humped beyond the fence, the slope on her right shadowed by trees, the driveway snaking around the juniper on her left, and the great spread of land between them. The house, windmill, and barn waited for her around the bend and out of sight, their images hovering behind her eyes, dim and quiet as old photographs in a family album.

"Oh, Mimi," she whispered, and drove through the gate.

Secrets

Cassie jounced along the rutted dirt road toward what was to be her home for the next twelve months.

Behind her, a shaded woodland. Before her, a meandering creek spanned by a narrow wooden bridge. Beyond, the house, barn, and windmill in a valley of scrub-covered hills – the time-battered barn slumped into itself as if it yearned to lie down and sleep, the windmill dry and splintery as long-buried bones. But it was the house her eyes sought, shaded under the limbs of a live oak. She slowed to a stop, wanting to see it from afar.

She remembered the house as a charming hodgepodge of construction with rooms added or demolished over the years at the whims of those living in them. The older rear section was made of stone and the front of wood, joined in a cockamamie fashion that would make an architect shudder. Yet it once held warmth and welcome. Now the place ached with loneliness. Mold stained the stone. Paint peeled from the wood. A sagging porch supported a swing that should have become firewood long ago.

Although sprawling and topped by a cupola with windows all around, the house was dwarfed by the massive live oak arching over the roof, engulfing stone and timber. Gnarled roots pushed from the earth, heaves and bumps splaying outward toward the creek.

How long had it been since she spent the night here with Mimi? Fifteen years? Twenty?

Six years ago she had paused on this very spot, her tears transforming the landscape into a misty watercolor painting. She had just buried Mimi in the little family cemetery sheltered in the woods, and hadn't the heart to linger. Nor had she the time, since the trip from and to Houston ate up almost eight hours. So she had turned away, seeing only the yesterdays.

The house peered at her with empty eyes.

A shape flickered behind an upstairs window, as though someone had been watching her before quickly drawing away. Cassie held her breath until she noticed the oak leaves tossing in the breeze, throwing quick, fluttering images against the glass.

A trick of the light, that's all. Nothing else.

She laughed unsteadily and headed for the bridge. Rickety, creaking with age and too narrow for comfort, it reminded her of a battered raft swept up in a storm and left adrift. Gripping the steering wheel, she rattled across.

"Oh, dear God!"

She groaned at the sight greeting her. Trash. Mounds of it, piles, stacks, a mini-garbage dump spilling from the carport. The tin lean-to squatted under a cluster of pecan trees, vomiting rubbish: busted rakes and shovels and wheelbarrows, rolls of barbed wire, lawn furniture with rotted wicker seats, a tin washtub, a twisted bicycle frame, firewood, a jumble of cardboard boxes covered with tattered quilts. Cassie's spirits sank. What other mess awaited her in the house and barn?

What did I expect? A genie with a power vacuum?

Her tires bumped over knobby roots as she parked in the shade of the oak. When she stepped from the car, she couldn't help but glance up at the huge hill looming behind the house, so rotund and scruffy Lillian had dubbed it Mount Bubba. "If this ugly thing sprouted legs, it would wear a silver-buckled belt under a fat paunch," she had said, "and drink cheap beer by the case."

Cassie had been fascinated by it when she was young, imagining caves and mysteries hidden among the bulging planes and thorny bush, but didn't dare explore. "Rattlesnakes big as a man's arm hide under the rocks," Lillian had warned, a gleam in her eyes as if relishing the terror this would induce. "They attack in a flash, *zap-zap!* until your legs swell like balloons and bust open." Yet it was something else her mother had said, something that still gave Cassie the chills. "A restless spirit wanders around up there," Lillian had whispered. "Dripping blood and crazy blind and mean as a rabid hog."

Cassie had never gathered enough courage to venture more than a yard or so up the rocky incline. Images of writhing snakes and a moaning ghost with gaping eye sockets sent her back, running. *I'll climb when I'm grown,* she would think, *when I'm big enough to stomp on any snake and holler at any spook.* Well, here she was all grown up and big enough to stomp and holler. Yet the sight of any hill close enough to climb made her want to run in the other direction. Ever since Colorado she had loathed the sight of them, preferring city streets on flat, solid ground, a bright and busy life of noise and concrete and man-made lights drowning out the stars.

She had been avoiding reminders of her past and now was forced to live among them. She wanted to turn around and go right back… where?

Nowhere.

She had no home waiting for her, no special love, no other responsibilities. Just this, right here, right now. *This.*

The screened front door had black iron hinges big enough for a drawbridge. Cassie opened the screen and slipped the key into the lock. As metal brushed against metal, she leaned in for a closer look. The lock and key tip were exact replicas of one another, differing only in scale. A matched pair of hearts! Why had Mimi never spoken of this?

"Secrets," she murmured. "Too many secrets!" This house and all that created it were unknown to her, except for the life and love that Mimi brought. The unanswered questions about her ancestors, about what came before Mimi entered this world and after, all the questions unasked or even unthought-of, were manifest in this single key.

A mystery to solve! Her spirits lightened. Surely answers lay among Mimi's belongings.

I'll take my time and look at each item, no matter how small.

She had an entire year to explore and decide what should be tossed, sold, or given away. Maybe searching for clues to Mimi's past would take her mind from the unpleasant tasks that lay ahead – as well as from the memories of what she left behind.

Cassie pushed the door open into a room of shadows. Half-remembered shapes appeared: the horsehair sofa, the wobbly coffee table, a floor lamp with its lopsided shade, the brick fireplace. A ceiling fan, the frayed cord dangling. To the right, through the doorway into the kitchen, Cassie could see the blue and white pottery canisters Mimi had inherited from her own grandmother, some chipped, some pieced together with glue.

For a moment it appeared as though Mimi were still there and simply had forgotten to turn on a light. Her grandmother's presence was so strong, so terribly real, that she half-expected to hear Mimi's voice calling from another room. Goosebumps prickled her arms as her senses awakened, alive to the touch of air against her skin, the musty scent of age biting into her tongue, the uneasy stillness of the house broken by her own quick breathing.

A scrub jay's chatter stirred her to open a drape, inviting the western sun to cast an evening glow upon clean longleaf pine floors and recently dusted furniture. It wasn't at all what Cassie had expected. No piles of clutter, no tossed rubbish in corners. Although she recognized the efficient hand of the

Grumms, it felt wrong, as though a stranger had intruded and rummaged through Mimi's personal belongings.

Cassie strolled through the rooms of the front part of the house, reacquainting herself – the kitchen, with a table carved by long-ago hands and curtains sewn from fabric scraps; the bath, with a claw-footed tub and a toilet tank that hung high on the wall, operated by a chain pull. Her footsteps, click-clacking on the wooden hall floor, paused in front of the room her grandmother had slept in for decades. She was almost afraid to enter, as though by doing so she'd see Mimi once again lying there, pale as dust, whispering, "The ghosts are singing." Or, worse, rising into the air, arms open for an embrace, while the walls and window glimmered through her bones.

The door wouldn't budge. She pulled the knob, pushed with her shoulder, and finally kicked. It flew open with a jerk, as if yanked from the other side.

The bed, emptied of the beloved person who once lay among its sheets, was freshly made, the patchwork quilt folded neatly at the foot, the coverlet turned, the pillow plumped. A jar of wildflowers sat on the dresser, next to a framed photograph of Mimi as a young woman. Dressed in white, she held the hand of a little girl who looked toward the camera with her head tilted as if to show off the big bow in her curly hair. Cassie's grandfather stood with arms wrapped around them both, handsome in his army uniform. Mimi buried him in it shortly thereafter. His gravestone lay beside hers in the family plot among the trees on the other side of the creek. The only thing Cassie knew of him was etched in the stone:

Johann Ruff, 1903-1941, husband, father, warrior
May his spirit fly with the winds.

Holding the picture to the light, Cassie studied the face of the girl, Lillian. Poised, aware of her beauty even then, flirting with the camera. Her lips were set in the fetching pout Cassie recognized, one her mother still used whenever she wanted attention – an act that should be ridiculous for a woman three years shy of seventy-five. Yet it must be effective bait, since a series of unsuspecting fish were still caught by its lure.

Cassie hesitated, drawn by Mimi's quiet gaze and the pride apparent in the face of the grandfather she had never known. The child they protected gripped her mother's hand and leaned into her father as if grounded by their combined strength.

If love had a color and shape, it would be exactly this – a family captured within a yellowed black and white photograph surrounded by a tarnished brass frame, lovely in its rightness, poignant in its passing. Something once treasured, now gone.

Loss! Loss! It caught Cassie unaware, punching her beneath the ribs, slicing cold into her veins.

There would be no picture of herself wrapped in the arms of protective parents. No picture of a proud father or mother standing beside her. Rather, there would be a series of photographs taken over the years with a variety of different "uncles" and step-dads, most of whom she couldn't recall. Nor could she remember much about her real father, except for his rumbly voice reading *Winnie the Pooh* while she sat in his lap. The last she had seen of him was on her sixth birthday. He had given her a ring with a blue stone in the shape of a heart. "Love you, Sugarfoot," he said, then walked out the door and never returned.

Her mother had wept, torn his photographs to shreds, tossed his clothing in heaps outside and burned it all. The bonfire blazed high, shooting sparks like falling stars.

Love you, Sugarfoot.

Cassie put the picture on the dresser and left the room. Whatever yearnings rose with the memory of her father's voice she pushed aside, burying them amid all the others.

She continued down the hallway, her footsteps changing to a sharper rhythm once they hit flagstone. The gray-black stones were uneven and joined with thick grout. Cassie's sandals jammed against one of them and she stumbled, slamming into the limestone wall. "Got to watch it!" she exclaimed. "God, I'm muttering like an old woman."

More carefully now, she approached the threshold leading to the older section. All was in darkness, except for shafts of light from the shuttered windows and shapes vague as draped phantoms. The arched stone fireplace hunched in the shadows. She waited for her eyes to adjust, but the longer she waited the darker it seemed to become.

A loud *ping!* shot through the gloom, followed by a rattle.

Cassie spun and dashed down the hallway. She knew the sounds were a normal part of the house, timbers contracting or expanding. Yet she still felt unsettled, as if someone or something lurked in that murky room, hovering beyond eyesight.

ꕥ

The chorus of clocks announced the arrival of twilight while Mr. and Mrs. Grumm sat in their usual places at the table, eating the last slices of blueberry pie. Berta fiddled with hers, shoving it around the plate.

"She has a sadness about her, don't you think?"

Justin shrugged. "Maybe she's the serious sort, and keeps a smile for special times."

"I worry about her, up there all by herself."

"You worry about every lost chick that finds its way into our yard."

"She's too young to be a widow. It isn't right."

"You going to tell her that?"

"Of course not. Don't be silly." Berta tapped her plump fingers on the table. "Does she have any children?"

"Not that I heard."

"She's alone, then." Berta pushed her uneaten pie toward Justin, who tucked right into it.

"No one should be without family. Especially here, among all this space and wind and loneliness. Neighbors are miles from each other with houses so well hidden from the road you could pass by and never know one was there."

"*Schatzi!*" Justin's fork slipped from his fingers and clattered on the table. "Are you lonely?"

He looked so startled Berta smiled and patted his cheek. "How could I be, when I have you? I'm concerned about Mrs. Brighton, that's all."

"She'll be just fine. With us around and with your good heart, she'll not be without a friend."

"It's a pity she doesn't have a neighbor nearby, someone closer than us, in case she needs anything."

"Aren't you forgetting Tatty?"

"She's too addled in the head!" Berta rose, using the table for support, and began to clear the dishes. "What help could she be to anyone?"

"Maybe none. I don't even know if she can talk anymore. She sort of grunts."

"How did you get that idea?"

"I saw her at Pete's fruit stand a couple of weeks ago. When I said hello she growled like a sick dog, and when Pete asked her what she'd like for her basket, she pointed to a melon and grunted, *Ugh*, and then to a couple of peaches, *Ugh. Ugh.*"

"Oh posh!" Berta laughed. "Maybe she's lived alone so long she's out of practice."

The dishes rubbed against one another in the suds while Berta washed and Justin dried them. It was a comfortable routine done without haste, the silence unbroken until Berta said, "Maybe we should warn her about what she might find out there."

"Why?" Justin dried the last plate and put it on the shelf. "Tatty may be peculiar but she's no harm to anyone."

"I'm not talking about her! I'm talking about what's been happening in and around that old place."

"What old place?"

"Mrs. Brighton's, of course! What did you think?"

"Nothing's happening."

"But you told me…"

"Nothing. A wind playing tricks, an odd shadow, and an old man with bad eyes and only one good ear."

Berta yanked the plug from the sink. "Hogwash!"

"Ah, *Schatzi*. I've got cobwebs for brains and you fuss too much." Justin hitched up his glasses and walked from the room.

"I still worry about her," Berta mumbled to no one in particular.

ꕤ

Cassie had forgotten how deeply the night falls when unbroken by city lights. And noisy! Crickets and katydids, strange rustlings, an owl. If she listened closely she could hear the chirrups of tree frogs and the *harrumph* of their larger cousins down by the creek.

The clay flowerpot banged against her shins while she carried it from the shade of the oak up the porch steps, careful not to disturb the rose blossoms as the sky rushed past, stars, clouds, moon flowing like a fire-lit river. The breeze quickened and lightening flashed in the north, illuminating the hills.

Maybe it will rain and cool things down a bit.

A lone howl from deep within the woods soared through the trees and over the meadow. The cry came again, answered by another from somewhere on Mount Bubba, a lingering, eerie yowl that sent shivers down her spine. "Just coyotes," she told herself, "yapping at the moon." The howls followed her inside, gliding through the windows. She began to shut the nearest one, her hand reaching for the sash. In the city she'd close everything up at nightfall with thick drapes, deadbolt locks, and an alarm system. It felt unnatural to be exposed to whatever lay in the dimness beyond, yet she hesitated, the wood rough on her fingers. Her image stared back at her in the glass, hand raised as if waving.

The parlor was stuffy, redolent with stale oil polish and a scent she couldn't quite place, faint but pleasant, akin to flower petals crumbling with age. Violets, perhaps. Or lavender. The ceiling fan whirred, attempting to stir it all about. Better to breathe than suffocate in the heat, she decided, and left the windows open. Hopefully a breeze would wander the rooms, seeking passage from one to the next.

She walked into the kitchen, hungry enough to eat the wallpaper. The refrigerator was a boxy affair the Grumms had stocked with eggs, bacon, and coffee cake. "There goes my diet," Cassie groused, and searched for a frying pan. Fumbling through a low cupboard filled with battered pots and filmy jelly jars, she found a cast iron skillet so heavy she almost dropped it. Encrusted by the accumulation of years, its age could probably be determined by the rings, like the sawed-out trunk of a tree.

She had never cooked on a gas stove, much less one so archaic, and eyed it suspiciously. It had four cast iron plates like blackened wheel spokes and a single unlit pilot light. An oven drawer, another beneath, all sorts of knobs. She gave the stove a leery nudge, struck a match, and held it to the pilot moments before a mouse popped its head out of the grate.

"Aaaak!" Cassie grabbed a broom as the rodent retreated into the bowels of the oven. "Out! Out!" she cried, whacking the stove and jabbing the bristles down the burner. The broom erupted into flame with the glory of a Fourth of July fireworks. "No! No! No!" Cassie thrust the torch into the sink and turned the tap. Water burst with the force of a geyser, splashing everything within sight and reducing the broom to a soggy, blackened mess. The entire kitchen stank of scorched straw.

There was no way she was going to eat on a single plate or use a single fork or cook from a single pot until the kitchen was completely rid of that creature and its relatives, and every item and inch scrubbed and disinfected.

She sat at the table in a cozy nook with a bay window. The live oak pushed against the screen, the massive trunk a silhouette, the limbs swaying. She ate coffeecake with her fingers, eyes wandering over the worn cupboards, the jumble of china and jars, the stove and refrigerator surely as old as she was herself, the chipped porcelain sink, the cockeyed drawers and their mismatched contents.

When had this place grown so shabby? It used to be a haven of sunshine and laughter, a place made happy because Mimi was there. How long had it been since she last walked through the kitchen door, sat at this table, ate from these plates, opened the cupboards and drawers?

Another lifetime ago.

Mimi had grown old amid these decaying things, never complaining, never asking for help, doing what she always did as best she could.

A choking regret welled up inside Cassie's throat. *Oh, Mimi, I'm sorry. I was so involved with my own life I neglected yours.*

The person looking back at her from the bathroom mirror bore little resemblance to the one she had studied so carefully that morning. This one had hair sticking out like an agitated porcupine and a face the color of oatmeal. Cassie leaned in toward her pale twin. The light from the single overhead bulb emphasized each downward turn. Maybe old age was catching, like the measles. Stay here much longer and gravity would claim the rest.

She brushed her teeth, knowing she should bathe, wash her hair, soak the ache away. But exhaustion demanded she wait until morning.

I'll worry about tomorrow… tomorrow.

She lay in Mimi's bed, under Mimi's sheets. It felt as though other eyes and other ears were nearby. She could almost sense a collective breath, as if an unseen crowd gathered around her bed. So she kept the lights on – not all, just enough to chase away the shadows. Thunder rumbled, growing closer. The house answered with thumps and grumblings, and the floorboards creaked as if someone were tip-toeing toward the bedroom.

"Can't you shut up for one minute?" Cassie shouted at whatever was or wasn't there.

A clap of thunder exploded at midnight, the sound roaring through the house. Cassie awoke with a start and sat upright. Lightening flared, rain hammered the roof, wind rattled window panes and charged into the room. Cassie leaped off the bed, rain spattering over the sill and onto her bare feet.

She rushed to close all the windows. The bedroom. The bathroom. Down the hall for the kitchen and parlor.

The lights flickered, then went out.

She waited, arms outstretched in the pitch black, for the next flash to light her way. When it came she ran in fits and starts, careening into furniture. The curtains whipped with the wind as rain sluiced through, soaking the floor. She stumbled from window to window and wrestled with the drapes, the wet fabric clinging to her arms. Lightning shimmered and burst over the meadow the very moment she touched the glass. The power of it jolted up her arms and she reeled backward, shaken.

Thunder vibrated along the floor and through her feet and up her thighs. The house shuddered and groaned. She lurched through roiling shadows into the kitchen, reached for the bay window and with a final heave shut it. The oak tree thrashed outside, limbs cracking on the roof and scraping the walls. She bumped into a kitchen chair and abruptly sat.

Dark. Light. Dark. Spots floated in front of her eyes as the storm raged.

A terrible wail careened down the hall, a wheezing shriek ending in a sucking moan. Cassie curled inward, reminding herself over and over that it was just a quirk of the wind finding an opening in the original fireplace and pushing through ancient stone and mortar. Sometimes it whispered, sometimes wept, and sometimes, like now, it wailed. Mimi had called it the voice of Firewind.

Shivering, Cassie put her hands over her ears and closed her eyes, willing the storm to cease, willing the darkness to end, willing the voice to silence.

Something shifted in the air, in the wind, in the room.

A burst of light split the night. Its brief glare revealed a man standing in the doorway of the kitchen. Tall, wearing a hat, face hidden.

Too frightened to move, too frightened to speak or cry out, Cassie sat, rigid, her heart racing. She felt suddenly cold, so very cold she couldn't think.

Another flash, and he was gone.

Every sense awakened, she waited for the next lightning strike. It revealed the parlor floor lamp, visible through the kitchen door – the same height as the shadowed man, its shade the shape of his hat. A floor lamp. A flash of light. A too-vivid imagination.

It took a moment before she realized she had stopped breathing. She forced air into her lungs, one long breath, two, striving to calm her heart while thinking how silly she was, how foolish, to get so riled up over a lampshade.

She tried to stand and walk hand-over-hand across the counter for a match and candle. But she couldn't remember seeing a candle. Besides, her knees were shaking.

Tomorrow. I'll find one tomorrow.

She wrapped her arms around herself and looked through the bay window as the old oak lifted its limbs and beat against the walls.

Small Blessings

CASSIE AWOKE, STARTLED TO FIND HERSELF ASKEW IN THE STUFFED PARLOR CHAIR. She looked at the lamp beside her, its crooked shade an unpleasant reminder of the shadow-man her fears had conjured the night before. She set it aright, shrugged away her stiffness, and opened the door to a new day. Morning had dawned upon a windswept sky, the only trace of the storm seen in the dripping leaves and puddles glittering in the meadow.

Tomorrow had arrived and with it a slew of things that needed doing.

She lingered in the shower until the water ran cold. It sloshed around her feet as she stepped from the tub and wrapped in a towel, wet hair clinging to her face. Exhaustion sat heavy on her shoulders, nothing a cup of strong coffee wouldn't cure – something she'd have to do without, thanks to that damn mouse. *Today's the day that mouse meets its maker, even if I have to take that stove apart bolt by bolt.* She reached for the hair dryer, thinking none too happily of those beady mouse eyes and squirmy mouse body as she plugged the dryer into the single outlet, a wonky affair that jutted from the wall, and turned it on.

Clack! the fuse popped.

"I don't believe this!" She stomped into the parlor, sodden hair spattering the floor, with no idea where to search for a fuse nor what to expect once she found it. Much of her life had been spent in apartments where management took care of such prosaic things as fuses. Thankfully, she had management of a sort in Justin Grumm. All she needed to do was call.

The telephone was a squat black rotary, the kind featured in old black and white movies, usually on the desk of a detective wearing rumpled suits while growling at sexy blonde clients in form-fitting skirts. A far cry from Mimi's life.

No dial tone.

She stared at the receiver as if it were purposely misbehaving then slammed it into the cradle. One more thing she needed to do – get the line connected. Why hadn't she thought of that earlier? Nor did her cell phone work, likely due to interference from the surrounding hills. Whatever the cause, she had no way to talk to the Grumms until she joined them for lunch at noon.

Her mother's voice scolded from the recesses of her mind: *Stop being a lollygagger and look for the darn fuse.* One of Lillian's favorite words was *lollygagger,* along with *slothful* and *lazy bird* and *drama queen,* each used one time or another to chastise Cassie for not doing what she should quickly enough. Cassie tossed the towel aside and slipped into her terrycloth robe, wondering where to search. A closet seemed as likely a place as any, but each was jam-packed with stuff. Didn't Mimi ever throw anything away? She yanked clothing aside, shoved boxes and shoes and snarled wire hangers away from the walls, but found nothing remotely like a fuse box.

"Ridiculous!" she cried, and "Where the hell is it?"

Earlier she had noticed a pair of ugly mismatched rubber galoshes stored near the side door. Perhaps the fuse box was outside. She pulled on the cumbersome things and ventured onto the muddy yard. Grateful no one could see how outlandish she looked swaddled in terry with grungy rubber boots up to her knees, Cassie high-stepped over pools of muck and began to inspect the walls. Her feet made sucking sounds in the quagmire, *thuck thuck.*

"This stuff is thick as horse glue," she muttered. And as tricky; it grabbed her foot and wouldn't let go, as if winning in a game of tug-of-war. She lost her balance and down she fell, landing on her hands and knees.

"Damn it all to heaven and back!" Mud squished between her fingers and toes and oozed around her mucked-up legs. "Damn damn DAMN!" She smacked the ground in what Mimi would have called a hissy fit, sludge flying and spattering her face and hair like globs of chocolate pudding.

Somewhere from behind came the unbridled sound of laughter. Cassie stopped in mid-damn. The sound came again, unmistakable. Startled, she looked over her shoulder. Standing in the partial shade of a cedar on the far side of the creek was what appeared to be a bag lady, a bedraggled creature scooped from the dregs of a city and dropped into the meadow. She was tall and knobby as a hackberry tree, and dressed in a hodgepodge of clothing in odd sizes and patterns. Twigs and scraggly weeds stuck from bulging pockets and dangled from a straw hat askew on a mop of flyaway hair, while combat boots stuck out from underneath it all.

They gawked at one another, the woman grinning and Cassie with her mouth ajar. Finally Cassie cried, "Looking for the fuse box." Bag Lady shrugged, putting a hand to her ear. Cassie tried again, shouting, "FUSE BOX!" The woman pointed to a vine-covered trellis leaning against the wall, did a "thumbs up" gesture, and turned into the woods, her chuckles trailing after.

Cassie stumbled upright and tucked the dirtied robe around herself, flushed with indignation. How dare that woman trespass! How dare she wander onto land that didn't belong to her, acting like she had a right to be there! "Knock next time!" she yelled at the empty space across the creek.

Sunlight glinted on metal partially hidden by honeysuckle vines. If it proved to be the elusive box, the bag lady knew what Cassie had not – proof that the odd woman had a habit of snooping around. Where else had she stuck her rude nose? The barn? The house? *Inexcusable!* Cassie eyed the meadow as though expecting to see the culprit skulking behind the trees or submerging in the creek with a reed for a breathing straw clamped between her teeth.

A gray shape emerged from the dimness of the wood. It blended into the surroundings so perfectly had it not moved she wouldn't have noticed. Amber eyes stared at her with unnerving interest.

A wolf!

Wolves hadn't been seen in a century or more. Maybe it was a coyote. Or a dog with weird eyes. "Go away!" she yelled, waving her arms as if to shoo him like an errant chicken. "Get out of here!" The animal didn't flinch. She threw a blob of mud that fell apart the moment it left her hands. "This is private property!"

He twitched his ears as if to say, *So what?*

Cassie clasped the robe close, her mouth suddenly dry.

The wolf-thing moved toward the bridge, sunlight glinting on powerful haunches. "All right, then," she said, her voice quavering. "Stay, for all I care." She stepped back, intentionally looking away as if she didn't give a damn, thinking it might be best if she were safe inside the house. One step, two, another.

When she dared a second glance, it was gone. She waited. The morning continued as usual, wet leaves glistening, birds flitting among the treetops, a breeze teasing her hair. A dog, that's all it was. And if not? No matter. She was in the country now and should expect to see all sorts of wild creatures – maybe even a dog that looked like a wolf.

She turned her attention to the trellis. Honeysuckle crawled in heavy layers over the wooden frame, the fragrance syrupy as fruit ripened too long in the sun. After a bout of furious tugging and creative cursing, a slew of vines sprawled at her feet, revealing the box in all its corroded glory. She pried it open, the metal door squealing. Four fuses lined up inside, the glass button tops reminding her of miniature doorknobs. One was blackened and off-kilter; she twisted it and the fuse tumbled into her hand. Fragments of aluminum foil clung to the squat, mottled brass body like dried-up skin on a bone. She picked them off, screwed the fuse back in, and hoped for the best.

Five minutes later she resorted to towel-drying her hair, wondering how the heck she was going to find a replacement for a dead fuse so old it likely belonged in a museum somewhere.

The ground was still soggy when Cassie drove toward the Grumms a bit before noon. Evidence of the storm lay all around – broken limbs, scattered leaves, water pooling in the fields – but she paid little heed. Her mind was occupied with all the things that needed doing. The house was deteriorating around her, complaining with voices and shapes stirring in the shadows, with stubborn drawers and rodents in the stove and faulty wiring and an amazing amount of clutter spilling from the carport, closets and cupboards. Adding a deluge, a meddlesome vagrant and a wolf-creature made her wonder whether coming here was such a good idea after all.

She was making a mental list of items she should purchase – fuse, cleaning supplies, groceries – and at first didn't notice the red pickup rushing from behind. The driver blasted the horn in triplets, *Honk-honk-honk! Honk-honk-honk!*, evidently oblivious to the fact that the road was barely wide enough for one car, much less two. *Honk-honk-honk!* Cassie glared at the driver through her rearview mirror, seeing only a blurred figure in a cowboy hat. On he came, as if he intended to run right over her. Cassie yelped and tugged at the wheel, spinning to a stop as her rear fender crunched against a fence post. The truck sped past, throwing pebbles in its wake.

"Hey, watch it!" She leaped out to investigate. Sure enough – a dent. "Idiot driver!" she shouted, and ran after the truck. "Come back here!" The pickup didn't hesitate as it sped recklessly down the road. A floppy-eared dog stuck its head out the window, barking as it continued downhill and away.

The last thing Cassie noticed was a hawk painted across the rear window, wings opened in flight. She shook her fists, feeling helpless and hating it. "I hope you crash into a ditch and land with cactus up your butt!"

Berta pulled the lace curtains aside as the yellow car skidded up her driveway. The bantam cock flapped his wings and skedaddled across the lawn, squawking as the wheels rolled past. The car came to an abrupt stop and Mrs. Brighton leaned her head against the steering wheel as though she might be crying.

"Something's wrong," Berta murmured, and hurried outside to see what she could do.

But the young woman greeted her with a smile. "Hi! Thanks for inviting me to lunch. It's been a long morning and I'm starved." No tears – in fact, her eyes were snapping. "I'm sorry I startled your poor chicken. I was mad at a cretin in a red pickup with a hawk painted over the rear window. He ran me off the road."

"Goodness! That must be Hawk. But he seems like such a nice fellow, I can't imagine him being rude. He's the quiet sort, hardly ever around. I see him sometimes walking the hills."

"He made me smack into a fence and ding my car."

"Let Justin take a look at it. He's good at fixing things."

"A lot of things need fixing, I'm afraid. I'm a bit overwhelmed by it all."

"I'd be overwhelmed too, wandering around alone in a big drafty place like yours, Mrs. Brighton."

"Call me Cassie, please – or Cassandra."

"No formalities for Justin and me either, dear girl. So call us what you will."

A mobile of angels fashioned from silverware jangled a welcome as they walked up the steps. Berta flipped her hand at the two rockers on the porch. "Come sit awhile, and I'll fetch iced tea for us both." She hurried inside, leaving Cassandra to mull over which rocker to choose, and shook Justin from his nap on the couch. "Cassandra is here. Take a look at the dent in her car, would you, while I fix the tea." She kissed him on the forehead and turned to the kitchen as he mumbled a reply, something that was becoming a habit of late. Her hearing was less acute than it used to be but the sound of his footsteps and the slam of the screen door registered just fine. More than likely he was developing a bad case of lazy lips.

She prided herself on the prettiness of the tea tray, with glasses on doilies, sugar and lemons in crystal bowls, and a single rose. Blessings could be found in small things, simple pleasures. She placed the tray on a little porch table and arranged napkins while Justin and Cassandra looked at the damage on the fender. *She's truly beautiful,* Berta thought. There was a charisma about her, a certain intangible something Berta had sensed the moment she had answered the door and found the young woman standing there yesterday afternoon.

But sorrow was evident too, and loneliness, and perhaps anger.

The wooden rocker bit into Cassie's tailbone and wobbled with a lop-sided *whump* on the floorboards. The frosty glass was cool in her hands, and the tea tasted of mint and lemon. "This hits the spot," she said as Mrs. Grumm's hazel owl-eyes regarded her from behind thick lenses. The eyes were kind but astute as well, and Cassie suspected that Berta could see what lay beneath bone and sinew if she had a mind to. Unused to such focused scrutiny, she didn't know quite where to look – the porch, the angel-strewn yard, Justin attacking her fender with a toilet plunger.

"Good heavens!" Cassie exclaimed. "What's he *doing*?"

"Don't worry. Justin's got a knack for things even if it does look silly." Berta cupped her hand to her mouth and called, "You about finished, *Schatz*? Time to eat."

Justin waved at them with the plunger. "Almost done!"

Berta sighed. "You'd think after sixty years I could get him to stop and eat of his own accord. If I didn't nag, I swear he'd starve to death working on his angels or clocks or whatever else tickles his fancy."

Sixty years? Cassie couldn't fathom what it must be like to live with someone that long. "How did you two meet?"

"When he almost killed me."

"What?" Cassie choked, dribbling tea onto her chin. "How? Why?"

"He threw me in the Alm, a mountain stream in Austria. We grew up nearby."

"Why did he do such a thing?"

"I provoked him." Berta chuckled and smoothed her starched apron over her equally starched and ironed dress. "We were children. I was eight, I think, and Justin three years older. As a treat my parents took me to the Alm to search for the first rose of spring. Other families were doing the same, all of us enjoying the day." Berta's face glowed with remembrance, her faint German accent deepening. "I saw Justin poking the water with a stick. It looked dangerous, leaning so near he could tumble in, and I marched right up and told him so. The winter's thaw turned the spring rapid enough to carry him away if he wasn't careful. I told him that, too. He laughed like it was funny and tossed a dead fish in my lap. So I took that stinky fish and snacked him with it. He called me a cowardly pug and pushed me in the water."

"Were you scared?"

Berta shook her head. "The current caught me. All I remember is the fierce cold and the land rushing past, and my mother running alongside, screaming."

"You must have had nightmares long after."

"Not really. It was as though I went to sleep and when I woke up I was lying on the ground with Justin leaning over me, wet and gagging, and Papa pounding him on the back. I didn't learn until later that Justin forgot he couldn't swim and jumped in after me, and Papa rescued us both."

"That's amazing!"

"It is, isn't it? Papa swore to the day of his death that he rested on the back of an angel who powered his lungs and limbs, bringing us safely to shore." Berta leaned forward, as if sharing a secret. "And I swore to get my revenge on Justin by marrying him when I grew up."

"I'm sure he considers it just punishment."

"And so you see," Berta swept her hand at the collection of metal scrap angels populating the yard and roof, "ever after Justin has honored the angel that saved us."

Cassie helped set the dining room table, touched by the care Berta had taken to make lunch a special affair, using china painted with a flourish of tulips, and a centerpiece of tiny roses. Serving dishes held a whipped concoction of potatoes and apples called Heaven and Earth, roast beef, carrots simmering in nutmeg, yeasty rolls. It all rested upon a fragile lace tablecloth that had deepened into the ivory hue of age. Perhaps it was a heritage piece handed from one generation to the next. The idea of being treated to something so treasured made Cassie's throat tighten and she gulped, surprised at herself.

"Justin!" Berta called. "Time for lunch!" She motioned to a chair at the table's head. "Sit there, Cassandra, between us old folk."

"All fixed!" Justin entered, wiping his hands with a towel. "Couldn't have been easier."

"No more dent?" Cassie asked.

"Nope. All it took was a good pop. Handy invention, the toilet plunger." His grin reminded Cassie of a garden gnome with a glint of mischief and eternal good humor. "Anything else needs doing, just say the word."

Cassie opened her mouth to say the word *fuse*, but wasn't fast enough.

"*Schatz*, would you give the blessing?"

Berta clasped Cassie's left hand and Justin held her right as he began to pray. Lowering her head, Cassie peeked from beneath slit lids at the two faces on either side of her – one long and bony with feather-tufted hair circling a bald patch, the other petite and rotund as a puff ball with rosy cheeks. "Our heavenly father, thank you for the blessings of this good food," Justin intoned, his voice falling into rhythm with the clocks. "Thank you for the blessings of our home and all that rest therein. And thank you for the special blessing of our new friend. May she find happiness here among the hills of Willow City. Amen."

Soon all was silent, save for the ticking clocks and the clinking silverware. Strudel the cat glowered from under the china cabinet, unforgiving for having been so rudely dumped from this new person's lap yesterday.

"Ambrosia," Cassie said between mouthfuls.

"Take some home for later," Berta said. "You probably haven't had time to shop for groceries."

"There's a mouse in my oven. I don't dare buy anything edible until it's found and everything scrubbed."

"A mouse in the *oven*?" Berta exclaimed. "Good heavens!"

"Probably a nest somewhere underneath," Justin said. "Won't take a minute for me to take care of it."

"Oh, thank you! You're a knight in disguise."

"Armed and ready to face the rodent dragon."

Berta collected the empty plates and busied herself in the kitchen. "Is everything else going well?" she called from around the corner.

"Okay, except the lights went out and I need a fuse, the kind with a glass knob on top that screws in. Mine is blown or corroded or something."

Justin put his hand in a pocket and pulled out a penny. "Here."

"A penny for a fuse?"

"Stick it in first and screw the fuse back in place. It'll work just fine."

"*Schatz!*" Berta stood at the doorway. "Why are your reading glasses in the flower pot?"

Justin rubbed his bare nose. "Well, what do you know. I guess I wanted to grow a new pair."

Berta plopped his glasses on the table. "You'll be the death of me yet."

"You fuss too much," Justin teased. "Just bring out your butter cookies and all will be forgiven."

"They're too hot from the oven, so we'll have to wait a bit."

Justin scooted his chair back. "Time enough for me to go find that mouse. You two girls visit in the meanwhile, enjoy yourselves." He turned to Cassie. "Can I borrow the key?"

"Of course!" She hurried to fetch it from her purse. "Are you sure you don't want me to come and help?"

"Stay, keep Berta company. I'll be back before you know it." A minute later he was gone, his lanky frame loping down the front steps.

"Thanks!" Cassie called after him. "You're an…" She meant to say *angel,* but a riot of cackles erupted from the back yard, followed by a barking frenzy.

"Not again!" Berta hurried to the rear entry, her slippers flop-flopping on the wooden floor. "Stop it, you two! Behave, or I'll sic the pound on you!"

Cassie watched through the window as Berta scolded a pair of dogs almost as big as she was while a black and white goat leisurely chewed a sunflower alongside the barbed-wire fence. Standing guard were a half dozen angel sentries fashioned from iron scraps, wings unfurled, wielding swords and hubcap shields. One of them perched upon a post, knees bent as if preparing to launch upward.

"Is that where Justin makes his angels?" she asked upon Berta's return, pointing to a shed attached to the side of a barn. Pyramids of rusty metal odds and ends lined up against its outer walls in neat formations.

"Good heavens, no. He's taken over the entire barn. The other is where he fiddles with clocks."

"A man of many talents, your Mr. Grumm."

"That he is," Berta said, sounding pleased. "Sometimes I forget."

"Maybe that happens when you live with someone for a while." Cassie returned to the task at hand, gathering dessert plates and napkins while Berta ran water into the sink. "Do you have any children?"

Berta nodded. "Two, a boy and a girl, with one granddaughter and two great-grandbabies." She pointed a sudsy finger to a photograph on the windowsill. "There we are. That's my daughter standing beside me, and her husband with their kids and grandkids all around."

Cassie gazed at the faces smiling at the cameras. Berta sat on a bench with Justin beside her, his arm over her shoulders. A baby cuddled in her lap and another hung onto Justin's leg while the others crowded close.

"Was your son taking the photo? I don't see him here."

Berta scrubbed a platter with undue concentration. "No. He's in New York. He doesn't visit much."

"You and Justin must miss him."

"There have been... disagreements between those two. And so my boy stays away."

"I'm sorry." It was all Cassie could think of to say.

"Justin wants him to be an engineer or a doctor or just about anything other than what that boy truly loves." She thrust the platter at Cassie. "Frederick waits on tables when he's not acting in a theatre somewhere. He calls himself Jason now, a stage name, Jason Wells."

Water dripped unnoticed onto Cassie's shoes as she looked with dismay at the saddened face of Mrs. Grumm. "Any grandkids there with him?"

"No. He doesn't have children. He'll never have children. He'll never have a *wife*." Berta wrung the dishrag as if hoping to strangle it. "He prefers a... man friend."

Cassie wanted to respond but couldn't find the words.

"Life goes on, and so must we," Berta spoke with a forced brightness. "Thanks for helping me tidy up. Work is better with two, don't you think?" She tugged at her apron and hung it on a hook shaped like a kitten. "But enough about this old woman. How about you?"

"Me?" Cassie wasn't used to talking about herself and found it awkward. "Well, I don't... Oh, look at this!" She gaped at a picture frame she hadn't noticed earlier, hanging between two cuckoo clocks. "A collection of arrow heads!" A familiar excitement prickled her scalp as she studied the stones and flaking pattern "Where did you find these?"

"Scattered around here and there. Justin likes looking for them." She peered over Cassie's shoulder. "Seem like chunks of rock to me."

"They're stunning."

"You think so?" Berta looked at Cassie with an odd little smile. "There's so much about you I find interesting. Let's sit in the parlor now that the dishes are done. Would you like that?"

"Absolutely."

Berta led Cassie into the other room and with a soft grunt plopped onto the sofa. "Come sit next to me," she said, and pushed aside a half dozen pillows of needlepoint cats. The real cat hopped into the cushy lap of its mistress and watched through wary eyes as Cassie joined them.

"Now then," Berta began, "Justin tells me often enough I have a bad habit of snooping where I oughtn't, but I truly would like to know more about you."

"There's not much to tell."

"Well, let's begin with your interest in arrow heads."

"I'm interested in the whole shebang, actually."

"The whole *what?*"

"All of it, any of it. If it's Native American, I'm hooked. I've been fascinated ever since I read a prayer written by a Sioux holy man. His name was Black Elk. It affected me so much I started collecting books about American Indians, so many I lost count. And things like jewelry, paintings, blankets, and fabrics – until I figured, why not do this for a living? So my husband and I opened a store and did just that."

"Gracious! Where?"

"On the top floor of the Galleria in Houston, overlooking the skating rink. I named it *Spirit of the Southwest.* A small place, really. A boutique."

"My daughter Victoria took me to the Galleria once. I never saw a mall so fancy."

"Does she live in Houston?"

"In Rice Village near the University. She teaches German."

"How impressive! I admire people who master other languages."

"And I admire people brave enough to follow their heart's desire, like yourself. So tell me about this store. Do you sell arrow heads?"

Cassie nodded. "*Did* sell. Past tense. Also silver and turquoise jewelry signed by the artist. Hand-loomed blankets and shawls, Kachina dolls, one-of-a-kind belts and bags." She gestured to her soft leather purse lying where she had tossed it on the footstool, the silver spider clasp gleaming. "This was my favorite, even though I loathe spiders. It's a memento of sorts. Of the shop, of my hopes for it."

"The place sounds... unique."

"I like unique. My partner didn't."

"Oh? You have a partner?"

"*Had,*" Cassie replied tersely. "I sold my share this June. June sixth, to be exact."

"Why?"

"A difference of opinion. Diane thought we would bring in more money by selling cheap trinkets for tourists: Tee-shirts decorated with rhinestone boots, plastic chili pepper mobiles, fake war bonnets with purple chicken feathers. That sort of thing." She glanced down, remembering the unhappiness of the last few months. "I was scraping by, glad to make each month's rent, until I faced the truth and passed what I had hoped would be my life's work into the hands of someone else.

"It was best we split. Now Diane can go her own way and follow her own tacky dream."

Berta leaned forward, almost squishing Strudel as she rested her elbows on dimpled knees. "And your own un-tacky dream?"

"It's still in the making." Cassie smiled, embarrassed. How could she say what had first come to mind? *I lost my husband, lost my boutique, and somewhere along the way I lost my dreams, too.* "To find myself. To put my life in order. To begin again."

Berta began to speak, then seemed to change her mind. Cassie pulled a cushion into her lap and hugged it close, wishing the conversation would end yet enjoying it all the same.

"It must be difficult, living alone," Berta finally said. "I'd be lonely all by myself. I've been married to Justin for so long I don't know what life would be like without him."

The words slipped from Cassie's mouth, as if pulled by an invisible string: "I had love once and can't imagine another as wonderful. My time has come and gone."

"Oh, my dear!" Berta clasped her hands over her heart. "You're still too young to know what life will bring! So let's not hear about time coming and going!"

The older woman looked so stricken, so warmly sympathetic, that for a moment Cassie was tempted to shove Strudel off of her lap and claim the spot for herself.

The Emperor Tree

JUSTIN OPENED THE SCREEN DOOR WITH A GRAND FLOURISH AND WIDE GRIN. "I found a nest behind the stove. It's gone, as is the beastie. How about celebrating? Let's have ice cream with those cookies. Cranked some up this morning, put strawberries in it."

"That was yesterday," Berta said. "Last night, in fact. Remember? We talked about the storm coming on."

"Well, no difference. It tastes just as good."

"It sounds tempting but I'd best get going. Every inch of that kitchen has to be scrubbed before nightfall." Cassie hugged Berta, then stood on tiptoe and hugged Justin, too. "Lunch was wonderful."

"Take a little something along to help you settle in." Berta hurried to the kitchen, and despite Cassie's protests filled her arms with leftovers and extra cleaning supplies.

"I need to stock up on just about everything," Cassie said as they walked to the porch. "Is a grocery store nearby?"

"Fredericksburg, if you don't mind the drive."

"Anything closer?"

"There's Pete's at Ranch Road and Crabapple Creek. Just turn right on the loop and follow it along for a bit. It's small with little to choose from, but I like it just fine."

"You can't miss it," Justin added. "Look for the sign, Pete's Gas `n Grub."

"Gas `n Grub?" Cassie burst into a giggle, lost her footing, and stumbled down the bottom step. Sponges and a can of cleanser slipped from her grasp and rolled across the lawn. "I'm sorry," she said, laughing while trying to gather them up. "I don't know why that name tickles my funny bone."

Justin chased after a sponge. "It's always nice having laughter in the house. When the grandkids are here the place fairly rings with it."

"We miss it, you know," Berta said. "Sometimes I'm surprised it's just the two of us rattling around all by ourselves. I'd go crazy without Justin taking up space and making a nuisance of himself. I think he riles me up just to keep away the quiet."

Cassie pulled out of the driveway, watching the Grumms through her rearview mirror. They stood together, Berta's head barely up to Justin's shoulder as they waved farewell. A mobile of silverware angels that had hung on their porch now rested in Cassie's lap. Berta and Justin had spoken over one another in their eagerness to give it to her. "To watch and protect you," and "Whenever it chimes, your guardian spirits are listening," and, "If it's specially merry, make a wish."

As the road curved and the house disappeared behind a clump of trees, she thought of the photograph on Berta's windowsill with several generations gathered together. The only family Cassie had was her mother. No father, no grandparents, no sister, brother, aunts or uncles or cousins – at least none she knew about – and no husband or child. Just Lillian. Their relationship consisted of telephone calls with token words: Nice to hear from you, chat-chat, goodbye. Frowning, Cassie tried to recall the last time they had spent more than a few hours face-to-face. It must have been during Mimi's funeral, and even then Lillian dashed in too late, full of apologies. She had been in Africa, ballooning over the Serengeti on a honeymoon with new husband Whoever, and had not known. Cassie faced Mimi's death alone, and buried her alone.

The memory rose and played before her eyes like the rerun of a familiar movie.

Lillian is traipsing over the rugged grounds to the family gravesite in four-inch stiletto heels, puncturing holes in her wake, long after the scattering of mourners are gone. She pauses by the weather-worn picket fence enclosing the small space deep in the woods beyond the creek and house. Cassie stands in the tree-cast shadows, waiting as her mother opens the wooden gate and steps past the old headstones to the fresh mound of dirt. "Dearest," Lillian whispers, her voice ragged and thick. "We have lost our heart." Swaying, she drops to her knees beside the mound and places her hands upon it, as if in a blessing.

It is silent for a time, broken only by the songs of sparrows and the wind rustling through the leaves. With her black shoes, black stockings, black dress, hat, and veil, Lillian in her stillness looks like a giant raptor come to rest. An unkind thought, Cassie knows, provoked by anger at Lillian's absence and neglect.

Abruptly, the black figure wails and pounds the grave, beating it with her fists as though to punish the earth for what lay hidden beneath. The face that looks up at Cassie contorts behind its thin veil. "I can't remember if I ever told her I loved her," she cries. "I can't remember."

Cassie's resentment wilts in the heat of her mother's anguish. She kneels, wrapping her arms around Lillian's slender shoulders and presses her lips against Lillian's hair, afraid that one day it will be she *pounding on a gravesite, weeping for the loss of words left unspoken.*

Cassie's eyes burned with unshed tears as she gripped the steering wheel, annoyed. Almost forty-five years old and she still missed her mother.

Thoughts of Lillian jumbled with thoughts of the Grumms as she drove back to the house. She found it difficult to phrase the return. Usually someone says, *I'm going home.* But this place wasn't home. *I'm going to the house* seemed... indifferent. Lonely, even.

She drove over the rackety bridge and parked under the old oak. Moments later, using a kitchen chair to stand on, she hung her silver angels from the porch eaves. They stirred in the breeze, the chimes sweet as rippling water. "Louder!" she commanded. "Time to make a wish." For what, she didn't know. She felt as hollow and haunted with the past as the house. Maybe they belonged together, she and it, in ways she didn't yet understand.

The mobile hung directly above the rosebush, as though protecting the blossoms below. She studied the potted plant with a critical eye, knowing that roses needed the right amount of sunlight at the right time of day in order to thrive. She scooted the bush here and there and back again, seeking the perfect spot. A petal trembled against her skin. So soft, so lovely. A good resting place for what lay beneath, long buried among the roots.

Her intent to disinfect every inch and item in the kitchen faltered after several hours of scrubbing. There were too many dishes in different sizes and patterns, too many glasses and jelly and canning jars, too many pots and pans so old the sides had buckled, too many and too much of everything.

Twilight fell in its usual slow summer grace. Shadows deepened, tumbling into darkness. The house seemed to expand around her as night descended, her footsteps echoing in strange ways. Whatever Cassie touched resonated in the quiet, as if breathing. She turned on the lights and sometimes sang, trying to fill the emptiness. She was used to being alone. But this was a different sort of aloneness, something she couldn't define. As if the walls had ears and listened.

One last chore for the evening and she would call it a night. She found a tin bucket among the carport junk, hauled it inside, and stuck it under the faucet. The bucket clanked against the sink and pipes grumbled in the wall.

A ray of light bounced along the counter and hit her in the face. She stiffened as it slid to the floor and crawled over the sill and out the bay window, brushing against the tree. She forgot the bucket, forgot the water as it overflowed and gurgled down the drain. She forgot even to breathe as the light traveled in the darkness beyond, then was suddenly no more. The mantle clock wheezed and bonged the hour. *One, two, three…* After the fifth she moved to the window, cupped her hands to her eyes, and peered into the night. *Seven, eight.* Moonlight threw silver onto the trees, the creek, the meadow. One final bong. Nine o'clock. Yet still she stood, pressed against the glass.

There! The light, swinging to and fro from the hand of someone close by, someone wearing a floppy hat. Wind tugged at a long, voluminous skirt, lifting it above a pair of cargo boots.

Good Lord, it's the bag lady!

The figure stepped back into the darkness.

"Wait!" Cassie ran into the parlor, through the front door and down the steps, crying, "Wait!"

The bag lady scurried over the bridge into the shadow of the woods.

"What do you want?" Cassie yelled. "Coming to watch another hissy fit? Let me know when you'd like an encore and I'll supply the popcorn!"

She stomped into the house, slamming the screen door. *What an odd creature, spying like some sort of pervert!* She peered through the screen, seeing nothing but moon-splashed meadow. Crickets and tree frogs chirruped and the windmill squawked in the wind as if nothing unusual had happened. Retreating to the kitchen, she turned off the faucet and mopped the floor in a fury, acutely aware of how silent and still the house seemed against the night sounds. How strange that face staring from the shadows. How vulnerable and exposed she felt.

"I need somebody around I can talk to," she muttered.

A fairy godmother must have been sitting on her shoulders, for as soon as the wish had left her lips headlights flashed through the bay window and played over the walls. Startled, Cassie paused while the vehicle growled closer, the bridge clattering, the racket abrupt and out of place in this too-quiet house. The motor coughed and came to a stop, followed by the squeal of a door opening.

Dropping the mop into the bucket, she rushed to the porch the moment Mrs. Grumm's rotund, petite self clambered out of Justin's blue pickup. It looked like a free-fall leap to get from the driver's seat to the ground.

"You actually drove that thing?" Cassie asked.

"Do it all the time." Berta thrust a frosty container into her hands. "Justin insisted I bring this tonight, with orders for you to eat it right away while the cream's fresh and the strawberries tasty."

"How thoughtful! Thank you."

"Other men have a passion for cars or football. With him it's clocks, angels, and ice cream."

Cold crystals bit Cassie's fingers while she stood, bemused. She had received so much kindness from the Grumms in such a short period of time she didn't know quite how to respond. She settled with, "Can you stay awhile, have some with me?"

Berta nodded, smiling. "I was hoping you'd ask."

"A weird thing happened a while ago," Cassie said while ushering her inside. "A woman in a floppy hat spied on me through the window, then ran away when I saw her."

"It was Tatty, I'm sure. She lives in a tumble-down house in the woods, all alone."

"She's peculiar, then?"

"My, yes. But harmless. I feel sorry for the poor thing."

Cassie scooped the delicacy into bowls and carried them to the swing. The rusty chains complained as Berta settled upon the seat, her short legs dangling. Cassie pushed with a nudge of her foot until the two of them rocked back and forth. Dots of flame scattered like embers across the meadow.

"Look," Cassie said. "Fireflies."

"Pretty things, lightning bugs. Wouldn't it be something if we could do that – have our own built-in flashlight?"

"Where would it be? In our stomach?"

"Maybe our forehead, like a third eye."

They laughed quietly. After a moment, Cassie said, "Once I tried to catch fireflies and put them in a jar, but my grandmother said that was a wicked thing to do. She believed everything has a spirit, that the stars, the rocks, the wind – all we see, and all we do not, hums with life."

"She must have been very wise.'

"Yes, I think she was."

"I used to tease Justin that he was a tad in love with her. He'd say, 'Her eyes are like blue hyacinths.' And he'd work up a lather doing stuff for her around the house and such."

"She obviously liked and trusted you both, or she wouldn't have asked you to be the caretakers."

"I wish I had known her better, but never had the chance. Justin and I moved here about six years ago, glad to find a quiet place far from the city even though our daughter kicked up a fuss about us old folks being alone. Your grandmother went to the hospital a short time after, I think."

"A nursing home," Cassie said quietly. "Mimi hated it. She wanted to be in her own home."

"I'm sure I'd feel the same way."

Leafy shadows waltzed through the moonlight, dancing on the ground and porch railing. Cassie glanced at Berta, remembering the times Mimi had sat in that very spot with the very same shadows dancing the very same patterns, while eating ice cream just like now. "We would sit here on the swing or on the steps, and she would tell me stories."

"Oh? What kind?

"Outlandish ones, funny, happy, sad ones. All sorts." Cassie motioned to the old oak sprawling over the rooftop and rustling in the wind. "My favorite is about this tree and how it came to be. Mimi called it the Emperor Tree because it stands regally above all the others, as if guarding its realm,"

"I remember stories from my childhood, too. Oma would hold me in her lap long into the night whispering long-ago legends, fairy tales about little people, pixies and such."

"Oma?"

"My grandmother. Small like me, and with a lap just as ample." She chuckled softly and asked, "Do you remember the tree story?"

"Word for word. I rarely let a visit here pass without hearing it at least once."

"Oh, do tell me!" Berta clapped her hands as eagerly as a little girl. "I'd love to hear it."

"Well then, I'd love to tell it." Cassie's lips moved, recalling the words of many yesterdays:

Once upon a time, there was a prince so handsome maidens leaned from their balconies and sang as he passed. When it was time for him to be crowned, people cheered at the gates, rang tower bells, and flung kites into the skies. Everyone thought someone so beautiful to look upon must surely be equally so in heart.

Cassie licked the last dollop of cream off her spoon. "I'd usually interrupt right about now and ask Mimi, 'Will I ever meet someone so handsome?' And she'd say, 'A beautiful heart is better than a beautiful face.' I never liked that answer. I wanted both together."

Berta nodded, waiting for Cassie to continue.

No one knew that his heart had shriveled into a blackened lump. Nor did they understand why sadness followed in his wake, or why flowers lost their bloom when he breathed upon them, or why those who gazed into his eyes were suddenly afraid of the dark.

His favorite hobby was to collect gifts of a maiden's tears captured in crystal vials, which he lined up on shelves for all to admire. At first he would dust the display, saying, "That one's from Francesca and this from Caroline, or Missy, or Rebecca." But after a time the shelves grew crowded and the glassed tears tumbled together, covered with cobwebs. He added shelves but no longer bothered to look at the tears or remember who had shed them.

Late one evening in the darkness of the night when the moon hid her face, the prince demanded, "I need room for more!" and swept vials off the shelves and ground them under his boot. The glass turned to powdered dust but the contents did not. The tears moved along the floor in a fast-flowing stream, gathering and transforming into a snake with glittering scales. The prince screamed as the serpent slithered up his legs and thighs and wound around his chest, squeezing life from his lungs.

"Goodness!" Berta interrupted. "This isn't a very pretty story, is it?"

Cassie looked at the face of Mrs. Grumm, pale in the moonlight, hands clasped tightly around the bowl as if it would fly out of her lap.

"Would you like me to stop?"

"Oh, my no!" Berta exclaimed. "I'd worry all night, wondering how it ended."

"All right then."

> "Your heart and spirit have long been hardened to the gift of love," the serpent hissed. "By your actions are you judged. Henceforth your skin will be tormented bark, your arms branches, your fingers twigs. You are destined to remain forever rooted to the earth, protecting those you once scorned."
>
> "Have mercy!" the prince begged. "Will nothing save me now?"
>
> "Only the love of a fair princess."
>
> With a magical poof! and a smattering of sparks, the once-handsome prince changed into a tree. Centuries passed. The tree grew old, his limbs heavy, his trunk twisted and thick. With each passing year, the shell of his heart crumbled bit by bit, until nothing was left but the pulsing core of grief and loneliness.
>
> Still he waited, hoping for a princess.

"What happened next?"

"I don't know."

"That's not a proper ending at all! I want a happily-ever-after."

"Me too, but Mimi never gave me one. 'Ask the tree,' she'd say."

"How sad!" Berta gave her bowl to Cassie and wiggled off the swing, hanging onto the chain until her feet hit the floor. "A powerful story, but it's time for me to go home. Justin is probably getting lonesome. He doesn't do well by himself."

"Thanks for the ice cream." Cassie put the bowls on a step and followed Mrs. Grumm to the pickup. "And thanks for listening to my story."

"I'd like to hear more, but only if you promise a happily-ever-after."

Laughing, Cassie helped hoist Mrs. Grumm up to the driver's seat. "Maybe I'll think up a better ending for this one."

"Yes, I'd like that." Berta slammed the door and leaned from the opened window. "You're a dear girl, Cassandra. I'm glad we met." She gunned the truck and drove over the bridge much too fast, chubby arm waving in the moonlight.

"I like you, too." Cassie called, although she knew her voice would be drowned by the truck's rumble. She waited until the headlights disappeared into the darkness, beguiled by the woman's spunk and energy, and hoping she herself would be half as sassy at eighty-odd years.

She returned to the porch, passing under the old oak. She patted the rough bark as one would a friend, her mind wandering and playing with Mimi's story. What would happen if love finally penetrated the Emperor Tree's crusty shell? Would he turn young again, morph into a prince and frolic into the sunset, streaming leaves like rose petals along his path? If so, he would leave behind a great hole where his roots had once burrowed, a hole almost as deep as the one in her heart.

The angel chimes trembled in the breeze while Cassie gazed at the fireflies, wishing for the impossible.

ꟿ

She lingered over coffee the following morning, leaning against the kitchen counter and gazing out the narrow window above the sink. She could see the barn and windmill, the hills far behind them, the clouds skimming above. And to the left, between the house and barn, the remnants of Mimi's garden. Parts of the picket fence had broken away, revealing weeds where tomatoes and squash once had flourished. In the far corner a single daylily struggled in the sunlight, leaves wilted.

It's all so desolate and sad and forgotten.

She tried to block the ruined garden from her mind's eye as she drove along the farm road toward Crabapple Creek. She knew if she kept going she'd eventually end up near Enchanted Rock, a mystical place some folk claimed was haunted by the Comanche, or was the center of an energy vortex, or just plain beautiful.

Justin had been right. The sign couldn't be missed. *Pete's Gas `n Grub,* painted in fluorescent pink, rose from the back of a cement armadillo. She turned into the dusty lot, easing past the single gas pump, and parked beside an outdoor fruit stand boasting a poster announcing peaches and blackberries guaranteed home-grown delicious. She turned off the ignition and began to open the door, hesitating when a red pickup abruptly backed away from its parking space and sped close by, gravel spitting from the tires. A floppy-eared yellow dog stuck its head out of the passenger window, yapping into the wind. She twisted around in her seat, squinting at the truck's rear window as it passed. Sure enough, a soaring hawk was painted over the whole thing.

That's the clod who forced me off the road yesterday, pounding on his horn as if he couldn't wait to shove me into the fence!

"Have a lousy day," she muttered, and tapped her own horn in triplets, *Honk-honk-honk!*

Stepping from the car, she turned toward the store – and realized the pickup had stopped, idling mere yards from where she stood. A tanned patch of arm from elbow to wrist poked from the open window as he looked at her, face shadowed beneath the rim of his cowboy hat. Although his eyes were masked behind sunglasses, she could feel him staring, as if laser beams cut through to her bones.

Oh my God, what have I done?

She had to admit it – she was spooked. *Maybe he's a temper-challenged jerk itching for a fight. Maybe he's wondering who the hell I am and why I honked at him. Maybe he just stopped for a sneeze.* She began to consider making a dash for it, when he raised a hand and tipped his hat, nodded, and drove down the road – too slow for her liking, those laser-beam eyes likely aimed at her the entire time.

It came as a surprise to discover she was gripping the car door handle, as if planning to throw herself in at the first hint of danger and race away.

The store itself was a sun-bleached green. A sagging porch supported two rockers and a dented Coca-Cola cooler, with faded letters *oca-Col.* An overgrown gray dog with paws big as softballs slept on the steps, barring access. "Nice doggie," Cassie ventured. Doggie opened one eye and growled. When she tried to maneuver around it, the growls grew louder and the fat lips quivered.

"*Hellooo,*" she cried, cupping hands to her mouth. "There's a problem out here!"

The door opened with a clang from an overhead cowbell, revealing a man who looked like a cross between Santa Claus and Paul Bunyan. Geniality glowed from every massive pore. "Pooh-Bah!" he roared, "get your lazy ass off these here steps so the lady can come in." He nudged the animal with the tip of his lizard boot.

"Pooh-Bah?" Cassie eyed the dog warily as it retreated huffing with the indignity of it all. "He looks more like a Rover or Big Jim or something."

Santa Bunyan opened his bewhiskered mouth and guffawed, showing rows of perfect teeth, all of them stained brown. "Pooh-Bah is fine for a dog who thinks he's grander than he is and gets puffed up over his own importance." The giant leaned down and whispered in a soft bellow, "He's really a cupcake under all that pretending."

"Sounds like some people I've known."

"Yah. Sometimes I forget he's a dog." Grinning, he stuck out a hand. "Pete Addle here. And who might you be?"

"Cassandra Brighton, but please call me Cassie."

"Welcome to Gas `n Grub, Miss Cassie. Take your time, walk around, have a cup of hot coffee there on the back counter. It's free to all customers, slice of pie's extra. Peach today. Mighty good, too. Wife makes `em. If you need anything, got any question, just holler." And with that, he plucked a glowing cigar from an ashtray, stuck it in his mouth, and left.

"Thank you," Cassie called to the retreating back. "I'll do that." She looked for something to put groceries in. Quarter-bushel baskets were stacked on the floor nearby, apparently for that purpose. Grabbing one, she wandered along cramped aisles so narrow she almost had to shuffle sideways on a wooden floor that sloped uphill or down like a wave in a petrified sea, reminding her of a quotation from Alice in Wonderland: *Curiouser and curiouser.*

Selections consisted mainly of canned goods arranged in no discernable order, with tick spray alongside baby food. Mingled amid it all were oddities such as mustang grape jelly or jalapeño pepper jam or beef jerky. She chose a jar of honey with a bumblebee sticker that read, "Sweet Miracles by Maude."

Bins of fresh vegetables pushed against a rack of hunting gear and auto supplies. She selected a few tomatoes and reached for a flashlight when a voice rang, "Hey, Ed, you done it again!" followed by raucous laughter. For the first time, Cassie noticed the din around her – the rattle and hum of the freezer, the *fup-fup-fup* of the ceiling fan, voices – and a guitar. Curious, she dropped the flashlight into her basket and headed toward the strumming.

Several men gathered around a cardboard table at the rear, playing dominos amid coffee mugs, half-eaten slices of pie, and crinkled bags of potato chips. Peanut shells littered the floor. A coffee pot rested on the counter behind them, as did a scattering of cups and what was left of the pie. Sitting alongside on a barstool was a boy around fifteen or so, playing a guitar.

It was like a scene from an old Western, complete with cowboy boots and hats. It even had one of those barroom double-doors opening into another room, the sort a gunslinger would fling open with a scowl, spurs jangling. A plaque hung overhead, its letters burned into the wood, *RAZORBACKS.*

The only things present that wouldn't be seen in a tavern from the Old West were the paintings on the wall – landscapes, floral arrangements, farm animals – likely by local folk hoping to make a small profit. A tag thumb-tacked beside each noted the price in red ink, the most expensive being sixty dollars.

"How you doing, Miss Cassie?" Pete's head appeared over the barroom doors. "Find what you need?"

"Yes, thank you."

"Everybody, this here's Cassie Brighton."

Heads popped up, hands extended, mutterings of Howdy and Glad to meetcha, the names going past rapidly – Ed, James, Rupert – the last names forgotten as soon as they were spoken. Then back to playing dominoes or whatever. Cassie stood awkwardly, feeling dismissed.

"Hi. I'm Billy," the boy said shyly.

Cassie smiled and shook his hand, thinking it was too big for the rest of him, as were his feet. By the looks of things, he had a lot of growing to do. "I heard you playing the guitar. Very nice."

"I'm practicing, trying to get good enough so Pete will let me join the band."

"He has a band?"

"Razorbacks. It's radical. Drums, guitars, fiddles, piano, bass or banjo or mandolin, sometimes a flute – not high and twerpy but kind of sad, even spooky. They get great gigs – Fredericksburg, Gruene, Blanco, even the Old Settler's Music Festival a couple months back."

"Now don't you go parading our colors, Billy." Pete's head once again popped up behind the double doors. "We play for the fun of it, amateurs all of us. Bluegrass, country-rock, blues, gospel or some such, depending on who shows up to jam." He winked at Billy. "Go ahead, boy. Twaddle them strings for Miss Cassie. Show her you ain't no dumb-ass who can't do nothin'."

A faint blush crept up the boy's neck and into his cheeks. "Would you like to hear something?"

"Sure!" She sat on a bar stool beside him. "What sort of music do you play?"

"I like all kinds but make up a lot." He struck a few cords, experimenting.

Cassie thought he looked like a Norman Rockwell painting of a country boy: tousled red hair bleached by the sun, freckles, eyes deep as pond water. He glanced at her briefly and began to sing:

A lady walked in the door, wearing a smile
She sits next to me now, lady stranger.
Pretty like my mama was, is she sad too?
Maybe she knows that love is in all the yesterdays,
And love is gone in all the tomorrows,
Lady stranger wearing a smile.

Cassie clapped, not trusting herself to speak.

"Was it really OK?"

"More than OK. It was..." Words stuck in her mouth, and so she tried again. "Wonderful. It was wonderful and I loved it. How did you make it up so fast?"

He shrugged. "I just let the words and music come out like they wanted."

The cowbell jangled as the door opened. Pete's voice bellowed from the next room. "Billy, customers! Break's over. Stop lazing around."

"Yes, sir." He leaned the guitar against the counter, and with a quick salute in Cassie's direction, hurried away.

Cassie watched as he disappeared behind a stack of goods. She didn't move for a moment, aware that this boy had touched her heart. She glanced at the domino gang. They were still hawing at one another, having a good time, paying no attention to her or Billy.

Good. Some things were best kept private.

She rushed through the aisles, tossing items into her basket. On the last round she passed the barroom doors and glanced over them. At the far end of the room was a platform with a drum set and piano. Pete, cigar clamped between his teeth, was busy arranging chairs and benches in rows, as if for an audience.

"Hey there, Miss Cassie," he said, waving her in.

"Is this where your band performs?"

"Yuh, sometimes. It used to be storage. Lots of stuff I keep behind that there." He gestured toward a self-standing screen in need of a paint job. On one side of it was a beat-up refrigerator and on the other a door opened to a jumble of boxes and a rag mop. "Guys hereabouts like to jam on Wednesday nights, bring whatever instrument they're handy at. Folks come to listen, have a good time. Starts at eight, goes on `til we're done." He placed a stool on the platform and closed the piano lid, revealing something that had been hidden on the wall behind it.

A painting. Small, the canvas perhaps a foot square, framed in roughened mesquite. "How interesting," Cassie murmured, and drew closer.

It was rendered in oil, sparse in strokes as though the artist had crafted it quickly in a burst of inspiration. At first glance it appeared to be a simple landscape of the hill country – a craggy plateau in the background, a field of bluebonnets, a large, twisted oak. She was about to turn aside when she noticed the phantom caught within the oak's crusty interior. Subtly drafted within the texture of bark was the figure of a man, face contorted in a cry, body embedded within the prison of the tree's limbs, struggling to break free.

Cassie caught her breath. Pete must have heard, for he raised his bushy eyebrows in mock surprise. "You like that? Not many folk do. They think it's peculiar."

"It reminds me of a story, a fairy-tale."

"Eh-yah? I never was one for fairies and all that."

"Who's the artist?"

"Nice fellow, bit of a loner. Travels way out in the country, disappears for days, sometimes weeks. Then comes back with stuff like this." He pointed at the painting's low right corner. "Name's Hawk. See? There's his signature – no name, just that there hawk. Usually it's got wings open like it's flying around. Even drew it on his windshield, big as life. But in this here the hawk's just sitting there, all solemn-like. Kind of creepy, if you ask me."

"I've met him, sort of."

"Eh-yah?"

"By sight. In that red pickup, coming and going." She spoke quietly, the anger forgotten, captivated by how the picture transformed when she neared. Loneliness and despair, captured with a strange beauty. Hope was there, too. She felt the promise of it, invisible and unspoken, as if the imprisoned figure had whispered to her in a dream.

"Is there a print of this available? I'd love to buy one."

"You can buy that there original if you want. Been hanging here for over a year. Nobody else around here cottons to it much, like I said."

"Are you sure?" Cassie exclaimed, almost jumping with pleasure.

"Need to get the darned thing off the wall anyway. Spooks everybody. Hate to say it costs a bunch. Hawk thinks a lot of himself, won't come down none."

Steeling herself for the bad news, Cassie asked, "How much?"

"Hundred fifty."

"You've got to be kidding! It's worth a lot more. I'd be stealing it at that price."

Pete looked at her oddly, as if he wanted to speak but thought the better of it, and took the painting from the wall. "That's the only time I ever had a customer complain because I was charging too little." He pressed it into her hands, brushing aside her words of thanks. "It's Wednesday jam tonight, with people coming from all around. You'd be welcome any time."

"I'd enjoy that, but another Wednesday," she said with genuine regret. "I've moved into my grandmother's house and have just begun to settle myself in. There's not much time for anything else."

"I heard you were there."

"Really?"

"Small town, that's the way it goes. She was really something, your grandmother. She had a special way about her. Could never put my finger on it exactly, sort of like she was younger than she looked but older than she seemed. I liked her. Miss her, too. We all do."

"I still feel like she's still there, in the rooms with me."

"Ghost-like?"

Cassie laughed. "In a good way."

"Don't know about ghosts. Gives me the jitters. Well, you got heavy things need moving – boxes, furniture, stuff like that?"

"Too much of it. The carport is overflowing with so much clutter there's no room for my car. I dread looking in the barn. It's probably worse."

Pete walked to the double doors, warily looking over them. "Miss Cassie," he whispered, "I have a suggestion."

Cassie whispered back, "What?"

He leaned forward, resolute. "Billy can do it for you. He's a good boy, a hard worker."

Cassie found herself so close to Pete she was in danger of bumping noses with his cigar. "He seems awfully young."

Pete nodded. "Yuh. You won't be disappointed." Glancing once more at the doors, he continued, "Work would be good for him, give him something else to think about. He's having a hard time since his mama died."

A burst of laughter from the domino players startled them both. Cassie almost dropped her basket and Pete hurried to the doors, speaking loud enough to be heard clear to the front and probably outside as well, "Miss Cassie, you come back now."

Her full basket landed with a thump next to chewing tobacco and snuff on a counter crowded with an eclectic assortment of goods. Billy waited behind it, hair stirring in the tepid breeze of a fan perched on a coffee can. "You find what you need, Miss Cassie?"

"Not everything, but enough." She could make do for a while but a trip to Fredericksburg was definitely in order. As Billy punched the cash register keys, her eyes wandered the area around him – the curling fliers advertising church or school events long past, the faded notice *Cash or Check Only,* a framed photograph of the store with a younger, slimmer Pete standing proudly beside the banner *Grand Opening Today.* Taped to the wall beside it was an advertisement scripted in purple longhand and decorated with gold star stickers: *Nails by Nan,* the number and address below. "Crabapple Creek," Cassie read aloud. "Must be nearby."

"Nan?" Billy asked. Cassie nodded. "Right next door, up a ways behind a bunch of trees. She's real nice, makes great pies, too." He turned and lifted a framed photo off of a cigar box. "See, here they are at their wedding. Pete says he likes to keep this nearby to remind himself every day how lucky he is."

Husband and wife squinted in the sunlight under an arbor of flowers, he in a suit and she in a simple white shift, her dark hair fastened with blossoms. "I can see why Pete thinks he's so lucky," Cassie said. "She's lovely. They look happy together."

"She's from Vietnam but won't talk about it much." He punched the keys one more time. "That comes to fifty-two dollars and three cents, Miss Cassie – not including the painting."

As Cassie pulled out her checkbook, and in as casual a voice as she could muster, she asked, "Billy, I have a slew of heavy things that need sorting or hauling away, most of it junk, pay negotiable. Could I interest you in a job?"

"Really?" His face lit up in a huge grin. "No problem! I'm your man!"

Twin Souls

The front door swung open as soon as Cassie touched it. She stood motionless at the threshold, certain she had locked it earlier. Perhaps she had forgotten.

The mantle clock tick-tick-wheezed, the lampshade cocked to one side, and the telephone sat awry on the side table. All was as she had left it yet felt amiss, as if someone had come and gone while she was shopping at Pete's. She half-expected to see the crazy bag lady pop up from behind the sofa, floppy hat askew. What had Berta called her? Patty, maybe.

Tatty. That's it.

Wary, she walked toward the kitchen. An oak leaf, kin to thousands of others outside, lay on the floor by the hall. She stared at it as though she had never before seen such a thing, as though it had dropped from another dimension. Had it been there earlier? Or had feet other than hers shuffled it in?

"I'm turning into a nut case," Cassie muttered as she put her groceries on the counter and lifted the mesquite frame from its wrapping. She held the painting to the light, inspecting it from different angles. From a distance the tree appeared like any other, but when she brought it closer a metamorphosis occurred, one so subtle a casual viewer might miss it altogether. The face of a man appeared in the gnarled bark, his mouth opened along the crack lines as if silently screaming. Arms merged with branches, fingers stretched into twigs, legs fused into the trunk. He seemed to be struggling against his confines, desperate to break free. Surrounding him were land and sky so lovely it felt almost sinful to put the two elements in the same frame – pain and beauty confined, each forced to share a part of the other.

She studied the hawk perched on the roots, facing the horizon. *Why so still? Why not with wings outstretched and soaring?* Thin black lettering woven between strands of grass on the lower left read, *Hidden Shadows*. Yet the picture held no shadows. The painted landscape blazed clear and hot and still, just as her own meadow had moments earlier.

She hung it in the narrow space beside the bay window. The Emperor Tree outside mirrored the smaller image inside, like twin souls.

The feeling of things being off-kilter remained, nibbling at the back of Cassie's mind as she washed and sliced tomatoes, the water singing in the pipes. Something moved – a shape, a breath – and a stealthy footstep creaked on the floorboards. She spun around, the plump tomato slipping from her grasp and splattering into the sink, but of course no one was there. It was simply the house settling and complaining.

Red pulp oozed down her blouse, a favorite in lime green. Reaching for a dishtowel to mop the damage, she discovered that her chinos were spattered as well. She flung the towel across the kitchen in a temper and undressed then and there, leaving the blouse and chinos to soak in the sink. The washing machine was out of the question. It was a dinosaur that would surely chew up anything not made of hardy stuff.

She had emptied Mimi's closet late last night, heaping musty clothes and dusty hat boxes and scuffed shoes into the hall to sort through later. Her own things now hung inside, perfectly arranged and perfectly impractical: a wardrobe suited for work in the Houston Galleria, for restaurants, for museums – not for getting grubby in a moldering old house.

Clothing of any sort had been far from mind when she signed away her shop. She'd felt lost, truth be told, and realized she couldn't stay in Houston one moment longer. The sale of her boutique had severed the last concrete thing that held her to Thomas, the last binding tie. She yearned to return to the one place where the lingering hurt might subside, where she could gather her wits and somehow begin anew. So she had shoved belongings into a warehouse, tossed random clothes into suitcases while packing away the rest, said goodbye to her old life, and left.

Now here she was, unprepared for the reality of country living and paying for it.

Rummaging through her grandmother's belongings, she flung together an outfit of sorts: baggy pants too short at the ankle, a scarf for a belt, an oversized shirt with a flashy tropical print and missing buttons. She rolled the pant legs up to mid-calf, tied the blouse at her waist, stood in front of the mirror, and laughed.

"Thank God no one's going to see me like this!"

She loaded her arms with soiled linens and towels, intending to use the doddering washing machine in what Justin had called the olden part of the house. She liked that word. It suggested comfort and welcome. "*Olden*," she murmured, and walked down the hall until her bare feet met the cool flagstone of what had once been the front porch of the original stone house. The cedar pillars were still there, plastered into the wall. The front entry was there too, minus the door. Carved with a heart and birds, the door now graced the porch in the wooden addition, its ornate iron key safe inside Cassie's purse.

She hesitated at the threshold, peering into the shadowed great-room where she had played as a child. Now shafts of light crept through the narrow slats of the shutters, running pale fingers along the darkened mounds of draped furniture. Even in the summer's heat a cold seeped from the dim corners like a winter's mist. She hurried to the window, soiled linen slipping from her arms and trailing behind, and yanked the cord. The shutter opened with a disjointed rattle, chasing away things unseen.

The space was large, with a high beamed ceiling and mottled limestone walls. The huge fireplace that had moaned its Firewind voice during the storm soared upward as though carved from a cliff, its mouth yawning into a wide arch almost big enough for her to stand in. On her right was a basin that looked as though it had been hacked out of a boulder and fused to the wall. Next to it was the washing machine, a primeval Maytag metal drum with a mangled On-Off knob. A drain hose poked out of the side and coiled into the basin like a fat, ill-disposed snake. She poured laundry soap into the tub's belly, closed the lid, and turned it on.

The machine whined and shuddered, whisking the soap around without a drop of water. "Oh, good grief!" She whacked the lid in frustration before turning it off. The washer stopped its painful contortions while she searched for the feeder hose. There it was, poking out of the washer's back. She pulled it toward the faucet and the pipes creeping up the wall like a metal fungus, screwed the hose to the worn threads of the tap, and turned the handle. Water sputtered into the Maytag, burst from the spigot, and spat her in the face.

Cassie smacked the faucet handle off as water dripped from her chin and eyelashes.

Three hundred-odd more days with this junkyard house.

At least she could make things more comfortable. Find a decent washer, a TV, a microwave – and an electrician and plumber to make it all possible. Thank heavens finances weren't a problem, not for a while, anyway. She had a decent profit from the sale of her boutique in addition to the funds provided by Thomas' life insurance policy. She had argued with Thomas about the cost of insurance at the time, telling him they were too young, that nothing was going to happen, that they were tossing money down the drain. Now she was grateful he hadn't listened.

Newly resolved, she tied a rag around the faucet and tried again. This time around it didn't spray; it drizzled. But at least it drizzled more into the sink than on the floor.

While the washer thumped its anguish, Cassie tugged at the sheets and blankets covering the furniture. Dust powdered the air, clung to her skin, coated her tongue. Coughing, she found two couches sagging like tired work horses put to pasture and a variety of chairs, tables, and lamps, and put them all in a cozy grouping as if anticipating an evening of conversation with friends. It felt strange to wander around alone in a large room set up for many, but her arrangement brightened up the place and made it more inviting.

I should probably chuck this battered relic into the trash. Cassie gazed at the chair she had once imagined to be the enchanted throne of a woodland queen. It was made of interwoven grapevines twisting and turning to form arms, legs, back, seat. And roses, too, winding among the vine. Jagged cracks showed where the chair had split and shattered, as though someone had attacked it before relenting and patching it back together.

The peculiar chair had been here as long as Cassie could remember, yet she still didn't know its history. "Where did it come from?" she had asked long ago.

Mimi hadn't answered right away, perhaps framing the words in her head before they came out of her mouth. "My father made it."

"Why is it all banged up?"

"Hush, child. You ask too many questions."

"But I want to know! Why keep a chair if nobody can sit in it?"

"It reminds me of… certain things."

"Good things, Mimi?"

"Yes. And bad ones too. Good and bad mixed together so strong I can't throw the chair or the memories away."

Those were the last words Mimi would ever say on the subject.

It was still beautiful in spite of its wounds, a haunting image of what it must have been when first formed by her great-grandfather's hands. Cassie placed it near the hearth, as if to keep its wooden bones warm.

The great-room didn't feel as ominous now as it had in the dark. It was simply part of an old building with a catawampus personality. Doors in different sizes and shapes opened to rooms equally odd, and steps went every which way as floor levels changed. Crooked hallways, unexpected corners, and a narrow stairwell curving out of sight to a space above made it all the more eccentric.

She opened a thick plank door with iron hinges and found a fusty room with items neatly arranged: an ornate headboard, the remaining pieces of a four poster bed bound with twine, a wardrobe with a black-speckled mirror. A china bowl and pitcher sat on a table, a braided rag rug on the floor, a chamber pot in the center of the rug. Cassie laughed at marbles glistening in the pot like colorful, fossilized poop. Another sign that Mimi rarely threw anything away.

When Cassie was a child, the huge bed with its tall, barley twist posts had filled the place with comfort. She walked inside, the rug bumpy under her feet, reliving the morning Mimi had first led her there:

"This is where I came into the world," Mimi had said. "Right here, in that very same bed. Your great-grandmother, too, and the one before her." She opened her arms to embrace everything around them. "This room, this house, bless us."

"That's silly! It's just rock and wood."

"A house is a living thing, Cassie, with a spirit vital as ours. The windows are its eyes, the walls its ribs, the ceiling its breastbone."

"What about its heart?"

"The heart, sweet girl, is the people who live within."

"Like you and me?"

"Like you and me, and everyone before and after."

Cassie had climbed onto the patchwork quilt that smelled of lavender, wondering what it felt like to have a baby while lying on the big, lumpy mattress, wondering if all the mothers who had once birthed on that gracious old bed were watching from heaven and smiling.

Everyone before and after. Mimi's words spoken so long ago whispered in Cassie's thoughts as she turned to leave, stubbing her toe on the chamber pot. The bowl rolled across the rug and rattled over the flagstone floor, spewing marbles everywhere. She knelt to gather them up and reached under the wardrobe, but something blocked her way. Curious, she peered between the stubby legs. A book lay on the floor, grayed with dust. *Look at each item, no matter how small,* she had promised herself. It was stuck between the floor and furniture as if forcibly shoved there. She tilted the wardrobe up and tugged at the book until she had it firmly in her grasp, the wardrobe settling with a dull thump.

The binding was raveled, the leather cover dull and dry. She sneezed, blowing dust from the gold letters *Heilige Bibel.*

A German Bible!

She sat on the floor with her discovery and opened it carefully, the fine papers yellowed and worm-eaten. On the inside cover was a list of names written in different inks and in different styles – unusual names like *Inge Osterman* and *Edel Schuster* – with marriage, birth and death dates noted beside them. She read the first aloud, *Idetta Grinde, 1743 -1786.*

An envelope slipped from the pages and fluttered onto her lap. She studied her new find, browned and crisped with age. An address on front was penned in an ornate fashion and difficult to decipher: *Viktor Dorst*... something-something, the ink water-stained... *Oldenburg, Niedersachsen.*

The name *Dorst* was vaguely familiar, like a half-forgotten lyric. She lifted the wax seal clinging to the outer lip and pulled out a letter. A signature scrawled at the bottom – *Gustav.* Above that was the date, *10 Juni 1846.*

Baffled, Cassie turned the letter over as if expecting answers to suddenly appear on the backside. How did a letter written in German and addressed to someone in Oldenburg end up under Mimi's wardrobe thousands of miles away and a hundred fifty-odd years later?

Did this letter belong to my great-whoever? Was this his family Bible?

She opened the Bible again and found the name she was seeking: *Viktor Dorst, 1810 -1848.* The poor soul died when he was only thirty-eight, two years after receiving the letter. *Gustav Dorst* was listed next, *1803-1879.* The same last name! Perhaps they were brothers. Whatever their relationship and whatever Gustav wrote, it was important enough for Viktor to carry it with him all the way across the Atlantic.

She refolded the letter, returned it to the envelope, began to slip it inside the Bible – and hesitated. The last page, once blank except for a colorful design stamped in the center, was covered in script. The letters crammed together and jostled for space, even running up the sides. Squeezed in at the bottom almost as an afterthought was the signature, *Rosine.*

"Rosine, Rosine," Cassie murmured as she flipped to the list of names. There it was: *Rosine Dorst, 1835.* Nothing else – no death date, no notice of marriage, nothing.

Like she just vanished. Or was disowned or something.

It must have been around three o'clock in the afternoon; the air had that particular glow, a softening around the edges. It made the room seem less abandoned. Her eyes traveled over the headboard, the bedside table, the wardrobe, imagining Rosine or Gustav or Viktor using them, imagining them stepping on the rug she now sat upon, or drawing the drapes.

Cassie gazed at the treasures cradled in her lap, possible voices from her ancestors. The only trouble was that she didn't know a word of German.

She carried the Bible and letter into the great-room and placed them on the vine chair for now, all the while fighting the urge to drive to the Grumms that very moment and ask if they could translate. Now was not the time. She hadn't looked in all the rooms yet. Or the barn, for that matter. Or at the land itself. It had been years since she walked these halls or strolled along the meadows, and she needed to know the state of things.

Where next? Stepping up one level and down another, she paused by the cellar door. It was a heavy, plank-like thing slanting up from the floor about forty-five degrees. She grasped the large iron ring and pulled until it opened with a groan, banging against the floor. Steep flagstone stairs led into the gloom below. She clutched the door for support and eased down a couple of steps. A bulb hung from the ceiling about an arm's length away, a precarious stretch before she pulled the cord. The bulb swung to and fro, sightless. "Must be out," she muttered, peering into the darkness. Light from the hallway fell upon clutter heaped at the bottom of the stairwell, evidence that Mimi had thrown things down rather than carry them.

Dear Mimi, Cassie thought with a pang of guilt. *She just couldn't do for herself anymore, even though she tried.*

Her grandmother had never wanted to live anywhere other than in this house. As she grew older and her body finally betrayed her, Lillian had tried to move her into assisted living. Mimi refused to go. "When it's my time to give up the ghost, I'll do it at my own home and on my own bed, not at some nasty-smelling place filled with old people waiting to die!" She spat the words, *old people,* as if they tasted foul.

Her frail body finally overcame her spirit the day she fell and broke her hip. Days lengthened into weeks, and weeks into months as Mimi slept in a metal frame bed in a nursing home, small and lost underneath her quilts. "Take me home," she begged. "Please take me home."

When Mimi finally understood that her new home was now within the confines of cold, white walls, behind a door where rubber-soled shoes whispered on linoleum and plastic trays clanged and the air smelled like loneliness and bleach, she closed her eyes and gave up. Her joy in each day, the vibrant life force that had defined who she was for ninety-two years, died on a strange bed in a strange place, with no one by her side except for the lone company of her granddaughter.

The memory never left, nor the lingering guilt.

Please take me home.

Cassie climbed out of the cellar and shut the door, wishing it could be as easy to shut the door on Mimi's last sadness.

A cramped stairwell some yards away was so narrow she could span it with a shoulder brushing one wall and her outstretched elbow the other. She clambered up the winding steps to a small room with wall-to-wall windows. This had been a favorite place when she was little. She'd sit on the wide wooden sills and watch birds whirl from the trees into the sky. Sometimes she pretended to sprout wings, and dreamed of flinging herself into space and flying among them.

The room, bright with sunlight, was empty except for an iron bed frame with strung-together springs, a wooden end table, a chair. A porcelain vase of a Dutch boy wearing a blue hat and yellow neck bow perched on a shelf. Smiling, Cassie picked it up, recalling the times she had filled the small urn with yellow flowers the size of thumbtacks. They were beautiful only for a short while, usually dying before the day was done. "Wildflowers aren't meant to be cut away from their roots," Mimi would tell her, "so enjoy them where they are."

She was about to put the figurine back on the shelf when something jangled inside it.

She tipped it and a ring fell out. A ring with a blue heart-shaped stone.

Cassie sank onto the bed, the springs bowing under her weight as she gawked at the miracle in the palm of her hand – the ring her father had given her on her sixth birthday.

She didn't know what to think. She couldn't think at all. She simply sat there, staring out the windows. The tin roof of the carport shaded by pecan trees. Mount Bubba. The barn, windmill, and outlying hills. The sloping front meadow bordered by the creek and woods.

Then she was six again and at home in Dallas with her mama and daddy, all dressed up in a white party dress and socks with lacy ruffles at the ankle. Pink balloons and crepe paper streamers floated above a birthday cake shaped like Cinderella's pumpkin chariot, with gold frosting wheels and tiny mice coachmen in blue caps.

She opened her presents, wadding the gay wrapping papers and strewing them underfoot. Playmates gathered around to get a better view of the last, a package so small she almost missed it. A silver ribbon poofed from the top and wound into a tag bigger than the gift itself. *To Sugarfoot,* it said. *With love from Daddy.* She could feel the breath of her friends upon her neck and arms as she unwound the ribbon, peeled the delicate wrapping, lifted the hinged box.

Inside was a ring all her own, with a blue heart stone.

"Ooooooh!" Her friends cried, crowding close as she slipped it from the velvet. "How pretty!" they squealed, "Let me see!" and "Can I try it on?" and "Me first!" The ring made its rounds from one girl to the other, each claiming she'd like to keep it for herself, until finally it came home to Cassie's finger. It was a perfect fit.

"Oh, Daddy!" She rushed to her father as he knelt, arms open wide in welcome. "I'll never take this off and will keep it forever and ever."

"Love you, Sugarfoot."

After the party had ended, after she gobbled the last bit of cake and waved goodbye to the last guest, her father blew her a kiss and walked out the door, closed it quietly behind him, and never returned.

Three weeks later the ring disappeared. Gone! Gone! Cassie searched the house, weeping. She crawled along the floor and swept her hands under the beds and couch and chairs, looked in the closets, in the drawers. She hunted outdoors, parting the grass with her fingers. Sleep came fitfully, bringing dreams of loss. Food lost its flavor, and she grew thin and pale.

"Eat!" her mother demanded. "Snap out of it!" Lillian raged and stormed from room to room, ridding herself of every scrap of evidence that her husband had ever existed and hurling them into the back yard. "Stop sniveling! It's just a stupid ring."

"Daddy gave it to me," Cassie's voice trembled.

"So what? He doesn't love either one of us."

"Yes he does! He said so."

Lillian leaned in close, her eyes squinty and black. "Listen to me girl, and listen well. Never believe a word any man ever tells you. If you know they're all liars, you're well ahead of the game." She stood up tall and straight and angry. "He's not coming back. Not ever. So get used to it."

"He will come back! He will, he will!" Sobbing, Cassie ran for her bedroom.

"Stop it, right now!" Lillian grabbed her by the shoulders and spun her around. "Your daddy doesn't want us. He wants to be somebody else's daddy. Somebody else's husband. Is that clear?"

"Somebody else's daddy?"

"I gave him a choice: Stay and keep our family together. Or leave, and be dead to us. He left."

"But why?"

"Because he's a selfish bastard."

"But I'm his Sugarfoot!"

"Forget him!" Lillian shook Cassie, her fingers gripping the small shoulders so hard Cassie could feel them pinching her bones. "I never want to hear the word *Daddy* come from your mouth ever again," Lillian hissed. "Nor will you ever shed a tear in my presence. Do you understand?"

Cassie nodded at the stranger her mother had become.

"Good." Lillian caressed Cassie's cheek. "I'll call you when dinner's ready and I expect you to eat it."

Cassie chewed the tasteless food, swallowed, and hid her tears.

She sat upon the rusty springs while time drifted by, the ring clasped in her hand. Sweat trickled into her eyes. The room was stuffy and hot and closed up tight, but she couldn't muster the energy to do anything about it.

A flicker outside caught her eye.

A lone cedar on the top of Mount Bubba swayed, perhaps touched by the wind, and a man slipped from behind. A golden dog followed, bounding among the brush as they climbed the steep incline. The stranger walked with ease, probably born of experience among rough terrain and whatever creatures it hosted. He stopped, rolling up the sleeves of his red shirt while gazing down at the meadow. The dog waited beside him, he and his master appearing to study the landscape before continuing on their mysterious way.

Who in the world...?

Hadn't Pete said Hawk was a wanderer among these hills, often disappearing for days? And the two times she'd seen his pickup, a yellow dog had been in it.

Hawk! It's got to be him!

Even so, what right had he to tramp all over Mimi's property? Just like the nutty bag lady Tatty, who moseyed around as she pleased. Didn't anyone have the common decency to at least *ask*?

Then something gave way underfoot – a loose rock, perhaps – and Hawk skidded down the hillside into the brambles, disappearing among them.

"Oh!" Cassie exclaimed, and hurried to the window. Had he fallen? Was he hurt? He could be lying helpless, maybe with a broken leg.

She leaned against the windowsill and peered through the mottled glass, waiting to see if he would return. The memory of Thomas, of his fall from the Colorado mountain, nibbled at the corner of her mind. She ignored it, pretended it wasn't there. Reminded herself that Mount Bubba was no mountain, that skidding down the side and landing among the brush was likely harmless. Painful, perhaps. But harmless.

She waited as the minutes passed. And waited.

What if he's hurt, lying under the hot sun, alone?

The thought propelled her downstairs and through the side door. Briars and rocks stabbed her bare feet, forcing her to return. She grabbed the mismatched galoshes and stuffed them on with fumbling haste and tore back outside, calling to him. Her blouse untied at the waist and flapped in the mounting breeze as she trotted the length of the hill, staring upward, searching for a splash of red lying motionless on the ground. And then she saw it, a crimson spot near the crest, likely too far to hear her cries. She scrambled toward it, rocks tumbling underfoot. The sun burned into her back and arms while she squinted into the glare, struggling up a rise so steep it felt as though she were scaling a cliff.

The higher she climbed, the more difficult it became. The air seemed to thicken and turn solid, as if she were trying to penetrate an invisible wall. Images flickered behind her eyes, vivid images of coiled rattlesnakes, of phantoms rising from the dust, of Thomas falling, falling, falling, of his body broken and bloodied far below, of the soaring helicopter carrying him into the rising sun.

And then it happened. Fear slammed her in the stomach and knocked her backward. She gagged, panic squeezing her chest. Turning away from Mount Bubba and the terrible memories it evoked, she stared at the house below, the thrust of its chimneys, the rambling walls, the spreading oak. *Count to ten, count to ten. One, two...* Telling herself to breathe, to keep her eyes on the familiar and safe, she retreated, stumbling over the rough terrain, feeling as though she were in the throes of a heart attack and dying. *Five, six, seven…* Trying not to run, not to fall, pebbles clattering from beneath her feet. Suffocating. *Breathe! Breathe!* Dust rising, the sun piercing her eyes, a striped lizard scrambling from her path. Right foot, left foot, right foot, keep counting, *eight, nine...* When at last she touched flat ground, a whimper curled in her throat and she sank to her knees, head so low to the earth she could smell its dry hunger.

After her heart stilled, she glanced upward. Hawk had climbed up the crest. He turned, slapping dirt from his jeans with his hat, and abruptly stopped, looking down at her. Perhaps he was as surprised to see her as she had been to see him. He raised his hand in greeting. Hesitating, she slowly raised her own. They remained like this for a moment, hands raised, gazing at one another from a distance. All was silent, save for the wind whispering through the trees.

The man put the hat back on his head, tipped it in farewell, and walked over the summit to the opposite side. The dog followed, tail wagging.

As far as Cassie knew, no one lived for miles past Mount Bubba. Nothing but wilderness sprawled on the other side, a rugged landscape of boulders, jagged outcroppings, cedar and spiny brush populated by snakes and scorpions. The giant hill loomed in the sunlight, its parched scruffiness so stark it appeared etched in crystal, mocking her for trying to scale it. She felt like a fool, a fear-besotted fool ruled by things long past.

Something bit into Cassie's palm. Startled, she realized she still clutched the ring.

Sleep did not come easily that night. Cassie lay on the bed, staring at the ceiling. It was yellowed in spots with lines spreading outward like roads on a map. She humored herself by naming the spots as if they were continents in an alien land: *Big Splotcha, Smalldotti, Wigglesworto.* Moths fluttered in the moonlight, drifting among the strange worlds like minute ghosts.

Too many shadows lurked in the darkness, too many whisperings. As soon a she turned off the lamps the house felt inhabited by unseen others, voices, mutterings. Her mind told her it was just the usual – the wooden floor snapping, a ceiling popping, night sounds beyond the windows – that stirred her imaginings. But although her mind accepted this, her heart did not.

She picked up the ring from the small table beside the bed and held it close. Not trusting it to stay safely on her pinkie finger, she had threaded it through a ribbon from Mimi's sewing basket, planning to wear it around her neck. Never again did she want to lose the only tangible evidence of a father who had once loved her.

The dream sweeps her into its world.

She runs through a field under a sky as blue as the flowers crushed by her feet. There is no wind, and although the sun blazes yellow no heat reaches her. Her breath is harsh and rasping, and her heart hammers against her ribs.

A black shape forms in the air, glittering and whirling, eagle talons extended, wings like helicopter blades. *Whap-whap-whap!* Death dances in its wake; the ground singes, streams shrivel, birds drop in feathered heaps.

Safety, where is safety? Nothing is in sight other than a giant oak with roots stretching beyond sight. At the base is her rosebush; scarlet petals unfurl as she approaches, exposing tiny faces within. Their mouths open, crying *Mama! Mama!*

The roar of wings spur her on. With a last burst of energy, she leaps under the tree's shelter, rips into the bark, and burrows inside its protective shell. The sap runs warm against her skin and in her blood.

Twin souls, the tree sighs. *You and I, twin souls.*

Song in the Walls

THE TELEPHONE HICCUPPED AN ERRATIC *BRRRRR- BRIP,* AS THOUGH CLEARING ITS long-silent, corroded throat.

"All right, I'm coming!" Cassie tossed the bedcovers aside and stumbled into the parlor. The only bad thing about having the telephone re-connected was that it could ring at inopportune moments, like this one. She glanced at the clock. Six-thirty in the morning. *Who in the world...*

"Hello?"

"Miss Cassie? It's Billy."

For a moment her mind went blank. "Who?"

"Billy Wilkins, from Gas `n Grub. You still want me to come work for you?"

"Billy! Yes, of course! Please excuse my foggy brain. It hasn't had its coffee fix yet."

"I'm sorry, Miss Cassie, did I wake you up?"

Before she could respond, a deep voice interrupted from further away. "Call the lady by her last name, boy!"

"I don't remember it, Dad!" The words were muffled, as though Billy had put his hand over the mouthpiece, but Cassie heard well enough.

"*Ask* her goddamit! You got to learn some respect."

"Pete calls her Miss Cassie."

"You ain't Pete! Now stop arguing and do as I say or you ain't going over there."

After a few moments, Billy asked, "What's your last name?"

The father barked, "Christ, gimmie that phone." A shuffling on the other end, then: "Ma'am, this here is Guy Wilkins. My boy don't mean nothing disrespectful."

"Well, I don't..."

"He's got to learn some manners."

"Whatever Billy wants to call me is just fine."

"It ain't fine with me. Now, if it's agreeable, we'd both appreciate knowing how to address you proper, with your last name and all."

"Okay. Mrs. Brighton, then."

"Thanks, Miz Brighton. Billy tells me you got stuff for him to sort and haul. That right?"

"Yes."

"More than a day's worth?"

"Lots more, depending upon how things go."

"Well now, that's a problem. I got to have my pickup. Okay with you if I bring a open trailer? I can tow it in and leave it there until you don't need it no more."

"Sure, that's just..."

"I'll bring Billy the mornings you want him and pick him up when he's finished for the day."

"I don't mind taking him home."

"That's right kind of you, but I don't want he should be a bother. This morning okay?"

"Today?"

"As good as any and better than most. I'll need Billy later on, when things get busy in the shop. Right now he's got some time on his hands."

"Well, I suppose."

"We better get going. Be there shortly."

"So soon? I..."

"Boy!" Guy yelled. Cassie flinched, even though the man had turned away from the mouthpiece. "Come tell Miz Brighton goodbye. And say thank you."

Another moment passed, followed by a subdued, "Goodbye."

The father's voice again: "Damn it all, do it proper like I told you."

"Thanks for the job, Mrs. Brighton. I'll work real hard."

"I know you will, Billy." In a mock whisper, she added, "And call me Cassie any time you want. I won't tell a soul."

Too vexed to care about her appearance, Cassie grabbed another pair of Mimi's stretched-out slacks and an over-sized shirt and dressed quickly, not once glancing in the mirror. The thought of Billy, so serious and sweet as he sang for her, being subjected to the sharp tongue of this brute of a father made her heart ache.

She found a pair of scruffy lace-up shoes in the closet, the sort she always thought of as old lady orthopedics. The heels were worn to nubs and her toes complained but she put them on anyway. Better those than open-toed sandals or fine leather flats. Why the heck didn't she have sneakers? Idiotic. A trip to Fredericksburg was definitely due.

A quick comb through her hair, the mandatory jolt of coffee, and she was ready.

He's probably bald and fat and farts in public.

She knew the thoughts were unkind as she sat on the porch steps to wait. No matter. She would greet the man with a smile, for Billy's sake.

The day had hardly begun and already it was hot. The sky had that particular sharp, steely glaze of summer, as though pounded from metal. Sunlight sliced through the trees and hilltops, and the air smelled both sour and sweet – a combination of wild grass and honeysuckle baking in the dry heat. Boulders lay exposed along the creek bed, proof that the stream had begun to draw away from the shore. By summer's end it could shrivel to half its size, sucked away by the sun, stranding turtles and crawdads in muddy pools.

At first she didn't realize that the gray shape on the opposite shore was not part of the natural landscape. It blended in with all around it, and was as silent.

The wolf-dog moved closer with a gaze so intense she could almost feel it touch her skin. She didn't shout, didn't wave him away, but simply stared back. For a fleeting moment, she had the oddest sensation that the wolf spoke to her. Not in words, not aloud, but from within. A greeting of sorts.

A flock of raucous grackles burst from the trees and spun like black fireworks, startled by a pickup pulling a trailer. The wolf slipped into the woods as the truck approached the bridge and paused, motor rumbling. Billy hopped from the passenger side and ran to the rear. The driver stuck his head out the window, looking down at the rattling boards as the wheels edged across and Billy shouted and waved directions.

Cassie jumped up, alarmed. The truck was a big one and the trailer it towed seemed even bigger, in danger of straddling the narrow bridge or jackknifing and spilling over, dragging everything down with it into the creek. Yet in spite of her misgivings, both truck and trailer cleared the bridge safely and bumped along the path toward the carport as Billy trotted after. The trailer was a lumbering slat-boarded contraption on two wheels, but it was the truck that tickled Cassie's funny bone – dented hood, missing fender, paint reduced to patches of rust. A barely legible sign printed on the side read *Guy's Auto Repair.*

With a roar and final *ping,* the truck settled to a stop and Guy stepped out with practiced ease. He wasn't the big-stomached hulk Cassie had imagined, but slim and weathered, with skin tough as leather left too long in the sun.

"Mornin'." He spoke around a toothpick lodged between his lips.

Cassie offered her hand. His grip was firm and calloused. "Good morning to you, too, Mr. Wilkins."

"That there some of the stuff you need help with?" He jerked his head toward the mounds of rubbish in the carport. "If so, I reckon I can park the trailer right nearby."

"Yes, thank you."

"All right, I'll do her," he said, and returned to the truck.

Low-slung jeans, snakeskin belt, scuffed cowboy boots. A sleeveless tee-shirt exposing lean muscular arms with a scorpion tattoo crawling along his left bicep. An easy-limbed swagger. Everything about this man shouted, *Don't mess with me.*

"Hey, awesome view." Billy gazed with obvious delight at the meadow and hills and the far plateaus shimmering in the west. "I bet at night you could see every star in heaven."

"Boy, stop blabberin' and help me with this thing," Guy called as he settled behind the wheel.

Cassie leaned against the porch railing and watched father and son maneuver the trailer and free it from the hitch. She could see the similarity between the two – wiry, red-haired, determined. But the man was dour, the boy light-spirited.

Gesturing to the piles jumbled under the carport, Guy said, "Sure enough a heap of stuff. You want all this here moved or tossed?"

"Just moved for now, to make room for my car. Then I want to go through it all and see what's there."

"You forget?"

"What? No! I mean, this clutter isn't mine. Well, it is now, but it really belonged to my grandmother. Mimi kept everything she ever owned so no telling what I'll find. I'd hate to throw anything away without looking first."

Guy shifted the toothpick from one side of his mouth to the other. "Well," he said, "seems like your grandma was sure enough a packrat."

Cassie surprised herself by laughing. "I can't argue with that."

"A real nice lady, though. Gave me some flower seeds once, don't remember what kind. Daisies, maybe." He leaned back on his heels, looking around. "Any more stuff someplace besides here?"

"Practically every room in the house. I haven't been in the barn yet, but I'm sure it's stacked to the rafters."

Guy whistled. "Barn's a big'un. House, too. Billy's gonna be needed around here for a good while. What do you think, boy?"

But Billy wasn't listening. He had walked to the live oak and now gawked at the car parked under it. "Dad, look at this!" he shouted across the space between them.

"Well, now, what've we got here?" Guy strolled to her car and Cassie followed, inwardly cursing herself for wearing shoes that pinched with each step.

"She's a beauty." Guy ran his hands over the hood and grill. "Thunderbird, 1959. Right? Hardtop coupe."

"Right," Cassie replied, averting her eyes from his gnarly hands. His fingers appeared to have been stomped on and left to heal as nature would have it.

"Body's been done up nice." He peered through the windows. "Updated innards to go with it, I reckon."

"Dad really knows his cars," Billy said. "But I've only seen pictures of the classic ones, not real, not up close like this. It's..."

"Miz Brighton," Guy interrupted, "why you driving with the spare?"

"I had a flat," Cassie replied, dismayed by her neglect. Her car was a mess: mud-splattered, covered with oak leaves, and christened with bird droppings. "It's not usually this dirty," she added lamely.

"There a hose somewhere?" Billy asked. "I can wash it, easy."

"You can change the tire, too." Guy spit out the toothpick, grinding it into the dirt as he turned to Cassie. "You still got that flat?"

"Yes. In the trunk."

"I'll take it to the shop, patch it up. Billy can bring it back tomorrow, put it on for you. If it's too blown, you might need a new one. That'll cost you some."

He stood not much taller than Cassie, squinting at her about an arm's length away. She fought against an impulse to step back. Something about this man and the way his lips barely moved when he spoke made her uneasy. The scorpion tattoo didn't help matters, either.

She forced a bright smile, said, "I appreciate it, thanks," and kept the smile plastered on her face while he carried the tire to the truck and drove away in a trail of dust and clatter.

"Well, Mrs. Brighton, where do I start?" Billy tugged at a backpack that hung from his shoulders and tossed it on the ground.

"Cassie, Billy. Call me Cassie. I'd like that."

"Okay."

"First things first, which means the carport. I guess the best thing for us to do is dig in and clear enough space for my car." She motioned toward the jumble. "Maybe we should try to place similar things together as we move them, obvious throw-aways in one spot, unknowns in another, and so on."

"You want to *help*?"

"Of course! I don't expect you to do it all by yourself."

"But that's not right! You shouldn't have to lift any of this stuff or muck around in the dirt. I can do everything just fine." Cassie must have looked skeptical, because he continued in a rush. "Dad says I'm stronger than he was at fifteen, and that's when he worked at a construction site hauling loads of bricks which were damn heavy. Darn heavy," he corrected himself, "and I'm responsible for a lot of things at the shop, have been since I was ten. No problem."

He stood with legs straddled wide and arms akimbo so much like a tough guy twice his age and size that Cassie had to bite her lips to keep from grinning. He surely was in a hurry to grow up.

"All right, I'll leave you to it. But please come get me if you need anything."

"Yes ma'am. I'll be fine, so don't you worry."

The day was going to be almost supernaturally bright. The sun seemed to hover, throwing flames against the rocky ground and ricocheting from the barn roof. Cassie shaded her eyes against the glare. An idea had popped into her mind, one that had been there before but never truly heeded.

"Billy, how about a small adventure first?"

"What kind of adventure?"

"What do you say we put the carport on hold and explore the barn? I've never been in there, not even when I was a child."

"Really? Why not?"

"My grandmother kept the doors padlocked. What's inside is a mystery to me."

Billy grinned. "Well, then let's go play detective!"

A lizard scuttled alongside and dry weeds crunched underfoot as they walked. Billy seemed full of energy, almost dancing along, whereas Cassie felt like an old crone hobbling in Mimi's orthopedic uglies.

"Weren't you ever tempted to go inside?" Billy asked.

"Only once. I ran into a bunch of tarantulas jumping along the barn wall, bopping around like fuzzy rubber balls with legs. After that I never went back."

"I like tarantulas, Miss Cassie. I used to stick them in jelly jars. Did you know they rear up on their hind legs if they're upset? It's awesome."

Cassie stopped in her tracks. "That, young man, is something I definitely did *not* want to know."

"Their big body and hairy legs and weird mouth makes them look meaner than they are."

"Maybe this isn't a good idea. Maybe that old barn can wait."

"C'mon! I'll scope the place out, stomp every spider in sight."

"Maybe bashing them with a shovel would be better."

Billy giggled – a free, bubbling ripple of sound. Cassie couldn't imagine Guy laughing like that. The man probably never laughed at all.

"Actually," she mused, "it will be good to know what sort of work will be in store later on. 'Forewarned is forearmed,' as my mother used to say."

"For *what*?"

"Forewarned and forearmed. It means that knowing the facts will help us prepare for whatever danger lies ahead."

"The danger," Billy said, "will be to open those doors without them falling on our heads or the whole barn toppling over."

The barn *did* seem about to collapse. The sides buckled outward, gray and dry with rot. A single window, warped as though it had melted in the heat, opened to a loft above the double doors. The doors themselves were massive, two stories tall and just as wide, drooping from their hinges. A hasp held them shut, fastened with a tattered rope.

"I'm almost afraid to touch it," Cassie murmured. "Looks like the barn died and left its ghost behind."

"Let me do it." Billy picked at the rope. "Pretty stuck," he said, and yanked hard. The hasp groaned and pulled away from the wood as the doors rattled, the walls they were attached to rattled, and something small and brown flew out of the window and darted over their heads.

"A bat!" Cassie flung out her arms as if to repel Dracula.

"I must've woke it up."

"There might be a crowd of them, hanging from the rafters or something." The image of winged bat bodies squirming upside down above globs of guano made her cringe. "What will happen when we force open these doors? They could all come swooping down like black rain."

"I don't know, but we'll soon find out."

Cassie eyed the weathered doors. They'd need several good heaves in order to open, likely shaking the whole barn in the process and alarming any nesting, creeping, or flying thing. "Maybe we should just burn the place down and forget about it."

Billy laughed and wrestled the hasp free. A screw popped out and flipped to the ground as he tossed the padlock aside and gripped the edges of a door. It cracked open with a prolonged squeal, the bottom scraping the hardened dirt. Cassie held her breath. Sure enough, two more bats flew into daylight – one from the window, another from the doorway. They zigzagged a dance around one another before joining their companion in the wood.

"Great. That's all I need – an infested barn." Cassie shuddered as she peered into the dim interior. "It probably isn't safe to walk around in there."

Billy didn't answer and stepped inside. The air smelled rank and moldy, and the taste of something like frayed rubber filled her mouth.

"Billy?"

"Miss Cassie! You gotta see this!"

"Are there any more bats?"

"I can't tell. Might be some in the loft."

"Well," she muttered, "here's hoping they stay there."

Light spilled through the cracks, landing on layers of cobwebs and grime thick as ash. The gray powder crawled into Cassie's nostrils the moment she entered, making her sneeze.

"Bless you!" Billy called from somewhere. "Come see what I found!"

"In a minute!" There were so many grit-shrouded things everywhere, Cassie didn't know where to look first. They spilled from corners, hung from pegs on the walls, dangled from overhead beams. There was a crazy sort of order to it, as though everything had been carefully organized long ago and forgotten, left to crumble under the weight of time.

Craning her neck to inspect the dark recesses of the rafters, she missed what lurked directly in her path and bumped right into it, scraping her shin. "Tarnation!" She rubbed her smarting leg and glared at her adversary – a coal-burning parlor stove resting lop-legged on one side, its ornate grate door hanging from a single hinge.

"There's tons of cool old stuff here," Billy said as he stepped from behind a ladder reaching to the loft, "like a museum with hardly enough room to walk around in."

"More like a junkyard. All it needs is a mangy watchdog nipping at our heels."

"A paradise of a junkyard. I found saddles and a plow rake and I think a butter churn and something you're gonna like even better." He hurried away, looking over his shoulder with a grin. "Hey, Miss Cassie, want to see something really super?"

A large, tarp-covered heap squatted in the middle of the barn. Whatever was underneath had been well protected. Except for one loose corner, the tarp was secured to the ground with rocks and pulled tight, like a makeshift tent.

"I peeked underneath," Billy confessed. "Interested?"

Cassie nodded, her curiosity mounting. They tossed the rocks aside, gripped the tarp, and tugged. "Pull it thataway, toward the rear," Billy said, pointing with his elbow as they heaved the tarp up and over what lay beneath: A touch of green, dull and muted as old velvet. Windows, filmy and white-ashen as cataracts. A stocky metal carcass, graceful now as in memory, propped on four concrete blocks.

"Isn't this something?" Billy crowed. "A Studebaker!"

Cassie clasped the latch, opening the door with a slow squeal. Acorn shells littered the seats, now split and shredded, the original fabric lost amid the stuffing. "It's a mess inside."

Billy popped the hood and raised it up. "This car sure must be tasty to some critters. They've gnawed through all the wire and rubber."

Cassie peeked over his shoulder. Nutshells scattered like dead leaves over wire shards.

"Not much left," Billy said. "Almost like a goat got in there, chewed everything in sight."

"I remember this car. We called it Methuselah. I sat in it many a time, while my grandmother drove us around here or there." Cassie wiped her hand across the roof, then trailed a name in the grime with her fingers: *Mimi*. "It's been sitting here for years and I never knew. Now it's just a pile of rubble."

"It's no such thing!" Billy cried, slamming the hood shut. "Look at the solid condition of the chassis! Why, any auto mechanic with an ounce of skill could put this baby back together in prime condition." He circled the car, eyes alight, pointing out the merits of this or that, much like a preacher anxious to convert a disbeliever.

He seemed so energized and excited that Cassie got in the spirit of things, too. "Would it actually work?" she asked. "It would need a new motor and a tremendous amount of skill and attention. And cash."

"But it would be worth it!" He opened the door and sat in the driver's seat. "This is so cool!"

Cassie opened the other door, pushed the acorns aside, and sat next to him. The barn faded from sight through the grit-glazed windows, making Cassie feel as though she were suspended in space and time. Part of her wouldn't have been surprised to find Mimi sitting in the back seat, waiting for a ride.

Billy gripped the steering wheel as though playing driver. "Someday I'm going to be an automotive engineer. I'd like to design cars like this or your Thunderbird – classic kind of – but have a devil for an engine under the hood and so much intelligence packed into its brain that it could do everything but yodel."

"Then start with this one," Cassie blurted. "Use this as your practice model. The barn will always be open, so you can come and go whenever you like."

"Oh, wow. What if I goof, mess up something?"

"So what? If you goof, you goof."

"You wouldn't mind if I made a bunch of mistakes?"

"Billy, you'd be doing me a favor no matter how many mistakes you think you've made or how it works out in the end. I'd have to pay someone to tow this to a dump anyway, where it would just disintegrate into a pile of rust. So if you want to try and give this poor, dead auto a second chance at life, then do it! I'll pay you, of course," she hastened to add. "Maybe you can put some money aside for college."

"Oh, Miss Cassie, it's the most wonderful thing anyone ever… But my dad, I don't know… I'll have to ask Dad."

His fingers danced along the steering wheel. "I've always wanted to do something like this for real, not just dream about it. I even have notes and diagrams and sketches and things, ever since I was a kid and so small I'd have to stand on a stool to see under a hood. Or I'd spook Dad out by crawling underneath a car when he didn't know, to study what was there."

His sudden smile lit up the whole interior of the shell-strewn Studebaker.

Billy worked with steady concentration as he cleared the carport. Cassie kept busy around the house, trying to be unobtrusive as she watched him now and again through the windows. He was slow but meticulous, peeling away clutter and re-organizing it into neat stacks under the pecan trees.

The morning sun climbed steadily and the shadows traveled with it, growing shorter as the hours approached noon. The boy had taken off his shirt in the rising heat, exposing a freckled, slender chest with ribs so prominent she could probably count them all. He sat in the shade of the trees, drinking a bottle of water. A rumpled brown paper bag lay alongside.

Water! Chagrined, Cassie realized she hadn't offered him a single thing to drink. She opened the refrigerator, wondering what would appeal to a teenager. Whatever it was, she probably didn't have it. And lunch! Why hadn't she thought about lunch?

She poured a glass of iced tea, dropped a slice of lemon into it, and went to find Billy. She walked carefully, the comfy slippers flop-flopping over the rough ground. The old lady orthopedics lay where she had tossed them on the porch. If she didn't get a pair of sneakers soon her feet would be forever ruined.

"Hey, Miss Cassie! What do you think? Is everything okay?"

"Absolutely. You're doing a super job."

A flush spread from his cheeks down to his inflamed shoulders and chest. "Good heavens, you're getting a sunburn!"

"Happens every summer. I get red as a lobster then it settles down into one big freckle." He took the proffered tea and downed it in four noisy gulps. "Thanks, Miss Cassie. That tasted real good."

"Are you about ready for lunch? How about sandwiches?"

"I thought… I mean, I brought one with me." He opened his sack and pulled out limp white bread with brown filling seeping from the layers like putrid glue. "Peanut butter. I made it last night just in case, when Dad said we might be coming in the morning. I didn't want to be late."

He gave the glass back to Cassie. She held it, looking at him, at his sunreddened face and grit-streaked hair and skinny young self. She imagined him in his kitchen, the bread slices spread on the counter while he slathered them with peanut butter. It may have been dark outside; the window glass would have reflected his image, head bowed in concentration. Perhaps the TV could be heard in the next room, or his father's voice calling to him. Was anyone else living there, brothers or sisters? Or was it just the two of them, father and son, alone in a home with no wife or mother to soften the emptiness?

"Billy." She spoke quietly. "I realize you went to a lot of trouble to make that sandwich, but I surely would appreciate your company at lunch."

He sat across from her at the kitchen table, hands and face damp from scrubbing. She took great care with the sandwiches, nestling slices of turkey and cheese in layers of lettuce and tomato, and adding crisp bacon for good measure. She made two for Billy and one for herself, arranged them on glass luncheon plates, and folded cloth napkins alongside. The napkins were threadbare but she favored them nonetheless, and the yellow daisies embroidered on the hems.

"This is super nice." Billy unfolded the napkin as if it were made of fragile stuff. "Mama would've liked this napkin with the flowers on it. She loved flowers, especially daisies. Daisies and honeysuckle."

"She must have been very special."

He nodded, but said nothing more.

Cassie hesitated before beginning to eat, not certain whether Billy wanted to say grace beforehand. He seemed to feel a little awkward too, glancing at her sideways rather than straight on. *What the heck. Just jump in and do it, even if I am out of practice.*

"Give me your hand, Billy."

"Huh?"

"Your hand. That five-digit appendage dangling on the end of your wrist."

He reached tentatively toward her, his fingers warm and calloused at the tips. "This is a prayer my daddy used to say, long ago." The words surprised her; she hadn't meant to say them, hadn't even known she would. "I was little then, but it's so short and simple I remember it well."

Billy's pond-water eyes rested upon her face, his body so still he seemed sculpted in the chair. Cassie lowered her head. "Dear God, for food and drink and all our blessings, we thank thee. Amen."

"Amen."

They began to eat, silent except for the clink of ice in the glass. The kitchen settled around them comfortably, the refrigerator humming an antiquated tune, the curtains stirring in the breeze.

"I like your house," Billy said, wiping crumbs from his chin. "It feels like a house should feel."

"How is that?"

"Like it welcomes you in. Like it has a heart and feelings and a voice almost, if we could hear it."

"It's a noisy house, I'll give you that. The boards pop and groan, and the stone fireplace howls in a heavy wind."

"All old houses do that." Billy stuck a finger into his emptied glass, swirling the ice around. "My house used to be happy when Mama was in it. Sometimes she would sing, and I think the sound got into the walls so the house sang, too. I could hear it and feel it, even when she was gone to work or to the store or something." He took the napkin from his lap and refolded it, his touch lingering on the silken daisies. "When she died everything died with her. Dad and I live in a house that feels empty now, with no songs in the walls."

"Oh, Billy, I'm so sorry."

"Like Dad says, what's gone is gone." He shrugged, a brave try at bravado. "Would you like another sandwich?" Billy shook his head. "How about a banana?"

"No thanks. I'm full, really."

"Or a cookie?"

"You got chocolate chip?"

"Chocolate chip coming up." She rose to fetch a tin of cookies. "I bought these at Pete's but haven't tried one yet, so can't vouch for how they taste. There's an assortment in there, so if you get tired of one kind you can always switch to another."

She leaned her elbows on the table as Billy plucked a cookie from the tin, and then another. He chewed with thoughtful deliberation, as though he were a judge in a cookie-tasting contest and this was the final event. By the time he reached for a third, Cassie figured they had passed muster.

"Mama used to put big chunks of chocolate in her cookies," he said between bites. "Dad would tease her about that, saying, 'Why goop up candy with a little flour?' And then he'd pat her bottom and grab a bunch to eat up himself."

The mantle clock bonged in its off-kilter fashion, rasping acknowledgment of a single hour. *One o'clock,* Cassie thought. *Where has the time gone?*

Billy glanced out the bay window at the sun streaming through the great oak. "He killed her, you know."

Stunned, Cassie couldn't respond.

"He didn't mean to. It was an accident. But she's dead just the same."

Cassie waited, silently urging him to continue yet dreading to hear.

"It was early in the morning. I was asleep when Dad started screaming. It was an awful sound, like an animal, and went up and up and on and on with no breath in between, just going and going and going. I remember weird stuff, you know? Like how cold the floor was on my feet when I jumped out of bed, and how I thought I was going to throw up, and how I shook all over and could hardly work my hands right to open the front door and go outside where the screaming was."

He brushed the back of his hand across his eyes. "It was dark and I couldn't see much right away, just a shadow kind of, rocking back and forth. It was Dad on his knees, holding Mama. She lay in his arms, her head wobbly like a rag doll dressed in her fluffy blue robe. Blood was smeared all over it and one of her legs was cockeyed.

"Dad yelled, 'Why? Why?' and buried his face in her chest. Her hair was bloody, too. I stumbled over one of Mama's slippers and landed beside her. Dad didn't look up but knew I was there. 'I didn't see her!' he said. 'Backing out the truck when she was bringing me the sack lunch I'd gone and forgotten. I didn't see her, didn't see her, didn't see her and ran right over her!' Then he sort of crumpled, like the weight of Mama was too much to carry, and lay on the ground on top of her."

"Oh, Billy, I… I'm…" What could she say? The words had been sucked out of her.

"It happened right before Christmas. Not last Christmas, but the one before. Dad trashed the tree and all the presents and threw out the turkey. You remember the banged-up truck he drove here today?"

"Um-hum."

"It's a spare he kept behind the shop for me to use sometimes. He had a brand new pickup, heavy duty, really loaded. After Mama died he couldn't stand looking at it no more. I mean, any more. He said he could see Mama's blood all over it. So he sold it and swears he'll drive the spare until it falls apart or he does, whatever comes first.

"He won't let me talk about her, say her name, even. He put her pictures and clothes and things in boxes and keeps them in the attic. He says it all hurts too much, and so he tries to forget. Sometimes he drinks to keep her memory away and then gets crazy.

"But I won't forget. I keep a photo of her in my shoe. Do you want to see?" He unlaced his sneaker, pulled it off, and handed Cassie a creased photograph.

A sweetly smiling woman with short, fluffy hair stood in the middle of a dozen or so youngsters. Whoever had held the camera had been too far away to capture exact features, but it was clear that Billy's mother had been petite and winsome, and pleased to be exactly where she was. "Goodness, who are these children? They can't *all* be hers!"

"Students. She was an English teacher." Billy slipped the photograph back into his shoe, tucking it in. "She wanted me to talk proper, so I try."

Cassie waited a moment before trusting herself to speak. "You do her honor, Billy. She must have been very proud of you. Any mother would be proud to have a son like you."

Billy kept his eyes down on his shoe as he tied the laces, taking more time than necessary.

He's crying! Dear God, he's crying!

Billy turned his face away. Aghast, Cassie rushed around the table and knelt beside him, putting her arms around his thin shoulders. He slowly leaned into her, tears slipping silently down his cheeks. "It's okay, Billy," she murmured. "It's okay."

But it wasn't okay. Nothing was okay.

Billy pulled from her embrace, wiping his eyes. Cassie took that as a hint and reluctantly returned to her own chair. After a time he asked, his voice thick, "Do you have kids?"

Cassie shook her head. "No."

"Brothers or sisters or anybody?"

"Not a one. Do you?"

"No. It's just me and Dad."

"It's just me and my mother, except she lives far away, somewhere in Spain."

"Do you ever get, you know, kind of lonely?" He looked at his hands, at the cookie tin, at the tablecloth, anywhere but at Cassie.

"Yes, sometimes."

He glanced up briefly, a young man's face with an old man's haunted eyes.

Cassie reached across the table and squeezed his hand. "Billy," she said, feeling her way through this, not knowing what to do, what to say, how to comfort. "Can I share something with you? Something I don't talk about very much?"

He nodded.

"What happened to you kind of happened to me, too. I lost a parent I loved, my father. He didn't die, although he might as well have. He walked out the door and never came back."

"Why?"

"I don't know, not really. Mother wouldn't let me say his name, either. Or talk about him. She burned his things, trying to burn away memories, I think. Like searing a wound so it wouldn't fester. Maybe it's like that for your dad.

"Look." She pulled the ribbon from around her neck. The ring it held was absurdly small for such an important thing. "Daddy gave this to me."

"Real pretty," Billy said, studying the blue heart stone.

"You hide your mother in your shoe, and I hang my father on a ribbon around my neck."

They laughed together, a bit shaky but a laugh all the same.

Sarah's Creepers

Cassie wiped the kitchen counter for the umpteenth time, watching Billy through the little window above the sink. He had moved her car to the outdoor spigot and thrown himself wholeheartedly into the job of washing it. He whistled as he worked, rainbows arcing in the water spray and sunlight gleaming off the metal. Yellow car, yellow sun, copper-haired boy, whistling. The afternoon seemed golden.

Who would have imagined the terrible things that had happened to that same shining boy, or the memories he relived?

There's so much courage in him.

The telephone sputtered, ringing. Cassie glanced once more at Billy before going into the parlor to answer.

"Hello?"

"This here's Guy Wilkins. Time for Billy to be home."

Cassie was about to say that the afternoon had barely begun, but thought better of it. "Of course. I'll bring him right there."

"He done good for you?"

"Very good. He's a fine boy, Mr. Wilkins."

She was met with silence. The only thing she heard was his breathing, followed by a sharp clink, as if he had set a glass down too hard. Finally, a ragged intake of air, then: "His mother thought so, too."

He hung up before Cassie could respond. She slowly replaced the receiver, unsettled. Something about his voice and manner wasn't quite right. Something...

"Billy, this car is so nice and shiny it almost looks new."

Cassie smiled at him with such warmth Billy could have washed her car all over again. He leaned back against the cushy leather seat, wondering if he would ever have anything as fine as this Thunderbird. He had dozens on paper, all designed, built, and stored in the garage of his imagination. The Studebaker, however, was real and waiting. An opportunity out of nowhere, like a gift.

He could hardly wait to tell Guy, although his father had been prickly lately and snapped at the world like an injured turtle. But surely he would be pleased that Billy could follow a dream and be paid for it, too.

The afternoon sun sparked off the car hood as Cassie drove the country road toward his home. He stretched his legs, not quite certain how to arrange his dirty sneakers on the fancy little rug placed there. It had a curlicue design with tassels on the ends. He ended up putting his backpack on the floor and resting his feet on that instead.

She's really pretty, he mused. She was kind, too, and didn't make him feel like a sissy when he cried. He hadn't cried in front of anybody since he couldn't remember when. Or talked about that awful morning, or how he felt about things.

"Look at that sky, Billy, deep and blue as a river."

"Guess that means we're driving underwater."

She laughed a little. He liked the sound of it, and liked her molasses-colored hair with strands of silver, and the way it kept creeping back every time she pushed it behind her ears. His mother's hair had been light and curly and fluffed around her head like a dandelion, but Cassie's was thick and straight and flowing like a dark stream.

She tapped the steering wheel, the sound filling the space between them. Her fingers were long and slender, much like the rest of her – long legs, long arms, long torso. His dad had noticed that, too. It made Billy feel weird, remembering the way Guy had acted around Cassie, pretending he didn't give a damn what she looked like. But his father had put a swagger in his walk when he met her and stood up real straight and was extra polite, like he was trying to hide what he really felt.

Her fingernails were long, too, and painted bright red. Some were chipped, and one was broken down to the quick. He hoped it didn't hurt.

Cassie must have seen him looking because she twiddled her fingers and said, "These are a disaster in need of a good manicure. I should give Nan a call."

"Everybody likes her. Even Darla, and Darla doesn't like most people right off, though she talks all bubbly and calls everyone names like Sugar and Sweetie Pie."

"Who's Darla?"

"Pete's sister. She's lives in Marion, near Woman Hollering Creek. Whenever she comes for a visit she acts like she owns the place, bosses everyone around, says things like, 'Do it *this* way not *that,*' or, 'You got chiggers in your britches?' "

Cassie looked at him and grinned, her brown eyes flecked with gold and green. Billy shifted his gaze to the side window, pretending an interest in the passing scenery. It was difficult for him to look into her eyes for long. It was like they walked right inside him.

"What sort of place is Woman Hollering Creek?" Cassie asked. "It sounds like something from an old western movie."

"It's more of a trickle than a real creek. I've never heard anyone hollering, but people say they've seen a woman in the morning fog, water streaming from her hair and clothes, wailing something fierce and carrying a drowned baby in her arms."

"I don't know about you, but that gives me the chills."

"Me too. The sad thing is that she's supposed to have drowned the baby herself."

"How awful! I wonder if that really happened,"

Billy shrugged. "Maybe something did, but the story got twisted with too much telling." He paused, then said, "I had a crazy thought once."

"Oh? What kind of crazy?"

"That whatever really happened got all mixed up with the telling of it, making a new story so powerful it developed a life of its own. Whatever wanders the creek might be part real and part unreal, but there just the same."

They rattled over cattle guards, following a pasture filled with scrub grass and cows resting in the shade of twisted mesquite. "Turn here," Billy said, leading them onto a pitted dirt drive bordered by a barbed-wire fence shrouded with mustang grapevine. Potholes and sizable rocks cluttered the trail, gravel clanged the underside of the car, and grit spewed from behind. Cassie drove slowly, her hands clenched tight on the steering wheel.

"I'm sorry." Billy raised his voice over the racket. "The pickup handles this drive just fine. You should have let Dad pick me up."

"Maybe next time," Cassie muttered as they jounced along.

"Your car is too nice for roads like this one. Have you had it a long time?"

Cassie didn't answer right away. "It was a gift," she finally said. "From my husband. It was our anniversary."

"Oh," he gulped.

"How much further?"

"We're almost there, around the bend coming up."

Trash cluttered alongside: beer bottles, fast-food containers, paper cups, a rubber tire, a fender. It hadn't always been like this, back when his mama was alive. Then they kept it clean and encouraged wildflowers to grow in the fields. Why hadn't he noticed how barren and ugly everything had become? It was as though junk had sprouted wings and flown there overnight.

I've got to clean this place up, he thought, glancing at Cassie. *She must think Dad and I live in a pig pen.*

They stopped in front of the house. Billy tried to see it through Cassie's eyes: a plain clapboard with sun-scorched paint, a porch barely large enough for an empty flower pot and rush-bottom chair, scabby grass, a tired flower bed running the length of the driveway and around the house. His mother had been proud of her flowers and spent hours digging into the earth, bringing them to life. Now they were bedraggled and wilting in the heat, with empty spots where some had died away. Guy's rattletrap truck was in front of the garage, so he was home. But the living room window blinds were closed like nobody lived there.

It was a sad little house. It looked sick, like it had a bad case of the flu and hadn't quite recovered.

"You were a big help today, Billy."

He grabbed his backpack and opened the door. "I'll be back tomorrow morning, but can't say exactly when after that. I work at Pete's a lot and school starts in a couple of weeks."

"You're welcome at my house anytime you can get there." Cassie touched his shoulder lightly. "Would you bring your guitar? I'd love to hear you play again."

"Really?"

"Really. And remember, the barn will always be open so you can work on the Studebaker whenever you like, day or night, even if I'm not there."

Billy stepped outside and leaned against the car door, wanting to find the right words to let her know how good she had made him feel, how happy he was. "Thanks," is all that came out of his mouth, but she smiled back, so maybe that single word was right enough.

He waved as she turned the car around and headed down the rock-strewn road, disappearing around the bend. A muggy breeze played with his hair as he fished his house key from the backpack. Lately Guy locked the front door all the time, even if he was inside, and kept the window blinds shut and the house shadowed.

The warped door scraped against the floor, the sound sharp in the darkened room. "Dad?"

"In here."

Billy found his father in the kitchen, sitting at the table with a bottle of beer. Guy didn't like cans, the look or feel of them, and so always drank from bottles. Several empty ones now sat neatly on the table, lined up like toy soldiers at attention.

A limp ruffled curtain hung over the opened window overlooking the back yard. It, too, was desolate – scruffy grass, a chicken-wire fence, a doghouse built for a pet whose bones now lay buried in the fields. The one bright spot was the yellow honeysuckle, reveling in neglect and growing with profuse abandon. It sprawled over the fence, spiraled up the utility pole, climbed the back wall to the roof. It spread over the kitchen window, too. He had to squint through the tangle of stuff to see anything outside.

His mother had loved the vine and made giant bouquets for each room, filling the house with a fragrance so thickly sweet Guy opened the front and back doors and went through the house with a leaf blower, knocking things about and saying, "I'm airing out the damned stink." He called the honeysuckle "Sarah's creepers" and clipped it back periodically over her gentle protestations, so that it kept mainly on the fence. But after her death he left it alone to grow as it would wherever it would, ignoring the heavy strands slowly encasing the back windows. One day, Billy thought, he'd wake up and find the entire house covered from one end to the other so thoroughly he'd have to hack his way out the door with a machete.

The kitchen smelled of cigarette smoke. Stubs piled in an upturned jar lid, and ash sprinkled the table. Guy sipped his beer and looked out through the vine-cracked window.

"Miss Ca… Mrs. Brighton said I was a big help today. Lots more to do, though."

"Tire's patched. Remember to take it with you tomorrow."

"Okay."

"You was polite, like I said?"

"She's so nice, Dad," Billy blurted, and sat on the chair opposite. "She fixed me sandwiches with cookies and tea." Guy swallowed the last of the beer and placed the empty bottle next to the others, carefully arranging it to line up in perfect order. Billy rushed on, "She's pretty, don't you think?"

A slight smile tweaked the corners of Guy's mouth. "You gettin' growed up, noticin' such."

"Someone pretty like her is hard to miss."

"Hard to miss is any two-legged female if you're somewhere between twelve and twenty."

"Then what about after, when I'm old like you?"

Guy snorted. "Then hard-to-miss is rightly rare. Now you got chores to do, so get goin' before it's too dark to see proper."

"Dark won't come for a good while. It's not even three o'clock."

Guy swiveled around to look at the cat-clock on the wall next to the refrigerator. It had eyes that moved and a tail that wagged with each tick-tock. "I could of sworn it was near dinner time."

"That's because it's always dark inside. We should open the blinds and chop away that honeysuckle from the windows to let the light in."

"I like it just fine."

"It's gloomy."

"I said I like it, so shut your mouth and do your chores."

Billy rose from the table as his father reached for a cigarette. "Dad," he ventured, "something really super happened today."

Guy struck a match with his thumb and looked at him over the flame.

"Mrs. Brighton has an old Studebaker stored in the barn. The motor's fried but the body's in great condition. Solid, with hardly a dent."

"Yeah?"

"It could be fixed up fine, a classic look with an updated engine and interior."

Guy slipped a cigarette into his mouth and lit it, letting the flame run up the matchstick to his fingers before stubbing it out. "So?"

"Restoring cars, fixing them up, designing them, is something I've dreamed about. And now I have the chance to really do it."

"Don't go gettin' reckless with your dreams, boy. Miz Brighton ain't likely to hand her car over to you wrapped in a big ribbon, like Santa Claus."

"No, but she'll let me work on it whenever I want!"

"Sure enough? That's right generous, but it won't come cheap. Last I heard you ain't no Rockefeller."

"She'll pay me, Dad, enough for supplies and labor. I'm so happy to do it I feel like I ought to pay *her.*"

"Well, how about that." Guy leaned back, tilting the chair on two legs. "All right, then. Can't see no harm, long as you do whatever else needs doin' and are here when I need you."

"I will, I promise!" He was so happy he wanted to shout for the joy of it. "I'm going to save most of that money for college."

"You ain't going to no college."

It took a moment for this to sink in. "Why?"

"You got your future right here with me. There's nothin' you can learn from books you can't learn in the shop."

"But..."

"We'll be partners, you and me. *Guy and Billy's Auto Repair.* Or just *Wilkins Auto.* Whatever you like best, how about that?"

"I don't know. I..." He couldn't think straight, as though the world had turned upside-down and left him hanging in the air.

"You'll get along just fine. Hell, you almost know about as much as I do already."

"Mom talked about college all the time. She wanted me to go. We had it all planned."

"God Almighty!" Guy shouted, rising as smoke spurted from his nostrils. "I lost your mother and I sure as hell don't intend to lose you, too!"

"Please, Dad." He put all of his heart into those two words.

"Shit." Guy groaned, sinking back heavily into the chair. "Every time I look at you I see her looking back – her eyes, her mouth, the shape of her chin, even the way you hold your head. It hurts me to look at you and it hurts me to look away.

"You're staying, and that's it. I'm done talking. Now get the hell out of here and go do your chores."

Billy closed the door to his bedroom and locked it from the inside. He dropped to his knees, reached under the bed, and pulled out a shoebox.

He sat on the floor with legs outstretched, opened the lid, and counted the money inside. Nine hundred fifty dollars and twenty-three cents, his entire savings since he'd begun working odd jobs two years ago. He figured at this rate he'd have three, maybe even four thousand by the time he finished high school – not nearly enough for college, but enough to begin. He could find a job and work his way through.

Whatever he earned from Miss Cassie would help make it possible.

I'm going. I am, no matter what. I'll not say anything until it's time. Then I'll pack my bags and walk out of here and never come back.

He lay on the bed, watching the light fade from the vine-encrusted window until darkness cloaked the room. He waited patiently, letting his anger build. When the front door creaked and slammed, and the pickup sputtered and backed out of the driveway and away, he walked into the garage and got the ax.

It was past midnight when Guy returned. Billy hid outside, crouched behind dried-up wild grass around three feet high. Guy walked into brightly lit rooms with windows opened wide to the wind and moon, free of entangled honeysuckle vine. Billy's eyes followed his father's shadowed form as it bumped into the walls.

He's drunk. Maybe he won't even notice.

Guy froze to a standstill, then staggered to a window and leaned out, groping the bare frame like a blind man. Billy watched in the darkness as Guy rushed from room to room and window to window, each time leaning out, each time reaching for the non-existent Sarah's creepers.

The vine still climbed the fence and the utility pole. But the house and windows were free, exposed to the moon glow. Ragged piles of ripped vegetation lay in heaps upon the ground, like drifts of yellow snow.

"Damn you, boy!" Guy howled. "Damn you!"

Billy sat amid the weeds in the field, his arms wrapped around his knees, and looked up at the stars.

Spirit Song

CASSIE WATERED HER ROSEBUSH, AWARE OF AN EMPTY SILENCE. THE WINDMILL creaked in the morning wind, birds chattered, a motorcycle growled from afar – but no pickup truck clattered over the bridge, no bright young face called a greeting.

She never knew when to expect him. Billy came and went at odd hours as the days slipped past, frequently disappearing into the barn after the work was done. She often found herself glancing out the window or loitering on the porch, hoping to see the battered truck approach and hear the cheerful, "Hi, Miss Cassie, I'm here!"

She rubbed a rose petal between her thumb and forefinger, worried. The flowers seemed droopy. Perhaps the bush wasn't getting enough sunlight. She lugged the heavy pot down the porch steps and out of the shade, placing it on the ground against the railing. The blossoms looked brighter there, shining dark red against the white wood. If they didn't perk up soon she'd try a dose of her special plant food, a mix of crushed black tea leaves and aspirin, a trick she had learned from Mimi.

Her eyes wandered to the neglected picket fence beyond the Emperor Tree and to the bedraggled daylily in Mimi's forgotten garden. Once upon a time the fence had been pristine and the earth it protected filled with growing things.

Maybe I'll try the mixture on that daylily. It deserves a little loving attention.

She'd think about that later. Right now she needed to head into Fredericksburg for jeans, sneakers, and hopefully a washing machine. She hurried back to the house and snatched her purse, ready to be on her way.

The German Bible stopped her. It lay in a shaft of light on the coffee table, the letter sticking out from between the pages.

Cassie drove up the Grumms' driveway, the Bible cradled in her lap, and parked beside a metal warrior angel wearing a copper basin helmet adorned by a flange plume. As she stepped from the car, a goat meandered into the yard with a bantam rooster atop its back, clucking and ruffling feathers as though demanding a faster ride. Cassie burst out laughing, startling the goat so much it jumped and did a sort of jig, the rooster squawking all the while.

"Hello! Anyone home?" The doorframe shook under her knock but the room behind the screen was still, except for Strudel the cat. He lay on the footstool, yawning. "Nice to see you too," Cassie murmured and headed toward the back yard. Perhaps Berta was puttering in the garden.

The gate was an odd conglomerate of metal scraps latched by a bolt that resembled a hooked nose. As soon as she reached for it, two large dogs bounded from around the barn and erupted into a barking frenzy, throwing themselves against the gate until it rattled. Cassie gulped and stepped back. They were so *big*, with big teeth, big jaws and big slobbery lips.

"Cassandra, what a nice surprise!" Berta called from the kitchen window. "Come on in."

"I can't!"

Berta rushed out the back door, clapping her hands. "Behave yourselves, or off to the pound you go!" The animals quieted, jostling for a whiff of Cassie's ankles as she opened the gate, then wandered elsewhere, tails wagging. Berta stood on tiptoe and wrapped her pudgy arms around Cassie. "What are you carrying? Plan on reading to us?"

"I hoped *you* would read to *me*." Cassie handed her the leather-bound book. "There's something scrawled all over the last page and a letter inside, both in German. I was wondering if you or Justin might translate them for me."

"Why of course! Go tell him hello while I make coffee, maybe warm up some cobbler."

"I'd love to. Where is he?"

"In the barn playing with his angel scraps, where else? Now go on."

The barn was a cavernous affair, stuffed to the rafters with piles of metal odds and ends. Justin stooped in the middle of it all like a gaunt giant surrounded by iron mountains, head bent over a long wooden table. A baseball cap sat on his head and goggles covered his eyes. A spit of fire ran from a rod he held, welding parts together. As he moved, a toilet plunger stuck into his rear pocket slid from side to side, appearing at one moment about to tip out then at another to slip back in again.

She watched him for a while, mesmerized by the dance of fire and rod and plunger, until he paused, as if contemplating his next move. Rapping her knuckles on a beam, she called, "Knock, knock!"

He spun around and the toilet plunger fell to the ground. Lifting the visor of his helmet, he immediately picked it up, stuck the handle back into his pocket, and grinned at her. "Cassie! Come to see an old man make a mess of things?" He stood with legs outstretched and fire rod in hand, reminding her of the angels he created.

"A beautiful mess, by the looks of it. I love your sculptures, every one."

"Every one, eh? Maybe you haven't seen them all."

Cassie gestured to the heaps around them. "You should have enough here for hundreds more."

"Not really. Metal is just metal until it decides to be something else. Then it talks to me." He picked up the fork end of a rake. "This, for example. Just a tired piece thinking about crumbling into rust. But it's not ready to die yet, it's waiting. So I wait. Maybe tomorrow it will say something, maybe the day after, maybe never. "

"I see," Cassie replied, although she didn't. As Justin tidied up, she asked, "Have you been inside Mimi's barn?"

"Maybe three, four times, *ja*."

"I'd like for you to have whatever you fancy that's in there, except for the Studebaker. I'd especially like for you to have the parlor stove with the ornate wrought-iron doors." She paused, teasing, "I don't know whether it speaks."

"Well, then, I'll just have to listen, won't I?" Justin's smile was crooked, one side rising higher than the other.

How strange, Cassie thought, that she hadn't noticed it until now.

She sat at the kitchen table, the apple cobbler on her plate half-eaten, anxiously waiting as Berta reached for the letter. Justin leaned back in his chair, the plunger on the floor beside him, slurping his coffee.

"*Schatz*, hush now, or she won't hear a thing," Berta scolded.

"Sorry." He set the cup on its saucer then picked up the plunger and put it in his lap.

Berta settled her glasses more firmly on her nose, peering all the while at Justin. "Can you tell me why you're carrying that thing around?"

"Keeping it warm." He winked and kneaded the rubber. "Got to keep it in good working order."

"Oh, for heaven's sake. Where do you get such cockamamie notions?"

"They just pop into my head. A rare talent," Justin teased, smiling in his lopsided fashion.

If the smile was different than usual, Berta didn't notice. She smoothed the letter on the table, careful not to tear the pages. "Ready?"

Cassie nodded. "Please."

"This is written in Old German script, but I think I remember well enough." Berta cleared her throat and read, sometimes stumbling for the right word:

June 10, 1847

Dearest Viktor,

Please come. I have found God's country. Fertile, beautiful, with surrounding hills and spreading sky not unlike our childhood home in Germany. Yes, it has been difficult – but our lives have always been difficult and we are used to trouble and bad times, and so look to the future with gladness in our heart.

We are our own men here, free to make of ourselves what we will. Food and game are plentiful, and the garden flourishes with each new planting. There is a hardy tree of leafy shade that produces excellent wood and nuts called pecans. Strawberries and dewberries abound wild in the fields, and my peach and apple trees bear sweet fruit. Your Katarina and little Rosine enjoy flowers, and here they carpet the spring earth with blue and purple and red.

I have one hundred thirty acres of land, and although the soil is rocky and troublesome, there is life and goodness in it.

Come, brother. The land speaks to me as it will speak to you. This is my home and I offer it to you. My wife Mattie died with the fever and I am alone, save for my son, Hans. We have built a solid house of stone and will add rooms for you and your family.

Come, Viktor. A new and better life awaits us among the Texas hills.

Your loving brother,

Gustav

"Oh, how wonderful!" Cassie cried, leaping from her chair. She pulled the letter from Berta's hands and danced around the kitchen. "Now I know for certain who built the house, who was the first to lay the stones – my great-great whatever granddaddy Gustav Dorst! Whenever I go in there, in the olden rooms, I can look at the stone walls and floors and that huge fireplace, and say to myself, that's part of who I am, too."

She pressed the letter to her chest and laughed at the dazed faces of the two Grumms. "Don't you see? The only thing I've ever known about my ancestors was that they sailed from Germany and traveled in an ox cart along the Guadalupe and overland to here. Nothing else. Nothing about the house, nothing about the land. I've always felt... disconnected, alone somehow, except for Mimi and my mother. And now I'm holding in my hands a piece of my family, a voice from the past."

"Speaking to you," Justin said.

"Yes. Speaking to me." She kissed Berta's plump cheek. "Thank you. I'm so happy!"

She sat down again, letting the joy flow through her, touching the paper. "This land *is* beautiful just like Gustav said, isn't it? When you remember to look at it, to really *see* it."

Berta nodded as Justin said, "I've always thought so. Although the red ants drive me crazy and Berta could do without the dirt getting on everything."

"More coffee?" Berta pointed to Cassie's empty cup.

"No, thanks. I'm too anxious to hear the rest!"

Justin raised his bushy eyebrows. "There's more?"

"Here, in the back of this Bible." Berta opened it to the last page. "The writing is small and squeezed together. But I'll do my best."

Cassie leaned forward, resting her elbows on the table, as Berta began:

> *Papa died at sea today. Mama and I watched as the captain said a prayer and threw him in the water. I held onto Mama's skirt but did not cry. Baby Theo did though, and clung to her neck. Papa was wrapped in canvas. He looked like a big white fish that sank under the waves and was soon gone. I ran to the railing, hoping not to see him, hoping he really was dead and not just deep asleep, hoping he would not wake up and find himself alone with no ship and no family to help him.*
>
> *Mama keeps asking, What are we going to do now?*
>
> *Rosine Dorst*

"Oh my," Berta sighed.

"How did she survive?" Cassie blurted. "How did they all? Traveling to a wild, unsettled part of the country, not knowing the language or the people, with no husband or father to protect them. How did they manage?"

"Maybe they didn't." Justin said. "Maybe they went back home."

"I want to know the truth of it!" Cassie exclaimed, surprised at how fiercely she felt about this.

"There's more, something written in the margin." Berta turned the Bible sideways, peering through her thick lenses:

> *Papa was going to give me a diary for my birthday next week, but Mama is not sure which trunk he put it in. I hope she finds it.*

"A diary!" Cassie exclaimed. "I'm going to search every inch of that house, every corner, every drawer and box and suitcase. If there was a diary and if it survived and if it's there, I'll find it."

"I wonder how old she was," Justin mused.

"Who?" Berta asked.

"The girl. What was her name, *Rosine*?" Berta glanced down at the page and up again, then nodded. "If it was her birthday, I wonder which one."

"Did she write a date?" Cassie stood and leaned over Berta's shoulder. "I think I saw one earlier."

"Here." Berta pointed a stubby finger to lettering scrawled at the top, barely legible: *September 18, 1848*."

"Now find her birth date. It should be in the front someplace."

Berta flipped the pages. "My, just look at this list. So many names, so many generations."

"There, see?" Cassie exclaimed. "*Rosine Dorst,1835*."

"Thirteen years old on her birthday," Justin said, "just a wee girl."

"How strange." Berta pulled the book closer. "Here's the date of her birth, but where's the one for her death? All the others have both dates recorded, but there's none for her."

"Maybe she's still alive," Justin said, daring to take a quick slurp of coffee. "One hundred sixty-five year old woman wandering the halls at night and sleeping during the day, so dwindled down by now she's invisible to the naked eye."

"*Schatz*," Berta muttered, "sometimes I wonder what planet you're from."

Cassie turned the car radio up and her window down and sang along with the music, her hair blowing in the wind all the way to Fredericksburg.

Girl, you're for me, girl.
Ain't no other can send me the way you do.
Ain't no other can slay me the way you do.
Girl, my heaven and hell girl, that's you.

Her hair was in tangles and her blouse clung to her skin in the heat, but it didn't matter. She felt wonderful. The diary had to be in the house somewhere, and with it the answer to the mystery of her family's past, of tales never told, of why Mimi or Lillian would say, "All families have secrets best kept in the closet" and nothing more.

Fredericksburg was a charming small town celebrating its German heritage with quaint gingerbread houses, wide streets lined with shops and boutiques and enough restaurants and *biergartens* specializing in bratwurst, schnitzel, and imported beer to feed and hydrate a city three times its size. She enjoyed browsing, and by noontime her trunk was filled with jeans, shorts, tops, and two pairs of sneakers – one pair bright pink with yellow daisies. *Why not?* she asked herself. *Step out of your mold, girl, be a heaven and hell girl, and wear bright pink shoes.*

Quite by chance, she wandered into a cobbled alley off of East Main and discovered *Grady's Goods and Betters.* It was hard to miss; appliances and machinery of all descriptions, ages, and conditions spilled from what once must have been a garage. There were so many things it was difficult to find a pathway to the door. A buck-toothed fellow with a defined lisp assured her that *yeth,* they had a pre-owned washing machine, several in fact, warranty included, and *yeth,* they had a microwave, one hardly used by a little old lady recently passed over, God *bleth* her *thweet thoul.* Fifteen minutes later she left, the owner of an almost-new washer and microwave, guaranteed delivery Tuesday of next week. Hallelujah.

Joining the throng of tourists and town folk, Cassie leisurely strolled the streets until she ended up beyond the multitude of boutiques and cafes. She stopped, wondering whether to turn back, when a blue jay hopped across her path. It nipped something with its beak and flew upward, landing on the peaked roof of a cottage out of a child's storybook: brown beams against whitewashed walls, blue-gray shingles overhanging red-trimmed bay windows, a curvy sort of front door, a brick path bordered by pots overflowing with yellow and purple flowers. All it needed was for Hansel and Gretel to appear, dropping breadcrumbs for a trail.

A sign dangled from above, swinging from a gold chain: *Whistle Pik Gallery.*

A gallery! Intrigued, she studied the paintings on display, many with western themes. She turned aside, ready to be on her way, when she noticed the lone painting illuminated by a spotlight. She stepped closer, holding her breath.

Oh, she whispered. And again, *Oh*.

It was a watercolor, rendered in shades of earth and spring, of an enclosed meadow in the woods bordering a small pond. The view was from above, as if the artist had painted while on a hill and gazing below. The sky, the trees, the water shimmered with life.

It was familiar to her somehow, this scene, this place, this feeling it evoked. She couldn't say how or why, except to repeat Justin's words: *It speaks to me.*

A brass plate attached to the polished cedar frame read: *Spirit Song.*

The longer and more intensely she gazed, the more it revealed itself. The landscape shifted, opening. Hidden figures emerged, rising like phantoms from within. Galloping horses rode among the clouds and shadow warriors curled among the treetops. In the water was a woman; her long blonde hair formed the current, surrounding and protecting a girl child swimming amid its golden strands. A wolf materialized from a boulder beside the shore, looking up directly at Cassie. Not just any wolf, she thought, but *her* wolf.

The partial shadow of a man spilled upon the hilltop, as though he stood beyond the picture frame – a profile, arms raised, playing a flute. The feathers in his grassy hair twined with a cactus flower.

The artist's signature was as she suspected: a hawk in flight, wings outspread.

A strip of bells hanging from the inside knob jingled a cheerful greeting as Cassie opened the door. A slim, aristocratic woman with prominent bones and thin lips approached, leaning on a silver-handled cane. "You were looking at Hawk's latest. Marvelous, isn't it?" Her voice was crisp, but her smile welcoming.

"How much does it cost?" Cassie ventured, almost afraid to ask.

"Twelve hundred, plus tax." Cassie must have blanched, because she added, "I can offer lay-away, if you're interested."

"Thanks, but no. I'll take it with me. I like it too much to leave it behind."

The woman laughed lightly. "I have several of his other works here. Would you like to see them?"

Cassie followed her into an adjoining room, the woman limping but using her cane with grace. Overhead spotlights drew her eye to five paintings, two in oil and three in watercolor, framed in pecan or cedar. All had figures woven into landscapes. "They're like a haunting," she said quietly, "as though the spirits of the past are here among us, living in the present."

"True," the woman replied, and extended her hand. "I'm delighted to meet another admirer who seems to appreciate his work as much as I do. Rebecca Stanch."

"Cassandra Brighton." Although Rebecca appeared to be in her mid-fifties, her grip was solid and strong, as if she could have wrestled Cassie to the ground in seconds. "I have another of Hawk's paintings, a smaller one, I like very much. If I could afford it, I'd buy them all."

"You have another?" Rebecca asked, her voice somehow too bright. "Which one?"

"*Hidden Shadows*. I found it in the back of a grocery store, behind a piano."

"How curious. A grocery store." She turned away abruptly, her cane tapping the wooden floor as she walked, thrusting her hip sideways in a swaying motion. "I'm not acquainted with that particular piece. I thought I knew everything that came from his hands, but obviously I'm mistaken." She lifted the painting from the bay window and began wrapping it in brown paper, her lips compressed into a tight smile. "He's unique, you know. No other artist quite like him."

She said not a word more, waiting until Cassie signed the credit card receipt before adding. "Genius like his must be God-inspired. I could never be a fraction as good."

"You're an artist?"

"I haven't a shred of talent." She handed the wrapped painting to Cassie and said, "I sell what others create. Thanks for coming. Have a nice day."

The bells jangled as the door shut firmly behind her. Cassie stood on the landing beside a pot of purple flowers, puzzled. *Friendly one moment, then all business the next. Strange.*

Cassie stepped down the brick path and onto the sidewalk, the wrapping paper crinkling under her touch. The weight pulled on her arms and she couldn't remember where she had parked the car, but it didn't matter. She was too delighted with her new-found treasure to care. A tune bubbled to mind from a musical, the name forgotten: *I feel happy, oh so happy, so...*"

A flute. The plaintive, drifting notes carried in the breeze.

Cassie stopped in the middle of the sidewalk, listening. The melody seemed to come from everywhere and nowhere, as though brought to life through the mouth and fingers of a phantom. It danced around her, then vanished.

For a moment longer she didn't move. A trick of the wind, she told herself. Or a radio turned up and then as quickly off. Yet she lingered.

A woman holding a child by the hand hurried past and glanced at her oddly. Stirring herself to action, Cassie shifted the weight of the painting from one arm to the other and continued walking, hoping to find a place for lunch. The only thing she'd eaten all day was Berta's cobbler. Even then, she'd picked at it, so excited about the translation of Rosine's note and Gustav's letter she couldn't manage more than a few bites.

An elderly couple tottered around the corner, bundled up too warmly for such a hot day. Each held a plastic bag printed with the words *Smithy's Barbeque.* Suddenly the idea of rich, tangy beef dripping juice from a thick sesame seed bun seemed too appealing to resist.

"How do you like Smithy's?" Cassie asked the old woman.

"Just fine, except the portions are too large. We always have to take some home."

"What?" the man said.

"She wants to know if we like Smithy's," the woman shouted in his ear.

He looked at his watch. "It's five minutes `til two."

"Thank you." Cassie replied, trying not to giggle. "Is it nearby?"

"Thataway," the woman pointed to the street behind her. "Turn right at the blue fire hydrant."

The two old folk wobbled away as Cassie turned down the street. In less than three minutes she stood before the reincarnation of a building from the past – a rectangular, flat-roofed structure of rough-hewn plaster and huge chunks of blue and gray stone. Yellow-shuttered windows framed the double door entry, which had *Smithy's* painted on the left in red and gold, and *Barbeque* on the right. A single step led up to the porch, the two weathered blue wooden benches placed there, and the three young men sitting on them with typical western attire and attitude: boots, cowboy hat, jeans, testosterone. One of them winked at Cassie, tipping his hat.

She pretended not to notice and looked up at the original sign tacked on one of the square stone pillars supporting the porch. It was so cracked and worn with age the only visible letters remaining were: *BLA KSM TH.* A blackboard hung beneath it, the day's menu written in chalk. Along with barbequed ribs, beef, pork, and chicken with all the trimmings, Smithy's offered sauerbraten, something called *calesbash-tumbas*, hot German potato salad and pastries, Blue Bell ice cream, and a breakfast menu with biscuits, gravy, and grits.

The entire thing – building and food – seemed to be an eclectic mix of Luckenbach and Heidelberg, as though a town from Germany had mated with one from Texas and sired a renegade.

"Miss, you comin' or goin'?" The boy-man who had winked at her grinned as the one sitting next to him said, "Come on up. We ain't gonna bite." His buddy added, "Might wanna try it, though," and they all snickered.

Oh, for heaven's sake…! "Going," she said curtly, turning aside.

And stopped.

The flute, once again.

Low, haunting. A sweet cry that sang directly to her heart. It floated through the open windows, through the double doors, through the walls of a building that ought to house guitars or honky-tonk piano or just about anything other than the music now coming from it. The young men didn't react, as if they didn't hear anything at all. Or if so, they were so used to the flute they no longer found it extraordinary.

Cassie forgot them and followed where the music led her.

Night Winds

SHE PUSHED THE DOORS OPEN AND STEPPED INTO A ROOM REDOLENT WITH HICKory smoke and sausage and onion. A hazy glow drifted over the weathered plank floor and timbered walls, the rough wooden tables and mismatched chairs. People gathered about, some sitting, some standing alongside a bar hacked from a tree trunk. A stuffed bobcat crouched on a log beam above them all, haunches raised and mouth stretched in a perpetual snarl, as if preparing to leap upon the man below.

He sat on a stool in a pool of light, head down, face shadowed under the brim of his hat. It was strange yet familiar, what happened to her when she first saw him, the instant stillness within. Everything around her seemed to ebb as through retreating into dim corners, except for the man before her: Denim shirt with the sleeves rolled up over muscled arms. Worn jeans on lanky legs. Scuffed western boots. Cowboy hat slouched low, revealing only his jaw. A shock of white hair – *white!* – curled at the nape of his neck.

The flute was a simple, hand-carved wooden thing lustrous with the patina of age, a feather dangling at the tip. The music soared, mellow and pure, as if coming from the throat of a living creature while his fingers stroked its stem, while his lips kissed its heart.

The final notes lingered, sighed, and quieted.

He lifted his head and looked directly at Cassie. His eyes were piercing and deep green, the green of oak leaves. They burrowed through her skin and marrow, filling her with green. Something in them – a connection, an unspoken communication, a *challenge* – made her hesitate to speak or even breathe.

He smiled at her then, slow and easy, as if thinking, *Come here girl, let me hold you. Come here girl, let me play you like a flute.*

She smiled in return, acutely aware of his lips, of his shoulders and arms and hips.

He rose, gaze never wavering, and moved toward her.

"Pappo!" A little girl with a pink ribbon in her white-blonde hair burst into the room. "Mama said to come home. We're having chocolate cake with strawberries on top."

"Hey, Rabbit, how's my sweet girl?"

His voice, oh his voice! Deep and vibrant with love for this child. He lifted the girl up, swinging her around. She squealed with delight as Cassie stepped backward, left foot, right foot, left again, until she turned and pushed through the doors. The sunlight hit her face and she blinked as if awakening from a dream.

The testosterone-plagued young men who had occupied the blue porch benches earlier strutted down the sidewalk, probably intending to make pests of themselves with whomever happened not to be male. Cassie sat down abruptly, feeling as though her knees were about to buckle.

A single moment, was that all it took? One glance? *Green-green eyes.*

She set the painting in her lap and wrapped her arms around it, as though it could comfort her. Married. The man was married. He was beautiful, mesmerizing, and married.

How remarkable, she thought, for a cowboy with sun-weathered skin to play something as un-macho as a flute. Had she been a movie director, she would have cast him taming wild horses or riding bulls in a rodeo or branding longhorns – not sitting quietly, breathing into a narrow tube, creating magic with his lips and fingers.

She gazed unseeing at the small yard and street beyond, feeling not a part of this world, as though she had appeared from another time or place. Footsteps approached, accompanied by the happy chatter of a young voice. Mr. Beautiful came through the double doors and down the porch step as the girl chased after, raising her hand to catch his. They walked side by side, he looking down at her and she looking up at him, to a red pickup parked nearby. A woman with long wheat-colored hair leaned against the fender, a slender picture of beauty in tight jeans, a sleeveless tee-shirt, and boots with armadillos tooled into the leather. Cassie glanced down at her beaded sandals and white linen slacks, feeling ridiculously out of place.

They all piled in, the child cuddled next to a floppy-eared dog in the back seat, and drove away. The last thing she saw was the translucent painting on the rear windshield of a hawk in flight.

Oh my God, it's him!"

She had stood in the darkened cafe, holding a painting she treasured created by the very man who captivated her with his music, and had not known it.

How could she reconcile the image of the impatient clod who almost ran her off the road to the pensive artist in Smithy's? The two seemed vastly different. Maybe he had a twin. Maybe he was bipolar. Maybe he was cursed with a short temper.

It doesn't matter. His paintings and his music speak far louder about the true nature of the man than the ding in my car.

She left the protection of the porch and headed toward Main and, hopefully, her Thunderbird. Sundry boutiques, specialty shops, and cafes slipped past as she walked, her reflection in the windows shadowing her every step. She looked frazzled and wind-blown and every inch the over-dressed tourist. Her image rippled over the glass, pausing as she stopped to gaze at a particular display – a dazzling array of western boots, intricately hand-tooled with flowers, hummingbirds, cactus, a rattlesnake. Twenty minutes later, she walked from their doors, boot-box in hand.

Ain't no other can send me the way you do. Ain't no other can slay me the way you do. I'll be a heaven and hell girl in cowboy boots.

She hung *Spirit Song* above the sofa. The room seemed to gravitate toward it, as though the sole purpose of the space was to honor what hung upon the wall. The painting murmured to her, urging her to look every time she passed through the parlor. When she succumbed and let her eyes rest upon it once again, the shadow-flute sang Hawk's music, the child of the water became the child of his blood, and the oak leaves turned into his green eyes.

She tried to ignore the pull, to squelch the threads of music, to shut her mind against the changing images. Yet they were all interwoven: the painting, the man, the music, the child, the woman with golden hair. And with it came a longing for something lost – a family of her own, a child, a husband, a *belonging.*

Cassie stormed around the house, fighting against the loneliness. *Maudlin*! she scolded. *Do something. Keep busy. Fuming over the state of things doesn't help matters.* She scrubbed the floors, washed the windows, emptied the trash. But the longer and harder she worked the worse she felt, as though her efforts to keep sadness at bay only drew it closer.

She sat on the porch steps, her face raised to the evening breeze. *The winds at night are tamed by the moon.* Where had she heard those words before? Daytime winds on the Texas hills chewed her hair, but in the soft darkness they caressed her cheeks and breathed the fragrance of sage and honeysuckle.

Frogs croaked along the shore, bass accompaniment to the frenzied chorus of crickets and katydids. *Every living creature seeks a mate. It's the way of things.*

The memory of Hawk and the little girl walking hand in hand toward the woman waiting for them was like a tender scab she couldn't help but pick. There seemed to be such perfect togetherness among the three, she ached with the lack of it in her own life, for the happiness she once envisioned for herself, for the dream that had slipped away along with the years.

"Why?" She asked aloud.

The silverware angels jingled in response, glittering in the moonlight. What was it Justin and Berta had said? *If the chimes are especially merry, make a wish.*

Oh, what she wished! If only, if only...

And remembered, not wanting to remember:

While sorting through his clothes some weeks after Thomas had fallen from the cliff, her spirit too drained for more tears, it suddenly struck her – those weeks had passed without a drop of blood. She was long overdue. A raging joy shuddered through her, a thundering hope. She would see her beloved in the face of their child, feel him in the comfort of her arms, sense him in the touch of her breath.

Three days later the trickling began, the familiar dampness. She found the beginning, and the end, of what was almost a child – a round, gluey pearl the size of a marble in the palm of her hand.

She buried her small treasure in the rosebush among the ashes of its father. From that day onward she tended the bush carefully, replanting in bigger pots as it grew, carrying it from one apartment to the next.

The years passed, but sorrow did not. Sometimes she imagined holding the child in her arms – a girl one time, a boy another – the texture and smell and weight so real, so pronounced, it was as though she truly had birthed, truly had held, and only now found her arms emptied. Dreams chased after her – laughter, the never-spoken, "Mama!" the small hands reaching for her. In the rounds of daily living, sometimes a youngster would dash from the muddle of bodies in the grocery or department store, in the church, library, wherever people congregated – giving a glimpse, a momentary sense of what might have been, had her life been different. And the loss would strike her anew.

As it did now.

A tree frog chirruped nearby, sweet and clear, but Cassie found no comfort in it, and curled inward as though the night dark had seeped into her blood.

She sensed more than heard it – a sound, a presence.

A woman stood before her, illuminated by the moonlight, skirt dragging the ground, floppy hat, hair riotous around her face.

Startled, Cassie asked, "How did you...?"

The bag lady stepped closer, holding something in her hands. "Here." She thrust it at Cassie.

"What is it?"

"For you." Her voice was raspy and deep-throated. "I'm sorry I startled you the other night. I like walking when the moon's up." She pushed the offering into Cassie's lap. "Take it."

Bewildered, Cassie did as she was told. The gift was a small nest, a miracle of hand-woven twigs embedded with crystals, feathers, and chips of turquoise. An egg of polished stone nestled inside, painted with a vine and tiny red roses. This was a work of art, as beautiful as anything Cassie had ever seen. During all the years she had searched for unique, one-of-a-kind items to purchase for her store, Spirit of the Southwest, she had never come across anything quite so remarkable.

"Oh, it's exquisite!" she exclaimed, but the woman had already left.

"Wait!" Cassie cried, leaping from the step. "Please stay!"

"Another time." She was a silhouette moving over the bridge, long skirt flowing.

"You're Tatty, aren't you?"

"That's what they call me." The silhouette paused, turning toward her. "I have another, but Tatty will do for now." Then she quietly blended into the night shadows.

"Will I see you again?"

Words carried with the breeze, sighing, "Peace, Cassandra."

Cassie slowly sat down again, gazing at the nest. Who was she, this Tatty, this artist, this crazy bag-lady apparition? She had appeared silently, as if dropped from the sky. Didn't the woman weigh enough to make footsteps?

I should have heard her walking over the bridge or stepping on the brittle grass.

Tatty had disappeared into the woods as if the purple-dark trees had claimed her, as if she belonged among them, rooted to the earth.

How did she know my name? Why did she give me such a lovely, perfect thing?

Sleep came slowly that night. Clouds swam over the moon, splashing ever-changing shadows against the bedroom walls. Through half-closed eyes, she imagined the dark shapes merging, forming hands and a flute. When the dreams came, they moved in music. Music winds, music hills, music hawks flying. She was running in a stream, water swirling around her legs, struggling against the current. The face of a little girl with a pink ribbon in her hair rose from its depths, bubbles between her lips. Cassie took her by the hand, and the child pulled her under, down and down until she was covered in darkness and drowned in music.

Daughter. Daughter, wake up.

Cassie awoke with a gasp, bolting upright. Someone had whispered to her, she was sure. Whispered there beside her bed, leaning close, the breath still warm on the tip of her ear. A man? A woman? She couldn't tell.

She gripped the sheet and pulled it under her chin, shivering in the heat and in the dark, eyes skittering around the room.

No one. Nothing. Simply the moon-shadows weaving upon the walls. It had all been a dream.

Yet still she heard the music.

She wrapped the sheet around herself and moved from the bedroom to the porch and down the steps, the sheet trailing after like a bridal gown. Stepping lightly, her feet bare on the meadow grass, the notes surging and fading, lifting and falling, buffeted by the breeze.

It's Hawk, playing on the hills.

She sank slowly to her knees, captivated by the flute's song. The notes drifted from one direction and then another, as though Hawk lifted his great wings and flew from hilltop to hilltop, from a far-flung plateau to the nearby wood, playing all the while.

Sighing, she lay upon the ground and gazed up at the clouds galloping through a field of stars.

The Trickster

"HOWDY, SUGAR LUMP." A WOMAN WITH A CURLY MASS OF BLEACHED BLONDE hair leaned on the counter behind the register at the *Gas `n Grub*, her pillowy cleavage in the low-necked blouse displayed to full advantage. "You need anything, just holler."

Cassie peeked from behind a display of canned soup as the woman smiled with red-red lips at a short, skinny fellow who blushed up to his balding head, mumbled, "Thanks ma'am," and bumped into the freezer before joining the domino game in the back of the store.

"Hey, Ed," one of the domino-players teased, "Darla given' you a hard time?"

"Don't mean nothin'."

"Gettin' a mite hot in here," another chuckled.

"Y'all behave, now!" Darla cried, and the laughter subsided.

She became all business the moment Cassie put her groceries on the counter. "Just lay `em right there and I'll take care of the rest," she commanded, and began to announce each item while punching the cash register. "Oatmeal. Raisins. Light bulbs. Bananas." Her fingers paused as she looked down at the bananas. "These here still greenish. You want I should get you some better?"

"No, thanks."

Darla sniffed and whacked the register keys, her fingernails the impossible pink of plastic flamingos and so long they curled at the end like claws.

"I've never seen nails quite like yours," Cassie ventured. "How do you get through the day without poking yourself in the eye?"

"Hardly know any different. Had these since forever, so using 'em is natural." She pronounced it with three syllables, *na-chur-al*. "I wouldn't be so lucky without Nan to keep `em in shape." Glancing at Cassie's hands, she added, "Maybe you should give her a try."

"Hey, Miss Cassie!" Pete lumbered up the aisle, whiskered face grinning around a cigar. "This here's my sister, Darla. I already told her about you."

"Nice to meetcha in person," Darla said. "Flour. Chocolate chips. You baking cookies or something?"

Pete wrapped his huge arms around Cassie in a boisterous hug, practically lifting her from the floor. "Ain't it about time you come to one of our Wednesday night shindigs?"

"I keep telling myself I will every time I walk through your door."

"Billy's gonna play his guitar next time around. I know he'd like to see you there."

"Fourteen dollars thirty-two cents," Darla interrupted.

Cassie handed her a twenty dollar bill as Pete reached over and flicked cigar ashes into a coffee cup. "He's been happier since comin' to work for you, seems to me. I ain't never seen him smile so much. It hurt him hard when his mama died the way she did."

"Billy's been a Godsend. I don't know what I'd do without him."

"Five dollars sixty-eight cents change." Darla counted it into Cassie's palm, maneuvering her flamingo nails around the coins.

"Hell, it's *you* that are a Godsend to *him*, Miss Cassie." Pete lifted the sack from the counter, giving it to her. "Hope to see you Wednesday."

"I'd like to hear Billy play. And you, too."

Darla's voice carried over the squeal of the screen door as Cassie pushed it open, nudging the Pooh-bah dog aside with her foot, "Come again, y'hear?"

Cassie walked past Pete's cement armadillo to her car, tempted to give the next musical gig a try since Billy would be there. All his free time had been spent in the barn working on the Studebaker, so she had yet to hear him play or sing again.

She put the groceries in the back seat, aware of the small, neat house on a rise nearby, partially hidden by a profusion of plants. A sign hung from a sprawling poplar in front of the porch, *Nails by Nan*. Darla was right. Her nails were in serious need of attention, so why not now? She rolled the car windows down in hopes the chocolate chips wouldn't melt and followed the stone pathway to the house, stepping around or ducking underneath the multitude of potted plants sitting and hanging from everywhere, and rang the doorbell. After a moment the door swung open and an exquisite gamine face looked up at her.

"Yes?"

"Hi. I'm Cassandra Brighton. I haven't called for an appointment, but..."

"Mrs. Brighton! I've looked forward to meeting you. Please, come in."

If Pete was a blustery Santa, Nan was a serene Asian elf with skin flawless as puréed silk. Cassie followed her through a spotless living room into an equally spotless kitchen, feeling clumsy in comparison to this delicate creature.

"I'm so glad you came by, Mrs. Brighton."

"Call me Cassie, please. Or Cassandra."

"*Cass-aie.* A pretty name," Nan said with a charming musical lilt. She gestured toward a black lacquered chair with a red leather seat, one of four around a matching table. "Perhaps we could visit a little first, if you have time. Hot tea?"

"That would be lovely."

"Pete says so many nice things about you. A lot of people do, you know."

"Really? But I've only met a few here and there. "

"It's the nature of a small town to want to know everything about everybody."

Nan moved with a quick grace as she handled water, cups and so on, the silence broken by the clink of dishes or the squeal of a cupboard door as it opened and shut. The kitchen was simple but pleasant, with little decoration other than framed photographs on the wall and a miniature bonsai in a red and gold planter on the window ledge. A rolling cart with fingernail polish and other items sat in a corner next to an arched doorway opening into what appeared to be a sewing room. Cassie glimpsed shelves of fabrics and a dressmaker's form wearing a silvery gown.

"You're making a dress?"

"Yes. It's almost finished, except for pearls on the bodice."

"It's gorgeous. The pattern must have been complex."

"I don't use patterns. I drape fabric this way and that, and come up with something."

"You *designed* it? I'm impressed. The only thing I do well with a needle is stab myself."

"It depends upon the fabric, the feel of it, the..." Nan searched for the right word, then shrugged.

"The way it speaks to you?"

"Exactly."

"Justin told me that's how he designs his angels. The metal *talks* to him."

"Maybe that's why they're so magical. To me, anyway."

"Especially the huge one in the front yard. Whenever I drive by, I half expect it to fly after me with sword and shield in hand, protecting me along the way."

The china was white with red winged dragons. Nan placed a platter of almond cookies on the table and sat opposite with her teapot. It, too, had a dragon, the handle forming the body as if the reptile were trying to climb into the pot.

"Enjoy, *Cass-aie*."

And so she did, cookies and tea and company alike. After a while, Cassie turned to the photographs on the wall. The closest showed two people, one stocky and one slight, wearing matching raincoats in front of a torrent of cascading water. "Is this you and Pete?"

"Our honeymoon at Niagara Falls." Nan leaned forward as if to share a secret. "I feed him too well, as you can see. Sometimes I don't know what he loves best, me or my pies."

"And this?" Cassie pointed to the smallest photograph, a blurry black and white with the edges curling. In it, a young woman cradled a baby in her arms while another clutched her long skirt. She stood in a field, facing away from the camera. Ragged clouds darkened the sky behind her, interspersed with a flash of lightning.

Nan gathered the empty cups and put them into the sink. "Me. My children. Long ago, in Saigon."

"Do you have family there?"

"No. Only ash and memories."

"Of course. Please forgive me. I wasn't thinking." Cassie felt terrible. How could she have been so stupid? Saigon must have been Nan's home before the war changed everything.

"No need to apologize." Nan smiled as she placed a glass bowl of sudsy water on the table. "Do you want polish?"

"Clear only, thanks."

Blue pebbles lay at the bottom of the bowl, along with a tiny jade turtle. "I feel as though I'm reaching into a fishbowl," Cassie said as she put her fingers into the warm water to soak. "All you need is a little goldfish swimming around in there."

"How about yourself? Do you have children?"

"No. There was a time when I thought… But no."

"A boyfriend, then?" Nan selected a cuticle stick and began to ply her magic. "Pete told me you were widowed, so I hope I'm not intruding."

"You're not intruding, and nope, no boyfriend."

"I don't believe it. You're much too beautiful. There are probably so many men swarming after you that you have to swat them away like flies."

"Not a chance," Cassie said with a quick grin. "Ever since my husband died any interaction with the male species has been disastrous. I keep... I kept comparing everyone else to him, I think, and they all came up short."

"It's difficult, sometimes. Letting go."

"Yes." The warmth Cassie saw in Nan's dark sloe eyes encouraged her to say more. "We were hiking in the Colorado mountains, and he fell into a canyon. I've been leery of heights ever since."

"And here you are, surrounded by hills."

"Surrounded by hills," Cassie repeated. "As long as I don't climb them, I'm okay."

"But when you do?"

"I'm there again. That morning, that mountain."

It was soothing, having her hands clasped and nails attended. Nan began to file them, the sound a soft *whish-whish*, like a comforting whisper in the dark. "It stays with me," Cassie said quietly. "The memories. The life we shared. All the beautiful moments. And then gone, so fast, so unexpected, as if God had plucked Thomas off the face of the earth on a cruel whim."

"I'm sorry, Cass-*aie*. Life isn't always fair."

"No. Or a fairy-tale with a happily-ever-after."

"True, although sometimes an unexpected ending makes a better story."

"You sound just like my grandmother."

Nan laughed suddenly, a big, bright laugh that didn't fit the dainty body housing it. Cassie laughed in return, wondering at the strangeness of life, how unforeseen and rare, to form an immediate kinship with someone who by all rights ought to be a stranger. Yet there she sat, feeling as though she were in the company of a friend she'd known for years.

"I heard you're staying at your grandmother's and tidying up the place to sell," Nan said as she reached for the nail polish. "She lived there most of her life, didn't she?"

"Almost every day of it. She was born in the old stone house on a splendid four-poster bed that's still there. It belonged to her own mother, and maybe her grandmother and the one before that."

"It's a treasure, then."

"One I could never sell." She sighed, adding, "I feel the same about several of Mimi's things, and may end up hauling them around with me for years even though most have little value. Like a crippled chair made out of twisty vines and a clock that wheezes more than bongs. Throwing them away would be like throwing away pieces of my grandmother."

"I'd probably feel that way, too."

No more was said for a while, nor did Cassie feel the need to speak while Nan's deft brush strokes transformed her nails. Light from the window cast leafy shadow patterns across the table and their hands as the breeze teased the hanging plants outside. Nan glanced up and smiled, and suddenly words slipped from Cassie's mouth, words she hadn't realized were waiting to be spoken.

"Something happened recently and I don't quite know what to make of it."

Nan nodded, bending her head to her work, listening.

"I met someone, a man. I didn't talk to him, just saw him, really, maybe ten feet away or so. And I surprised myself, the way I responded. The way I felt, so immediate, so damned *physical*. Like a feral cat in heat."

"Oh, this sounds promising!"

"It's not. He's married. I didn't know it at the time. It's crazy. *I'm* crazy. I haven't felt an inkling of desire for anyone since Thomas, so what the heck was going on?"

"Maybe *life* was going on."

"I know how stupid this sounds, but I feel like I've besmirched my husband's memory."

Nan unfolded a paper fan and whiffed it over Cassie's nails to help them dry. "My grandmother once said love never ends. It just puts on a disguise and changes direction."

"Why a disguise?"

"It likes surprises."

"Love as a trickster!" Cassie exclaimed, delighted with the idea. "In Native American lore, Coyote is a trickster. Guess that makes love a coyote."

"I can see it now: valentines with pink coyotes."

Their laughter was swallowed by the puttering growl of a motorcycle passing down the road and by a few lazy barks, probably from Pooh-bah. Cassie waited until the racket faded and said, "I've been talking too much about myself. It's your turn now. Tell me anything. Favorite music? Adventures, bad or otherwise?" She pointed to the black and white photograph. "Your children must be grown by now. Do they live nearby?"

After a moment, Nan said, "I lost them."

"Lost what?"

"Lo and Tuan, my children. The missing pieces of my heart."

Cassie looked again at the two small figures, a babe hugging its mother's neck, a child clutching the hem of her skirt. "What happened?"

"I watched them fly away until the airplane melted into the clouds. I've not seen them since."

"Why?"

"The war took them. April, 1975. I'll never forget that day. Rockets blasting so close the ground shook. I ran down the tarmac at Tan Son Nhut airport through fire and dirt and smoke with both children in my arms. The plane shut its doors and started to move but I ran alongside and screamed for them to stop and take my babies to safety. And so they did."

"Where did they go?"

"I don't know. Nobody knows. There are no records, no identification papers, nothing." Nan touched the face of each child, as though a kiss lay in her fingertips.

Aghast, Cassie exclaimed, "Why couldn't you go with them?"

"The plane was to rescue orphan children only – in open boxes, on the seats, on the floor, anywhere one could be placed. Operation Babylift. Have you heard of it?"

"No, I never..."

The doorbell chimed, startling them both. Nan glanced at the clock. "Where did the time fly? It's already my next appointment."

"I must go," Cassie rose from the table. "Although I'd rather kick whoever is out there off the porch and keep you all to myself."

Cassie turned onto Spring Creek, the car jouncing over the ruts. The sack of groceries toppled over in the back seat, spilling bananas and raisins.

Nan's words murmured in her thoughts: *The missing pieces of my heart.*

Pete couldn't have been the father of the two children Nan had been forced to send away. The honeymoon photograph at Niagara showed a woman older than the one standing against the storm clouds of Saigon. Had Nan been married before her life with Pete? It seemed so. What about a family, parents, brothers, sisters? She never mentioned anyone else. Perhaps they all died in the war.

How could she have endured such unspeakable loss and yet remain intact? Why hadn't grief eaten her soul? Cassie shook her head in wonderment.

Whenever I feel sorry for myself, I'll think of Nan and count my blessings.

She drove past the Grumm's cottage, the metal archangel glittering in the afternoon sun. The day had a lazy feel to it, hot and golden, the light soft upon the ground. A flock of migrating ducks swam through a water-blue sky. Where had the time gone? Summer was making an exit as autumn lurked in the wings, ready to walk onstage far too soon.

Down the road and through the gate she drove, the air redolent with prickly pear and wild grass. She clattered over the bridge, startled to see Justin beside the barn. Guy's battered pickup was there, too, the bed piled high with odds and ends. Billy stood on top of it all, lifting a plow claw from Justin's upraised hands before placing it with the rest. They turned and waved, continuing with their work as Cassie rescued her spilled groceries and hurried into the house.

It didn't take her long to fix a tray of iced tea and peanut butter cookies and carry it outside.

"Hey, Miss Cassie!" Billy hollered. "Mr. Grumm asked me to help him load up some of the junk you don't want."

"How about a cookie break?"

"Never could resist a pretty girl with a platter," Justin said with a lopsided grin.

"I hope you're finding stuff you can use for your angels, something that *speaks* to you," Cassie teased, placing the tray on the open tailgate.

"Well, now, I've been carrying on a pretty good conversation with several chatty items, especially that there." Justin pointed to the parlor stove. "Those wrought-iron doors are fancy beautiful."

"Mr. Grumm already knows what he's gonna do with them," Billy said as he snapped up a couple of cookies. "He told me."

"All right now." Justin winked. "Don't go giving away secrets."

They settled into the business of eating – Billy with his usual deliberate attention and Justin with an absentminded air. Cassie sat on the tailgate, enjoying the easy camaraderie. A lightness filled her heart, a pleasure in the company of these two friends, and it suddenly occurred to her that she was happy. "Billy, I'm glad you're here to help Justin, but why aren't you in school? It's a week day."

"You playing hooky?" Justin asked.

"No, Dad would whup – I mean, whip me good. There's only teachers today, no students."

"Has he done it before?" Cassie blurted. "Whip you, I mean."

Billy took his time to reply, wiping crumbs from his chin. "He takes his belt off and waves it around when he's really mad. It's mostly just yelling, but if I don't duck fast enough he'll whack me good. I know he's sorry after because he'll get quiet and not talk much."

Cassie felt the anger flare in her chest and she clenched her teeth to keep it inside. She yearned to hunt Guy down and lash him with his own belt until his skin peeled like seared onion.

"Miss Cassie, what do you want me to do with that bent-up bicycle frame still in the carport? I've been meaning to ask but keep forgetting."

"Throw it in the trash." She spoke more sharply than intended, and Justin raised his eyebrows in surprise.

Billy didn't seem to notice. "Okay if I take it home?"

"I don't know what good you'd get from that old thing."

"I got something in mind."

"Oh? What?"

"Just something." Billy shrugged. "You coming to Pete's tomorrow night? Mr. Grumm said he might. I'm gonna be playing."

"You bet. Wouldn't miss it for the world."

"Cool!"

His face lit up with such pleasure that Cassie decided not only would she go, she'd sit on the front row and clap like crazy.

The Crack Between Worlds

Cassie stood in front of the full-length mirror, a critical eye on her outfit: slim jeans fitting in the proper places, a tank top, concho belt, and the new cowboy boots with tooled roses.

With turquoise earrings and bracelet and her father's blue stone heart on a silver chain necklace, she was ready to wow the world – or at least meet it head-on.

"Billy boy, here I come!" she sang as she hopped into the car, glad that Berta and Justin had accepted her offer to act as chauffeur.

They were holding hands and waiting for her on their porch, he gangly and stooped and she a puffball of smiles and fabric. Berta's full skirt with overlapping red and blue checked ruffles made the plump woman look as if she were sprouting from a gaily-frosted cake. They quarreled as usual, each wanting the other to sit in front, until it was decided that Justin might have more leg room if he stretched out in back. Berta settled next to Cassie, her voluminous ruffles fluffing around her like the feathers on a fat hen.

"You look festive tonight," Cassie said, touched by Berta's look of eager anticipation.

"Do you think so? I used to wear this square-dancing since I forgot when." Berta twisted around to look at Justin. "When was the last time you took me dancing?"

"Let's see now." After a moment's reflection, he said, "A year or so ago, when I turned eighteen and you were twelve."

"Silly old man," Berta grumbled.

Cassie glanced at Justin in the rearview mirror, startled to see that his eyes were weepy.

"This is the first time we've been to one of Pete's musicales." Berta held her purse in her lap. It was hefty, with a thick strap and bulging pockets. "It's been a while since we've gone socializing."

"Talked about nothing else all day long and scolded me, too," Justin added. "She's afraid I'll forget my manners and revert to a Neanderthal."

"That's because you've been carrying the toilet plunger around like a club! For a while there I thought you wanted to take it with us."

"Well, now," Justin chuckled, "that plunger can be fairly good company. It thinks I'm a genius."

ꟷ

The parking lot in front of Pete's was so full it barely left room for a bicyclist trying to maneuver through it. Cassie let the Grumms out by the cement armadillo then parked on the roadside a good walk away, passing a multitude of parked cars, vans, pickups, a motorcycle.

She pretended that it didn't matter and she wasn't really looking, but not one of the red pickups had a hawk painted on the rear window.

Sounds greeted Cassie first: the rumble of chatter broken by an occasional burst of laughter, the creak and slam of a door or two, footsteps. A tantalizing aroma of barbeque and sausage mingled with the tang of cigars and cigarettes and beer. People milled on the front porch. For once Pooh-bah was nowhere in sight, except for two canine eyes peering from under the steps. Reluctant to elbow her way to the front door, Cassie followed others walking to the back yard. It was spacious, hemmed with a picket fence pushing against a tumble of brush and trees, the entangled limbs glowing purple in the darkening light. Japanese paper lanterns, swaying slightly in the evening breeze, hung near a barbeque pit fashioned from an oil drum. A noisy throng meandered among tables and chairs, eating spareribs or plucking iced beer and soda from tin water troughs.

"Hey, sugar lump!" Darla's voice rose above the clamor. She leaned on the checkout table, thrusting her cushy bosom toward the same skinny Ed fellow as before. Her amplitude was magnified by an appliquéd strawberry placed on the two strategic spots of her stretchy knit overalls. "See anything you like, darlin'?" She flicked her flaming pink nails at the cash register near her hip. "Just bring it to me, and I'll ring you up good."

Instead of stumbling away as he had earlier, Ed lingered longer than necessary, thumbs hooked in his waistband, gazing at her from under his eyebrows. She seemed flustered by his attention, preening one moment then fussing with the table the next.

"Cassandra!" Justin's head with its feathery tufts of silver poked above the crowd. Berta's small hand lifted up almost to his chin, the fingers twiddling. "Come join us!" she called.

"On my way!" Cassie stepped toward them just as a youngster with white-blonde hair bolted out of nowhere and crashed into her. "Oops!" The little girl squealed and dashed away, chased by a young woman crying, "Come back here, you monkey!"

White-blonde! Cassie spun around, trying to keep the child in view, and stepped onto a discarded paper plate slicked with barbeque sauce. It skidded across the grass as her foot shot out from under her, and she instinctively reached to grab whatever she could on her way down – which happened to be the person behind her. They both plummeted to the ground, landing in a tangle.

"Looky here," a familiar voice growled in her ear. "Not often a pretty woman throws herself at me." Stone gray eyes regarded her with amusement. "You steady now or want to keep hangin' on?"

"I'm perfectly fine, thank you, Mr. Wilkins." Mortified, she realized she was gripping his thigh.

"Name's Guy. No need to be so formal-like, seein' as how we've gotten so close." His voice was teasing as he helped her to her feet, his hands strong and his touch sure. She pulled away, averting her eyes from the scorpion tattoo on his left bicep undulating as if crawling to his shoulder.

"Thanks for the rescue, Guy. I promise not to throw myself at you again."

"Wouldn't mind if you did." He tapped his forehead in farewell.

Cassie paid little heed to his retreating back. *White-blonde hair!* If she were here, her daddy might be, too. It wouldn't hurt to see Hawk again. From a distance, of course.

Guy watched from the corner of his eye as Cassie strolled through the crowd, looking around like she was trying to find someone. She walked smooth and graceful as a damned cat, which was why her tumble was so unlikely and funny, throwing her right into him.

Christ, she was good-looking. Shapely legs going on forever in those tight jeans could wrap themselves around a man and hold on good. And her lips, the fullness of them, the way they up-tilted at the ends and moved when she spoke, made him want to eat them whole.

Good God Almighty, I'm getting unhinged.

He'd dressed special tonight, knowing she'd be here.

Billy had come running into the house yesterday, yelling that Mrs. Brighton was coming to hear him play. Rare thing to see Billy so out and lively. He'd been distant lately, keeping to himself. Maybe it was just a part of growing up, although Guy suspected something else was the cause. Or someone.

Cassie sure enough had an effect on that boy. Maybe too much. He had better keep his eyes sharp, make sure she didn't encourage Billy's far-fetched ideas.

Look at her, smiling big at that old couple, the Grumm folk. So nice and warm it makes me want to go over there and talk to her myself. Or do something better that don't require no talking.

He yanked another beer from the tin trough and sat in one of the folding chairs scattered throughout the yard. He popped the lid with his pocket knife and took a swig, planning to pay for it later. Right now he needed time to think about things.

The child seemed to have vanished like a sylvan ghost. There was no sight of her or of the woman chasing after. Or of Hawk, for that matter.

"Cassandra, isn't this lovely!" Berta's face glowed and her eyes danced huge and happy behind their thick lenses. She and Justin carried plates loaded with barbeque and coleslaw. Justin carried two.

"We got a plate for you," he said, "and this here plastic do-dad fork."

They sat on a splintery bench by an equally splintery picnic table and said nothing more while they ate. Once Berta leaned over and dabbed Justin's chin with a paper napkin, and later he returned the favor. "How about a drink?" Cassie asked. "What would you like?"

"Lemonade would be nice," Berta mumbled through a mouthful of coleslaw.

"Lemonade coming up."

The ice had melted to almost nothing and the spigot container was about empty. Cassie tilted it to fill her cup. "Think I got the last drop," she said to Darla.

Darla beamed more than usual, her flamingo nails poised above the register as though she expected to have her picture taken. "One fifty each, plus tax. That's four dollars eighty-one cents." Her blue-glittered eyes slid from Cassie to somewhere on her right, then back again. Cassie followed her gaze to Ed ambling around partly out of sight – but not quite. And not too far away.

"Thanks." Cassie handed her a five dollar bill as Darla chirped and strutted, a bird in full plumage displaying her colors. The male bird, in this case, was the plain one – small and unspectacular and wary, but circling within range.

Balancing the three cups, Cassie left Darla to her designs and passed Pete manning the barbeque pit. He waved at her with a red-smeared brush, splattering his apron. "Hey, Miss Cassie! Enjoyin' yourself?"

"Having a great time. I had no idea there would be so many people!"

"Someone popular hereabouts will be playin' tonight. Go find yourself some seats. I'm about ready to close shop and start jammin'!"

Cassie opened her mouth to reply. And left it open, words unspoken.

The fleeting moment when daylight sinks into darkness and shadows shimmer with an opalescent light is oftentimes magical. Mimi used to call it the crack between worlds, when what is real and what is dreamed become one. So it seemed natural that the man who created magic with a paintbrush and flute chose that moment to appear.

Hawk stepped from the deepening darkness on the far side of the yard. Thick, white-shining hair, strong jaw and wide shoulders, gorgeousness in every slim-hipped inch. By his side was a slender aristocratic woman holding his arm with one possessive hand and a silver-handled cane in the other. She tilted her head up to him, sharp-boned face softened by something akin to worship.

Rebecca Stanch! The saleswoman from Whistle Pik Gallery, acting like a queen consort as a group gathered around eager to greet them. Chatting amiably, the handsome king, ever solicitous, helped his patrician queen up the porch steps and through the door.

What the. . .? Where's his wife?

"There aren't any decent seats left!" Disheartened, Cassie realized she had waited too long. The room was crammed with chairs and benches, all occupied except for a smattering of the most undesirable spots – such as a bench behind the freezer and a dilapidated crate.

Justin nudged Cassie. "Why is Guy Wilkins flapping like an agitated rooster?"

Gesturing broadly, Guy pointed to three chairs on the front row, unclaimed except for a pocketknife, Stetson, and beer bottle. Berta squealed, "We're in luck!" grabbed Justin's hand and hurried over.

Guy motioned for Cassie to sit next to him. "Billy told me to be sure and save you a good seat."

"Thank you. And thank Billy for me, too." She sat down and fidgeted, hemmed in on the right by Berta, whose plump self spilled from the confines of her chair, and on the left by Guy. She felt squashed between them, uncomfortably aware of his shoulder and hip brushing hers.

Pete and a half dozen musicians did last-minute preparations, rearranging platform stools, tuning guitars and a fiddle, tapping the drums, leaning an ear to the bass, getting ready to perform and obviously enjoying it. Darla's skinny Ed was up there, too, with a banjo.

"My, this is so exciting!" Berta exclaimed.

"Miss Cassie, you really came!" Billy rushed over, guitar hanging on a strap from his shoulder.

"What did you call her?" Guy asked.

"Oh." Billy flushed. "I got so excited I forgot."

"Forgetting ain't no excuse."

Cassie touched Guy's arm. "It's okay, really. I like it that way. I'd even like it better if he dropped the *Miss*."

"That right?" Guy asked.

Billy and Cassie both nodded.

"Alright then. But keep the *Miss*. Line's gotta be drawn somewhere."

"C'mon, Billy, let's get crackin'!" Pete called. Billy gave Cassie a quick smile before stepping up on the platform.

Guy snorted. "He's so happy you're here he can't hardly stand it."

Look at that! Cassie stared at the other end of the front row. Rebecca Stanch was sitting beside Hawk's wife and chatting nicely as you please. Hawk stood alongside, beaming down at his harem of two, the little girl on his back with her arms tight around his neck. If Rebecca was a friend of the family, that family was in trouble. She wanted Hawk in her own talons.

Her conscience jeered: *And you don't?*

The audience cheered and whistled as lights dimmed and the platform lit up. "Here we are folks!" Pete bellowed. "Let's have one hell of a good time!"

A riotous, joyful blast of foot-stomping music exploded into the room. Pete sat at the piano, head thrown back, hands pounding the keys as he led the way into gospel-flavored rock. His raspy voice was rich as old whisky, laughing or weeping or down-out wailing as one piece led into another. By the time Cassie came up for air, the music had slid into country, folk, scat-jazz, each leading into the other almost without pause.

How much time had passed? Berta looked dazed. Justin's head drooped, and even in the raucous cacophony his chin settled on his chest as he slept through it all.

Why wasn't Hawk up there? He sat beside his wife and Rebecca, evidently enjoying the evening as much as everyone else. Maybe he wouldn't be playing. This wild-out, boisterous musical explosion wasn't his style, at least not from what she'd heard at Smithy's.

As Pete launched into a rollicking blues, Billy perched on a stool, looking delighted to be there and half scared to death, playing his heart out. When the music paused, Pete announced, "A special treat comin' up, folks, written by our own Billy Wilkins, called *Ain't It Grand*."

"Wake up!" Berta hissed and poked Justin in the ribs.

Billy strummed a melody that reminded Cassie of fast-tumbling water, then sang:

Ain't it somethin', ain't it grand
How a stranger can walk in,
Take you by the hand,
Turn your life around?
Angels don't always need wings
And hearts don't always need words
When you've truly found
A friend.

The piano picked up the tune, the other instruments followed, and soon Billy led them all in an upbeat, swinging whatever it was. Cassie had no name for the music that followed, no niche in which to put it. It simply *was*, and it was wonderful.

When he finished, Cassie leaped up along with Guy and others as the room filled with shouts of approval. "Whoo-eee!" she cried, "Bravo, Billy!" He seemed stunned, sitting on his stool, cheeks flushed and eyes wide.

Guy was the last to stop clapping and the last to sit.

He loves that boy, Cassie thought, *although he's afraid to show it.*

"Okay, folks, let's give a big welcome to someone y'all have been waiting to hear!" Pete motioned in Hawk's direction. "Susan Anders!"

Hawk's wife! Slender and graceful, with wheat-gold hair streaming down her shoulders, she glided onto the platform amid cheers and whistles. Pete played an intro, then without further ado she began to sing. Sure, polished, silver and shining, her voice drifted into the ears and hearts of everyone present.

Stunning. Talented. No wonder Hawk loves her. If I were a man I would, too.

But she wasn't a man, and envy nibbled its nasty way into her thoughts. Something about Susan's name and voice were familiar, something she'd heard before. *Susan Anders. Susan Anders. Susan…* Then realization hit: *The* Susan Anders, promising country-western star! Susan Anders, with a first CD rising to the top of the charts and staying there. Susan Anders, featured in major magazines and talk-shows.

Susan Anders, Hawk's wife.

Dear God, it couldn't be much worse.

It wouldn't have mattered as much had he married someone unattractive and unknown. Then she could dream, perhaps. Imagine. Play the game of, "What if…?" But now?

Reality can be a damned ugly thing.

Up on their feet again, the audience stamped and whistled, some throwing cowboy hats. Laughing, Susan picked one up and put it on her head. Hawk laughed as well, blowing her a kiss in the bargain.

"Hawk, what're you doing restin' there on your haunches like the old buzzard you are?" Pete hollered through his beard. "Come on up here and join us!"

The crowd truly did grow wild. Berta gasped, "Oh my!" and Justin looked around, startled, as if he had been deposited into a football stadium by mistake. Hawk ambled onstage as Billy pushed his stool to the center and settled on the step, looking up. Hawk faced the audience, waiting for them to quiet before he sat, holding his wooden flute with the dangling feather.

"Thank you, everyone." God, his voice! It reached down inside Cassie, vibrating among her ribs like a tuning fork. "I'd like to play something along with my girl."

My girl! A silly, endearing term. Cassie wanted to leave right then, forget her manners, tramp over all the outspread legs, and haul Berta and Justin and herself back home.

Of course she sat right where she was, waiting for whatever happened next.

Wishes

WHAT HAPPENED NEXT WAS ENCHANTMENT — FLUTE AND VOICE ACCOMPANIED by the chirrups of a cricket in the wall. The audience listened with an electric silence that often happens when faced with something that grabs the heart and squeezes. Cassie closed her eyes, trying to pretend she was somewhere else, that the man playing was pudgy and bald and the woman singing was a plain, formless blob. That the two didn't look perfect together, weren't bound by the invisible threads spun in music.

Finally it was over. Susan with the glossy hair and glorious voice waved to her fans and returned to her seat. Hawk repositioned himself on the stool, lifted his flute, and looked at Cassie, directly at her with his green oak-leaf eyes. Cassie felt as though her chair were about to sink into the earth and carry her along with it.

A child's voice piped, "Mama, I want to sing with Pappo, too."

Gentle laughter rippled through the gathering as Hawk smiled at his little girl. "Sure, Meredith. Come on up here and we'll play a song for everyone."

Meredith. Her name is Meredith. Pretty.

She ran to stand beside her Pappo and rested against his knee. "I want to sing the one about wishes," she announced firmly.

"I'll start with the tune first. Okay, Rabbit?"

"Okay."

The melody was simple and sweet, reminiscent of *Twinkle Twinkle Little Star.*

Looking at ease and happy to be where she was, Meredith lifted her face into the light and sang while her father accompanied her:

I wish I were a little fish
swimming in the river.
I'd flip my shiny tiny tail
and make the water quiver.
I wish I were a kangaroo
with a pocket in my tummy.
Then I could hide all safe inside
the pocket of my mummy.
I wish I were a pretty bird
swallowing a worm.

I'd laugh and laugh because
Worms will tickle when they squirm.

Hawk bent toward the child, encircling her with love while he played. She leaned into him, hugging his knee until the final words were sung. "That was great, sweetheart," he said, and kissed her on the head. She scampered away to the sound of applause and into the waiting arms of her mother. Susan lifted her, whispering as she carried Meredith to the door.

"Night-night, Pappo!"

"Night, you two. Need help with the truck?"

"No, I'm fine," Susan said over her shoulder as she left. "Thanks, Dad."

Dad!

Cassie must have gasped because Guy glanced at her suddenly, his expression guarded. She mumbled something like "Isn't this fun!" and forgot him. Forgot Berta and Justin. Forgot every single individual filling that room, with the exception of Hawk.

Dad!

Colors and sound careened. Even Hawk seemed surreal. He glittered – white hair, white guayabera, white teeth – as though he had been dipped in the moon. A bubble of laughter rose from the depths of her stomach. It was all she could do to keep from leaping on her chair and tap dancing across the heads of everyone there.

Pete whammed on the piano with ham fingers, bringing it to startling life. His touch was surprisingly elegant, made the more surprising since the man was almost as wide as the piano itself. "Let's do it, Hawk!" he howled. "Go, baby, go!"

Hawk rose, resting against the piano as Pete threw himself into an improvisation, head thrown back, feet working the pedals. After a moment, Hawk lilted a counterpoint that at first seemed far different from what Pete began – two opposing forces, two competing voices, each going merrily on their own way until the final marriage. The other instruments joined in and *oh!* what music! A wild invention, a glorious dance, a soaring into the night that made Cassie want to weep for the pure joy of it.

She let herself be captured in the momentum, carried away to some far place, until she realized Hawk was playing to her. Looking and playing right at her, as if she were standing on the stage beside him. She shifted in her chair, trying to ease an inch or two away from Guy without poking Berta – a difficult task, since she was wedged between the two.

Hawk's eyes traveled from her to Guy and back again, a question couched within the green.

"Alright, folks!" Pete hollered as the music ended. "Save your clappin' for next time around! We're gonna take a break. Grab yourselves a beer and come back in ten or so. It's gonna be a long, rockin' night."

Berta spoke in Cassie's ear over the whoops and hollers. "We best get home before Justin slides off his chair and falls asleep on the floor."

She couldn't leave. She couldn't. She was riveted to the spot, pinned by a hawk's gaze.

The Grumms turned toward her, fatigue clouding their eyes. Cassie's heart lurched with regret. Duty called, as did love for these two. She smiled brightly, hoping to mask her disappointment and concern. "Of course. Wait out front and I'll get the car."

"Thanks dear. It was a lovely evening." Berta was pale, Justin dazed. The two helped one another up, Berta clutching her oversized purse, and slowly made their way through the mingling crowd.

"You leaving?" Guy spat his toothpick onto the floor beside several others he had chewed into splinters. "I was hopin'... Billy was hopin' you could stay awhile."

"I can't. Please tell Billy I'm sorry."

"Come back later. It ain't over yet."

"Maybe," she mumbled.

"I'll save your seat."

Cassie nodded absently, torn between the need to take care of the Grumms and her crazy desire to march up on the stage and introduce herself. She walked to the back porch, waving at Pete on her way out. The night had cooled, bringing with it the scents of cedar and sagebrush. A few remaining gardenias dripped from a bush by the fence, fragrant remnants of summer. One had fallen in her path, and on impulse Cassie picked it up and tucked it into her hair.

She glanced up before continuing on her way, and stumbled in surprise.

Hawk stood on the porch, looking at her. The light splashed onto his head and shoulders and threw shadows into the hollows of his face, but she knew his eyes were upon her.

He moved toward the steps, and Cassie's heart stopped.

He's coming to meet me!

Rebecca Stanch suddenly appeared, reaching for his arm. It was too far away for Cassie to hear clearly, but she caught the words, "Please, darling."

Hawk didn't budge. Rebecca followed his gaze then turned away as if she saw nothing of consequence, cooing something that sounded like, "Come, or they'll throw me to the lions."

"Cassie." Guy's voice. "It's late. I'll walk you to the car."

Guy emerged from the darkness alongside the house. He must have exited through the front door and hurried down the path. He approached with an odd angle to his shoulders, the usual swagger gone.

Hawk looked at Guy and then Cassie, his head turning from one to the other. He probably wondered if she and Guy were a couple. But what could she do? Bash Guy on the head with her boot?

Hawk lifted a hand in a gesture of farewell as he had done while standing atop Mount Bubba. Once again Cassie lifted her hand in response. They stayed that way for a moment and then he was gone.

The walk back to her car was quiet, save for the sound of gravel crunching under their feet. Guy was solicitous, warning her now and again of a dip in the road, and once steadied her over a rough patch of ground. He even waited while she fished for her key, standing patiently by until she got into the car.

She caught his reflection in the side-view mirror, watching as she drove away.

"God, I'm beat. This old mule can't keep kickin' like he used to," Pete sighed. "But hell, we rocked tonight." He sat heavily on the porch step, groaning as he went down.

"Look at this mess they left in the yard," Hawk muttered, "chairs overturned, dirty plates lying around, cans and beer bottles everywhere." A gust of wind lifted a paper tablecloth and sailed it onto a tree, where it dangled in the moonlight like a ratty ghost. "It'll take until morning to clean it all."

"Won't take no time with the two of us. I saved an apple pie and can put some coffee on. Interested?"

"If it's decaf, you've got a deal."

"You don't need no caffeine, that's for sure. I ain't never seen you so jittery. Why don't you sit down? Keep an old friend company `til I get a second wind."

"No thanks. I'm fine."

Pete gazed at Hawk, eyes bloodshot but sharp as ever. "You've been pacin' up and down the porch like you got a bee up your butt. Want to tell me why or should I guess?"

Hawk shrugged. "I'm just wired tonight. No particular reason."

"Um hum. " Pete raised his bushy eyebrows and waited.

"Don't give me that wise-old-owl look. It won't work."

Pete drew a cigar from his breast pocket and unwrapped it. "You aim on keepin' your thoughts to yourself, it's okay by me. But I've got big ears, in case you change your mind." He bit off the cigar tip and spat; it landed with a *ping* against a soda can.

"Right on target. You win the prize."

"Takes practice. Hawk, by God stop actin' like a caged-up hound! Sit down and let's talk without me having to twist my head around to see you."

"Just don't blow smoke in my direction. That stuff reeks like wet dog."

Hawk hated to admit it, but he *was* troubled. Haunted, actually – by a woman with dark hair and midnight eyes, a woman twice glimpsed from a distance until the day she emerged from the shadows of Smithy's Barbeque as if conjured by the music of his flute, lingering in his thoughts ever since. And now, tonight, she had come again, and once again had slipped away before he could speak to her.

Pete puffed on the cigar while Hawk stared at the moonlit clouds, words dry in his mouth. He wasn't used to talking about himself much, but if he was going to do it with anyone it would be Pete. Yet it still didn't come easy. "There was someone here tonight. Someone I've…" He couldn't finish.

"You sure close-mouthed, but I reckon I know the reason. I saw you lookin' at trouble. And it's lookin' right back at you. Am I right?"

Hawk grinned. "Right. Who is she?"

"Cassandra Brighton. Rumor has it she's a widow. Lives in the old Dorst place, belonged to her grandmother."

"Second time I saw her was at the bottom of that steep hill behind the house. She slipped and skidded down some."

"You're countin' times you saw her? Bad sign, my friend. So when was the first?"

"When she honked at me in your parking lot, glaring like she wanted to kill me on the spot. I couldn't figure who she was or why… Oh, shit!" Hawk smacked himself on the forehead. "It's the car! She's got a yellow vintage Thunderbird, right?"

"What you getting at?"

"No wonder she was mad. I practically ran her off the road near the Grumm place the last big storm we had. She was inching that Thunderbird over the mud like it would suck her under. I got frustrated because she was so damned slow." He shook his head. "I didn't know who was driving, man or woman, and didn't care, either. I just wanted to *move*."

"Why the hurry?"

"Meredith was in the hospital, sick. Turned out okay in the end, but I went haywire."

Pete chuckled. "Kids can do that to you." Puckering his lips, he blew three perfect smoke rings.

Hawk watched in the following silence, remembering Cassandra standing in Pete's back yard, looking at him. She had seemed to glow, as if moonlight had penetrated her skin and pulsed inside her. "Do you, um, know anything more about her?"

"Not much," Pete said. "But there's something special about her I can't put my finger on, a kind of sadness maybe. A gentle heart. She's different, that's for sure. Bought that odd painting of yours with the man struggling inside the tree. She called it *compelling*."

Hawk flushed, surprised and pleased. "Shows she has good taste, unlike some people. You hated that thing. Admit it."

"Glad to be rid of it." Pete grinned, spewing ashes on his beard. "I knew her grandma some, a good woman if there ever was one, stubborn and proud. Fanciful, too, with strange ideas of ghosts and fairies and stuff. Must of been a looker in her day; never saw hair so thick and glittery. Anyway, Cassie – that's what she likes to be called – aims to fix the house up for sale in a year or thereabouts. She liked Billy right off and hired him to help her. I reckon Billy took to her too. Misses his mother, that boy. Might be good to have someone look after him a bit."

Hawk nodded, half-listening. *Cassandra*. A name that had music and mystery in it, like those in legends and folk tales. He silently mouthed it, *Cassandra*, tasting the unspoken letters.

"She left too soon," he said quietly. "Ran away from the party like Cinderella to her pumpkin coach."

Cassie didn't return to Pete's after driving Berta and Justin home and seeing them safely into the house. She sat on the porch swing instead, a shawl around her shoulders, rocking to the sounds of crickets and frogs. A silhouette moved in the night darkness, coming slowly across the bridge. She froze, unafraid but cautious, knowing what it was. The wolf dog continued onward, venturing closer in a halting fashion until it met the light from the open door pooling onto the porch and beyond. He paused, yellow eyes unblinking.

Cassie didn't stir. After a while the wolf twitched one ear, as if expecting her to speak.

And so she did.

"He doesn't know my name, but he knows where I live. He'll find me. If he's interested, he'll find me."

The wolf sat on its haunches. No human shape emerged from the dark. Rag-bag Tatty with the floppy hat and beautiful bird nest didn't step from behind the trees. Evidently Wolf had decided to visit her on his own.

"Are you guarding me tonight? I'm fine, thanks. Feel free to go home."

Wolf lay down instead, resting its head on its paws. Cassie decided to ignore it – not an easy task, since the amber gaze never wavered. The swing squealed as she rocked to and fro, rusty whisperings of desire.

That evening Cassie dreamed of a horse with luminous white wings. She rode upon his back, thighs gripping the silken hide, arms wrapped around the neck, hair streaming in the winds as they soared through the star-lit darkness. As she awakened, the rhythmic cadence of him under her turned and moved upon her, a horse no longer. It was a man who claimed her, a dream phantom in the night, his panting soft in her ears before he rose from where he lay heavy and warm against her breasts.

With Appreciation

Cassie almost crumpled the big manila envelope without looking at it, expecting another seed catalogue. It seemed that Mimi had subscribed to every known gardening catalogue in the universe, and even after all these years a handful still flew into her mailbox.

But this particular envelope was different. On the front was an odd address penned in flowing calligraphy: *Cassandra Brighton at the Dorst ranch, Willow City.* Embossed on the upper left corner was the silhouette of a flying hawk.

Lately she'd thought about little else except Hawk. Everywhere she turned, he seemed to be there. She'd walk through the parlor and the painting *Spirit Song* called to her from its place on the wall, and she'd remember clutching it to her chest at Smithy's Barbeque, the brown paper wrapping crackling in her hands, Hawk's oak-green eyes looking up from the shadow of his hat, the flute between his lips. Whenever she went into the kitchen she couldn't help but glance at the small painting of the man struggling in the tree and think of the time she discovered it behind Pete's piano, and the night Hawk stood beside that same piano playing his flute, playing right to her. She tossed in her bed, listening for a flute echoing among the hills, sometimes telling herself that *yes*, there it was, and a moment later *no*, when it faded away.

But most of the time she kicked herself for mooning over a man who evidently didn't intend to moon back. Two weeks had passed since the night at Pete's, and she had yet to hear from him. Maybe she had misunderstood his interest. Maybe he was busy painting. Maybe he was occupied with someone else – namely, the aristocratic, possessive Rebecca Stanch, who would likely try to clip his wings and turn a wild hawk into a domesticated chicken.

Cassie opened the envelope and withdrew a single sheet of paper.

It was a penciled sketch of a glass slipper. Lying within it was a woman, eyes closed in sleep. A crown sat atop her flowing hair, which spilled over the shoe and trailed along the ground, forming the word *Casserella*. Fastened among the dark tresses was a white gardenia.

The sleeping woman was *her!* The face, the mouth, the everything that mattered was *her!*

Cassie hugged the sketch before looking at it again. Of course! Cinderella ran away at midnight just as she had at Pete's, leaving only a glass slipper for a befuddled prince. *Casserella* – a marriage of the two names.

Was Hawk telling her she was the princess he'd been searching for?

Then *damn it!* Why hadn't he called?

Billy propped Cassie's old bicycle in front of her house and stood back to evaluate his handiwork. The once-crumpled frame was now smooth and bright blue, the wheel spokes shiny. New tires, new seat – well, almost new. He got a good deal from a parts shop. New bicycle horn, too, a funny one he hoped would make her laugh. It had a rubber ball at one end, and when squeezed honked *Ooompa! Ooompa!*

He had wanted to do something nice for Cassie, to thank her somehow. The shoebox of savings hidden under his bed was so stuffed with money he earned from her the lid kept popping off. And the Studebaker! Each time he worked on it his passion for cars grew, as did his hopes for the future.

He looked at the bike with a critical eye. Maybe this wasn't such a good idea. Cassie could probably afford something new and sleek with multiple gears like the ones in fancy stores. What would she think when she saw her old bike hiding under a coat of paint?

"Billy! What have you got there?" Cassie smiled through the open bay window, her hair pulled back by a yellow scarf.

"Something for you."

"For me?" She disappeared for a moment, then the screen door banged open and she hurried down the porch steps. She wore a frilly apron with tiny pink flowers dotted all over, reminding him of old-time quilts and fussy grandmothers.

Cassie didn't say anything right away, but just looked. Walked around the bicycle real slow, looking. No words, no glance, nothing. Billy's stomach tightened. She hated it. It was just a stupid dressed-up old bike and she hated it.

"Oh, Billy." Cassie turned to him, her eyes unnaturally bright. "What a wonderful surprise!"

He whooped, he was so glad. "I hoped you'd like it."

"I love it." She hugged him, the scent of lemons clinging to her hair. He could have hugged her forever. "Well, now," Cassie said as she turned away and dabbed her eyes. "I should give it a try, don't you think?"

"That's the idea."

"It's been a while. I haven't been on a bike since I was around your age." She took off her apron, wadded it into the basket, and gripped the handlebars. "I hope I don't wobble into the creek and make a fool of myself."

"I'll be right beside you, so don't worry."

Off she started, the bike crazy at first, zigzagging along the rough ground every which way like a wacky carnival ride. Billy trotted alongside, delighted to see her giggling and acting silly as a kid. He reached over and honked the horn, *Ooompa! Ooompa!* Cassie laughed so hard she almost ran over him. They careened across the pasture, past the barn and back again, until Cassie pedaled from his side and flew away on her own, yellow head scarf fluttering.

Cassie leaned the bicycle against the barn and followed Billy inside.

"Look," Billy said, his voice light and excited. "It's not hardly done. But I've made sketches and bought parts and supplies and am about ready to start putting things together."

The Studebaker was stripped to the bare frame, empty of just about everything – including the seats, dash, and engine. The green paint was sanded down to metal and the hood opened in a gaping, toothless maw. Parts littered the floor, multitudes of odds and ends that took up a good portion of the barn in a madcap collection of stuff.

"See?" Billy ran his hands over the passenger door. "Not a dent here, not anywhere." Face alight, he circled the car, caressing all he touched as he chattered about the work done and the work ahead.

Cassie sat on a wooden crate, inserting a comment or question now and again. She enjoyed his excitement and the glimmer in his eyes but envied him a bit, too. When was the last time she had experienced such full pleasure in doing something? She couldn't remember.

"I'm taking pictures as things progress and keeping a log." Billy sat on the ground beside her, legs outstretched. "Maybe it will help when I apply for scholarships, show them that I'm serious, that I can do this."

"That's a great idea. What does Guy think?"

Billy shrugged. "I didn't tell him. Dad doesn't want me to go to college, so I keep quiet about it."

"He *what?*"

"He says we could be partners in the shop, that whatever I need to know I could learn right there."

"Baloney!" Cassie exclaimed. "Don't let the future you've dreamed about slip away because your father is acting like an... like he doesn't understand how important it is."

Billy traced patterns in the dirt, graffiti exploding with angry squiggles. "He said losing Mama was bad enough. He's doesn't want to lose me, too."

Cassie looked at Billy's lowered head, and laid her hand on his hair. It was the color of copper and curled around her fingers. "It's hard to let go of someone you love." She thought about what to say next as a daddy long-legs spider high-stepped across the ground and collided with Billy's boot. "Your mother wanted you to reach for your dreams, didn't she?"

Billy nodded, still not looking up.

"Then do! I know she'd be proud."

The barn door slapped against the wall in a sudden gust, and a spiral of dust drifted along the floor. "I'm like that wind sometimes," Billy said, "kicking up dust but going nowhere important."

"Me too, sometimes."

They sat among the strewn piles of automobile paraphernalia and said nothing more.

Cassie tugged the hose into Mimi's fenced garden and watered the newly-planted flowers. No longer was this the forlorn, forgotten space that had greeted Cassie when she first arrived. She and Billy had mended the sagging posts, uprooted weeds, and tilled the ground. Now pansies, mums, and rosemary kept company with the daylily, which had perked up and likely would sprout baby daylilies come spring. Although the garden couldn't compare to the profusion of glory that had blossomed under Mimi's hand, it still made her proud to look at it, neat and fresh and promising, as if Mimi had done it herself. Almost as if, were Cassie to glance away and back again, she'd find her grandmother in earth-stained apron and gloves, happily digging in the dirt.

A flock of grackles screeched in alarm, their dark shapes dipping into the woods as a familiar rumble approached. Cassie turned off the water, waiting for the truck to clatter over the bridge and park in its usual place beside the old oak. She waved, expecting Billy to hop from the driver's seat. But the truck stopped short of the tree, and Guy stepped from the door.

"Afternoon, Cassie." He lifted the rim of his hat in greeting.

"Hello, Guy. Where's Billy?"

"Shop duties. He asked me to come see if somethin' needs doin'." He peered at her through eyes slit against the sun's glare. "You been plantin'?"

Cassie nodded. "I'm trying to bring my grandmother's garden back to life, although the only planting I've ever done has been with pots."

"You plant pots?"

"What? Of course not. That's..." Guy's weathered face creased into a smile and Cassie laughed. "You're almost as big a tease as Billy."

Guy blushed and turned aside as if idly studying the roof. "Winter's comin' soon. You aimin' to use the fireplaces?"

"I was thinking about it, remembering the times Mimi and I spent in front of them."

"That right?"

"We'd drink hot chocolate and tell stories until the firewood crumbled."

"You need to check `em out first, clean `em good. Don't want your house burned up."

"Thanks for the tip. I'll do that "

"Got a ladder in the truck. Might as well do it now, while I'm here. Save a trip later."

Cassie chased after Guy on the way to his truck. "This is very kind of you, but it's dirty work. Maybe I should call a chimney sweep."

"Me and dirty work like each other." He hoisted a ladder from the truck bed. "You go tend to your flowers and let me take care of things."

The next day came and went with Guy still working on her roof. And the day after that. When he finished cleaning the fireplaces he began fixing shingles, sealing potential leaks, repairing worn eaves. His footsteps rattled overhead, following her from room to room as Cassie moved around the house. At first it was comforting, thinking that the house and she would be snug and safe. But as one hour dragged into another and day two melted into day three, the air thickened and pressed down from above. Guy's eyes seemed to penetrate the barrier between them, watching, watching.

The footsteps stopped at noon on the third day. Cassie rushed to the window as he carried the ladder to the pickup and tossed his bag of tools inside. *He's finished! Halleluiah!* She danced a little jig in the kitchen, her slippers slapping the linoleum.

Guy leaned against the truck and mopped his brow with a rag, his face red and blotchy. Cassie stopped in mid-tap, wondering what sort of selfish creature she had become. Guy sacrificed his own work to take care of hers and all she could think of was, Halleluiah, he's gone.

Heaven help me, I don't want to be like Mother.

She rummaged through a drawer for a pen and her checkbook, angry at Guy for hanging an albatross of obligation around her neck, and angry at herself for allowing it to happen. When she opened the screen door, he stood up straighter, tipping his hat as she approached.

"Thanks for everything, Guy. I really appreciate it."

"Anytime." He gave a final swipe to his neck and tucked the rag into a back pocket.

"I hope you'll accept this in return." She offered the check. "You surely earned it."

"No need."

"Please. I don't feel right otherwise."

"Don't want it."

The check fluttered uselessly in her outstretched hand. He avoided looking at it or her. Good God in heaven, this man was prideful! "Are you always this stubborn?"

"Can't say I ain't been called stubborn before."

Cassie wadded the check into her pocket. "At least let me make you lunch, a sandwich in return for days of hard labor. Fair enough?"

He nodded. "Fair enough."

He sat at the kitchen table, silently chewing ham and cheese sandwiches and drinking iced tea. He took care with his manners, placing the napkin in his lap, keeping his elbows off the table, thanking her for this or that. He didn't talk much, but seemed content to sit and listen to whatever she had to say.

He opened up when the subject turned to Billy.

"He talks about you all the time. Miz Cassie this, Miz Cassie that. Sometimes I think he's got the... a schoolboy crush. He spends more time here than he does in his own home."

"It's these chocolate chips he can't do without." She pushed a platter of cookies toward Guy. "I made a fresh batch for him two days ago and he's about gobbled them up already, so we might as well finish the rest."

Guy put two on his plate and bit into a third. "I don't always think to do special for him like his mother did. She spoiled him awful but he didn't seem the worst for it. Thrived on it like a weed in heaven."

"He showed me her photograph."

"Billy's got a photo?" Guy's voice cracked and crumbs speckled his shirt. "I should've known he'd sneak one somehow."

Damn! Me and my big mouth! "He told me in confidence and I just let it slip. I shouldn't have said anything."

"No, no you did right. It ain't his fault I got stirred up." Guy looked down, picking cookie crumbles off of his shirt and flicking them into his plate. "He misses his mother. I know for a fact."

"It must be difficult sometimes."

"I reckon it is. For us both."

The mantle clock bonged. "One o'clock," he murmured. "Time went fast."

A moment of silence fell between them. Cassie hesitated, afraid to stir the waters but feeling she must.

"Guy, I'd like to ask you something."

"Yeah?" He reached for the sugar bowl and poured another spoonful into his tea.

"Have you thought about which college might be the best for Billy, one that excels in automobile design and engineering?"

"Ain't gonna happen."

"Billy said you and he and his mother talked about it all the time."

"Things changed."

Cassie leaned over the table, looking intently into his wary eyes. "Wouldn't she have wanted that for him?"

"I said things changed." He swirled the tea until ice clattered against the glass.

"There are all kinds of scholarships."

"I'm done talkin' about this!" Guy slammed the glass on the table so hard ice flew out and spattered the tablecloth. "You keep your nose on your face and I'll keep my tongue to myself. Otherwise I'm like to say somethin' I'll regret."

Cassie slowly pulled away.

Guy cupped his head in his hands and muttered, "Christ, I'm sorry. I don't mean to be ugly or hurt your feelings none."

"It's probably hard to see him grow up, knowing he'll move away someday. But isn't that the nature of things?"

Guy lifted his head, his stone gray eyes unsettling. It was as though he wanted to say something intense and personal but kept the words tight inside.

"I'll do for him what I think best. Now change the subject."

Cassie began to speak of other things, trying to keep her voice bright and smile genuine, but it was a struggle.

A coiled presence seemed to lurk inside Guy, something powerful, like a tenderness gone awry.

Guy didn't leave after lunch.

When he started caulking the windows Cassie picked up her purse, locked the front door, and left. She waved goodbye as she drove away. He stood without moving – thin, sunburned, shadowed by the house. He looked lonely, desolate somehow, and she almost turned back. But the thought of his eyes prying through the windows, walking with her among the rooms and invading spaces that were normally hers alone, pushed her through the gate and down the road.

After several hours and errands had passed, and after she stopped at Gas `n Grub to buy a few groceries, Cassie walked the flower-crowded pathway to visit Nan.

The two friends smiled at one another across the black lacquered table, sharing a pot of jasmine tea while Cassie talked about Guy. "He's still there, Nan, after three days! And he won't let me give him anything in return except a couple of sandwiches." She glanced down at her napkin, tracing the fire-breathing dragon with her fingertip. "I'm not certain repairs were really necessary. That house has lasted for decades, and probably would have managed not to crumble into ruin the short time I'll be in it."

"Some men are better with actions than words, *Cass-aie*. It seems to me that Guy's trying to tell you something."

"Oh, Lordy," Cassie muttered. "I'm not sure how to handle this."

"You'll figure it out."

"I don't want to alienate him because of Billy. When I brought up the subject of college, Guy told me in a few choice words to keep my nose to myself."

"Ouch."

"If I'm not careful I might end up doing Billy more harm than good."

"Could be," Nan said quietly. "Guy's different since his wife passed away. More troublesome and quick to take offense. He used to laugh all the time and tell corny jokes or pull silly pranks. Once he hung a German sausage out of his britches and strutted around the store, pretending he had the biggest dong of anyone there."

"You're kidding!"

"Berta whacked it with her purse. It flopped off and rolled under the freezer."

"Oh, my God!" Cassie laughed. "I can't imagine Guy doing anything that outrageous."

"True. Sad but true."

"What am I going to do? I don't like being obligated. I didn't ask him to come over. I didn't ask him to stomp around on the roof or caulk windows. Maybe it wouldn't be so bad if I could repay him somehow."

"There might be a way."

"Really?"

"I tell you this in confidence," Nan said, waiting for Cassie to nod before she continued. "Guy runs a sizeable tab at the store. He pays in full the last Friday of each month."

It took a moment for the words to sink in. "I could pay his grocery bill?"

"Why not?"

"It feels a little peculiar to me."

"Think about it. You'll know what to do when the time comes."

Afternoon shadows stretched across the meadow as Cassie drove across the creek bridge. She groaned inwardly. His truck was still there, the ladder poking up from the metal bed.

A shaft of sunlight glanced against Guy rocking on the porch swing. He rose slowly to greet her, at ease with his surroundings, as if that swing were *his* swing, that porch *his* porch.

"Help you with these groceries?" Guy opened the car door and pulled items from the back seat.

"No, no thanks. I'll do fine." Cassie tried to retrieve a sack of goods from his grasp but gave up when it threatened to turn into a wrestling match.

"No trouble." He followed her up the steps, waited while she unlocked the door, then walked inside and placed his armload on the kitchen table. "I'll help put these away, save you stretching for them top shelves."

"I'd rather do it myself."

She must have spoken sharply because Guy blinked, and after a moment's hesitation tipped his hat. "I'll leave you be, then." He turned abruptly and walked out the front door, his shoulders high and stiff.

She hurried after his retreating back. "I appreciate your efforts to help this old house withstand whatever troubles the weather throws at it."

Guy lingered on the porch, saying nothing more.

"Will you please reconsider and let me pay you?"

He shook his head, lips narrowing.

"I want to do *something* to thank you!"

"Yeah. Maybe I'll think of somethin'."

The tone of his voice slid over her skin like oil.

Before sunset that evening she drove down to Gas 'n Grub and gave Pete a check toward Guy's grocery bill. She added a thank-you card with a smiling Halloween pumpkin printed on the front and signed it, *With Appreciation, Cassandra.*

The Cheshire Cat

CASSIE SLIPPED ON DENIM SHORTS AND PINK SNEAKERS, PLOPPED A STRAW GARDENing hat on her head, and headed out the door for an afternoon bike ride.

She pedaled over the creek bridge and through the gate, then turned right onto Spring Creek. It wound around the base of Mount Bubba and beyond as if hacked from the rock by machete. The journey along the rutted, rocky terrain was difficult, especially since the bike was an oldie with no hand brake or gears. But the effort energized her and she pushed onward, pausing now and again to rest.

It was a glorious day, the sunlight soft, the air brushed by the cooling hand of autumn. She swept her eyes over the magnificent view to the west: cascading hills, scattered plateaus, trees and pastures. Down below, thin as a shredded ribbon, lay Willow City Loop. The entire vista seemed unchanged from the times she had traveled this same route on this same bicycle when she was a girl and Mimi still alive. She could have sworn that the scattering of cattle and goats were the same, too, their shapes pressed forever upon the countryside.

Although high up, the immediate terrain on her left was made of gentle rises and wide expanses. If the fall brought rain, bluebonnets would be profuse in spring and a host of wildflowers would bloom yellow and red, the brilliant flames spreading across the landscape. But to her right was another world altogether, a tangled riot of scrub trees and brush at the base of rocky cliffs. No flowers there, except prickly pear. Just snakes and lizards.

She breathed in deeply, relishing the scent of earth and cedar and grapevine, aware her journey in this direction was about to end. Spring Creek would soon butt against a craggy bluff standing like the portal to a wilderness of spiny brush and juniper, then narrow into a rocky path cutting upward into the steep incline. Where *that* may lead she had no idea and no desire to find out.

Cassie stopped, squinting in the sunlight. Something sped down that bluff path, growling and spitting smoke. On it came, practically flying, disappearing from view as the road dipped.

What in the world...?

A rumble erupted from the scrubby wilds, growing louder as it drew closer. Cassie gawked as the apparition leaped into sight, dust billowing in its wake – a squat black motorcycle, the kind seen in World War II movies, usually mounted by German officers in crisp uniforms. A passenger cart was attached to the side, and a bright flag whipped atop a pole stuck in the rear. Whoever was at the helm wore a droopy hat bound to the head with a long scarf flapping in the wind, ballooning cargo pants, and combat boots.

The motorcycle sputtered to a halt and there sat Tatty, her face a windswept prairie, furrowed and cracked. "Any reason you're standing in the road with your mouth open?"

"Did you just drive down that rollercoaster hill?"

"I had to, seeing that I was on it."

"You must be nuts! It's dangerous."

"Not as long as you know what you're doing."

"Why risk it? Chasing rattlesnakes?"

"Just collecting things." Tatty pointed to branches sprouting ball moss stuffed in the passenger cart. "For my weavings."

Cassie glanced at the pile. It looked like a bunch of kindling. "Weavings like the bird nest you gave me?"

"Some, some not."

"The nest is beautiful, Tatty. I love it but haven't had a chance to thank you. You slip away before I get a word in edgewise."

"Glad you like it. Lots more where that came from."

"You ought to contact a gallery and see if you could get shown. Anything so extraordinary shouldn't be kept hidden."

"I have a few things showing round about."

Cassie lifted a prickly twig, inspecting it. "Oh? Where?"

"Here and there." Tatty smiled and stomped her foot on the gas. "Bye now." She zoomed away, waving goodbye over her head with a single flip of the wrist.

Cassie shook her head and continued on her way, thinking of crazy Tatty with her flyaway hair and strange clothing and odd ways. An old song came to mind, one of her favorites, and she sang under her breath, *Funny old clothes, she wears funny old clothes, thinkiiing anything goes…*

Everything changed in an instant. The bicycle abruptly gathered speed and hurtled her downhill. *Downhill!* She had known about this particular hollow – how could she not when she had just watched Tatty dipping in and out of it – but was so busy daydreaming it caught her unprepared. Gripping the handlebars, she back-pedaled while the tires bucked and the bike shimmied like a drunk colt.

"Stop, damn you!" she screamed. "Stop!"

Her feet slipped off the pedals as she sped helplessly onward, careening off the road toward a drooping willow tree. Good God Almighty, a man and woman were sitting there on a blanket, eating from a wicker basket! She plunged toward the startled picnickers, howling "Out of the way! Mayday! Mayday!" The startled couple leaped apart as she jounced onto the blanket, barreled past a streak of red, and charged toward something she hadn't seen – an easel and canvas. Yelping, she swerved aside, shuddering to a stop as the rear tire smacked into wood. The easel tipped over and the canvas flew upward like a wayward kite as Cassie fell, pulling the bike down with her.

"Training for a race? Quite an impressive tumble."

Cassie gawked through one eye. The other eye was covered by the squashed hat that had plastered itself to her face. But that single eye saw clearly enough: White-white hair. Leaf-green eyes. Lips split with amusement at the fool lying catawampus on the ground.

Hawk knelt beside her as Cassie plucked at the mashed straw. All she could think to say was, "What are you doing here?"

"Running for my life, looks like."

He kept grinning. What was he, the Cheshire Cat?

"What's so damn funny?" Cassie asked.

"Your painting!" A familiar voice moaned. "Your beautiful painting! It landed face down on the dirt."

Rebecca Stanch. How lovey-dovey.

"Need any help?" Hawk offered a hand.

"I'm fine!" Cassie snapped, and began a cautious untangling of legs, wheels, and handlebars, wishing she could disappear or turn time around and begin again.

"Just look at this! It's ruined!" Rebecca handed the painting to Hawk. "Grit all over, and leaves stuck to the paint."

Hawk turned the painting this way and that. "Not too bad."

"May I see?" Cassie stood and held out her hand.

It was an unfinished landscape of the willow tree and the hills behind, roughly sketched with slashes of color as though Hawk had rushed to get the image on canvas before the muse left him. It would have been beautiful, but for debris clinging to the fresh oil paint like exotic mold.

"She's right. I ruined it." Her voice cracked.

"Not ruined, just changed it a bit. Van Gogh had sand in his painting, no reason why I can't have dirt in mine."

Rebecca snorted. Afraid they could read the humiliation burning in her eyes, Cassie reached down to tie a loose shoelace. Damn it all, a bloody shoelace.

Blood seeped from her scraped shin and spattered the blanket. "Good Lord, don't tell me I've ruined your blanket, too." She stepped backward, stumbled over a rock, and landed on her behind.

Cassie tried to laugh, so mortified she probably sounded more like a dog upchucking than a human making merry. "Just a klutz, I guess."

Hawk seemed to agree with her. That Cheshire Cat smirk about split his face in two.

She started to rise, but stopped when Hawk gestured for her to sit. "Stay!" he commanded, as if ordering her to heel. He reached into the basket and withdrew a bottle of water and paper napkin. "It's only a scratch, so this should do it." He wet the napkin and started dabbing her shin.

Cassie sat so still she could hear the earth hum beneath her, the wind sigh in the willow. Somewhere on her right a beetle scurried under a leaf, the crackle crisp and clear, as if a tiny amplifier had been hidden in the undergrowth.

"Well, now," Rebecca chirped. "That looks good enough, doesn't it?"

Hawk leaned back on his haunches. "Think you can get through the next few minutes without crashing into something?"

Rebecca snickered as Cassie glowered.

"One more time," Hawk said, and offered his hand.

"I'm perfectly capable of standing, thank you." Cassie faced the damage strewn before her: stained and rumpled blanket, a downed easel, the dirtied painting. "God, what a mess. Let me help clean it up."

"Please don't bother." Rebecca's patrician face with its polished cheekbones and arched nose studied her with an expression that would look at home on an ice sculpture.

"That would be inviting danger." Hawk laughed, probably something he had been wanting to do all along.

Cassie mashed the straw hat back onto her head. "I apologize for spoiling your picnic." Squaring her shoulders, she lifted the bike with as much dignity as she could muster.

"You plan on riding with that?" Hawk pointed to the back tire.

It couldn't have been flatter or the rim more askew. Cassie shrugged, trying to act nonchalant. "I'll walk it back, no problem."

"I'd be glad to drive you home."

"That's kind of you, but I've already been bother enough."

"You'll end up having to leave the bike alongside the road. It's too far gone to push so far, especially with a scraped shin."

By now it was a matter of keeping whatever pride she had left. "I'll manage just fine, thanks." She turned and trudged up the incline, hauling the bike with her. The wheel rim squawked and the rubber sagged like a deflated baloon. It was heavy and awkward and about as easy as dragging a dead mule.

Hawk strode after her. "Don't be stupid. I'm putting this in the truck and driving you home." He yanked the bike from Cassie's hands before she could utter a word of protest. "Now get in without any more fuss."

Who did he think he was, calling her stupid and ordering her around? She fumed as Hawk put her bicycle in the truck bed. *I'm surprised he doesn't beat his chest and howl.*

Hawk opened the passenger door. "Well?"

Cassie nodded once, trying to look less clownish than she felt. "If you insist."

Before she could get in, Rebecca pranced forward, swinging her cane. "I'll come with you. It might be fun, the three of us all squeezed together. A little adventure." She accepted Hawk's hand and stepped up, moving her hip in a peculiar, sure motion borne of practice with getting in and out of trucks, probably this one in particular.

Cassie followed with whatever grace a bloody shin and bruised pride would allow. Hawk grunted and slammed the door louder than seemed reasonable. She stared straight ahead as the driver's door opened and shut. From the corner of her eye she glimpsed long legs reaching for the pedals, hands for the gear shift. His profile, stern now. Grim, even.

Rebecca settled closer to Hawk, glancing at Cassie with a smirk as the truck lurched forward.

The door handle bit into Cassie's ribs and the lock poked her in the shoulder. The bike rattled in the metal bed as they bounced along, soon accompanied by pebbles and clumps of dirt clattering on the underside. Each *thwang* or *patter-patter* jabbed little spikes into Cassie's nerves. Even her teeth hurt.

Eventually Hawk started to whistle. It sounded like a flute – tiny, maybe, but a flute all the same. He played with the rhythms clanging against the metal of his truck as if they were the percussion and he the soloist.

"I love it when you do that," Rebecca purred.

Oh, God! Cassie closed her eyes and pressed her forehead against the window. *I'm about to curl up and die before my time.*

Finally they came to a stop, motor idling. Hawk leaned past Rebecca to look at Cassie. "Want to open the gate, or is this close enough?"

"This is perfect. Thank you." Cassie jerked the door open and hopped out.

Hawk didn't say anything more as he lifted the bike and leaned it against the fence post. He tipped his hat in farewell, returned to the truck, did a quick spin-around and headed back to whatever was left of the picnic.

Cassie stood holding the bike as the soaring hawk painted on the rear window disappeared behind a cloud of dust.

Pushing the front door shut with both hands, Cassie leaned her forehead against it and closed her eyes.

She had made a fool of herself. A damned silly fool.

The mantle clock twanged the half hour. One-thirty. So early? It felt as though the day should be done. How could she manage the entire afternoon and evening, feeling so awful? She wanted to go to bed and huddle under the covers and forget that she'd been acting like a love-struck ninny over a man she didn't really know.

Cassie turned with a sigh and faced the room. It was comforting, somehow – the small parlor, the hallway with a floor of pine and flagstone, the kitchen on her right. The shabby furniture beckoned like the arms of an old friend, and she sank onto the sofa, pulling the cushions around her.

Time to face the truth. She had created a man who lived in her imagination. The real man, the man of flesh and blood, was different from the one she had dreamed.

Hawk was gorgeous, yes. Gifted, yes. And he could be kind. But he was also a Cheshire Cat commando draped with a clinging Rebecca vine.

She wasn't crazy about cats and could do just fine without this one.

Light fell upon a stuffed chair beside the fireplace, the flowered fabric sagging in the middle, and for some reason she wanted to weep. The chair was evidence of lives lived, of people now gone. Gone like her young husband Thomas was gone, leaving nothing but an empty place.

The empty place she had been trying to fill all the years since.

Shadow Memories

HAWK POSITIONED HIS EASEL TO CATCH THE LIGHT FROM THE STUDIO WINDOWS, placed a canvas upon it, and gathered his brushes and paints. He nudged the stool in place with his foot; it scraped along the wooden floor, the sound familiar and welcomed as the voice of an old friend.

He sat and cleared his mind as always before beginning a new work. His eyes wandered awhile, fastening on this or that before focusing on the canvas calling to him: Old Yeller snoozing in the corner, his fur the golden hues of an Arizona desert; the wild black cherry near the window, leaves ever-changing in the breeze; the glittering sky, bright as a frozen pond, cumulus clouds skating over the icy blue.

Then she came to him, her image superimposed over the surroundings as if he had painted her there: stomping pridefully away while towing that mangled bike, her back stiff and hat askew. The purple-dark depths of her eyes, pulling him like a riptide. Her shoulder pushed against the door of his truck as if she could hardly wait to leap out, her beautiful bare legs beside Rebecca's skirted ones.

Christ in heaven, he had wished Rebecca gone. Wanted to shove her out the door and dump her on the road. But there she sat, pressed next to him, happy as a lark while Cassie stared out the window and made it clear she wanted to be somewhere else. Anywhere else but with him, likely. So he had dropped her off at the gate, driven back to the willow, eaten the damned fried chicken that stuck in his throat as Rebecca chatted on and on and on, and later fell into bed alone and dispirited and confused.

He couldn't get Cassie out of his mind. She rattled around in his thoughts no matter the time of day, no matter what he was doing. Like a curse or a blessing or a little of both.

It was her face that most captivated him. And her eyes. And a *something*. He couldn't find words for what he felt and didn't try. His brushes and paints would speak for him.

He turned toward the waiting canvas.

Time had no meaning as he worked, aware only of the shifting light. At dusk he drew away and looked with some surprise at what he had done, as if it had been painted by someone other than himself.

ဢဢ

Cassie began to close the parlor drapes, and froze.

A stag with an impressive set of antlers had ambled onto the porch and was nibbling the rosebush. "Get away from my roses!" She shouted and banged on the window. The stag lifted his head, a red petal dangling from his lips. "Out! Out!" She stormed to the door, throwing it open as hooves clattered across the floorboards and down the steps. "I didn't put these here for your dinner!" He trotted over the bridge and paused, eyeing her over his shoulder.

Her poor roses! Scattered petals, two or three bare stems and ragged blossoms. She knelt and inspected the damage, relieved to discover it wasn't as bad as she had feared. "You'll be okay," she whispered to the bush as if it could speak and tell her its pains. "No harm done, you'll see."

The stag snorted and pranced along the shore. A golden shape moved behind a juniper and a doe slipped from the deepening woods. The two halted by the water and dipped their heads to drink before darting away, white tails flashing. Cassie shivered as much for the moment as for the chill in the evening air. The weather had changed almost overnight, riotous with leaves falling and spinning in whirlwinds of color. The moon swelled and dropped closer to the earth. Sometimes Cassie felt she could stand on tiptoe and prick it with a pin like a fat balloon, making it fizzle gold dust as it zig-zagged a crazy dying dance across the night sky.

A bird flew across the moon face, the wings a silhouette against the glow, and for a fleeting moment she wondered if it was a hawk. Then she spun around, hurried into the house, and closed the door firmly behind her.

She had tried to push away thoughts of Hawk ever since the day she crashed through his cozy picnic with Rebecca Stanch. If the sound of a flute seemed to float with the breeze, she shut the windows. If the green of an oak reminded her of his eyes, she looked elsewhere. And if the timbre of his voice or the turn of his head or the touch of his hand rose from memory, she grumbled aloud about her foolishness and rededicated herself to preparing the house for eventual sale. She found pleasure in seeing clutter gradually disappear and worked however her interests dictated. Her mind would wander, imagining those who had once sat in the chairs or wound the clock or eaten from the chipped china. Sometimes she thought she heard their voices in the next room or the soft tread of footsteps. Yet when she stopped to listen, only silence greeted her.

ജ്ഞ

The heavy cellar door creaked open and thumped against the flagstone floor. Cassie peered into the darkness below. She had delayed this unpleasant task far too long.

Gripping the frame for support, she stepped down and reached for the burned-out bulb hanging on a frayed cord. It grated as it turned, spitting rust. *Probably been stuck in there for years,* she thought while screwing in the new. The bulb swung, throwing light on the bumpy walls and floor, paved with an odd assortment of stones without regard to size or shape. The basement rambled under the olden house, with turns and twists outside of the light's range. Wooden shelves, clotted with dust-covered jars and cobwebs, disappeared into the gloom.

Mimi's pile of detritus lay haphazardly at the bottom of the steps, topped by a couple of blankets, a boot, a crumpled purse with a missing strap. Although tempted to lug it up by the armful and throw it all into the trash bin outside, she knew she wouldn't. *Look at everything, no matter how small.* She had repeated that refrain to herself so many times that by now it popped into her head automatically whenever she faced a new task. And always, in the back of her mind, she hoped to find a clue, a connection, to her ancestral history.

Something like young Rosine's diary, if it truly did exist.

The cellar was the only place she hadn't looked. She had already riffled through Mimi's drawers and closets and cupboards, and had a fairly good idea of what remained among the neatly stacked items that had once cluttered the carport. The cellar might be her last chance.

It was empty except for the jumbled mound of stuff Mimi had thrown from the top. Cassie had to climb over the mess to get proper access. After an hour or so, she had divided it into Charity or Toss, and allotted a space for Keep, just in case. Nothing of surprise was there, no windows to family secrets. But it was definitely a window to Mimi's final years, years that Cassie should have been there to help, and wasn't. Tired and dispirited, she threw a hairbrush onto the Toss pile, and missed. It knocked against a shelf and fell to the floor.

An eerie jangle drew her eyes to a jar tap-dancing among the cobwebs as if a little creature inside its milky confines was banging around, desperate to get out. The jar danced to the edge and fell without breaking, rolling around a corner. It landed against something solid, the final *thump* sudden and sharp, as though the jar had been caught by unseen hands.

Silence followed, so dense she could hear the blood ringing in her ears. The dim space pressed closer, quiet and cramped and filled with things unseen. She stepped into the shadows and walked with one hand grazing the wall, the edges rough against her fingers as she cautiously turned the corner. Enough light filtered through the darkness to illuminate a shape directly ahead. She moved toward it, hands outstretched. Her foot struck the jar, sending it skittering away as she bumped into a large wooden trunk. Even in the faint light she could tell it must be older than old, probably more than ready for the dumpster. She ran her hands over the sides, found a handle, and pulled. The crate was heavy, protesting with scrapes and squeals as she heaved it along the uneven floor into the light.

Its deep blue paint had faded into a sickly green, all but one of the brass clasps were missing or broken, and little remained of the leather straps intended for protection. A ragged crack ran along the lid and a lock hung from the single unbroken clasp, fastening the trunk shut. Cassie tugged it tentatively, concerned when the rotting wood began to crumble. She dashed upstairs for a screwdriver and back down again, stumbling over the bottom step. Willing herself to be patient, she unscrewed the clasp until it fell away with the lock still attached.

The lid opened with a squeal and puff of camphor, revealing a quirky mix of belongings. "Look at this!" she exclaimed, her cry bouncing off the stone walls. "A treasure chest!" She rummaged through the items, hoping to get an idea of what was inside, and hoping against the odds that Rosine's diary would be there, too. The assortment resembled strata, with different layers from different years. The further down she dug, the older everything seemed to be. She lifted several papers crisp with age, two of them ripped from a Red Chief writing tablet she remembered from her childhood. The first was a valentine, a lopsided heart scrawled in crayon and the words, *I Love You Mimi from Cassie,* with each "s" written backwards. Another was a drawing of the house surrounded by fluffy clouds and purple flowers, and the Emperor Tree smiling down at the stick figures of Mimi and herself side by side on the porch swing.

Oh, Mimi. You kept me in your heart as I keep you in mine.

One paper remained – a crumpled theatre program, smudged with a shoe tread as though it had been stepped on. *Countryside Community Theatre presents Oklahoma! by Rodgers and Hammerstein, Starring Lillian Ruff and Edward Fullerton.*

Cassie gaped at the program as if it were written in Sanskrit. Acting was something her mother did every day, as natural to her as brushing teeth. But *singing* and *dancing*? With *Daddy*? Was that how they first met? It sounded like the plot of a sappy old-time movie: singing lovers onstage become volatile lovers off, and here she is, Cassandra, the end result.

What else didn't she know? Her own parents were a mystery to her.

Buried near the bottom was a porcelain doll that fit into the palm of her hand. It had jointed limbs at the shoulders and hips, blue eyes that opened and shut, real hair bound with ribbons, and a delicate painted face. Her shoes and socks were painted, too, and she wore pantaloons with polka dots. "So sweet!" Cassie murmured, wondering whether Rosine was the girl who may have loved this, braiding its hair and sleeping with it beside her.

She gazed down at all that yet remained, disappointed not to have found Rosine's diary but still overwhelmed by the riches packed into this old trunk. More questions than answers, perhaps – but links to her past, to who she was and where she came from, were here, right in front of her, bound by crumbling wood and tarnished brass.

One thing at a time, one day at a time. Look at everything, no matter how small.

She took her time with each article. The motions soothed her, the touch of paper and fabric and wood and metal. Scattered photographs slipped through her fingers: somber men with long beards, bushy mustaches, and Sunday-best suits; women with upswept hair and an array of hats, lace, and high-necked blouses; children in knickers or bonnets. She touched the faded faces, the long dead souls gazing at her through the yellow haze of years.

Something was wrapped in a cloth napkin exactly like those in the kitchen upstairs, with yellow daisies sewn along the hem. She picked it up, beguiled. Nestled inside were baby moccasins the color of butter, decorated with glass beads and twisted fringe. The leather was soft, perfect for tender little feet. Who had worn these? Who had made them? Why were they in Mimi's trunk?

There was too much to take in all at once. Enough for today – except for perhaps a hinged keepsake box, the green paint long faded, the floral design barely perceptible. What made Cassie catch her breath was the heart encircled in its center with two yellow birds. It looked remarkably like the design etched into the front door.

A bundle of ink-smeared letters nested inside, bound with pink ribbon. Tucked into the top was a military medal shaped like a star, with a red, white, and blue ribbon attached. She put it in her lap and unbound the letters, careful not to ravel the fragile pink silk, and chose the first.

The penmanship was familiar – long, slanting strokes, sharply defined:

> *Dearest Johann,*
>
> *How I miss you! Especially now in the fall, the time of year you like the most. The moon is full and round as an orange. Lillian and I sit in front of the fire and drink hot chocolate and remember the times we all sat there together and how nice it was. I try to tell stories to take her mind away from your absence, at least for a little while, but she will have none of it. That's not real, she says.*

The paper crackled in Cassie's hands.

> *Our daughter grows more pretty and troublesome with each passing day. She has your eyes and thirst for danger, too. Yesterday she jumped from the roof and sprained her ankle and got a solid knot on the back of her head. She said she wanted to fly like her daddy. I hadn't the heart to punish her.*

A cold breath touched Cassie's bare neck. She jerked around, half expecting to find someone standing behind her. No one was there, of course. Just the stairwell, the bare walls, the room edging into darkness.

> *I keep your photograph beside our bed. Last week I found her talking to it, just chatting away, talking about her day like you were really there. I stood out in the hall and listened and felt guilty for it, like I was eavesdropping. Which I guess I was.*
>
> *Keep safe for us, my darling Johann. I pray for the war to end soon and for you to return home to our arms.*
>
> *Forever yours,*
>
> *Wilhelmina*

Cassie refolded the letter, placed it among the others, and retied the ribbon. She would not read the rest, at least not now. Maybe later. Maybe never. Some things were meant to be private. Her eyes misted, and she wiped them with the back of her hand.

She put the letters and medal back into the wooden coffer, lay it and the baby moccasins on the floor beside her, and tucked everything else into the trunk. She started back up the cellar steps with the chest and moccasins, her feet warm in woolen socks and quiet against the stones. Something nagged at her... Something... A photograph. Something in a photograph.

She back-tracked to the trunk and rummaged through the photographs, the faces and figures flipping past like images in a nickelodeon, and found what had haunted her: a sinewy man standing beside a horse, self-consciously posed with his right hand on the saddle, the left on his hip. He had long fair hair curled at the ends like General Custer, wore dress boots with spurs, and scowled from under a large-brimmed black hat. He looked perfectly pressed and starched. Even his spurs sparkled. The general effect was of a coiled dandy, the sort who would serve you poison on a silver platter.

She turned it over. *Jedediah on his birthday, September 12, 1898.*

Jedediah? She couldn't recall that name among the others listed in the Bible. She looked at him again. The nature of his hat, perhaps the way it tilted rakishly with the left brim rolled up, that reminded her of... what?

Shadow memories rushed toward her of the first night in the house alone, of the wail and moan of Firewind, of roaring thunder and crushing darkness. She had huddled in the kitchen chair as the storm thrashed about her and lightening flashed upon the silhouette of a man in the doorway – a man wearing a broad-brimmed hat.

Her imagination had run amuck. The shape had only been the parlor lamp, disfigured by her fears.

Still, it wouldn't hurt to find out who this fellow Jedediah was.

Child in the Tree

CASSIE SAT ON THE SOFA EARLY THE NEXT MORNING WITH JEDEDIAH'S PHOTOgraph in hand, trying to remember when she had spoken to her mother last. Weeks ago. Months, perhaps. She pulled her address book from the drawer and dialed Lillian's number.

"*Bonjour.*"

"For heaven's sake, Mother! You're in Spain, so why are you speaking French?"

"Hello, darling. Your usual cheery self, I see."

"Why not *Buenos Dias*? You always said, 'Do what the natives do.' "

A brittle laugh on the other end. Cassie recognized that particular laugh and visualized the gesture that usually accompanied it: an up-tilted chin, a forced brightness in the smile.

"Did I? How clever. In any case, I'm packing as we speak and leaving for Paris."

"You and Whatshisname?"

"The *Champs-Elysees*, the *Louvre*, sweet cafes on every corner. What could be more delightful? Not to mention the shopping."

"Sounds lovely. How long will you be there?"

"Until I decide to try someplace else. I've never been to Romania. Romania should be rather romantic, don't you think? Gypsies and all." A catch caught in Lillian's throat.

"Don't tell me you've broken up with him, too." Cassie closed her eyes, expecting to hear the proverbial refrain of heartbreak. Lillian hurdled from one man to the next, always believing that *this* one would be the last.

Lillian burst into a sob. "It was awful, truly awful. I never should have trusted that man. My heart is too big."

"What happened?"

"I don't want to talk about it." A loud sniff. "Men are beasts. They ought to wear animal hides, drag clubs behind them, and gnaw on bones."

"He cheated on you?"

"Worse. He *forgot* me!"

"That's hard to believe."

"He forgot our anniversary."

"Is that all?"

"I spent the entire day waiting for him to say something, *do* something. There's a precious necklace I specifically pointed out to him weeks ago, clusters of blue topaz set with the tiniest rows of diamonds, just lovely – but do you think he remembered? Hardly! He left to join his cronies for a spin on the yacht. Without me!"

"I don't think…"

"We married exactly two years ago today. I wore the most darling hat with feathers that framed my face. He said he loved the way my eyes looked at him through all the plumage, like an exotic bird."

"He's not…"

"You would think a man would remember falling in love with a bird, don't you?"

"It wasn't him."

"Don't be ridiculous."

"You're mixing up men and weddings. Someone else fell in love with the bird. Pedro or Placido or whoever he is…"

"Pirro," Lillian interrupted.

"… fell in love with the ice queen. Remember? Long white gown, diamonds in your hair, snow outside. He said you looked as though you were made out of winter. When you told me I thought it sounded poetic."

Silence.

"You married sometime after Christmas."

"Oh my God. Oh my God. I'm getting Alzheimer's."

"No, just too many husbands. I'm surprised you don't get their names mixed up during, um, intimate moments."

"I've got to run before he comes back."

"What are you going to do?"

"Bring his clothes back in. I threw them off the second-story balcony."

"Reverting to old habits?"

"Sarcasm doesn't become you," Lillian snapped. "So be nice."

"Sorry." Cassie murmured, pushing aside the memory of her father's clothes tossed into a funeral pyre in their back yard. Lillian had danced around it like a madwoman.

"Thanks for calling, but I simply must go."

"Wait!"

"Hurry it up. I've things to do!"

"I found some photographs inside a beat-up trunk stashed away in the cellar. Do you know about them?"

"Is that old trunk still there? I thought it would have rotted away by now."

"What about the dapper guy with long curly hair? He's leaning against a horse and wearing a large black hat with the rim curled up."

A long silence followed. Cassie could hear her mother breathing in rapid little puffs. Finally she muttered, "If that's Jed, his name is on the back."

"That's him. Who is he, friend or family?"

"A scoundrel married to your great-grandmother, Emilie."

"He's my great-grandfather?"

"God, you've got the tenacity of a ferret!" Lillian sounded thoroughly out of sorts. "There was some trouble and Jed disappeared. I'm saying goodbye now."

"Please, Mother. If you can't talk about the photographs, how about the baby moccasins? What do you know about them?"

After a moment, Lillian said, "Throw the damned things away."

"Why?"

"Throw the entire trunk away. Reminders of the past aren't always welcome."

"I'll welcome them. I know next to nothing about my ancestors, who they were, where they came from. I feel adrift, rootless."

"Grow your own roots, if you're so wilted. As I have."

"Is that what you're doing over there, Mother? Rooting?"

Lillian snorted. "Enough!"

"Please don't go yet. Tell me about the moccasins."

"You don't want to know," Lillian said, and hung up.

But she *did* want to know.

What could be so dreadful that Mimi never spoke of it and Lillian refused? Somehow, she would find out. Even if it meant reading Mimi's private letters.

Cassie put the photo on her bedside table next to the family photograph of Mimi, Lillian, and Mimi's *Dearest Johann* who came home in the arms of a coffin. The image of a childish Lillian smiled from within the picture frame. Young, assured of the love surrounding her, unaware that in a single war-ravaged moment her life would be forever changed. She must have felt abandoned by his death and betrayed, as she had when Cassie's father left them both.

The fear of abandonment likely still followed Lillian, a vengeful twin intent on devouring her soul. Maybe that's why she didn't stay with one man for long. Maybe she wanted to leave them before they left her.

Darkness settled as Cassie walked toward the kitchen, turning on a lamp here and there. Rooms looked different during fall evenings, truer and deeper, as though painted in oils. She welcomed the way lamplight seemed to melt across the wooden floors and walls, and the way colors glowed with an inward fire.

She fixed tomato soup and a toasted cheese sandwich, content with the rattle of cutlery and the creak of the cupboard doors and the grumble in the pipes, and sat in her favorite spot by the bay window. The Emperor Tree tapped a greeting against the outside wall. Smiling, she glanced at the old oak glimmering through the window, swaying under the gibbous moon.

It took a moment or two before she realized something was amiss. Leaning on the sill, she squinted into the moonlight.

Something strange hung from an extended tree limb, something that didn't belong there. Something the size and shape of a small child.

Not waiting to grab a shawl against the chill, Cassie dashed outside, the screen door ajar behind her, and ran under the tree. A silhouette adhered to a large branch above her head, moving as the breeze commanded. Shadows played upon it, appearing and disappearing while the limb danced.

The face of a little girl looked at her, mouth open in a perpetual giggle. Chubby legs straddled the branch as though she were astride a pony, while one hand gripped a stem for balance and the other lifted in a wave. Flyaway pigtails blew back from her face as though teased by the wind, almost touching the wings.

A child in the tree, riding the prancing limb and loving it. A metal angel, with ornate iron wings fashioned from the parlor stove.

Dear, sweet Justin! You read my heart.

He had sculpted a cherub with items from her ancestors. The people of her own blood resonated within this small figure.

Cassie knelt on the ground and watched her child fashioned from scraps ride the wind.

ꟹ

It had started out to be a great day. Billy and a couple of friends finished a cool jam session, practicing for the Halloween dance tomorrow night. It was going to be a big event, his first at the high school – first gig, first dance, too. The gym was already decorated with orange and black balloons and crepe paper streamers. Chiffon ghosts and monster spider webs hung from the ceiling, and a scarecrow straddled a pile of carved pumpkins. His band would play on the back of a wagon with hay stacks as seats. A full-sized plastic skeleton from the biology lab sat on one of them, a guitar in his bony hands. Billy tied a red kerchief around its neck and stuck a cigarette between its teeth, making the other boys laugh.

He rushed home in the early darkness, eager to share his excitement with Guy, when all hell broke loose.

"Where've you been?" Guy yelled from the kitchen. "It's late."

"At school, rehearsing." He walked through the dim living room and paused by the door. "I told you about it last night. Remember?" His voice wavered. He hated it when Guy looked at him with eyes all squinted up and mouth tight.

"I thought maybe you was with Cassie. You always seem to be there instead of here."

"She needs me, Dad. I've helped her with a ton of stuff."

Guy slapped dishes on the table. "That woman don't need nobody or nothin.'"

"She pays me real good, too. The Studebaker…"

"The hell with that damned car. From now on you be where I can lay my eyes on you while it's still daylight. Now sit down and eat dinner."

When Guy got quarrelsome there was no sweet-talking him out of it. Billy bit back the words he wanted to spit, found silverware and paper towel napkins for the two of them, and pulled out the chair.

Guy spooned a pile of spaghetti on their plates. Lukewarm and sticky as dead worms. Billy kept his thoughts to himself and choked it down.

Billy washed the dishes as Guy slumped at the table, smoking and drinking a beer. The kitchen was quiet except for the loud *tocka-tocka* of the cat clock that had been hanging there since the day Billy was born. The wallpaper was the same, too – except now it was blotched and peeling. Billy had never noticed any sad or ugly stuff when his mother was alive. Maybe everything else around here died when she did.

Guy set the empty bottle on the table, turning it so the Coors label faced front. "Cassie ever say anything about me?"

"No, not really."

"Not one stinking word?"

"Why?"

"No reason."

Guy looked out the window at nothing. Then he grunted, pushed roughly from the table, and rooted around in the trash can. Billy stood immobile, watching as his father grabbed a wadded-up card and tore a piece off and threw it in the trash.

"What you looking' at?" Guy snapped "Ain't you got homework to do?"

"Just finishing with the dishes."

"Hurry it up, then." Guy drew a cigarette from a pack on the table, flicked his thumbnail against the match, and walked outside without another word. The glowing cigarette ash marked his pacing in the night dark, like a firefly guide leading the way. Now and then he would stop and look down at the card.

Billy folded the dishtowel and went into his bedroom. He tried to study but couldn't concentrate. The heavy silence nearly choked the breath out of him. Then sounds penetrated: the screech of the back door as his dad came back in. The refrigerator opening, shutting. The bottle cap rattling in the sink. Footsteps from the kitchen into the living room and back again. Muttering, his voice rising and falling.

Billy tiptoed into the darkened hallway. Guy slouched under the kitchen light, his back turned, muscles bunched up.

"Dad?"

"What the hell do you want?"

Billy flinched at his father's red-rimmed, hurting eyes. "What's wrong?"

"Nothin' you can fix. Now go mind your own business."

Billy stared at the face before him, the contorted features suddenly not familiar at all, as though his father glared at him through a mask.

"Go on!"

Billy returned to his room and sat on the bed as the table clock marked the passing seconds. An owl screeched outside, as if it were crying.

"Damn it to hell and back again!" A crash, a shattering. Billy leaped to the doorway and looked down the hall.

Guy was throwing beer bottles at the wall, another and then another. They smashed onto the floor, liquid and glass flying. Billy pressed his hand against his mouth and backed up, peeking through a crack in his door as his father went crazy. Guy shoved a chair across the room and punched the wall, once, twice. The cat clock rattled and fell, rolling across the glass-strewn linoleum. "Shit!" Guy kicked it into a corner and left, slamming the front door.

Billy stood frozen, listening to the truck growl, the tires spin on the gravel, the motor fade as the stranger who was his father drove away.

The kitchen was a mess. Billy righted the chair, mopped the beer, swept the glass shards. The cat clock was cracked and something loose rolled around inside. He hung it in the usual place marked by a dark spot, a ghost of itself.

Aware that he was trespassing into something personal, Billy reached into the trash can and withdrew the crumpled paper Guy had discarded.

It was indeed a card, or had been. All that remained was a picture of a grinning pumpkin. The inside, the part that usually had writing on it, was gone.

ꕥ

Guy passed the turnoff to Spring Creek by a good mile before he stopped, turned the truck around and slowly drove back. The note was still clamped in his fist. *With Appreciation, Cassandra.* Formal and stiff and oh so ritzy polite. Even the penmanship was polite, perfectly looped and dotted like it would be a God-awful mistake not to cross the *"t"* just so. *Cassandra* she wrote. Not *Cassie.* Nothing else. Not one single Goddamned word except for *With Appreciation.* It was like he was a stranger who didn't matter none. Like he hadn't spent three whole days trying to be helpful.

But what especially galled him was the money. She paid his grocery bill, for Christ sake. Jesus! Did she think he was a charity case who couldn't do for himself? Was that how she saw him?

He gripped the steering wheel. *Damn her fancy ways and her fancy car and her money. And damn me for wanting her.*

He turned the truck onto Spring Creek and drove the rutted drive upward. He passed the Grumm's house and kept on going. He drove slowly, hoping to reduce the rattle of stuff in the truck bed as he hit the potholes so Cassie wouldn't know he was coming. He parked far from her gate and walked the rest of the way. The breeze slid icy fingers under the collar of his shirt but the cold didn't bother him. His skin felt hot. His breath fogged as he exhaled, thick as steam from a boiling pot, and sweat beaded his forehead.

The gate would squeal if he opened it, so he leaped over and landed quietly. Stepping from one shadow to the next, he crept toward the bridge.

The full moon hung right over her meadow, lighting the whole place so bright he didn't dare take another step. He ducked into the deeper shade of a cedar and leaned against the trunk.

She was awake. Light glowed from the windows and the open door. It took a moment before he saw her sitting on the ground under the big oak. Her knees were drawn up with her arms wrapped around them as she looked up at something. What the hell was she doing? So still, like she wasn't real but was painted there.

He waited until she rose and went inside and closed the door. He kept on waiting until the light went out from the bay window, then from the parlor, and then at last from the bedroom.

The house looked different at night. The place had a creepy feeling about it, with empty window eyes that seemed aware, as if the house knew he was coming and wasn't too happy about it. Jesus, if it didn't look like it was grinning, what with the shadows from the oak tree flitting over the porch rails.

He walked gingerly across the bridge, pausing to shift his weight whenever a board creaked. He didn't think about what he would do when he got to the house or even why he was doing it, but kept putting one foot in front of the other, slow, slow.

He got about half-way and stopped, muscles rigid. A dark shape with gold eyes slunk around the corner, looking right at him.

A dog? I didn't know she had a damned dog!

This wasn't any ordinary dog. These eyes burned and glowed in the dark. A shaft of moonlight glittered against the drawn lips and bared teeth. It moved closer, shoulders hunched and head low, ready to attack.

Bile bit into his tongue. This was no dog. This was a wolf.

There aren't wolves in these here parts. Coyotes, wild dogs, even feral hogs – but no wolves. Maybe way back in the days when nobody but Indians lived here. Maybe then.

He stepped back and kept on going until the fence bumped against his legs. Leaping over the gate, he ran fast as bloody hell down the road to his truck, slamming the door and locking it.

Shame boiled in his gut and he rested his head on the steering wheel, sick to his stomach. What had got into him? What sort of man was he, to sink so low he'd spy on Cassie? And how come his imagination played such tricks, making him think the house was alive and that a dog had turned into a wolf?

I drank too much. Things get screwed up when I'm drunk.

He swore to never sneak over there again.

Unless he was sober. And maybe had a gun.

Forever Yours

Hawk slumped on the stool in front of Cassie's unfinished portrait, his brushes clean and dry, his tubes of paint capped. He hadn't touched the canvas since the first inspired rush. Something elemental was missing. It looked like her well enough, he supposed: hair, lips, eyes, shoulders, and the background was what he had envisioned. Yet that unnamed *thing*, that essence he sensed, that particular quality within her, he hadn't yet captured.

Whenever he was stumped in the past, he'd step back and let his imagination simmer. Usually a break did the trick and the creative energy would burst through and flow like water surging over a dam. This particular break had lasted longer than most, yet still the muse slumbered.

He needed to be with her. Imagination and memory could only do so much.

He had imagined, of course. He had dreamed and wished. Just the other night he had looked up at the full moon, wondering whether she was doing the same, wanting to go see for himself. He had to hurry back inside the studio and shut the door to keep from hopping in the truck and driving toward trouble.

She did trouble him. Everything about her troubled him. He hadn't felt this churned up in so long he had almost forgotten what it was like.

He returned to the easel and sat on the stool and gazed at the portrait, letting his mind wander, speaking to her without words or voice or conscious thought. Patience was all he needed. Patience, and an unruffled spirit.

All the while, he felt Rebecca's eyes upon him, as if she were in the next room and would walk through the door at any moment, her cane tap-tapping on the wooden floor.

Cassie dreamed of a train whistling from afar before she awakened to the insistent ring of the telephone and stumbled out of bed to answer.

"Hello?"

"Cassandra dear, this is Berta Grumm."

Berta always announced her full name whenever she called. Sometimes she would include her middle name, as if to clarify exactly *which* Berta Grumm from possible hundreds populating the planet was speaking on the other end of the line. Usually the habit brought a smile to Cassie's lips, but not tonight. Tonight the old woman's voice was choked with tears.

"Something is wrong with Justin," Berta sobbed. "He put his dress jacket on over his pajamas and sat on the floor and won't get up."

She sped through the darkness. Clouds covered the moon and paled the stars and obliterated the distant plateaus. Cassie felt as though she were driving in a shadowed cave, the headlights spearing the way through its winding passage.

The clouds parted the moment she drove up Justin's driveway. Moonlight glittered on the outspread metal wings of the warrior angel standing guard, a shield upraised against trouble. "He'll need you tonight," she whispered, running past and up the porch steps.

Berta waited by the front door, her gray hair tousled and fallen to her shoulders. She wore a fuzzy blue robe and matching fuzzy slippers and gazed through wide, red-rimmed eyes. "Thank you for coming," she said, reaching for Cassie's hand. "He's in the bedroom."

Cassie hugged her, the stout little body trembling in her arms. Berta pulled away and led her down the hall, her voice sharp with worry. "I called 911 like you said, but don't know what anyone can do to make a stubborn old fool get up off the floor."

Justin sat upright, legs spread out before him on the gaily-patterned throw rug, back resting against the mattress. Pajama bottoms pulled up at the ankles, revealing pale thin legs and black socks. He wore a tan suit jacket, a silk hankie neatly folded in the pocket, over his pajama top. A black dress shoe lay beside him. He grappled with the other, tying and untying the laces. His head was bent in the endeavor, the bald pate shining through thin wisps of hair.

Cassie's heart felt as though it would split in two.

"Hi, Justin."

He glanced up with a lopsided grin and for a moment seemed his normal self, caught in an awkward position. "Company. How nice."

Cassie knelt beside him. "What are you doing?"

"Tying my shoelaces."

"Wouldn't it be easier to put the shoes on your feet first?"

"If my shoes aren't tied right, all my trousers will fly out of the closet and Berta will fuss at the mess I've made. So I'm being careful."

Berta stifled a sob and ran from the room.

"It's cold on the floor." Cassie pretended to shiver. "Let's go sit in the kitchen and visit, maybe have some tea or hot chocolate."

Justin reached for the second shoe and tugged at the laces. "Nope. Got to fix these."

"Then let's take the shoes with us. You can tie them in the kitchen."

"Shoes should stay down here where my feet are."

Justin worked with quiet concentration, long fingers fiddling with knots and bows in strange configurations. Clocks rang the hour, a chorus of *cuckoo-cuckoo* and chimes and bongs. "One's off-kilter," he mumbled. "I'll look at it tomorrow."

Cassie placed a hand on his arm. "Berta's worried because you've been sitting on the floor for a good while."

"She worries about everything." He arranged the shoes side by side with toes facing the same direction, adjusting them until satisfied. "Alright. I'll get up if it makes her feel better."

"Can you stand?"

"Of course I can stand!" he snapped, stumbling as he tried to rise. Cassie caught him around the waist. They weaved back and forth in a clumsy dance as she struggled to balance them both. He fell toward her and then back, pulling her down with him onto the bed. They landed hard, the springs squawking and the headboard thumping against the wall.

"Oh my my, what happened?" Berta rushed into the room.

"I tried to help him up." Cassie untangled herself and rose, a dull pain throbbing at the base of her spine. "He got dizzy."

Justin lay as he had fallen, legs draped over the edge of the mattress, arms outstretched. "Grumble dust," he said, closing his eyes.

"At least put your feet up proper," Berta fussed, trying to lift his legs. "You're lying down half-way off the bed, crazy old man."

"Gumfeltz noodle."

"What?"

Justin lay quietly, mouth open. Berta shook his arm. "Wake up. I can't do this alone."

"Let me help." Cassie crawled up onto the mattress, gripped him from under the arms and pulled, dragging him across the bed while Berta pushed. Justin was heavy for such a thin fellow, and unresponsive. Finally he sprawled at an angle, fast asleep.

"The paramedics should be here soon." Cassie sighed, rubbing her aching back. "I could use some hot tea. How about you?"

Berta nodded and walked silently down the hall. Cassie turned and looked one more time at Justin. She stood awhile, breath caught in her throat, before slowly heading for the kitchen. She opened the cupboard for the cups and saucers while Berta filled the teakettle. They sat at the table with its starched blue cloth. A wooden bowl of apples and oranges rested in the middle, a bright touch of color.

They drank their tea and waited. And all the while Cassie thought of what she had last seen, and couldn't find the words or heart to tell Berta. The poor woman would discover it for herself soon enough:

The right side of Justin's face had drooped, as though the flesh were melting off his skull.

Berta shivered in her heavy winter coat, an overnight bag in her lap. Cassie turned the car heater up. The ambulance raced down the road, rear lights blinking and siren wailing in intermittent burps as Cassie followed.

"I wanted to ride with him." Berta sat on the edge of her seat, as if urging the car onward. "He'll wake up and wonder why I'm not there."

"You'll be with him soon."

"I wanted to ride with him."

Cassie bit the inside of her cheek, desperately trying, for Berta's sake, not to scream.

Except for a young man slouched in a chair on the far side of the room, Cassie was alone. A Fredericksburg newspaper lay on a table beside her, printed in German. She plucked it up, put it down again. A siren blared outside. Nurses and doctors in white coats moved back and forth behind swinging double doors. A sign posted on the doors read: *No smoking. No entry. Authorized Personnel only.*

Berta was Authorized Personnel. She had been inside those doors with Justin for several hours. Cassie fidgeted, the pain in her lower back starting to shoot down her legs.

Maybe Justin would be okay. Maybe this was just a setback. Maybe all he needed was time and therapy.

Maybe this was the beginning of the end.

Cassie felt sick.

ꕤ

"They told me to go home."

Berta sat beside Cassie, hands shaking. "He's behind a big glass window in intensive care, with tubes sticking into him everywhere. The nurses are very kind. They said there's nothing more I can do and they will take good care of him and go home and get some rest and come back tomorrow."

"What did the doctor say?"

"He had a stroke and maybe several little ones before this. Strokes! I never knew! And there I was all the time, fussing at him because I thought he was being lazy-brained!" Berta pressed her fists against her cheeks and moaned, low and soft. "I think they're afraid to say anything more because if they do I'll go to pieces."

"They probably want to wait until they know for sure what's happening."

"The house is going to feel strange without Justin in it."

"Maybe it won't be for long." Cassie rose, taking Berta by the hand.

The ride home seemed to take forever, winding through the night. In a few hours it would be morning. Berta leaned her head against the back rest and after a time began to snore. It was an funny sort of snore, a wheeze-puff-gasp that reminded Cassie of a cat about to throw up a hairball. She smiled, her eyes misting with unshed tears.

The Grumm house looked shrunken, as if Justin's absence had saddened and diminished it. Even with the porch light on, the place seemed cloaked in mourning.

Berta stepped from the car and made the same shooing gesture as she did with her chickens. "Go, go, Cassandra. I'm fine. Don't worry about me."

"Are you sure? I don't mind staying."

"I don't need a babysitter. Now go."

"I'll pick you up when you're ready. Just call."

But as she watched Berta walk slowly up the porch steps, slumped and forlorn and each footfall precarious, Cassie couldn't stand it and rushed to help. Berta seemed not to notice, fumbling in her purse and dropping the key.

"I'll get it." Cassie picked it up and unlocked the door.

Berta motioned for her to wait, disappeared into the kitchen and returned with a plastic-wrapped loaf in her hands. "I baked some bread and put one aside for you and forgot."

"It smells wonderful."

"Tomorrow, then. Goodnight."

Cassie returned to her car and reluctantly drove away. The warrior angel glimmered in her rearview mirror, the soft gleam a beacon in the approaching dawn.

ᘓᘐ

A few hours later Cassie knew she wasn't going anywhere. The slightest twitch stabbed needles into her spine and she walked like a crippled old lady, gingerly risking one step at a time. A heating pad helped. Lying down helped. It was the getting-up part that hurt like the devil.

"Don't worry," Berta said on the telephone. "I can drive myself."

"I'm so sorry. I'll probably be fine in a day or so."

"There will be plenty of time for you to visit. I'll call and let you know what the doctors say."

"Thanks. I love you both."

"We love you, too. Take care of yourself. Bye now."

Cassie stretched out on the sofa, plumping the horsehair pillows and adjusting the heating pad. Worry about Justin settled right down beside her, so sleep was out of the question. She needed to put her mind on other things.

She turned to the little hoard of treasures she had arranged on the coffee table yesterday – the tattered German Bible with Gustav's letter tucked between the pages, the keepsake chest with Mimi's letters inside, the baby moccasins, the photograph of Jedediah. Each was a key that could help unlock the mystery of her ancestors.

A sense of belonging, that's what she longed for. To be part of a loving whole.

She picked up the Bible, looking for the names listed inside. Jedediah wasn't included. There was, however, a blackened smudge. Something had once been written there and erased. Was it Jedediah? If so, what had he done so terrible it demanded that he be expunged from family memory, as though he had never lived or breathed among them?

She flipped through the pages until she came to the last: Rosine's message scribbled in haste while sailing across the Atlantic, her father claimed by that same sea, her mother newly widowed. Cassie remembered from Berta's translation that in spite of troubles the note held courage and hope. The stroke of the pen, the slant of the lettering, the way the words rushed over the page and up the margin, seemed created by the hand of someone with passion, willing to fling herself into life.

What did she look like, this twelve-year-old girl? Closing her eyes, Cassie let her imagination draw a picture: slender limbs, yellow-blonde braids falling down her back. Wide blue eyes with pale lashes and brows. Freckles scattered on her cheeks and nose – a Roman nose, long and prominent and strong, as befitting a self-willed girl.

She is part of me, Cassie thought suddenly. *Her blood flows in mine. Her spirit and heart, too.*

Didn't Rosine mention a baby boy, her brother? Cassie glanced at the list of names. Yes, there he was: Theo Dorst. 1846-1848. Two years old! He died the same year Rosine was at sea, leaving his widowed mother and young sister as they traveled alone to a strange country thousands of miles from home.

She faced the window, her mind wandering among the meadow and woodland and the sacrifices it must have taken to travel here and begin anew. So many lives were lived among these walls and on this land, so many histories lost to time. As she looked away, her eyes sweeping through the kitchen doorway, over the cracked Formica counter and the cupboard drawer that jammed and the linoleum floor that had morphed into something indeterminable, a wayward thought drifted up from wherever it had been hiding:

After Mimi died, there was no one to fill the house or walk the grounds or tend the garden. Maybe that's what I sense sometimes – the old house remembering its past and wanting to be loved again.

The mantle clock whanged the half-hour. Eight-thirty. Startled, she realized that she hadn't had her morning coffee or breakfast and was suddenly ravenous.

It took a while and some maneuvering to get herself up and into the kitchen, then all she wanted to do once she got there was to turn around and lie back down again. Forget the coffee. Breakfast would have to be something easy she could eat prone, such as a toasted slice or two of the home-baked bread Berta had given her. A note was clipped to the wrapping: *This is good German potato bread and will put meat on your bones which you need because you are too skinny. It is nice with butter.*

Cassie's laugh stopped short, and she pushed the loaf aside. She'd eat it later.

Shortly after, with a few stops and groans, she was again on the sofa, a banana and glass of milk within easy reach. The keepsake chest was within easy reach, too. Maybe she could use this forced in-house time to read some of Mimi's letters. It would help take her mind away from what had happened to Justin and what might happen next. She opened the chest lid, dipped her hand inside and lifted the first one she touched:

June 12, 1940
My Darling Johann,

I baked a strawberry pie today with sprinkled sugar on top just the way you like it, and Lillian and I had a picnic by the creek. I put out the yellow checkered tablecloth and we sat on it and ate chicken sandwiches with lemonade, and then the strawberry pie. Lillian put an extra piece on a plate and set it aside. "That's for Daddy," she said. It sat there untouched for the longest time. Finally we decided to eat it ourselves, and with each bite we told a story about you, lovely memories or silly ones – like the time you tripped over that pesky rooster and sent it flying into a mess of hens, remember? Those hens came chasing after you, angry as could be, as if you'd done it on purpose. I still laugh, thinking about it. Lillian talked about the hobby horse you made for her at Christmas when she wasn't yet four years old. You made it from a tractor spring, I think. A big, flat spring maybe three feet long with a small saddle-seat on the top, attached to a wooden base. Somehow you put it all together so there was a horse head with a grin and a handle for her to grip, too. She could hardly wait to get herself on that saddle and bounce up and down while you sang, "Little Lillian, riding far, clippity-cloppity, here and thar." Now here she is going on eleven years old, and she sat on the tablecloth pretending to bounce on her hobby horse, singing, "Clippity-cloppity, here and thar." It made me want to cry. We both miss you so very much.

Forever yours,
Wilhelmina

Cassie hugged the letter close, as if the words could sink through the paper into her blood and become part of her. No thoughts came to mind; she simply gazed at the old clock on the mantle, the brass pendulum swinging with each *tick-tick-tick*. Seconds slipping by, the present sliding into the past. Time gone, so quickly gone.

She reached inside the keepsake chest and choose the next letter at random:

> *September 14, 1940*
> *I'm enjoying the porch swing you made for me, especially when the sun rises or sets and everything is so beautiful. That...*

Footsteps clattered onto the porch.

"Morning, Miss Cassie!" Billy peered through the screen.

"Hi! I didn't hear you drive up."

"I rode my bike. It's nice out, not too hot, not too cold. "

"Come on in. I'm playing old lady today and can't move around much."

"Are you sick?" Billy's smile wavered as he hurried toward her.

"I'm fine, really. Just wrenched my back a little. No big deal."

Billy knelt beside the sofa. "You sure?"

"Positive." Cassie pointed to a paper bag in his hands. "You bringing doughnuts?"

"Something better. Look!" Billy spilled the contents on the coffee table, careful not to disturb Cassie's things. "University catalogues! I've been writing to schools with programs in automotive design technology. There aren't many around, but if I plan it right I might could go somewhere like Cincinnati or San Francisco. Maybe I could try for a Masters in Industrial Design! Wouldn't that be cool?" He leaped up, eyes alight.

"Yes, wonder..."

"They're all way too expensive. I could never tell Dad. He'd go ballistic. But I'll find a way. I'll work, I'll get loans and scholarships. My grades are pretty good." He paused, shoving his hands in his jeans pockets in a gesture much like Guy, then said quietly, "Maybe he'll change his mind and not be too mad at me when the time comes."

"He'll be proud of you. He might not say it, but he'll feel it."

Billy nodded. "He keeps a lot of stuff locked up inside himself, like a pressure cooker Mom had that exploded all over the kitchen. Dad's like that sometimes, pushing everything down until he explodes."

"How about you, Billy?" she teased. "Are *you* a pressure cooker?"

"I'm more of a whistling tea kettle. Get me boiling and I steam and make a lot of noise."

Cassie laughed, then winced as she tried to sit upright. Billy rushed to her side, helping fluff the cushions while she made herself comfortable.

"How did you hurt yourself? Fall off the bike again?"

"It was Justin. He's had a stroke, I think. I was helping Berta get him onto bed last night and something gave way." Her eyes began to burn, and she looked down at her hands still clutching Mimi's two letters.

"That's awful. I like Mr. Grumm. Is he in the hospital now?"

Cassie nodded, not trusting herself to speak.

"Is there anything I can do?"

Cassie shook her head.

"How about some coffee? I know you like coffee in the morning. I make it for Dad and he says it isn't half bad."

"Great idea."

It *was* a great idea. Cassie felt herself relax as Billy moved around in the kitchen. Sounds comforted her: the water gurgling in the pipes, the clang of the coffeepot, the rattle of cups and saucers. No matter if his coffee was spiked with grounds or thick as syrup, she would savor it and love the boy who made it for her. How exceptional he was, how intelligent and deserving of every good thing life had to offer, particularly the education he so desperately wanted.

That's when the idea came to her. Why hadn't she thought of it before?

"Billy," she called, trying to keep the excitement from her voice. "How long have you been saving for college?"

"Three years or thereabouts." Billy stuck his head through the kitchen doorway, wiping his hands on a towel. "Mowing lawns, washing cars, odd jobs like that. I work at Pete's store every summer and on weekends during school. He pays me good. Pays me for playing in the Razorbacks, too. I babysit sometimes and once I tutored a kid who was lousy at math."

Billy busied himself in the kitchen, talking while he worked. "I do stuff for Dad, helping at the shop. Sometimes he pays me a little, but mostly not. We're family and I shouldn't expect money for helping out. Hey, Miss Cassie, want toast with peanut butter?"

"If you'll have some with me."

"Peanut butter tastes great with coffee. I could eat it right out of the jar it's so good."

He was silent for a while. The toaster squawked when he pushed the ancient lever. For a moment Cassie wondered how old that thing was. She couldn't remember ever having seen another in Mimi's kitchen.

"Billy, I know I'm asking a personal question and you don't have to answer if you don't want to. Do you have a college savings account?"

"You mean, like in a bank? I keep everything in a shoebox under the bed. You want cream or sugar?"

"Just cream. Don't you think a bank would be better than a shoebox?"

Billy carried the two cups into the parlor, handing one to Cassie. "Dad said I was a minor and if I had something to put in the bank I could use his account. I love my dad but don't want to put my money in his account or anybody's. I want my own. I keep a ledger real neat, with the name of the job and the date and how much I earned for each and a grand total of everything."

"Does Guy know about your under-bed stash?"

Billy shrugged just as the toaster spit, tossing the bread onto the counter. He dashed into the kitchen and fussed around, eventually returning with a platter of toast and a jar of chunky peanut butter. He slathered the butter on Cassie's toast, handed it to her, then settled on the floor beside the sofa.

All the while Cassie lay propped on the cushions, silently fuming at Guy. "Billy," she said, keeping her voice light, "I'd love to go to the bank with you and help open your own personal account. I'll co-sign, if you like, so you or the bank won't have to worry about a thing."

Peanut butter shot from Billy's mouth as he exclaimed, "Really? Wow!" Laughing, he grabbed a napkin and mopped up after himself. "Look at this, I'm a pig. When can we go?"

"How about early next week?"

"Yeah." Billy grinned. "Right after school." The toast crunched as he took another bite, licking his fingers.

Cassie nibbled, too busy thinking to eat. "I have an idea."

"You're full of `em today."

"How much have you got tucked into that shoebox? I hope you don't mind my asking."

"Two thousand one hundred forty. And sixty-five cents. I have to check the ledger but I think that's about right. A good part of that is from you."

"You worked hard to earn every cent of it."

"I like working for you. It's nice here. When I'm at home I miss it."

A piece of toast stuck in Cassie's throat. She sipped the coffee to urge it down.

"Well, what's your idea?" Billy leaned against the sofa, gazing at her. Cassie could never quite describe the color of his eyes, a mix of gray and blue and green, ever-changing.

"Billy, for every dollar you earn here or at Pete's, I'll match with another dollar, including what you've done for me since the first day."

He jerked upright, looking so stunned Cassie had to laugh. "It's for college, Billy. The bank can advise you how to invest it, maybe a certificate of deposit or a savings account, that sort of thing. So by the time you graduate from high school you'd have gained some interest."

"That's... that's got to be several more thousand right off."

"It's a start."

"Miss Cassie, you are the most wonderful person I have ever met in my entire life except for my mother."

Cassie smiled and drank the rest of her coffee. Guy was right. It wasn't half bad.

"Hello, dear. It's Berta Grumm. I would've called sooner but time got away from me."

For a moment everything seemed suspended in motion: the empty cups on the coffee table, the keepsake chest, Bible, moccasins, and Jed's photograph alongside them. Her eyes were gritty from napping too long. She blinked in the afternoon light and held her breath, afraid of what Berta might say next.

"Justin spoke to me a while ago. 'Take me home,' he said. Not in those exact words, but I knew what he meant. He was lying there nice and peaceful, not worrying about shoelaces."

"That's great news, Berta!"

"He's weak and fuzzy-brained and his tongue gets tangled up, but the doctor said he's doing well as can be expected and called him a tough old bird!" Berta half-laughed, half-cried. "Imagine, a tough old bird."

"He'll get through this just fine, you'll see."

"If he keeps improving he might go to a rehabilitation clinic next week.

And maybe," Berta's voice stumbled. "Maybe he can be home for Christmas."

"That's next month! Oh, I'm so glad!"

"Me, too."

"Can he have visitors?"

"No, not yet. But soon." She sighed, long and slow. "He keeps looking for you, I think, his eyes going to the doorway like he expects you to walk through it."

Cassie said her goodbyes and lay there for a good ten minutes more, listening to the clock tick or the refrigerator hum or the house beams pop and crack. The pinch in her low back let her know that like it or not, she was bound to these scratchy horsehair cushions for a while longer, so might as well make the best of it.

She picked up Mimi's letter she had been reading before Billy came, and continued:

> *I'm enjoying the porch swing you made for me, especially when the sun rises or sets and everything is so beautiful. That swing is an outrageous flirt, did you know? It squeals, "Love you, love you!" Or, "Hubba-hubba, cutie-pie!" So you better hurry and come home before that swing seduces me altogether and we run off and have a torrid, woody affair.*
>
> *Be safe. Be well. Write!*
> *Forever Yours,*
> *Wilhelmina*

Cassie tugged the chest closer, wanting suddenly to grab every letter it held, to gobble each one down in a feast of reading.

Her hand hovered over the letters, hesitating. Something unusual caught her eye, something carved on the lid's underside. Initials? She sat up carefully, swung her legs over the side, and lifted the chest. Letters tumbled out, the World War II medal plopping on her knees.

Initials were cut deep into the wood, the gold paint inside still visible: *RD.*

Rosine! Rosine Dorst! It's got to be her!

Maybe Rosine had carried it with her during her journey. Maybe she had kept her diary inside, with pens and ink. And maybe Mimi had known about it, and wanted to keep it for that very reason. A treasured item handed down from generation to generation.

Why didn't Mimi say anything about it? Why keep it a secret?

So many things were a mystery. But bits and pieces were coming together, like random puzzle parts. If Cassie were lucky, maybe some of it would start to make sense.

She scooped up the medal and letters, almost missing one that had slipped between the cushions. A single sheet of stationery, a single paragraph. Mimi hadn't even signed it. Cassie looked at the envelope; there was no stamp, no return address, no sign of wear like the others, as if Mimi had changed her mind and never mailed it:

> *February 1941*
>
> *The shadows whispered again tonight. I could feel Jed skulking there, almost hear the hiss of his breath. I pulled the quilt over my head and squeezed my eyes shut and told myself he was harmless. But I remembered what I saw as a little girl, and the unspeakable horror of it, and so it haunts me to this day. Likely I will carry the secret to my grave, except for your ears alone.*

Cassie put the letter back into the envelope along with the rest and placed the chest back onto the table. Jed's photograph was only a hand's breadth away. It seemed to leap up at her, his face in the black-and-white background no longer handsome, as if an evil twin had taken his place.

Whatever Mimi had seen, whatever Jed had done, whatever the secret hidden all these years, Cassie would never know. Nobody would know. And Mimi couldn't tell them.

One Day at a Time

BILLY HURRIED INTO HIS BEDROOM AND SHUT THE DOOR QUIET AS HE COULD, heart beating so hard he reckoned it was about to leap right out and bounce around the room like a pink rubber ball. He sat on the edge of the bed and hugged the bankbook to his chest.

His own bank account. His very own.

And here, in his other fist, was the envelope holding the papers that proved it. A savings account. A certificate of deposit. All signed by him and Miss Cassie and the bank.

He jumped up, not daring to laugh or shout for fear his father would come stomping in and ask what was so damned funny. Guy was in the kitchen, sitting at the table as usual, three empty bottles of Coors lined up like toy soldiers on parade. It wasn't yet five o'clock, early for Guy to drink so much. It must have been a lousy day at the shop.

Billy pulled the shoebox from under the bed and opened it. The spiral notebook was inside, his ledger, divided into columns with every entry neatly written in ink. Only a few loose dollar bills lay underneath. Spare change, Miss Cassie had said. It's always best to have a little cash on hand. The rest was now in the bank – four thousand six hundred eighty dollars. Almost five thousand! He could hardly believe it.

A college fund. A real, honest-to-God college fund.

Billy placed the bank book and envelop on top of the ledger, secured the lid, and slid it back under the bed. He looked at the rectangular shape in the under-bed shadows, thinking he couldn't remember ever being so happy.

℘☙

The hospital linoleum was a pattern of gray and white squares. Cassie's footfalls echoed along the corridor. The place felt ominously quiet, as if she were expected to tiptoe and speak in whispers, as if the figures glimpsed through the opened doors, lying or sitting in silence, were ghosts caught in limbo.

"Cassandra!" Berta rushed forward, hands outstretched. "Justin will be so glad to see you! Come."

His room was small, with a single bed and chair. The narrow window overlooked an inner courtyard scattered with crepe myrtle, branches bone bare and the color of ash. Justin sat in a wheelchair, gazing through the glass at a scrub jay strutting among the fallen leaves.

Berta bustled toward him and fluffed the blanket across his knees, her voice unnaturally bright. "You have a visitor, *Schatz*. Isn't that nice?"

He looked pale and diminished in the chair, a thin bundle of his former self. His feet, clad in slippers that stuck out from the bottoms of his pajamas, seemed too big for the rest of him.

"Hi, Justin."

He turned from the window and smiled with such a terrible sweetness Cassie's heart lurched. "Fiddle wax."

"What?"

"Castle come, Castle me."

Berta's eyes reddened, their penetrating, silent plea shouting, *Help me.* "He's glad you came," she said.

For a fleeting, insane moment, Cassie imagined yanking this impersonator out of the wheelchair and shaking him until his bones rattled. *Where is the real Justin?* the secret part of herself hissed. *What have you done with him?*

She knelt beside him, the floor cold against her knees. "I'm happy to see you, too. Now give me a hug."

The arms that wrapped around her were tentative and unfamiliar. Gone was the quick squeeze hard enough to knock the breath out of her.

The jay flew upward, wings bright in the morning sunlight. Justin's hand lay on Cassie's shoulder as he watched the bird rise into the sky. He seemed so wistful Cassie blurted, "Would you like to go outside?"

Justin didn't respond, but looked longingly at the clouds.

"I think he might like that," Berta said. "He's always gets jittery being inside for too long a time."

"All right, then. Let's go! I'll be the chauffeur."

Berta lifted another blanket from the bed and tucked it around him. "Don't want you to catch a cold now, you hear? Last thing I need is a sick old man to worry about."

Justin chuckled. Berta paused, her face flushed, gray hair tumbling down her cheeks. "Well, listen to that," she said. "It's good to hear you laugh again."

Cassie pushed the wheelchair out the door and down the hall. Maneuvering the chair wasn't as easy as it looked. The thing was unwieldy with a mind of its own, and she struggled to keep it from bumping the walls. A crack in the linoleum floor snagged the wheel. Grunting, Cassie rocked the chair to and fro, then gave a giant push. Down the hall they careened. Justin's bald pate bobbed as she veered this way and that, and he grinned as if on a crazy ride at the county fair. "Whoop!" he cried. "Whoop, whoop!"

"You like that? Okay, hang on!"

One more shove and away they hurtled. Berta opened the French doors and stood aside as a delighted Justin burst over the threshold into the sunlight.

Cassie parked him next to a concrete bench. Berta sat beside him, smoothing his few tufts of hair. He smiled absently and gazed up at the sky. It was an icy blue, misted with clouds thin as gauze. Several black buzzards slow-danced in the high distance, dipping and swirling. Justin watched until they vanished from sight, then nodded and closed his eyes.

Signs of life outside the enclosed garden walls drifted lazily downward – the hum of traffic, an abrupt blare of music here and then gone, a shouted greeting. Berta tugged at her drooping nylons. "Thanks for coming, Cassandra. It's lifted his spirits. And mine, too."

"I'm sorry I couldn't be here sooner."

"Our daughter Victoria wanted to come, but she's got so much to do at the university I told her to wait until Christmas, that her papa was doing fine." Sighing, Berta added, "I leave messages for Frederick but he doesn't answer."

"He's the actor in New York?"

"He's very busy, you know. Working all hours of the day and night."

Cassie sat on the bench, fighting the urge to grasp Berta and Justin in her arms and hold on tightly. She wanted to wrap the two of them in blankets and settle them in front of a fire and cook them something delicious and promise to care for them always. She wanted to say she loved them, but the word itself was too small to accommodate the sharp ache in her chest.

Justin began to snore. After a short while the snore grew into a put-put muttering.

"Listen to that," Berta whispered. "Sounds like a dog about to choke."

The two women glanced at one another and burst into laughter. The giggles rose and subsided and rose again until Berta slapped the bench and cried, "It's unfair! Unfair!"

"Well, now!" A broomstick of a woman with peroxide hair poking out of her scalp like cropped straw spoke from the doorway. "A bit chilly for us to be outdoors, don't you think?" She strode into the courtyard, her frown at odds with the grinning cartoon cats printed on her shirt.

"Maybe so." Berta wiped her cheeks. "But he wanted to come, and he's happy out here."

Cassie squinted to read the nametag pinned to the nurse's pocket: *Ima Twerpe*. If she hadn't been so taken aback by the woman's curt approach, she would have felt sorry for her. What kind of parents would stick such an awful name on their own child?

Ima leaned over Justin and chirped, "Mr. Grumm, time to wake up now." She shook his shoulder three times in quick succession.

"Umph?" Justin blinked and looked around, as if startled to find himself in strange surroundings.

"How are we feeling, Mr. Grumm? Time for us to be inside now, and for our session with the physical therapist." She reached for the wheelchair. "And so here we go!"

"Castle help!" Justin called over his shoulder as he was carted away. "Turtle soup!"

"Now let's be a good boy and stop fussing." Ima wheeled backward, evidently planning on going through the doorway fanny-first and pulling Justin after.

"Wait," Cassie said. "He wants me to do it." She held the chair arm, and for a moment expected Ima to yank it from her grasp like a child playing tug-of-war.

"You can't know that, not with aphasia," Ima sniffed. "Mr. Grumm may have a mild form, but it's gibberish nonetheless. I know about these things." And with that Nurse Twerpe did indeed yank the chair and pull it over the threshold with her fanny leading the way.

Berta and Cassie followed as Ima marched down the hall. Each of her thick-soled white shoes squeaked. Justin seemed entranced by the sound; he kept looking down at the floor as if searching for a pack of mice running underfoot.

"He'll be all right, won't he?" Berta whispered. "Tell me he'll be all right."

"We're here. Say goodbye, Mr. Grumm." Nurse Twerpe waved, sang, "Bye-bye now!" and propelled him through an open door. It shut with hardly a sound.

Cassie slammed the car door and glared through the windshield, wishing her eyes could pierce the hospital walls and stab Ima in her twerpy heart.

Something about the nurse got under Cassie's skin. Maybe it was the bright sing-song of her voice, as if Ima were talking to a little boy instead of a grown man, as if she could barely restrain herself from patting him on the head and cooing. "No dignity!" Cassie spat, whacking the steering wheel with her fist. Just because he had a stroke didn't mean the whole being wasn't inside the shattered brain, waiting to be healed. Justin was still Justin and worthy of respect.

Berta lingered by the hospital window, watching as Cassie drove away. Her face, framed with hair the color of fog, seemed faded through the glass, sad and dim and unsubstantial. "Like a ghost," Cassie mumbled, "staying behind to guard a loved one."

What if Justin died? How would Berta survive living alone after so many years together? Berta's words, spoken months ago, murmured in her thoughts: *I could never rattle around in a house without Justin in it.* Sixty-odd years of loving someone, sixty-odd years of being inseparable. A burning sensation flared in Cassie's stomach and seared the back of her tongue.

She'll die soon after from heartbreak. I'll lose them both.

The thought was too ugly, too frightful, yet she couldn't shake it. Ima Twerpe's cheery voice sang in her imagination, *Lose them both, Lose them both.* "Shut up!" Cassie growled, and drove faster. By the time Pete's Gas `n Grub appeared, the car had developed a shimmy and stones rocketed from under her wheels and the scenery flashed past. She didn't care.

Pete was outside near the gas pump, hauling trash to the corner. He leaped aside as Cassie roared by. She glanced at him running after her and shouting, thick legs pummeling the ground. Only then did she come to her senses and stop.

Pete banged on the window. "Lord have mercy, girl, are you plain crazy? You're driving like a maniac." Cassie smiled, her lips trembling as he opened the car door. "Now come on out of there and let me fix that flat."

"I've got another flat?"

"Right rear. One more inch and you'd be riding on the rim."

"*Cass-aie!*" Nan called from her porch, a watering can in hand. "Come on in. I've baked apple crumbly."

Pete pulled her from the car and nudged her toward the pathway. "Go have some of that apple stuff Nan's been cooking up."

"But what about…?" She pointed to a slice of rubber hanging from the tire like a serrated tongue.

"Leave it all to me. Shouldn't take hardly no time at all."

"Thank you," was all Cassie could think to say.

"Ain't no problem. What are friends for, anyway? Go on, now."

Nan called again from the porch, and as Cassie turned toward the pathway and Nan's welcome, the ache in her heart eased.

Nan piled the apple crumbly in warm heaps in two red dessert bowls and scooped vanilla Blue Bell ice cream on top. "Ummm," Cassie sighed after one bite. "Fabulous."

"Pete's favorite. He eats enough to stuff a horse and then asks for more."

"It's so good I'll probably do the same. Maybe half a horse."

Nan chuckled. "I'll pack some up for you to take home."

Cassie paused, spoon half-way to her mouth. The aged black and white photograph of Nan and her two babes seemed to pounce from their position on the wall, demanding attention. A young woman, a boy and girl, a darkening sky.

"Nan," she said quietly, "how do you handle it?"

Nan's sloe eyes turned inward as they, too, found the photograph. "I just do."

"Your children, your family, your home. Everything you knew and loved. Gone."

"I think of them every moment of every day."

"Do you think you'll ever see them again?"

"No."

Cassie leaned her elbows on the black lacquered table. Nan seemed delicate as a porcelain figure, as if she could break into a million pieces with a single blow. Yet buried within that perfect, small frame was a backbone of steel.

"I never forget." Nan said. "Never."

"How do you stand it then?"

"I look outside at life, *Cass-aie*. I look at green things growing. I surround myself with reminders that life can be beautiful."

Cassie glanced out the window at the multitude of plants hanging from the porch eaves and tree limbs and clustered in pots along the walkway. "You must spend a good deal of time taking care of them all."

"It takes a lot of work. Pete teases me about it sometimes." Nan spoke quietly, her lovely face pensive. "Sometimes I think I'm like a plant. I need to be pruned and weeded and fertilized to keep from withering into a dry stalk and crumbling into dust."

A breeze danced among the trees and greenery, casting shadows across the table and upon Cassie's arm, and she thought of Justin sleeping in the sunlight under the bare branches of the crepe myrtle.

"Justin's had a stroke." Cassie's voice shook.

"Yes, I heard."

"He looks awful and can barely speak. What if he dies? I'm not ready for him to die. And what about Berta? What will become of her?"

"I know how hard it is to lose someone. One day at a time, *Cass-aie*. One day at a time."

Guy worked a toothpick between his teeth and leaned against his pickup. The metal was coated with dust that rubbed off on his shirt. No matter. The crappy heap of junk was old as God anyway.

Good thing he was in the store when Cassie drove by. Soon as she walked up to Nan's he came on out and told Pete he could take over, no trouble. "Go on to your customers and don't worry," he had said, real polite. Pete didn't seem too inclined at first, but after chewing the bull a while they shook hands and Pete ambled back to the store, looking out the screen door now and again like he maybe thought Guy would steal the car and drive off.

It was also a good thing that his shop was close by. He rushed there and back with a new tire since Cassie's was shot. He changed it in a hurry, hoping she'd stay inside long enough for him to get the job done. Now he was anxious for her to come on out.

Then he saw her stepping around the tons of plants Nan strewed outside every which way like some plant store. For a brief, bitter moment an image shimmered in his mind: Sarah kneeling in the dirt, planting flowers alongside their house. Yellow ones with red centers. Dozens of them.

Now Sarah was gone and so were the flowers.

Cassie carried a plastic container and lifted her free hand in a sort of wave. Christ, she was beautiful. She walked easy and graceful as a blasted cat. Maybe a panther, what with her dark hair and all.

He spit the toothpick on the ground. "You got some of Nan's pie in that box? Nobody can cook up pie like she can. I buy a slice almost every time I walk in Pete's store."

She looked at him kind of funny. "Apple crumbly."

She had a freckle on the side of her mouth. He wanted to lick the damn thing.

He couldn't think of anything else to say. Words got all jumbled in his head. He looked away and kicked the tire like a dumb-ass kid. "Got you all fixed up here, Cassie."

"A new tire! Thank you."

"You got two others a mite worn. I could replace `em."

"No need for you to go to the trouble. I'll ask Billy to change them when he's over next."

A hot flush spread up Guy's neck and cheeks and scalp. He pushed the rim of his hat down until his face was in shadow. "Sure, no problem."

A flat-out lie. Why the hell didn't she want *him* to do it?

Cassie fished in her purse, a weird thing with a silver spider clasp, and pulled out a wallet. "How much do I owe you?"

He wanted to say, *Nothin'*. "Tire costs sixty-five. It's a good one, last you a while."

She paid then tried to give him more but he pushed her hand away. "Jesus, Cassie, keep your damn money. It only took me ten minutes." Her smile faltered so he added real quick, "Billy would kick up a fuss if I took your money for somethin' so easy. I got enough trouble with him as it is."

She looked startled then laughed a little. "You're probably right," she said and got in the car. Before she shut the door she glanced up at him with those powerful glittery eyes of hers and said, "Thanks again, Guy. You have a kind heart."

She drove away nice and slow. Guy stood as she had left him until the Thunderbird was no longer in sight.

A kind heart. She thinks I have a kind heart!

Maybe she liked him good after all. Maybe all this fuss and consternation in his head was something he stewed up himself. It had been a long while since he felt anything for a woman, and he was kind of raw at it.

Jesus, stop being a coward and ask the woman out. The worst that can happen is for her to laugh. But what the hell.

Shattered Glass

THANKSGIVING ARRIVED, ANNOUNCING ITSELF WITH A SKY CLEAR AND POLISHED as a mirror. Cassie walked along the cracked sidewalk to the nursing facility. Justin had been deemed well enough to transfer there for rehabilitation. Red brick, paned windows, white pillars at the entry, and mature trees all around made it seem more like a rambling home than a hospital.

The activity room had been decorated for the holiday with white tablecloths and little pumpkins and mock turkeys wearing pilgrim hats and buckled shoes. Cassie sat with Berta and Justin at one of the small dining tables. Other families were at tables scattered throughout, filling the air with chatter – except for a wizened old lady wearing a blue straw hat and glasses with rhinestone rims. She sat alone, eating in silence.

Cassie averted her eyes. The loneliness was too frightful to contemplate. Hopefully this fate was not in store for the Grumms. If Justin died, their children would care for Berta, wouldn't they? Or for Justin if Berta were to precede him?

Berta tucked a napkin at Justin's neck. "There, that's better."

"Glory," he said, smiling. "Tender hooks girl."

"I love you, too." Berta turned to Cassie, her face shining with hope. "I think he'll be home for Christmas. Victoria is coming, and maybe Frederick."

"He answered your calls, then?"

"Not yet, but he will."

Cassie nodded and kept her thoughts to herself.

"Justin misses Frederick even though he won't admit it." Berta touched his cheek. "Next year we'll have Thanksgiving at our own table, won't we *Schatz*? I'll cook your favorite things and all the pie you can eat. Peach and blueberry and whatever you want."

Justin grinned and chewed. The food was the usual bland, tasteless fare. Limp carrots and cold mashed potatoes and turkey pale as boiled turnips. Justin didn't seem to mind. Cassie pushed it around on her plate. *Let him be well. Let him be home for Christmas.*

Let the two of them live happily ever after.

&

Groceries slid around in the back seat as Cassie drove the rutted road home the following week. She dreaded passing the Grumm's house. It looked abandoned and silent. Even on the days Berta was home there seemed to be no evidence of her presence. The dogs hovered by the back gate as if waiting for Justin to return, and the rooster and goat wandered aimlessly around an unkempt yard. Only at night did a bit of warmth come with the lighted windows.

The scrap angels hovered over a lonely place.

Berta was there now, sleeping in the rocking chair on the porch, a shawl tucked around her knees. Cassie hadn't the heart to awaken her and drove on. The day was mild, the air calm and fragrant with woodsmoke. She took her time, jouncing over the potholes as thoughts of Berta and Justin drifted to Mimi and the holidays they had shared in front of the fireplace. Sometimes a storm would arise and they cuddled on the sagging couch and listened to Firewind moan through the stone chinks.

A knot burned in her throat. There were times when she missed her grandmother so much it hurt, as if she had swallowed shattered glass.

The car idled behind her as she pushed the gate, the wood warm against her palms. It swayed open, the rusty hinges singing. Each time the lyrics were different from the time before.

It's silly to be saaad, silly to be saaad.

"Not exactly Shakespeare," she grumbled.

Rotting timbers creaked as she drove over the bridge, surprised to see the wolf sitting under the old oak. Usually he came after dusk for his rare visits. But never at mid-day, alone in full sunlight, unless Tatty was around. She parked near the house, half expecting the odd woman to appear; perhaps she had wandered through the unlocked doors and was even now peeking through a window.

She picked up her purse and groceries and walked toward the porch. The wolf leaped up and followed. Cassie paused, startled, and the wolf froze in mid-stride, one paw raised.

For a crazy moment the wolf and surroundings felt surreal, as if the meadow were a painted landscape and the wolf superimposed upon it. Somewhere in the corner would be Hawk's signature, a shadow of opened wings.

"Hey, there. Where's your friend?"

The wolf spun around, loped toward the bridge and halted at its edge, his gaze upon her unwavering. For a moment Cassie could have sworn he was trying to speak.

She hurried up the steps and shouldered her way inside. The wooden door opened easily as the screen door swung shut behind her. No one else was there. She was alone except for the presence she always felt within these walls. Sometimes tangible, sometimes elusive, it was as much a part of the house as the stone and wood.

She tossed her purse onto the stuffed chair, walked into the kitchen, and glanced through the bay window. The wolf had gone.

The wind rattled the screen door as she put apples and peaches in the fruit bowl on the table. They smelled like autumn at its finest. Even the colors reminded her of this time of year, golds and reds. Like turning leaves.

Leaves!

Not a single leaf had stirred when she was outside moments before.

Something was amiss. Uneasy, she looked again out the window. No breeze danced among the trees or played with the angel chimes. Even the clouds hung lazy and low, unmoving.

Yet the screen door clattered and banged.

Her senses on full alert, Cassie returned to the parlor – and faltered. Wolf had reared up on his hind legs and beat the screen with his front paws. He stopped when she approached, eerie yellow eyes blazing as if he came from another world.

"Go home," she muttered, and shut the front door.

Rattle. Rattle. The screen shuddered against the frame.

Cassie backed up, both fascinated and fearful. This wasn't happening. This couldn't be happening.

Rattle. Rattle.

"Stop that!" she called. "What do you want?"

Wolf whined.

Cassie grasped the knob and pulled. Light flooded the room as Wolf leaped from the porch, whirled toward her, and yipped. *Come,* he seemed to command. *Come.*

"Is it Tatty? Has something happened to Tatty?"

Come.

She opened the screen door, tentative.

Come now.

That did it. Cassie ventured down the steps, hesitant but willing to take the risk. She followed him deep into the woods. They hurried through places she vaguely remembered from her childhood: boulders like gnome bastions, a willow tree forming a leafy bower, a rivulet spanned by a fallen log. It was here she had once seen a possum swimming downstream with tiny baby possums hanging from its upright tail like pink ornaments.

A turtle watched from the water below as she stepped across the log. The rivulet marked the southern boundary of Mimi's property. Cassie stepped beyond the shore, unfamiliar with the land she now trespassed, so tangled and wild it could well have belonged to no one but God since the time of creation.

Wolf trotted ahead, sometimes in sight and sometimes not, silent as the shadows he seemed to favor. Cassie followed through clustered trees draped with vines so thick they blocked the sun. Interspersed among them were spiny thickets and scrub brush and rugged crags. Fallen leaves crackled with each step and shale loosened and crumbled underfoot.

All the while she worried about Tatty. She had no idea where the woman lived but never imagined that it would be here in the backwoods, isolated as a hermit. Animal life was abundant – birds flitting overhead, a porcupine rummaging among the leaves, squirrels scampering high among the branches. Yet there was no sign of human habitation, as if Tatty lived in a tree or a cave and sprouted wings and flew about without need to touch ground.

Cassie found herself on a pathway, if a narrow, trampled space could be considered such. Wolf had disappeared again and she decided to go on without him, thinking that surely this was where he had intended to bring her.

The path led to an archway of branches and vines. Feral and strange, the wooden fingers wove a pattern so off-kilter Cassie felt as though it had been designed by a loony architect. Everywhere she looked something beckoned within its walls: balls of tree moss, strings of red berries, strips of bark, dried sage. Cassie felt as though she had walked into a fairytale and at any moment would be met by elves playing among the fern.

The arch opened and she stepped into a spacious clearing. Sunlight fell upon a neat garden bordered by a fence of twisted mesquite, a cistern barrel with spindly legs, an opened shed. Tatty's motorcycle, straddling a puddle of oil, glistened in the dim interior.

At first Cassie didn't see the house for the ruin that hid it. What had once been a stone building lay crumbled in a wayward heap as though blasted by a bomb. Ivy and trumpet vine sprouted from the cracks. Yellow pansies, too. The creepers trailed up to a glass roof that rose from the fallen stones.

The glass rounded into a dome, supported and framed by metal supports glittering in the sunlight. One side attached to a cottage of sorts, made of rough-hewn timber and wattle and river stones.

"Tatty?"

A door was ajar. Cassie knocked and called again, "Tatty?"

From inside a muffled moan, "Here."

The room was semi-circular, its curved walls of tumbled stone and glass joined to one of wattle and weather-grayed cedar. Tatty lay rigid upon a narrow cot, her face blanched, her lips taut. An Indian blanket spread underneath her, vegetable-dyed, hand-woven, and quite old. "I knew you'd come," she said.

Cassie paid little notice to the piles of twigs and baskets heaped on the floor, cluttering a trestle table, or spilling from a shelf against the flat wall. She rushed to Tatty's side, stepping over scattered brushwood, and knelt. "Are you ill?"

"Shoulder's out of socket. Done it before."

"What happened?"

"Gathering mistletoe. Branch broke under me and I fell."

"Lord Almighty, Tatty. Up a tree! I'm calling 911."

"Don't want a damn ambulance! Called one years back. It skidded down a ravine and smashed into the creek. Siren wouldn't stop, screamed for hours." Tatty's eyes crinkled at the corners as if she were silently laughing. "It made the driver nuts. Stupid man clobbered the horn until it broke."

"What can I do?"

"An herbal mix in the kitchen. Blue pottery jar. Boil a cup of water and steep four scoops."

"Can I help push the socket back in place?"

"Got to numb it up some." Tatty smiled, an unsettling contrast to her constricted face. "Old injury, old girl. Gets worse with time." Without moving her arm, she lifted a finger and pointed to a doorway on the timbered wall. "In there."

The door was set low. Cassie ducked through into a room with shelf after shelf lining the walls from top to bottom, filled with pottery the hues of earth: browns, golds, greens. A kiln with the color and texture of a battered cast iron skillet squatted in the left corner. A pottery wheel and clay-splotched stool were on the right, near a window overlooking the garden.

Cassie turned slowly, gaping at all around her. *I know this pottery!* She had once dreamed of having works like these in her boutique, but couldn't begin to afford them.

The singular design of each bore an unmistakable thumbprint of the artist – a signature of sorts. The pieces had a particular tint and idiosyncratic twist to the forms, as though partly melted by the heat of the sun. The lip of jars, the handle of pitchers, the curvature of plates, all had the same unique warp.

If this is what I think it is, Tatty has a lot to tell me.

Resisting the urge to linger or rush back and pester Tatty with questions, she continued her search for the kitchen. The house was small, with thick walls and beamed ceilings and wooden floors that creaked underfoot. It was cozy, made comfortable with a multitude of clashing colors and scuffed, time-worn furniture Lillian would have scorned as "yard sale." Nothing matched. Each chair or table, each curtain or pillow or lap throw, each area rug might as well have been plucked from attics around the world. Even the dishes and glasses and cutlery looked like leftovers from a dozen different patterns.

Cassie loved it all.

The herbal concoction was thick as mud soup and smelled about as rank. Tatty leaned upright with her back braced against the wall, tilting the mug to her lips with a single turn of her wrist. She managed without a word of complaint or an outright howl against what must have been amazing pain. Shutting her eyes with lids crinkled as tissue paper, she drank the mess in loud slurps through closed teeth, perhaps to dam the floating bits. Cassie settled on the floor beside her, afraid of jarring the cot, and looked around. Glass soared from the fallen stone on three sides and from a timbered wall on the other, encasing the room in a crystal bubble. Vines wound up the transparent walls to the dome above. Oak floor, polished to a soft sheen. A braided throw-rug, faded and raveled. One tall lamp, the shade askew. It was not turned on, nor needed. The room was awash with sunlight. And baskets, baskets everywhere, woven from the woods. Stunning creations with crystals and berries and dried wildflowers and herbs intermixed among the grapevine and twigs.

Cassie recognized the baskets, too. They looked exactly like those known and valued among artists and collectors. She had yearned to include a couple for her boutique, although it was a lost cause. The baskets and pottery were normally sold in galleries or museums or upscale stores like Neiman Marcus, never in small boutiques with a limited customer base.

If she was right, the person sitting on the cot and drinking a foul concoction without a whimper, the one who lived in this tumbledown house and worked in this glass-enclosed studio and rode the antique three-wheeled motorbike leaking oil outside, wasn't the bothersome eccentric Cassie had thought her to be.

If she was right, there ought to be a web of silver threads woven into the bottom of each basket and cut into the clay of each pottery piece, the signature of the renowned, reclusive artist known as Spider Weave Woman.

Why didn't I think to look at the underside of the nest Tatty gave me?

Spider Weave Woman was a mystery to art critics. Little was known about her. No photographs, no biographies or memoirs. Reviewers called her The Enigma.

Tatty's eyes were still closed. The empty mug rested in her lap, fingers wound around it. Her hands were unexceptional: wide and stubby-fingered with knobby joints and prominent veins. Short, yellow nails with a residue of soil embedded at the quick. Rough, wrinkled skin splotched with brown. Unremarkable and ordinary, the sort Cassie imagined planting a garden or hanging laundry or scrubbing a pot.

Were these the hands of a famous artist? Cassie reached for the mug, determined to find out.

"You finished, Tatty?"

A nod.

"I'll take this back to the kitchen."

Tatty offered no resistance as Cassie lifted the mug from her fingers and carried it away. She ducked under the low doorway into the adjoining room and raised the mug up to the light, trying to look at the bottom without spilling any herbal residue.

There it was: a web, a simple spiral. Spider Weave Woman.

Cassie rushed from one pottery piece to another, yet still couldn't let herself believe it. She went into the kitchen and put the mug in the sink before returning to the glass-walled studio, her mind whirling. It must be true. It had to be true. And yet...

Tatty's head and jaw drooped, as if she were asleep. Cassie tiptoed to the trestle table and lifted a partially completed basket. Nothing unusual was woven underneath. She tried another. There, on the underside, a crochet needle dangled from a silver cord embedded in the vine. A web in the making.

"Find what you're looking for?"

Cassie jumped; the basket slipped from her fingers and rolled lop-lolly across the floor. "I'm sorry, I…" She chased after it, stubbing her toe on the table leg.

Tatty's eyes glinted under half-closed lids. "You always this graceful?"

The basket prickled Cassie's fingers. It was shaped like a large bowl and smelled of crushed rosemary. Dried yellow wildflowers wound within it, small as teardrops. Cassie looked it over carefully, hoping against hope that a stem hadn't snapped in the fall. "If I damaged this beautiful thing, I'd kill myself."

Tatty snorted. "Nonsense. It's just stuff from the woods. Nothing irreparable."

Cassie carefully lay it on the table, releasing her hold only when assured that the basket would stay put. Tatty watched, expression inscrutable, arms held close to her body. She had a strong face, Cassie thought – firm jaw, direct gaze, furrowed skin reddened by constant exposure to the sun. Flyaway hair was pushed behind her ears, exposing chunky turquoise earrings and a necklace. The jewelry had the patina of age but Tatty herself seemed ageless. She could have been fifty-five or eighty-five or anywhere in between.

Cassie took a deep breath and asked, "Are you who I think you are?"

"Depends. Crazy old lady? Yes. Rebel? That, too. Friend? Absolutely."

Cassie fumbled for words, trying not to pry – or at least not be so obvious about it. "I mean, um, do you have a name other than Tatty?"

Tatty studied a red-breasted finch that hopped along the glass rooftop, pecking at the vines. The seconds dragged on. Just when Cassie thought she couldn't stand it a moment longer, Tatty replied, "*Tatez Guaihpe.*"

"*Tatez Gua… Gua…*" The sounds were soft and cadenced and difficult to pronounce. "Sounds Spanish."

"Comanche."

Comanche! A sharp thrill danced up Cassie's spine. "Spider Weave Woman?"

"*Spider Woman*. I added *Weave*, poetic license and all."

Cassie sat on the cot, watchful of any motion that might jar Tatty's wounded shoulder. "I've loved your work for years. I'm honored to know you."

"*Psht!*" Tatty flicked her fingers, as if swatting away a fly. "I don't usually like people much. But you're quite tolerable." A low growl slid from her throat and she slumped sideways, her head resting near Cassie's thigh. She lay immobile, face the color of paste, fists gripping her elbows.

"Tell me what to do, Tatty. Can I pull your shoulder back in place?"

"Call my son. He's done it before, many times."

"Where's the phone? What's his number?"

"Kitchen. 844-2905."

844-2905. 844-2905. Cassie muttered as she once again hurried through the pottery room and into the kitchen. Where was the damned phone? *844-2905.*

There, on the counter, a streamlined, contemporary piece that looked out of place amid its surroundings. Cassie picked it up and dialed, fumbling in her haste.

It rang ten times before she slammed the receiver down and hurried back, so worried she forgot to duck and whacked her forehead on the doorsill. The sound exploded in her skull. Pain ricocheted from behind her eyes and sawed into her scalp. She staggered, bracing herself against the wall.

"No answer." Cassie strove to make her voice steady. "Now what?"

"Drive me there."

Cassie pressed a palm against her forehead. It felt hot, as if a volcano boiled under the skin and was about to erupt. "Where's your car?"

"Don't have one."

"Then how…? Oh my God, the *motorcycle*?"

The Precipice

"I'M GOING TO CRASH! I'M GOING TO CRASH!" CASSIE HOLLERED AS THE MOTORcycle shot along the path. It snarled and bucked and jounced over rocks and chuckholes with such force Cassie feared Tatty would hurtle out of the sidecar. "Hang on!"

They were traveling to God knows where for God knows how long. This was crazy, Cassie told herself. Insane. Pain ricocheted up her arms and shoulders and throbbed in the middle of her forehead. She gritted her teeth and focused on keeping them both alive.

Gas, rotate right handlebar. Clutch, squeeze left. Brake, hit pedal.

Just starting this archaic heap had been traumatic. She had to haul it from the shed and prop it with kick stands before Tatty could get in the sidecar and tell her what to do next. Then came the impossible business of adjusting the choke, fiddling with the fuel valve, advancing the accelerator. Finally she stood on the lever and stomped down hard. Once. Twice. Three times. The motor flooded, making her repeat the exasperating process all over again.

Tatty's face pinched into a mask of misery. "That way!" She pointed to an off-shoot directly ahead. It came at Cassie fast. She turned as directed, crashing through scrub brush en route while Tatty hunkered down, and burst onto a rutted trail. She struggled to keep within the boundaries as the sidecar swung to and fro like a wild ride at a county fair. It was attached to the main frame by something akin to a hinged spring, and with each jostle she worried it would rip off and rumble away on its own.

Gas, rotate right handlebar. Clutch, squeeze left. Brake, hit pedal.

The mantra reassured her. So far, so good. No dead bodies yet. Five more minutes, then ten. The searing pulse in Cassie's forehead subsided to a dull ache. The motor barked and spit smoke and kept on going.

Tatty's long yellow scarf slapped against Cassie's leg. *Thwap. Thwap.* She wanted to rip it off and tear it to shreds. The stubborn woman had insisted upon wearing a battered straw hat knotted under her chin with that scarf and refused to leave the house without it. Cassie risked a quick glance in her direction. The hat rim flapped up and down as they plunged along, whipping Tatty's nose and cheeks. Her skin had blanched to the color of glue. Yet not a single tear slipped from her eyes, not a single groan from her lips.

"You okay?" Cassie yelled over the barking racket.

Tatty nodded.

Cassie squinted in the sun's glare as they rounded a cluster of hills and rocketed onward. The terrain seemed familiar, not the landscape exactly, but the feel of it. The trail cut through cactus and cedar, and meandered in the shade of a great peak to her left. The mound rose and rose again, building upon itself.

Then the realization hit her. Mount Bubba! She was on the far side of Mount Bubba! It loomed above her, treacherous and beautiful, with jagged outcroppings and huge boulders and sheer cliffs blazing copper and silver in the late afternoon light. A section looked made of rubble, with sheared scars ending in piles of jumbled rock at the bottom showing evidence of landslides.

The trail slipped from the shadow of the hill and veered through thickets of juniper and stunted mesquite. Cassie eased her grip and risked flexing her cramped hands. This wasn't too bad, she thought. Sort of like riding a hybrid – half machine, half cantankerous bull.

"Dead end on road ahead!" Tatty hollered over the racket.

"Then what?"

"Right turn."

The words barely had enough time to leave Tatty's lips before the bike slammed into a rock, leaped a good foot off the ground, crashed through a strand of jimson weed, and landed on Spring Creek. The wheels smacked the road and kept on going.

"Turn around! Turn around!" Tatty yelled.

They zipped across Spring Creek and vaulted over the down-sloping field, picking up speed along the way. Gravel shot from under the tires like a round of fireworks. Cassie stamped on the brake as the motor sputtered and burped and farted rank oil fumes. It grumbled to a shuddering halt a hair's breadth from disaster – a prickly pear cactus taller than the motorcycle and bristling with needle-sharp spines.

"Well," Tatty grumbled, "that was exciting."

A familiar tree stood against the sky on the far left, its slender limbs brushing the ground. Cassie backed away from the cactus and turned the bike around, disgusted with herself. Once again she had lost control and raced willy-nilly downhill into the realm of the weeping willow, a place that triggered unpleasant memories of a warped bicycle and a ruined picnic. In her imagination, Hawk peered from between the flowing branches, eating a fried chicken wing. Rebecca Stanch was there, too, nibbling on his ear.

"Think we can try the road now?" Tatty asked.

Good God, she's laughing! Hurting like the devil and laughing in ragged, breathy gasps.

A lump bloomed on Cassie's forehead, a painful reminder of her collision with Tatty's low doorway. She could feel it taking root like a poisonous mushroom with tentacles that crept behind her eyes. She pretended it wasn't there and grinned. By damn, if Tatty could make light of things she could, too. "Both of us are idiots," she said, rumbling up the incline to the trail they had left moments before. "Has that path always been here? I don't remember seeing it."

"It's a back entry. Made it when I bought the place some years ago."

"The land is yours? What part?"

"Most of what you're looking at."

"My grandmother's property stops on this side of Mount Bub... that big hill over there. It's in a valley of sorts, but I never knew who owned everything beyond."

"I have a good piece and my son the other. If you don't get me there shortly he's going to inherit my share a lot sooner than I had planned." Tatty leaned sideways in the sidecar, her good arm cradling the shoulder of the other.

Cassie looked around, puzzled. Where was she to go? The road butted against a steep, craggy hill erupting from the earth like a prehistoric monster turned to stone, its angry head pushing up through dense woodland until the barren scalp emerged high above. A trail slashed through the trees, ascending straight and sharp before swallowed by shadows.

"Tatty, where to?"

"Up."

The inside of Cassie's mouth dried to dust.

She couldn't move. The world shrank, closing in on all sides, squeezing the air. Tiny firelights danced and sparked in the corners of her vision.

I can't do this.

A whisper of a moan. Tatty slumped into the seat, her head tilted awkwardly, her eyes closed. Cassie placed a gentle hand on her cheek. "Are you going to be all right?"

A bare sound, "Hurry."

Don't think. Go. Go. Go.

Another, separate part of Cassie, a reckless twin-self she never knew existed, arose from deep within, gunned the motor, and raced uphill.

Oak, juniper, and pine closed in on either side, forming high walls of bark and leaf that met in a canopy overhead. Darkness pressed from behind them, crawling between trunks and falling from branches like mutant spiders. The cycle bounced and rattled and roared up and up and up, veering into a mad zigzag toward the summit, left, right, left. The twin Cassie, the stranger, hung on for dear life and squeezed her eyes into slits. *Pretend you're in a forest,* the twin whispered in Cassie's ears. *There is only woodland here, no cliffs, no precipices, no chasm far below.*

A blur of greenery flashed past, framed by Cassie's lashes. *A forest, traveling through a forest.* The cycle rumbled on, vibrating in her bones and blood. Her head felt about to burst like an overripe pumpkin, exploding seeds. Tatty flopped from side to side in the sidecar, eyes closed, arms hanging loose. Her scarf had come undone, and the hat slipped to the side as if about to fly away.

"Tatty?"

She's fainted! Get her there, get her there NOW!

Cassie leaned forward as if to meet an onrushing wind and accelerated as much as she dared. Fear burned the air into dry cinders, clogging her mouth, searing her eyes. The memories of that fateful morning on the Colorado mountain crowded around her now, clamoring for attention – the sheer cliff, her feet in red hiking boots teetering on the edge, the horror awaiting below. She clenched her fists, struggling against the images, damning their existence.

The higher the path ascended, the thinner the woodland became until it fell behind her. She hurtled from its shaded protection into sunlight so bright it blinded her, and stomped on the brake before she careened into the unknown. The bike came to a shuddering halt. Gasping, Cassie realized the road clung to the side of the hill. Serrated rock in streaks of brown and green and gold rose on her left. To her right, beyond the road lip, was nothing but air as the ground dropped away. Precipices jutted from stone face, slate glittering like sunlit water.

A short span more, that's all she needed to travel. The road ended just ahead, at the hill's crest. So close, so very close. She shook the motorcycle, as if imploring it to defy gravity and levitate. *I've got to do this for Tatty! Move, move!*

She couldn't flex her fingers, couldn't release their grip on the handles, couldn't do anything except remember another place, another day, high on another mountain. The bright morning, the smell of coffee, Thomas crumpled far below, sprawled across the cruel rock. His blood pooled and dripped off the rim like red pearls.

Her body hummed as if plugged into an electric socket.

"Cassie?" Tatty had awakened, although she hadn't moved. The hat still sat lop-eared on her head, the scarf dangling over one eye. The expression on her face was hard for Cassie to define – a watchful stillness, a waiting.

"Just taking a breather." Cassie's voice shook and her lips felt nailed into her head.

Tatty nodded and said nothing more. Cassie ground her teeth, forced her fingers to release the brake and rev the gas. The bike bucked and plunged ahead, blue smoke billowing and wheels raining gravel over the rim. Seven seconds to cover the distance, that's all it took. Seven torturous never-ending seconds, a lifetime of seconds, a century.

The road ended on terrain flattened into a plateau. A low stone wall on the hill's summit enclosed rocky pastures of shrubs and trees opening to the sky. The world fell away, rolling into the horizon: buttes, hills, valleys, roads thin as threads, a smattering of towns. The sun would set in an hour or two, spilling a scarlet fire across the broad heavens.

I'm here. I did this. I actually did this!

Exhilarated, wobbly as a rag doll, Cassie followed the trail to the house at its end.

The house seemed to have grown from the land and trees surrounding it. Constructed with a combination of rough-hewn logs and stone quarried from the hill, it had a sweeping front porch and steeple roof and huge picture windows. Handsome, both rustic and contemporary, it was completely unexpected in a town of country homes built long before those now living in them were born.

She parked beside the porch and helped Tatty out of the sidecar as the motorbike growled a dying swansong. She expected someone to come running any moment, but the only thing that greeted them as they walked up the steps was silence.

"Hello?" Cassie called. "Anyone home?"

"Door's never locked," Tatty said.

The heavy door opened to a spacious, sunlit room with a stone fireplace, high beamed ceiling, and chandelier of intertwined antlers. Leather furniture in warm earth tones was complimented by hand-woven Native American rugs underfoot and artwork on the walls – particularly the fringed deerskin shirt with beaded embroidery.

"Hello?" she called again.

"He's not here." Tatty sank onto the couch, leaned against the plump cushions, and untied her hat. "Truck's gone."

A jolt of panic ran through Cassie's bones. She imagined having to drive Tatty all the way back to Mimi's house for the car, and from there to the hospital. "Does he have a cell phone? We could call. Reception ought to be great this high up."

"He'll be here soon. He comes and goes." She started to say something but faltered, her lips drawn tight against her teeth. "Water, please."

Cassie hurried through an arched entry into the kitchen, found a glass, turned on the tap. As the water ran, she glanced through an open doorway on her left. Light streamed from picture windows onto canvas paintings. Paintings everywhere, piled and stacked and hung, clustered in the corners and leaned against the walls. In the middle of the organized chaos was an easel, the back toward her, and a paint-splotched stool.

The sound of a truck approached, rumbling closer. Cassie turned off the water and carried the full glass with her over the threshold into a studio. The vehicle stopped at the rear of the house; its door opened and shut. Heart pounding, she walked around the easel and looked at the painting it held. It was an unfinished portrait, the oil glinting.

A woman, dark hair swept from her face by a blowing wind. Shadows swirled around her, a whirlwind, a storm. A single shaft of light fell from above, surrounding and protecting her in a nimbus of luminescent gold. She smiled, tremulous, beautiful, her eyes a suggestion of brush strokes, her hands opened to receive something not yet defined.

It's me! He's painting me!

Footsteps crunched over gravel. The back door leading to the studio flung open and Hawk walked into the room.

He tossed his hat onto a hook on the wall. It landed perfectly, swinging slightly as he turned and froze at the sight of Cassie. They stared at one another, unmoving and mouths agape in such a stunned, ridiculous fashion that for a crazy moment Cassie thought she would burst into a fit of laughter. Then she remembered Tatty.

"Your mother needs help. Her shoulder's out."

His eyes went from her to the portrait and back again. His face reddened, and he grabbed her by the wrist and pulled her after him. Water spilled from Cassie's glass as she stumbled alongside, too dazed to do anything except be led like an awkward puppet. He pushed her toward a stuffed leather chair with a matching ottoman. "Sit."

Dismissed, Cassie did as she was told. The soft leather settled around her as she watched Hawk tend to his mother. All the while the image of the portrait hung behind her eyes. She didn't understand the meaning of it, the dark, struggling shadows, the circle of light, the beauty and hope it radiated. And why *her*? What was it he saw in her that made him want to pick up the brush and put it on canvas? She wanted to go back in there and look again, but didn't dare move.

"Mom?" Hawk's voice was tender, his touch gentle. "How did this happen?"

"Not telling. You'll fuss."

"Fall from the roof again? Or was it the ladder this time around?"

"Not telling."

"One of these days you're going to kill yourself."

"You worry too much. Now stop yatting and get me fixed up."

Hawk lifted her off the couch, cradled her in his arms like a babe, and laid her on the rug-covered floor. "Ready?"

Tatty nodded. "Yes."

Cassie almost dropped the glass when Hawk slipped his boot off and put his foot on Tatty's shoulder. It happened quickly. He lifted her arm, paused, and yanked once. The sound of the socket popping back into place was unlike anything Cassie had heard before, sort of a muffled gunshot.

Tatty gasped, a ragged moan. Hawk knelt and placed her arm across her chest. "Stay quiet, now. You have to rest flat like this a while." He reached for a pillow on the couch, put it under her knees, and stroked her cheek. "Promise you won't move until I say so."

Tatty's lips quivered in a smile. "Maybe."

"You should have called instead of driving that shitty bike. Probably made things worse."

"Didn't."

"Then how...?" He looked at Cassie. "You?"

"Me."

He regarded her briefly, expression guarded. "Are you planning to drink that or water the floor?"

Cassie had forgotten about the glass. It dangled from her fingers, tilting dangerously downward. "It's for Tatty."

She was too amazed with the state of things to find fault with the way he snapped the glass from her hand and walked from the room without another word. Hawk, Tatty's son. Living here, in this amazing house on top of the world. Hawk, seeing her in a way no one had ever seen her before, illuminated on canvas.

She listened to him moving about in the kitchen, the scrape of a chair, the sudden quiet that followed. What was he doing, sitting at the table? Did he find it that difficult to be in the same room with her?

Tatty's eyes closed in sleep, her thin chest rising and falling, her mouth parted slightly. Reassured, Cassie sighed and leaned back into the cushiony chair, placing her feet on the ottoman. Exhaustion weighed her down. Every possible muscle and bone in her body ached. She lifted heavy fingers to the dull pounding on her forehead and felt a lump big as a plum. Probably as colorful, too. Her hands dropped to her lap, her eyes shut, and it was forgotten.

She dreamed of flying. Her body floated, light as air, high over great hills and buttes and rolling pastures. Over rocky precipices and deep chasms and streams narrow as yarn. The wind lifted her up and sang in her ear. A deep peace penetrated her heart, a quiet joy, without a shred of fear. Then she saw Thomas standing on the edge of a steep cliff. He looked at her, smiling, and leaped into the abyss. He fell in slow motion with arms outstretched, graceful as a dancer in an aerial ballet. His shirt billowed as he fell, fluttering like feathers, like wings.

Suddenly she was on the ground, in the meadow. It was snowing. The stream crackled against the bridge and hurled ice upon the shore. She lay on Mimi's comfy old sofa in the middle of it all, bundled up to her neck in quilts. The wolf sat close beside her, his breath warm upon her face. "Keep still," he said, and put a snowball on her forehead.

Whisperings. Rustling. A murmured word, a quiet laugh. Cassie swam upward from the recesses of sleep, and peered through half-opened eyes.

The sun had already set. How long ago, Cassie couldn't tell. The room was soft and dim, the light warmed by logs blazing in the fireplace and a single lamp. Tatty sat on the couch beside Hawk, her lap covered with a woolen shawl. They leaned in toward one another, talking quietly. Cassie watched them without stirring, watched the way Hawk smiled, the way he pressed Tatty's gnarled hand between both of his, the way she smoothed his hair. A yellow hound dog lay contentedly at their feet, his head on Hawk's boot. Firelight seemed to encapsulate them, like a halo.

A longing she couldn't name made Cassie turn her eyes elsewhere.

Her reflection glimmered in the windowpane: a woman slouched low in a chair, tired face drawn, hair a dark tangle. A blanket covered her from toes to chin. *A blanket!* Startled, she sat upright. A drop of water trailed down her cheek and something cold slid from her forehead, resting cockeyed over one ear.

"Don't touch." Hawk was there, pushing her back into the chair. "It's an ice pack to reduce the swelling." He repositioned it, green-green eyes so close she could see flecks of gold swimming within them. "Mom told me what happened. Thanks for helping, Cassie. I'm sorry you got hurt."

"I'm okay." Her voice cracked.

He lingered above her, arms on either side of the chair, looking down. There was a half-moon crease on either side of his mouth. A mole under his left earlobe. A bump on the bridge of his nose, as if it had been broken long ago. Heat emanated from him, tangible, reaching to her. It awakened something primal. Cassie had the oddest desire to bare her teeth and bite his lips, maybe even growl.

"How do you like your steak?" He grinned, slow, easy, and Cassie's heart lurched.

"What?"

"Rare? Medium? Incinerated?"

"Medium rare, no blood."

"Can do. Now take it easy and leave the ice pack in place until dinner."

"You want me to stay for dinner?"

"No. I'm going to throw you out in the darkness and insist you walk home by yourself with a nasty lump on your head and an empty stomach." He spoke lightly, teasing, and tucked the blanket around her, his fingers brushing her skin. "Keep still and stop fidgeting."

"I'm not fidgeting."

"Oh? And what do you call that?"

Cassie followed his gaze to her foot. It was jiggling, much to her chagrin. "Just… stirring up circulation, that's all." She flexed both feet. "Much better."

"You," Hawk said in a mock whisper, "are too damned stubborn."

"And you," she mock-whispered in reply, "are a bully."

"Touché." Tatty called from across the room. "Call it a truce and bring out the wine."

The Visit

"My husband was a charming two-legged rat." Tatty sipped her wine, smiling at Cassie over the rim of her glass. "I knew it but married him anyway."

"How long were you together?" Cassie had put the ice pack aside when it turned to mush, then slipped her shoes off and joined Tatty on the couch. They had both finished one glass of wine and now were working on the second while Hawk grilled steaks outside.

"Ten years, off and on. I don't regret it. At least not the good times."

"Maybe we can't help who we fall in love with. Maybe it happens in spite of ourselves."

"Hah! Don't believe that for a second. It's because of who we are, our secret self, wise or foolish or just plain greedy."

A log in the fireplace popped; sparks shot upward, bright, shining, smelling of oak and mesquite. Cassie tucked her bare feet under, pulled the woolen wrap they shared over her knees, and snuggled deeper into the couch. A perfect night, a perfect wine the brilliant hue of red roses.

A metallic clatter erupted from the kitchen. "Hoo-ha!" Tatty exclaimed. "Think he dropped the silverware?"

"Probably the entire drawer, with a pot thrown in for good measure."

"I heard that." Hawk's voice from the other room, bantering. "Now be nice or I'll toss your T-bone to Old Yeller."

Cassie mouthed *Old Yeller?* and Tatty gestured to the hound dozing in front of the fire. "Named in honor of the dog in a book he loved as a boy. He still has that book, or what's left of it, torn pages and all." She grinned, a mischievous glint in her sun-wrinkled eyes. "His birth name is Chayton. Chayton Walker. I thought you might be interested."

"Don't be a tease! Of course I'm interested."

"It means Falcon."

"Chayton," Cassie murmured, loving the sound of it. "Do you ever call him that?"

"Sometimes, when I'm feeling motherly."

"Why did he change it?"

"Hawk is his spirit name, given to him on a vision quest when he turned sixteen."

"A *vision quest*? I didn't know traditions like that still existed! Where did he go?"

"Deep into Big Bend. He was there for a week fasting and praying, alone in the wilderness. I can't tell you how glad I was to see him come home, or how proud."

The rear door opened, shut. Cassie looked through the window as Hawk walked to the grill in the shimmering night, his back turned to her. He moved like his namesake, with grace and a certain stealth. The full moon threw a spotlight on him, as if at any moment he would pull out a stool and play the flute for a shadowed audience. She couldn't reconcile her image of this man with that of a little boy. It was a startling revelation to discover she had never imagined Hawk younger than he was at this moment, as though he had slipped from the womb fully grown. She tried to picture him then: lanky, sunburned, perhaps a bit wild.

As if reading her mind, Tatty said, "He looks like his father except for the eyes. No one else in the family has eyes like his, the color of moss. Or hair pale as corn silk. My grandmother said he was a throwback from time before reckoning, when white strangers wandered the land."

"White strangers?" Cassie felt a thrill of excitement, the sort she experienced whenever she discovered a fascinating bit of Indian lore.

"Such a thing is spoken of in stories of our past. My grandmother's mother used to tell them to my mother when she was a child, and then to me when I was little."

"My grandmother used to tell me stories, too." Cassie paused, then added softly, "I never knew either of my great-grandmothers."

"Mine was so old her face looked like a crumpled rock with eyes poking through. Her voice was stone, too. Rough and crackly. Whenever she spoke I imagined words tumbling out of her mouth like pebbles."

"I'd love to hear a story about the white strangers, Tatty. Do you remember one?"

Yes, of course." Tatty tilted her head, as if listening to a distant voice. "It goes something like this." And so she began:

> In the time before remembering, gods sailed across the great waters in canoes with wings and lived among us. The sky rested in their eyes and the sun blazed in their hair. Magic was in their hands. They carved sacred figures in

> stone and tree, and hunted with strange bows and arrows until a sickness claimed them. Those who lived scattered and vanished from the earth, although some say their spirit lives in the corn.

"Vikings!" Cassie cried. "I've read about their explorations in the north, especially along the Ohio River, but never knew they were here in Texas."

It struck Cassie, then, the truth of Hawk's heritage. Like Tatty, he had Comanche blood. Perhaps that was why he surrounded himself with Indian-made things: the handsome items on the walls, the loomed rugs, the woven throws. And perhaps – she had to admit this to herself, even though she wanted to deny it – being Comanche made him even more interesting, more desirable, than before.

Guy straightened his four empty bottles of Coors beer and lined them up in an orderly row on the kitchen table, making sure the labels faced the same direction. He lit a cigarette, flicking his thumb across the match before placing the stub in the ashtray just so, then leaned back and looked through the window at the silvery night. The cigarette dangled from his lips, smoke trailing upward. Sarah had once said he looked like Bogart in some film or other, he couldn't remember which, smoking squinty-eyed and serious. Now and again he would glance at his reflection and wonder if she was right, but all he saw was a skinny guy with thinning hair.

The house was too damned quiet. Billy had gone to band practice with his pals. The only thing he heard was the tick-tick of the clock. It had developed a grinding sound that irritated the hell out of him. He sighed, aggrieved at the injustice of it all, at his lousy, lonely life, and reached for another beer. He stared at the bottle, at the moisture drops clinging like glistening parasites, and pushed it aside.

It wasn't another drink he wanted. It was company. *Female* company.

Maybe he'd give Cassie a call. *You have a good heart, Guy.* That's what she said. Made him feel good, remembering.

He eyed the old phone on the wall, a fake antique with brass bell things on top like mouse ears. The phone hung there, silent. He couldn't remember the last time it rang for him instead of Billy, unless it was business. Hardly never from a friend. Most gave up on him after Sarah died, what with his moodiness and all. He wasn't the easiest person to be with and his temper could get in the way of things, but shit! A friend was supposed to stick with you, bad times as well as good. They could go to hell for all he cared.

Except for Cassie. Her face hovered in his mind misty-like, as if glimpsed through the smoke curling around his head. She wasn't smiling exactly, just looking at him with those deep dark eyes. He should call, pay her a little visit. Apologize for the way he snapped at her when she talked about Billy going to college. She didn't understand proper, that was all. He could explain it to her, let her see his side of things. He'd take some beers; hell, he had more than enough in the fridge. They could sit on the porch swing and talk to each other. And if it got chilly out, he would warm her up some.

He stubbed the cigarette in the ashtray, rose, walked to the phone, lifted the receiver.

Put it down again.

He'd surprise her instead.

Cassie leaned her elbows on the wooden table and laughed at something Tatty had said. Maybe it was the wine, maybe the lovely night. Whatever the cause, everything seemed delightfully funny: a joke, a dropped fork, Old Yeller begging for a bone.

They sat under the stars, a fire in the brazier warming them against the evening chill. Cassie pulled a wrap over her shoulders and pointed her toes toward the flames as Hawk cut his mother's steak into bite-sized pieces and mashed her baked potato. "I don't want you using that arm for a good while," he insisted. Tatty sighed and rolled her eyes with exaggerated patience.

Cassie choked on her wine, trying to keep the giggles at bay. Hawk didn't seem to notice. She could likely have drunk an entire bottle and bonked her head on the table before he'd look directly at her for more than a second or two. But conversation among the three of them was lively and filled with good humor, and when he did look in her direction, his warm glance welcomed her.

She felt as though she belonged here, under the night sky on top of a mountain. As though she had sat at this very table sometime before, had patted the head of Old Yeller, had listened to the crackle of a fire while tipping one too many glasses of wine.

She couldn't remember when she had last been so perfectly content.

Guy drove with the windows open, the cold wind slapping his cheeks. He liked it that way, cooling him down some. His face was hot like he had been in the sun too long, and his heart was doing a trip-hammer in his chest.

He slowed down when Cassie's fence came into view. Her gate would be up ahead, around that clump of cedar. As if of their own accord, his hands turned the steering wheel, guiding the pickup onto the shoulder of the road. And further still, until it stopped under the limbs of a tree so old it was already half dead. Why he had the urge to hide was something he didn't think about much. He was just following his impulse. Going to be friendly. Everyone likes surprises. Didn't want to spoil things with the truck clanging over that rackety bridge.

He pulled the gun from the glove compartment, stuck it into his pocket, and tugged his shirt over it. Just in case the wolf-thing was there again, he needed something to protect himself. He leaped over Cassie's gate so it wouldn't squeal and made his way to the little bridge, keeping a sharp eye for the wolf. It wasn't around. Cassie wasn't there, either. It was still early enough but no lights were on anywhere. The place was bleak as a tomb. Guy hesitated, uneasy. The house looked like a big skull, with windows for eyes and steps for teeth.

"No reason to get spooked," he muttered. "It's just an empty house."

It just didn't *feel* empty. Like something was looking at him through those gaping eye holes.

He put his hand against the gun and walked up the steps when wind chimes hanging from the porch eaves got to jangling. *Shit!* The damned things looked made out of silverware, spoons and knives and forks bent and folded into angels that clattered loud enough to wake the dead.

A glint, a shape like something sneaking in the dark, made him spin about and squint into the night. But it was only moonlight falling through the leaves of the big oak, the shadows dancing around and reflecting off of Cassie's car. Maybe she was home after all and sleeping, although it was too early to sleep, not yet ten o'clock.

No polite person would knowingly wake somebody up. Best to check first.

Slow and careful, he crept around the side of the house to the bedroom window and looked in. He couldn't see much, so cupped his hands around his eyes and pressed close to the glass. The fat moon and sky bright with stars flooded the room enough to show the bed with no lump on it like there would have been if she'd been lying there. He moved to the parlor window and looked through that, too. From what he could tell, Cassie wasn't there, either.

Best to make certain. He stepped onto the porch and knocked on the screen door. It rattled under his fist. "Cassie?" He waited a little then opened the screen and knocked on the big wooden door behind it. The sound thumped through the house and down the hall; he could hear it echo. After a time, he turned the doorknob.

The door swung open and he walked inside, closing it after him.

It was time to go home. Cassie lingered, prolonging the inevitable. Tatty thrust a bag of food scraps into her hands. "For our four-legged friend."

"A guardian as well as friend, I think." She hugged Tatty goodbye, careful not to squeeze the wounded shoulder. "Take care. I'm glad you're not going to be alone for a while."

"That son of mine is worse than a mother hen," Tatty grumbled. "I'll stay with him a day or two and let him cluck and fuss. Makes him feel useful."

Hawk waited outside by the pickup. As Cassie turned to join him, her eye caught the glint of a picture frame on a small table nearby. It held a photograph of a slender woman with an elegant, arresting face. The face Cassie had first seen in the Whistle Pik Gallery in Fredericksburg. The face that had attached itself to Hawk with the determination of a festering pustule. There he was beside her in the photo, hat brim low on his forehead, arm around her waist.

Cassie had liked Rebecca when they first met. Had it been in other, Hawk-free circumstances, they might have become friends. Now look at the state of things. *Funny,* she thought as she walked toward the pickup, *how odd the path of life is, what twists and turns it makes. Who knows what's waiting around the corner?*

Hawk helped her into the cab, his touch firm but hurried, as if impatient to get her seated. As she stepped up, she saw the motorcycle and outrider in the yard. The bike took her by surprise, as though she had forgotten it. Had she really driven that thing all the way up here?

Tatty waved as they drove away, the headlights sweeping over her face before finding the road. The landscape glittered in the moon's glow. Rocks, trees, cactus seemed unreal, objects from a myth in ebony and silver. Clouds raced across the night sky, trailing fragments like ripped silk, and the trees on the mesa swayed to silent music. Hawk opened his window to the chirrup of crickets and the melancholy hoot of an owl, its cry answered by another. "I like to sleep outside on a night like this." He spoke quietly, as if careful not to disturb the chorus.

The breeze played with Cassie's hair. She wrapped her arms around herself, enjoying the night in spite of the chill. Hawk dove slowly as the landscape slid past. When the truck's wheels hit the narrow road along the hill's rim, she kept her gaze directly ahead and tensed against the paralyzing fear she hoped would not come. Stones rattled from under the truck as they had from the motorcycle, spinning into the emptiness below. A wild itching crawled along her palms and a tightness gripped her chest. *Breathe,* she told herself, *just breathe.*

Hawk reached for her hand and held it on the seat between them. Startled, Cassie turned toward him and the expanse of space beyond, the steep cliff and precipice visible in the moonlight. A perfectly framed moment, as if viewed through the eye of a camera and captured in a single flash, the colors and shapes sharp and clear as ice.

She was breathing, breathing slow and deep, the cedar-scented air cold in her throat as Hawk began the zigzag trek downhill, the trees arching overhead and blocking out the stars.

Guy waited until his eyes adjusted to the gloom then walked through the parlor into the kitchen, remembering the lunch he had shared with Cassie at the wooden table. He wanted another beer, surprised for having forgotten to bring them, and opened Cassie's refrigerator. It was almost as crappy as his, although a mite cleaner. Not a single beer inside. He selected a soda then pulled out a chair and sat at the table for a while, telling himself he would wait for her. He looked through the bay window at the weird baby angel statue in the oak tree, almost real, like at any moment she would jump off and come running in to join him.

It gave him the creeps.

He tossed the empty can into the trash and wandered down the hall into Cassie's bedroom, careful not to bump into anything. The moon was huge and low, like he could reach up and pluck it with his fingers, so he could see well enough to get around. He saw the stuff on her dresser, too: an old-timey photo of a man and woman and little girl with a big bow on top of her head.

A pair of moccasins so small they must be for a doll or a baby. A box with a curlicue design. He lifted the lid and found a bunch of letters. He tried to read one but the light wasn't strong enough, and so put it back.

He opened the top dresser drawer. Footsteps pattered down the hall. He froze, twisting his head around to look over his shoulder.

Footsteps, soft and shuffling, heading in his direction.

He couldn't move, his hand in the drawer and heart thumping so hard it seemed about to leap out of his chest. Then whoever or whatever was coming whispered, he couldn't tell if it was a man or woman or monster, whispered something unintelligible, like hissing water.

The sounds died away. Guy waited, so abruptly cold his hands felt numb.

Nobody was there. Nobody at all.

Headlights pierced the tunnel of trees down the hillside. They rode in silence. Cassie felt no pressing need to talk. She was too weary to talk much, anyway. The day had finally crashed down upon her, and she looked forward to a long sleep in Mimi's lumpy bed. They hit a rough spot and Hawk released her hand as the truck jounced along, the dark canopy of limbs rambling above them. Even without looking at Hawk she could feel him beside her, as if electrodes had been fused between them.

I wish I knew what was going on in this man's head. Rebecca's photo said one thing. Cassie's portrait said... what? She didn't know.

Maybe Hawk didn't know, either.

They were soon off the mountain and once again on Spring Creek, passing the junction where the motorbike had leaped off the trail and almost collided into that huge cactus. Now the willow tree appeared, ghostly in the night, wearing limbs like a shroud.

She felt him gazing at her. He had done it before, when he thought she wouldn't notice. His face was serious then, pensive, almost shy. Perhaps he was embarrassed she had seen the portrait, and didn't know how to explain it away, or even if he should. So she pretended to have forgotten, pretended it didn't matter, when in truth it mattered a great deal.

Guy slammed the dresser drawer shut and returned to the hallway, chiding himself for being scared of nothing.

Might as well take more of a look while I'm here. Can't hurt none.

He crossed the hall into the bathroom. His face floated in the mirror.

He didn't look at it right on. It was a face that belonged to a stranger, to an intruder. *I'm just a friend,* he reassured himself. *Here to visit. A kindly gesture.*

Cassie's nightgown hung on the back of the door. He buried his face in its folds, inhaling her scent. It was as he remembered, something deep and musky that flowed from her person like she was a creature from the sea or from secret parts of the earth.

Sarah had always smelled like honeysuckle. It had drifted after her like a mist, seeping into the pores of the house and into his bones. But Sarah was gone. The honeysuckle was gone, too. Nothing remained but memories and guilt.

Life had to be lived, didn't it? No need to stay stuck in the past.

He took the gown off the hook and draped it around his shoulders, as if he were holding Cassie in his arms.

A pickup rumbled down the pathway and clattered over the bridge. Guy could tell it was a pickup without looking, even the make of it; he had worked on trucks since he was a kid. Hugging the nightgown to his chest, he bolted down the hall to the side door, dashed outside, and ran behind the trees at the back of the house.

Hawk parked near the emperor tree and, much to Cassie's surprise, switched off the ignition and turned to her. She could only see his silhouette against the starlit sky behind him.

"Cassie." His voice cracked and he tried again. "Cassie." Then he simply sat there, saying nothing more. The cab space swelled with unspoken words, hundreds of them rocketing around Cassie's head, ricocheting off the ceiling and doors. The longer Hawk waited to speak them, the louder the silence.

"Cat got your tongue?" She meant to ease the moment, but it didn't help.

Guy slithered in the shadows, cautiously making his way around the house from tree to tree. He saw the truck good enough. Hard to say when he'd seen a night this bright. Seemed unnatural, like he was looking at a movie set and everything around was painted real perfect. Cassie's face was lit up, too, and turned to where he could see it clear. He couldn't make out the particulars of the person driving, but knew who it was. Nobody else on the planet had a truck like that, with the painting of a hawk splashed over the rear window.

He stuffed the nightgown under his shirt and crept as close as he dared. Why was she with Hawk, anyway? *What's he done, dumped that slick chick he's usually with? Playing around?*

He imagined Cassie lying naked under Hawk, skin damp with sweat, smiling like she was now. Even heard the sound of her voice, *ooooh* and *aaaah*, worse than a porno flick. It made him sick. He wanted to stop looking, but couldn't. It was like a magnet pulling at him. Like he knew what would happen next and hated knowing.

Hawk put his arm around Cassie's neck, drew her to him, and kissed her.

Guy jerked forward, pulling the gun from his pocket as Cassie finished the lip-lock and glanced in his direction. He dropped to the ground, landing on his stomach in a patch of chest-high johnson grass.

What the shit am I doing?

Muttered words. A door slamming. Steps clattering up onto the porch. The truck revved; headlights skimmed over him sprawled flat, cheek buried in the dirt. He lay still, every nerve in his body listening as the pickup crossed the bridge, as it exited the gate, as it turned at the road and kept on going. He waited a moment more, then peered over the grass stalks. Cassie was inside the house now; windows were alight in the parlor and bedroom.

Slouched over low like a damned ape on the run, he rushed out of there quiet and careful, the gun still clutched in his fist. His legs felt about to buckle at the knees and blood roared in his head so he couldn't think straight.

Christ, what a fool he was. What a rotten, half-assed fool.

His feet led him back to the pickup. He jumped in and tried to start the ignition but his hands shook, so he lay on the cracked leather seat. He stared up at nothing, his breath loud and choked up like he had a cold and couldn't breathe right.

Groveling in the dirt. Sneaking around like a thief. All because of a woman who didn't give a crap about him.

The Grotto

CASSIE LOOKED AT THE EMPTY HOOK ON THE BACK OF THE BATHROOM DOOR, SO flustered by Hawk's kiss she couldn't remember where she had hung her nightgown.

She wandered through the house, turning off the lights. Moon shadows played across the walls and slid into corners and crawled underfoot. When she moved the shapes moved, as if she were dancing among them. The thought tickled her fancy, and on impulse she waltzed on her way to the kitchen, pretending Hawk was waltzing with her, their reflections swaying together.

The whiff of a peculiar odor lingered in the room. The air felt strange, too, as though the house had caught its breath and waited to exhale. She paused in the semidarkness, watchful, listening. The oak tapped the windowpane, the refrigerator hummed, and once the ceiling popped. She heard the windmill screeching faintly through the walls and the jingle of the porch wind chimes.

Then she saw the glint of a soda can in the trash basket.

"Oh look, Billy was here!" She spoke aloud, as if someone were standing beside her and listening to the pleasure in her voice. Billy had been reluctant to accept her invitation to come into the house when she wasn't there and help himself to whatever was in the fridge – until now. She glanced out the window over the sink, hoping to see light glimmering from the barn. Sometimes he worked on the Studebaker well after dark, illuminated by a kerosene lantern propped on a rickety wooden crate.

The barn was a hazy silhouette against the night sky, the windmill standing sentry beside it. Billy was probably at home and asleep, as she should be. Yawning, she returned to the bedroom and undressed, letting her clothes pile on the floor, and slipped a flannel gown of Mimi's over her head. It was old-fashioned with lace at the neck and sleeves, and about as glamorous as a decrepit cat with a bad case of mange. She snuggled under the quilt and waited for sleep to claim her.

Hawk's face glimmered behind her closed eyelids, floating in the rose-tinted darkness. Sighing, she brushed her hand against her mouth, remembering his kiss. It had been tender but restrained, as if he feared what might follow. But passion *had* been imprisoned behind his lips. She felt the heat of it – his skin, his breath, his hand resting against the nape of her neck – as though he had stepped from an oven. She wanted to melt into that heat, to wrap herself around him, to be consumed by flames.

"What now?" she whispered into the darkness.

As she slept, the voice of a flute drifted in the night winds. Faint, so very faint, perhaps only a lone bird, its song captured by her imaginings. A terrible yearning gripped her dreams as the music embraced her. The notes glowed bright as cinders sparking upward from a fire. She reached to catch them like darting fireflies, to shove them into her mouth, to devour them. The music smoldered in her stomach and singed her blood and burst into flame, igniting her into a brilliant torch clear and shining as the moon.

ഇ൚

"It's almost midnight!' Tatty scolded. "What are you doing in there?"

"Just cleaning up, " Hawk called from the kitchen. "Go back to sleep. You need to rest that shoulder."

"How can I when you're making such a god-awful racket? Sounds like you're at war with the dishes."

"Sorry." Hawk tossed the dishtowel aside and turned out the light. "I'll wait until tomorrow."

"Good. You could use some rest, from the looks of you. All wired up." Tatty grinned at him from under a comforter on the couch. She seemed disembodied in the dying firelight, like a loving phantom come to pester him.

Hawk sat on the edge of the leather ottoman, hands between his knees. Truth be told, he didn't know what to do with himself. He felt juiced up. *Edgy,* that was the word. Rebecca's photo on the table beside him didn't help. He shifted position so he wouldn't have to look at it. The sight of her face made him feel guilty somehow. But why? There were no promises made between them, no talk of love.

But affection of a sort did exist, that he had to admit. Theirs was a longstanding relationship based upon mutual respect and trust. It was comfortable and familiar and suited him fine. At one time he thought that might be enough.

Until he met Cassie.

"You going to tell me what's bugging you?" Tatty asked.

"I'm not exactly sure myself."

"Hogwash."

Hawk shrugged and stood to look out the window. The moon was so bright it lit up everything. The tree by the porch appeared cast in silver, leaves and limbs and trunk glimmering.

"Maybe I should paint a night landscape. Never done one."

Tatty snorted. "Painting isn't what's on your mind."

"No." Silver, silver in the night. He remembered the silver moonlight in Cassie's eyes and upon her hair, her skin, her lips.

"I saw the way you looked at Cassie tonight, pretending you hardly noticed her at all. It's her you're thinking of, isn't it?"

"Maybe."

"Can't say I'm surprised." Tatty tilted her head, gazing at him sort of sideways like she did sometimes.

Hawk never knew what was really going on her in her mind those times, and it never failed to make him uneasy – as if she could see into his heart and read whatever was written there.

"You worrying about Rebecca?" she asked.

Hawk nodded and glanced at Tatty, the firelight shimmering in her eyes.

"So what are you going to do?"

"Damned if I know."

"Listen to your heart, to your true self. That's what I say."

"What if my heart and mind disagree?"

"Then you're in trouble," she said, and chuckled.

Hawk sighed and turned away. "Goodnight, Mom. See you in the morning."

"You're hiding from yourself. You know that, don't you?" Tatty's voice followed him into the next room.

He shut the door to keep it out.

ꕥ

Hawk turned onto Spring Creek and headed home, errands done. The afternoon hours lay before him, golden with sunlight, perfect for painting – if he could concentrate on something other than Cassie. She floated in and out of his thoughts, fragmented moments of sound and shape: the melody of her voice, the curve of her lips, the limitless depth of her eyes. Cassie, the luminous Cassie, had tugged at his heart since she first appeared from the shadows of Smithy's Barbeque joint like a seductive angel sent to torment him.

A retreat, that's what he needed. An hour or two in a special place he hadn't visited in a while. Perhaps there his mind would clear, his spirits lighten.

Dust rose and scattered along the rutted road, stirred by the truck. The air was crisp and dry; his skin felt tight on his bones. He drove past the Grumm's, slowing down as he neared Cassie's gate before speeding up again. He continued on, trying to fill his mind with something, anything other than the obvious, until the weeping willow came into view. He knew he wouldn't look at that tree ever again without remembering Cassie crashing through on her bike, and how he had been tempted to sweep her into his arms and run into the sunset like a ham actor in a corny cowboy movie.

He stopped suddenly. *What the hell am I doing?* He made a U-turn, headed back the other way, and soon found himself rattling over her bridge.

Cassie sat on the porch swing, eating an apple. The day shimmered with the slow promise of winter. The sky blazed pale, almost white, as if made of melting ice. She heard a truck rumble along the road and pass by. Moments later it returned, pausing at her gate. She stood with a smile, thinking perhaps it was Billy in his father's battered pickup.

She knew who it was the moment a flash of red emerged from behind the juniper. Her heart did a little skip and she tossed the apple core into the flower bed as the pickup approached. Why hadn't he called? Six days had passed since their meeting on his hilltop, six days of silence since his kiss. An irritating man, this artist, suddenly dropping in as if they were grand friends who had talked to one another just yesterday or the day before.

The truck came to a stop and Hawk stepped out, his white hair glinting, his eyes hidden behind sunglasses. Jeans, a khaki shirt rolled up to his elbows, a Stetson, boots. All this in a six foot-odd package of gorgeousness. And here she was, bare-faced except for a dash of lip gloss, wearing one of Mimi's kitschy holiday sweaters spangled with dancing reindeer. At least the jeans were her own, and fit as they should.

"Hi," she said. "Long time no see."

He grinned in that slow, maddening way. "You busy? I'd like to show you something."

"Show me what?"

"A special place nearby. I thought maybe you'd enjoy it."

"Right now?"

"Yeah. It won't take long."

Cassie's irritation evaporated. She could stew and whine about being ignored, but suddenly it didn't matter. He was here, he was smiling at her, he wanted to show her something special. So why not? "Okay, I'm game."

"Good. Come on, then." He opened the passenger door. "It's not far."

"Should I change? I hadn't dressed with company in mind."

"You're perfect. Every inch of you is perfect."

Cassie could have sworn that he blushed under his tan when she stepped up into the truck. Hawk settled in the driver's seat beside her, his shoulder almost touching her own. Soon they were passing through her gate, the breeze from the opened windows stirring her hair.

"No one else knows about this site," Hawk said as he made a sharp right turn onto Spring Creek. "It's kind of tucked away."

"How about Tatty? Has she been there?" She wanted to ask the same about Rebecca, but kept her mouth shut.

"With Mom you never really know. She keeps her secrets." He reached up to the visor, withdrew a slender case, and handed it to her. "You might need these."

"Sunglasses? So we're going to be trekking around outside somewhere, right?" The weeping willow slid by. Cassie watched it pass, wondering where they were heading.

"The man remains silent," she teased. "Oh, the mystery."

"No mystery. Well, maybe a little," he conceded with a grin. "It's a peaceful spot and calms my mind, especially if a painting is going nowhere and I'm stuck and can't think. And I just… I just wanted you to see it." His fingers drummed the steering wheel as the truck bounced on, something in the back clanging against the side. "I didn't realize that's what I wanted until I saw you on the porch. And you looked so… And then I wondered..." He paused, glancing at her. "Hell, Cassie. I sound like a teenage kid with his tongue all tied up."

"I've always liked teenagers, especially tongue-tied ones," Cassie laughed. She felt good, so very good, a happy warmth invading every cell of her being. The day was turning out to be spectacular.

"Almost there."

Oh my God, don't tell me we have to go up that again.

They were aiming directly for what she'd come to think of as Hawk's Hill; it loomed mere yards away. Cassie gripped the edge of her seat, dreading the moment they'd ascend, remembering the fear that had engulfed her on Tatty's motorbike up that steep zig-zagging path.

"It's going to get a little rough," Hawk warned. "Fasten your seat belt."

He veered abruptly to the left, jouncing away from the hill. Two parallel tire tracks slashed through brush and wild grasses where the truck must have passed countless times before. Hawk bounced and rambled this way and that among prickly pear and mesquite, and along a dry creek bed cluttered with rocks, knocking her about. Cassie hung on, laughing, suddenly afraid of nothing, rejoicing in everything, almost sorry when they left the creek bed behind.

One final jolt, and they came to a stop.

"Okay, out you go."

"Where are we?" She stepped from the cab and found herself on a precipice, a wide one, thank God, descending in a series of ragged slopes. The horizon spread to her left: bluffs and valleys and ribbon roads under a cloud-drifting sky. The wind tugged at her hair, whipping it around her face.

"My stomping ground." Hawk motioned to the mound on her right. It reared up, a rough-and-tumble thing surrounded by piles of rubble, as if in millennia past a portion of it had slid away. "One reason I chose this hill is the way it changes over time. No view is the same. Wherever I go, wherever I look, I discover something different."

"I'm turned around. This is your hill, the very same one?"

"The very same, just a different part of it. If you stand back far enough and look up, you'll see my house on top."

The idea of balancing on a cliff edge, no matter how gradual the slope below, gave her the shivers. "Another time, maybe."

"There's a path here, but be careful."

She made her way over a jumble of rocks and onto a narrow trail. Hawk walked ahead of her, long legs moving easily over the rugged terrain. She liked this back view of him almost as much as she did the front. Lean, strong, assured. Comfortable in a wild habitat, as if born there, as if part of it. He glanced over his shoulder at her now and again, smiling, offering his hand when the going got rough.

The boulders she stepped among were warm to the touch, and gleamed in the sunlight. Colors abounded, as if the seasons had been captured and held within stone: golds, ocher, silver, touches of green. A scent lingered in the air, dense and sharp. It suddenly occurred to her how magnificent this site was, old as time itself, teeming with color and life and the knowledge of centuries long past.

"It's beautiful here," she said. "Like we're among the bones of something ancient, something still alive and breathing."

He paused, tilting his hat back a bit to gaze at her. "You've just put into words what I've been trying to paint."

"Is that good or bad?"

"Good. Definitely good."

The trail led to a small clearing and a sudden end. A downed oak sapling sprawled against the hillside, gray and brittle dry.

"Little good this did," Hawk groused. "The tree was in full leaf when I put it here, so you can tell it's been a while since." He dragged it aside, limbs scraping the ground as pebbles scattered.

A mouth opened into the earth and stone.

"What is it, a cave?" Cassie peered inside, enthralled.

"The ceiling is low for a few steps in, so watch your head."

Hawk tucked his sunglasses into his shirt pocket and motioned for hers, then led her inside. A cool breath hit her as she entered, carrying a scent of moss and something she couldn't define, reminding her of crushed leaves.

"Here it is," he said.

Cassie found herself in a small cavern, the ceiling high above them. Bluish-dark, shadowed, the light diffused. "It's like a grotto," she murmured, eyes sweeping over the craggy walls, the multiple openings that lead elsewhere. "How did you find it?"

"I didn't. It was Old Yeller. I heard him barking and there he was, poking his nose inside and grinning!"

"Grinning?"

"He's good at that. He's good at pouting, too. Keeps me on my toes."

"I hope you thanked him. This is beautiful. Almost like a chapel, isn't it? I feel as if I should whisper."

Her words went right into him. Hawk felt them enter, sing in his blood. He smiled and took her hand. Long fingers, slender, strong. God, even her fingers were lovely. And they felt good, clasped in his own.

"There's a narrow ledge here, bumpy," he warned.

She followed, silent, her footsteps soft behind him. A dark glimmer on their right revealed a narrow stream, drifting into the darkness beyond. Long strands of tree roots plunged down from the ceiling, seeking the water below. He watched Cassie as she took it all in, looking at everything, the silver-tinted light reflecting in her eyes.

And then they were there, the site he considered his own. At least for now, while he walked upon this earth.

"This is it, Cassie. My favorite spot."

"Your secret place," she said, her voice hushed.

"My dreaming place, really. Inspiration, introspection, whatever."

They sat on the large boulder he often sought, the top flat and smooth. Sunlight from the opening fell upon part of the cavern wall and shimmered along the water, which flowed so close by he could have easily cupped a handful and taken a drink, as he had at times in the past. There was something about this site that grabbed him. He had tried to paint it over the years but was never satisfied; for some reason a picture refused to form, so he let it be.

"I can see us reflected in the stream," Cassie said. "Rippling, but there. Appearing and disappearing. Kind of spooky, in a nice way."

Startled, Hawk followed her gaze. "Sure enough. Maybe our doppelgangers are floating around down there."

"Floating doppelgangers?" Cassie said with a grin. "Mother always told me my imagination was running rampant. Wonder what she'd say about yours?"

"I'm more interested in what *you'd* say."

She laughed, but didn't take the bait. Damn. Clever girl.

And beautiful, oh very beautiful. Everything about her. Everything. She sat there, part of this place and this moment, and so part of him. He pulled her to him, gently. The fullness of her breasts pressed against him, and the silkiness of her hair brushed his chin. She lifted her lips to his and he kissed her, long and deep, wanting to pull the taste of her, the fragrance of her, deep within himself.

He wanted more. He wanted much, much more.

Not yet, he told himself. *Not yet*, and reluctantly drew away.

"Nice," Cassie sighed, "so very nice," although *nice* was too wimpy a word for how she really felt. The right word didn't exist, not at that moment.

She was about to say more when she glanced over Hawk's shoulder and saw something she couldn't quite believe. "Oh my God, is that what I think it is?" She released his hand and leaped up. "There, on the wall right behind you."

"A final surprise," Hawk seemed delighted, grinning like a kid who had waited until the last possible moment to share a special secret.

And what a wonderful secret, a tremendous secret. Cassie couldn't take her eyes off of it.

"How old?" she asked.

"No telling. Centuries. Eons, maybe."

Cassie resisted the urge to press her own palm against one of the three painted on the stone – two larger than her own, and one very small, perhaps that of a child.

"And these, look!" She found herself gaping, as if she were the one who had just now discovered the stick figures of men with arrows hunting deer and buffalo, and the scattered drawings of round faces with round eyes. "These belong in a museum, not hidden away."

"No, they belong here. Right here."

"Maybe so, but..." And then she saw it. How could she have missed? It gazed directly at her with ochre eyes. A wolf! Just the face, but still... She touched it lightly, tracing the lines that were simply wrought yet fully dimensional. "I could swear this is a picture of the same wolf that visits me almost every day. It's the eyes, maybe. Something about the eyes."

"Well, I'll be damned. There's only one wolf I know of in these parts, and it doesn't visit just anybody. I've only seen it a few times, from a distance. It must think you're pretty special."

"Really?" Cassie liked that idea, she had to admit.

Hawk gazed at her in his disarming way, his own eyes glinting. "There's a Cherokee legend about wolves. Want to hear it?"

"Of course!" Intrigued, Cassie returned to her seat beside him.

"It's a story a shaman in Sedona told me some years ago. An old guy called Cham, dry and wrinkled as a lizard, but with a big soul. He helped me when I... when I lost myself for a time."

He paused, perhaps remembering. Cassie waited in the silence, wondering about his "lost" time, knowing now was not the moment to ask. Water dripped from somewhere close, a constant faint trickle, echoing.

"Cham was just a boy when he first heard this, on a reservation in Oklahoma. I never asked how he ended up in Sedona, alone in a beat-up trailer. But he was true to his name, changeable as a chameleon, almost as old as the cliffs around him."

"You liked him, didn't you?"

"Yes, very much." He opened his arms. "Come here. We need a proper position for this story-telling time."

Cassie laughed lightly and leaned her back against his chest. He wrapped his arms around her, his breath touching her left ear as he spoke. "A little boy was eaten up with anger at something or other," he began, and continued:

> His grandfather saw that the boy was making himself sick with it, and it worried him. "I understand how you feel," the grandfather said. "So I'll tell you a secret. It is this: There are two wolves inside of me, fighting all the time. A terrible fight. One wolf is angry, like you are now. Its heart is dark with pride and envy, with greed and self-pity and hate. But the other wolf has a different heart, one bright with love and humility and kindness. He does no harm, and walks in harmony with all living things.
>
> "It isn't easy living with these two wolves fighting inside me," the grandfather said. "The same struggle is going on inside you, too. Inside everyone."
>
> The boy thought a moment, then asked, "Which wolf wins, Grandfather?"
>
> The old man smiled and said, "The one we feed."

It was silent, save for the distant *plink-plink* of dripping water. Sunlight drifted in patches along the cavern walls. Cassie didn't want to speak or move, feeling strangely lethargic, content nestled in Hawks arms. "A powerful story," she finally said, her voice quiet. "I've had my share of inner wolves, I think. Battling it out."

"Me too."

His arms tightened, and she rested her head against him. His scent embraced her, something undefinable. Earth, perhaps. Or a mixture of earth and wind, the fragrance of trees in autumn.

"Listen. Hear that?" he whispered.

"Hear what?"

"*Shhh*. Listen."

Cassie closed her eyes. Slowly the sound came to her: a lingering sigh, a faint melodic hum, wandering through the cavern depths.

"It's the wind," he said, "coming in from one place and leaving from another, passing through. It doesn't happen often."

"It reminds me of a lullaby."

"A lullaby?" Hawk chuckled quietly. "Mother hill, singing to us."

They didn't talk much from then on. Cassie felt the silence grow between them, an unspoken understanding, as if they had known one another in ages past. A lifetime of knowing. It felt right to her somehow, to sit close, to be there, to experience the sighing cave. The stream reflected their faces, side by side, the hand and wolf paintings shimmering on the wall behind them.

"Thank you for sharing your special place with me," she said. "It's peaceful here. It's magical."

Hawk murmured something and kissed her. His lips were familiar to her, as if she had kissed and lingered there hundreds of times before. She felt oddly comforted, as if she had been grieving for something unknown and only now felt peace enter her heart.

"Cassie," he whispered. "It's you who are magical." He released her, his eyes a golden green, as if the cave itself had entered him, and now gazed at her through those two mirrored pools.

Cassie watched from her porch as Hawk drove away, the painted hawk on the rear windshield seeming to fly with him. The touch of his lips lingered, the feel of his breath, the deep mystery of the cave reflected in his eyes.

She felt off-balance, as if awakening from a dream. Her time with Hawk had been so right, so very right – his sudden appearance, the secret cave, the wall paintings. His tenderness, the warm nearness. For that single hour or two, he had become part of her and she of him there in that ancient place, their side-by-side reflections rippling in the water.

Not a physical part, she reminded herself. That moment was yet to come. And she'd welcome it, gladly. She would have welcomed it then, in the hill's womb, had Hawk not pulled away before they both lost themselves.

She closed the door behind her, smiling into the shadows of home.

Hawk lay in bed that evening, restless, wondering why he had shared that cave with Cassie when he hadn't even shown his mother, much less Rebecca. It was his personal place, his secret, something that he felt connected to. Yet he had invited her, brought her, wanted her there. And it had felt right, not an intrusion. Like a joining. She had felt it, too. He was sure of it.

How was that possible? Two different souls walking separate paths unexpectedly meet and find not a stranger, but someone known and loved. Maybe the myths were true; maybe souls could meet in lives before this one, and so recognize each other when they met again.

His chest constricted, as if he were going to weep. Hell, what was going on? He wasn't the wimpy sort. Hadn't cried since… well, a lifetime ago. Was he experiencing a grief he hadn't known was still there, an unabated loneliness that Cassie had somehow released? Whatever it was, it was dangerous. He shouldn't let himself be ruled by emotion; it wasn't fair to himself or Cassie. Or Rebecca.

He wasn't thinking clearly, that was it. Maybe a good night's sleep would help clear his head.

Who the hell are you kidding?

He laughed. He had to. Jesus, he was an idiot.

Blown to Dust

Billy waited in the gloom of his bedroom, alert for the grumble of Guy's truck. The house always seemed to echo when his dad wasn't around, and ordinary sounds shouted at him – his bare feet patting against the linoleum floor, the closet door squeaking, the springs shrieking when he sat on the bed. His breathing seemed too big for the room and he could hear his heart beating, *thump-whoosh, thump-whoosh,* like a television documentary on the human body.

He walked to the window and looked up at the sky shining with a gazillion stars. His father had come home earlier and paced antsy around the house for maybe fifteen minutes, then left again. "Going to play some pool at the Knot," he had said. "Don't wait up." And off he went, tires screeching. Once again he probably wouldn't be home until after midnight, when the saloon closed. And once again he'd probably stagger in, slamming doors and bumping into walls, tetchy and maybe mean. Or he'd be teary-eyed and slouch in a chair like a tired old man.

I wish I could live with Miss Cassie in her house.

He sighed and sank to the floor, wishing and feeling guilty for wishing.

He especially liked the cupola bedroom at the very top of her old house. It had windows all around, almost like a lighthouse. Sometimes he imagined lying there in that little bed at night with the stars surrounding him and the wind whispering and moaning in the stone fireplace downstairs like a kind of musical instrument. A sax, maybe, or a cello, even a trumpet if it was stormy outside. Cassie called the sound Firewind.

She made him feel safe and welcomed and special. His mom had been like that, too. Life had been different when she was alive. Their house was a cheerful place then, with laughter in it, and smelled like honeysuckle. His dad had smiled a lot and sometimes sang real loud, air-strumming like a country star, *Honey you're my girl, don't fergit it, blue-eyed sugar babe.*

Now the house was bleak and smelled like rotting tires, and his dad didn't sing or talk much about anything. Sometimes Billy felt invisible.

Scrounging under the bed, he pulled out his shoebox and lifted the lid. There was his ledger and under it his bankbook. He didn't have to read the pages to know what was written inside each. He knew to the last cent. A few loose dollar bills scattered like leaves on the bottom. He brushed them to the side and ran a finger over the college catalogues lying underneath, wanting more than anything to share them with his dad but knowing he couldn't. He picked up the top one, replaced the lid, and pushed the box under the bed. Punching the lumps out of his pillow, he propped it on the headboard and sat against it, holding the catalogue close as if the promise of those pages could really come true.

He fell asleep, the catalogue slipping into his lap, his hands clasped around it.

The front door banged open, slapping against the wall.

"Goddamn!"

Billy jerked awake as Guy cursed amid the clatter, crash, and thumps of furniture being knocked about. Glass shattered, the sounds bright and stabbing. "Crap!" Guy roared. "I live in crap!"

Billy hurried under the covers, the catalogue pressed to his chest. He lay on his side with his back to the door, pretending to be asleep as Guy's clumsy passage down the hall aimed for the bedroom door. It jerked open, light slicing into the room. Billy closed his eyes and forced himself to breathe slow and natural. His father's footsteps came close, deliberate and quiet, like he was walking careful on his toes. After a long silence the springs squawked and the mattress gave as Guy sat on the edge of the bed.

"Son?"

His father said nothing more but just sat there, the sloping mattress feeling strange under Billy's legs. Then Guy touched his hair lightly, like the wind blowing against it, and leaned over and kissed him on the top of his head. The stench of too many beers and cigarettes crawled into Billy's nose and coated his tongue, making him want to gag.

Guy's hand brushed against the catalogue. "What you got there? A girlie mag?" He laughed and tried to pull it from Billy's fingers. "I ain't playing no tug of war, now give it here."

Billy rolled onto his back as Guy yanked the catalogue away and stared down at it, his grin stuck on his face. "This ain't no *Playboy*." Guy flung it on the bed as the grin melted away. "You ain't goin' to no college, so get that notion out of your head. You hear me?"

Billy nodded and pulled the blanket up to his chin.

"All right then. We're done talkin'."

Billy flung his arm over his face, willing himself not to cry.

Guy sat at the table, smoking a cigarette and looking out the window. He missed seeing the crazy honeysuckle vines that had crawled over that window and just about everything else before Billy chopped them all down. One more evidence of Sarah blown to dust. Now the only things he had were memories.

And Billy. He still had Billy.

There was so much of Sarah shining in their boy that sometimes he was afraid to look at him. She would suddenly appear in his eyes and wide smile, or in the way he shrugged his shoulders or turned his head or spoke. Downright creepy at times. Like Sarah was there, watching him. Seeing how lonely he was, how much he missed her and couldn't do a damn thing about it. Seeing what an idiot fool he was making of himself over another woman who wasn't nothing like her. Seeing how things were different between him and Billy.

Guy stabbed his cigarette in the ashtray. Something inside that boy had withdrawn into a secret place Guy didn't understand and couldn't touch. His own son was a turning into a stranger. Christ, he couldn't even talk to Billy anymore. Seemed like everything he said came out all wrong.

Guy shoved the ashtray across the table and smacked it against the wall. It was Cassie's fault. She had turned Billy's head, babbling about college when it wasn't any of her damned business. Keeping him over at the house and barn, where he was playing around with that shitty car all hours of the day and night.

He propped his elbows on the table, laying his head into the cup of his hands, and realized after a moment that he was looking down at the Formica table top, the pattern wandering every which way among blackened smudges where years of cigarette ashes had burned through. Jesus, how many were there? Why hadn't he noticed them before? What sort of father was he, that he didn't pay attention to burned spots on the table?

"Forget it," he mumbled, and walked toward the bedroom, lurching into the door frame. He tugged off his boots and sat on the tangle of unmade sheets and stared unseeing at the walls, welcoming the rush of sleep. It pulled at him, drawing him down until he lay backward and closed his eyes and sank into a pool of nothingness.

Sometime during the night he pulled Cassie's nightgown from under his pillow and wrapped himself around it.

At Odds with the World

The December morning dawned with the north winds. Frost covered the ground, sparkling in the sunlight as if a carpet of crystals had fallen to the earth. Cassie threw a shawl over her flannel gown and ran outside in her slippers, remembering her days as a child: Mimi calling from the porch telling her to keep warm, a fairytale wonderland destined to melt away before the morning passed, the satisfying crunch underfoot followed by a cup of hot chocolate. She stopped in the middle of the meadow and spun around with arms outstretched, the shawl rippling behind her, and sang the words Mimi had taught her:

Ice queen, ice queen, in a frosty cloak and crown,
Diamond shoes and silver hair and melting gown,
Where is your cold castle, your carriage and king?
Where your misty breath, your heart, the songs you sing?

She gazed at the glistening plateaus and hills, and at the frost-spangled house, and for a moment was a child again. In that second of time it was the Christmas season, and soon she would help Mimi decorate the porch and tree. Mother was there, too, watching from the parlor window, the reflection faint and crimped in the stippled glass.

Caught by the memory, Cassie impulsively raised her arm and waved as she had done so long ago. She paused, startled. Someone was there, waving back. A fleeting moment, glimpsed through the window before vanishing – a flash of color and movement, a lingering smile, a woman's face luminous as old pearls.

It's a trick of sunlight, Cassie told herself. *A simple reflection.*

But her heart knew otherwise.

She had the oddest sensation that another family lived within, walking along the halls or sitting at the breakfast table or warming themselves by the fire. Yet the windows once again looked as they always looked, reflecting what they normally reflected. Cassie smiled. She wasn't frightened, as she had been with the shadow-man in the wide-brimmed hat, but suddenly and wholly happy, as though she had been greeted by a long-lost friend.

She gazed at the house for a while, lingering over the high-pitched roof, the jutting angles, the mottled stone walls. The view seemed precious and transitory, as if she were gazing at a mirage, a reflection of a time past glimmering in the meadow frost. A shiver darted up her spine – whether from the cold or from the sight, she didn't question – and she knew she loved this place.

A party! A New Year's party to celebrate the dawn of a new era! She was giddy with the idea. Strings of lights all along the front, with a wreath on the door. A crackling fire in the olden house, and beside it a Christmas tree decorated the old-fashioned way with popcorn chains and peppermint sticks and sprigs of berries. A smorgasbord of food, with hot buttered rum and champagne and caramelized pecans gathered from her trees. She'd invite the Grumms – hopefully Justin could come, even if confined to a wheelchair – Pete, Nan, and Tatty. She'd put Tatty's woven nest in the tree, too, where everyone could see it. Maybe she'd invite Pete's sister Darla, and Ed, the scrawny fellow she liked. And of course Billy, which meant she should include his dad, even though something about Guy, something undefined, made her uneasy.

And Hawk? Not if he came with his clinging female appendage! "Arrogant pissy-faced diva," Cassie groused, then cringed when she heard her own words. The green monster had bitten her, and she was looking at Rebecca with envious eyes.

Hawk had disappeared after that lovely afternoon in the grotto last week. Vanished, presto! No telephone call, no unannounced visit, no note, no clever sketch like he had done with *Casserella.* As if their meeting had never taken lace, the cave a dream, the kisses a fantasy. Maybe Hawk didn't know how to tell her that he wasn't as interested in her as she was in him, and so found it easier to say nothing. *Well, that's the way the world turns. Enough already. Enough mooning, enough wishing, enough being pulled this way and that.* She would treasure those few hours they had shared, accept his friendship for what it was, and get on with life.

Hawk was a grown man and free to choose whomever he wanted, but it bothered her. She was so drawn to this man every minuscule fiber inside her yearned to merge with his. When had she last felt this strongly for anyone?

Not since Thomas.

A brisk wind tugged at Cassie's shawl and she absently pulled it close, remembering the years after Thomas died and her few disastrous efforts at dating again. She had felt like the weary hermit pictured on a tarot card, forever carrying a torch and searching for an honorable man yet doomed never to find him.

Maybe I was more like the card of the blindfolded fellow hanging upside down by one leg, sightless and at odds with the world.

A blaze of color interrupted her thoughts, a blur of red against startling white. Her roses, hoary with frost! She hurried across the meadow and knelt beside the potted bush, the ice cold and shattering under her knees.

Dry, crisped leaves, curling at the tips. Blossom remnants hanging limp.

Cassie gripped the clay pot and hauled it to the porch, the weight pulling on her shoulders. Murmuring, "Are you okay? Please be okay," she set it on the floorboards with a heavy thud, pushed it through the door into the parlor, and positioned it by the window to be warmed in sunlight. She brushed the frost away and plucked the dead leaves and wilted petals, rose debris dusting the floor. "Please, please, please be okay."

She sat amid the strewn foliage when her task was done, her relief profound. Although newly-shorn and ice-shocked, the bush was alive. Decidedly, beautifully, alive. Blossoms should bloom once again in spring.

It was amazing how well the roses had thrived throughout the years, as though the ashes of Thomas and their almost-child, long-buried deep within, had infused the roots with their spirit blood. Cassie fingered a stem, half-believing that she could feel a pulse throbbing through the skin of her touch. "Thomas," she sighed, and leaned against the drape, the velvet soft and warm and reeking of must and decay.

Her eyes wandered the room: the scuffed pine floor, the warped walls, the horsehair sofa and overstuffed chair, the cockeyed floor lamp, the corner fireplace with smoke-blackened brick. The mantle clock creaked and bonged the half-hour. Eight-thirty. Yet here she sat in her nightgown and slippers, as if waiting for someone to bring her a cup of coffee.

Dust motes spun in a column of light. As Cassie watched them her imagination took hold – it must have been her imagination, for she had no other explanation for what followed. The minute specks joined into a whirling cloud, from which the figure of a man appeared. Transparent, made of spinning dust motes, he sat on the sofa, at ease among the surroundings. His lips curled into a smile and formed the word *Cassie*, and again, *Cassie*. He leaned toward her, elbows on his knees, a question written across his handsome face.

Thomas.

She opened her mouth to speak, but he vanished under the force of her breath as if he had been made of dandelion fluff.

She fought the urge to weep. Although no words had been spoken, although his voice had been silent and his image of her own imagining, she understood the message.

"I've been looking for your reflection in others, haven't I?" She whispered, eyes burning with unshed tears as if Thomas were there, listening. "I couldn't see any other man for who or what he truly was, because it was you I wanted. It was you, my darling. And you were gone."

The screen door rattled, perhaps in response. She rose and walked onto the porch while the breeze tossed her hair, caressing her cheeks with cool fingers. She sank onto the top step, her gaze drifting to a rose petal on the frosty ground, and finally wept. Wept with her mouth wide open. The sobs were guttural, rasping, primal. She heard them as if from a distance, as if they were the howls of the wolf, the groaning of the windmill, the thrashing of the old oak. With every breath, she opened her heart to the memories hidden there. With every breath, she honored the love she had shared and the sorrow it brought. With every breath, the ghosts of the past lifted from her soul and drifted upward like smoke, like mist. They rose in a lazy fashion, spiraling around her body in a blessing before the wind carried them away.

All The Tomorrows

"LOOKS GREAT, DON'T YOU THINK, MISS CASSIE?"

She and Billy leaned against the old oak and gazed at their handiwork. Dusk had fallen and the festive house lit up the meadow like a second moon. Strings of Christmas lights framed the windows and hugged the porch pillars and dangled from the eaves, while electric candles flickered on each windowsill. Cassie thought it iridescent and magical, as if at any time Santa would hop out of the chimney and prance over the roof, laughing his big *ho-ho-ho*.

It hadn't been a simple task. The breakers kept popping until Billy found a dusty relic of a generator in the corner of his dad's shop and jerry-rigged it all. He grinned, cheeks flushed in the chill evening air. "If the generator conks out, just kick it good." He gave a cocky salute and trotted backward. "I gotta go. Don't know when I can come next, what with Christmas and all."

"Can you stay a few minutes? I have something for you under the tree."

Billy stopped short, a delighted smile spreading across his freckled face. "Sure!" He followed her up the steps. "I like the room it's in, with the big stone fireplace and beams and everything. So many cool things in there, like the twisty grapevine chair. I'm glad you decided not to throw it away, even if it was once all broke up." A wreath hung on a crossbeam of the screen door, with bells that tinkled as he opened it and stepped inside. "Sure smells good in here. You making cookies?"

"Roasting pecans."

They walked down the hall, footsteps pattering over the wooden floor and then upon flagstone. Billy led the way, talking over his shoulder. "I never heard of nobody baking pecans. What do you do, just stick them in the oven? Don't they get all dried out?"

"I bake them with oil and spices then sprinkle them with brown sugar. And no, they don't dry out unless I forget to take them out of the oven. Then it's a lost cause."

"I bet they're tasty."

"I'll give you some to take home."

He paused by the entrance to the large, stone-walled room. "The tree sure is pretty."

A gaily-wrapped package with a glittery silver bow waited under it, surrounded by jars of pottery and colored glass stuffed with sugared pecans and festooned with ribbons. Gifts lovingly made, and patiently, too. Cassie had hauled buckets of nuts from the yard and spent hours cracking and baking them. Her fingers were stained a putrid yellow-brown, as though she had dipped them in shoe polish.

Billy sat on the floor beside the tree. "Sure are a lot of jars here, Miss Cassie. These the pecans?"

She sat next to him. "Pick the one you like best."

"Dad didn't have time to buy a tree so I found a pine growing way out where nobody would miss it. It's not decorated fancy but smells good." He lifted a glazed pot in gold and purple, murmured "This is real nice," and glanced at her shyly. "I have a present for you, too. It's a song. I taped it so you could hold onto it like a real present. I was going to surprise you later at the party, but here I went and spilled the beans."

"I'm glad you did. Now I have something special to look forward to."

He started to rise, but plopped down again when Cassie gestured for him to stay. She reached for the package with the silver bow and put it in his lap. "Merry Christmas."

"*Another* present?"

"You want me to take it back?" Cassie teased, pretending to grab it.

"It's almost too fancy to open. Ought to keep it under the tree, like an ornament."

"You can wait and put it under your own tree for Christmas morning."

"It's nicer here, with you." He unwrapped it as if fearing a single unwarranted rip or wrinkle. "Hey, radical! Look at this!" he cried, as if Cassie hadn't known. "*The Encyclopedia of American Cars!*" He flipped happily through the pages, exclaiming over this or that until an envelope slipped from where it had been tucked inside. "What's this, a card?" He slit it open, drew out a slip of paper, and gasped. "Wow! Oh, wow!"

"Something for your college fund."

He gawked at the bank receipt, turning it over and back again as if to reassure himself that it was real. "I never got so much money all at once, not ever. I'll pay you back someday, I promise."

"No need, Billy. But there is one thing I'd like very much."

"I'll do it, whatever it is."

"Promise you'll write me when I'm gone."

"You're leaving?" His voice cracked.

"But you know that. You know I'm here for just a year."

He grew unnaturally still, then murmured, "I guess I kind of forgot." He threw his arms around her, saying, "I love you almost as much as my mom." Grabbing the book and jar, he leaped up and flung open the side door.

Cassie blinked and he was gone. At first her body wouldn't follow her startled commands. She sat where she was before her limbs moved her up and out the door. She paused under the arbor, then hurried along the side of the house and turned the corner in time to see Billy pedaling his bicycle across the creek bridge. "Billy!" she called as he rode from the glittering lights into the approaching night.

Cassie had "kind of forgotten," too.

The realization shocked her, as if the news of her looming departure came unbidden, delivered by a stranger knocking at her door. In a matter of months she would say goodbye to Billy. Goodbye to Berta and Justin Grumm, goodbye to Tatty and Nan and Pete. Goodbye to the ramshackle house which held so many memories and secrets and also held her heart.

Goodbye to Hawk, and to the love that lived only in her dreams.

It was just that, she knew – a fantasy of her own making. His attachment to Rebecca Stanch couldn't be denied nor altered. It would be silly to try. Nor would she grovel for his attention like a soppy woman in an afternoon soap opera populated with hysterical, sex-addled half-wits.

Yet, in spite of it all, she was glad to have met him, glad to know she was ready to love a man for who he was with a full heart, not as a shadow copy of what had been lost. It was a painful awakening but embraced nonetheless.

All my tomorrows will be different from all my yesterdays.

But what would she do with the rest of her life? Where would she go? Once she sold this land she would have enough to buy a home in Italy or France or Hawaii or wherever sounded exotic and beautiful, the rooms stuffed with exquisite furnishings, the closets with designer clothes.

Lord help me, I could turn into Mother – wandering the globe in Prada, the perfect country and home and lover always somewhere else.

Or I could open another southwestern boutique, maybe in Fredericksburg. Wouldn't it be great if I could offer Tatty's pottery and weavings with the Spider Weave Woman signature?

Enough! Cassie thought, excitement building. There was too much to do in the present to worry about the future. She vowed to open the land for bids at the dawn of the new year and get a feel for offers. Until then she'd enjoy planning her party and worry about tomorrow... tomorrow.

A Norther swept down from the panhandle on Christmas Eve, blustery and cold. The wind moaned through the hollows of the stone chimney, melancholy as a wheezing pipe organ. Cassie burrowed under the quilt and pulled it over her head to smother the sound. The screen door rattled and banged, pecans ripped from the trees and clattered over the tin carport roof, and the windmill shrieked with the plaintive cry of a gigantic wounded bird.

She couldn't sleep. Finally she gave up the effort and rose on her elbows to look out the window. Clouds flew past the moon like clumps of gray ghosts. The stark silhouette of trees swayed in their passing, as if yearning to disentangle from the earth and rise to join the flight. Their shadows thrashed along the ground and slapped against the windowpanes.

A movement sighing behind her, a breath touching the bare nape of her neck. Cassie gasped and whirled around. Her room was empty, the open doorway gaping into the darkened hall. She waited a moment, then got out of bed and shut the door.

This old house is too big for one person.

All the empty space, the empty rooms, the odd corners, the steps and twists and turns needed people in them. She felt her feet echo in their absence, her presence resonate from wall to wall. And so she was prone to imagining, or prone to sensing memories captured there. She fluffed the feather pillow and sat up in bed, wondering what was real and what imagined. So many questions were yet to be answered. She would leave this house knowing little more about the people who once lived here than she had when first stepping through the front door.

Since sleep was out of the question, Cassie turned on the bedside lamp and reached for Mimi's letters in the keepsake chest on top of the dresser. Let the winds kick up a fuss and the fireplace moan and the house creak and stir. She'd lose herself in Mimi's words, picturing her grandmother as a young woman writing to her husband far away at war.

She put the writing chest in her lap and chose two letters at random:

> *April 12, 1940*
> *My darling Johann,*
> *Lillian was a curse today. I swear, the older she grows, beauty shines on her like she was poured out of gold. And does*

she know it! Prances around with her nose in the air acting like she's a princess and I'm a servant put here to do her bidding. Sometimes I want to grab her by the hair and dump her in the creek mud. Then she does something sweet like this morning, when she surprised me with apple pancakes, and my mad intentions vanish.

What are we to do with her? I can see the blood of her grandmother Emilie inside her, and she doesn't know it. It worries me sometimes, the power of her feelings so strong they can overwhelm her if she isn't watchful. She must be watchful. But how can I tell her what I must about her heritage? She isn't ready to hear it yet. It will likely be many years before she will be ready to hear the truth.

Cassie put the letter aside, wishing she could conjure Mimi from her resting place in the little cemetery. What truth? Why watchful? "Damn it, Mimi!" Cassie muttered. "Why couldn't you tell me? Didn't you trust me? Did you think I'd go all to pieces if I knew?"

She sighed and reached for the second letter.

November 12, 1941

My dearest Johann,

The strangest thing happened this morning. The fog was up and rising from the creek so thick I could barely see the trees on the other side. Then a shape appeared, growing more plain as it drew closer, and I about fainted with happiness because I thought it was you stepping over the bridge, home at last. Then the fog swirled and you were gone.

I hear you calling me across the miles. Sweetkins, you say. Sweetkins. I imagine you lying beside me, your head on the empty pillow, your body filling out the quilt, your presence so strong I could swear you left but a moment ago and would soon return.

I feel you are here with me. As if when I turn around I'll see you standing in the doorway. Last night I thought I heard your voice outside the bedroom window. You sounded so sad, my darling, so terribly sad and alone and far away. I ran to the window but of course you weren't there. I even ran outside, but heard only the wind.

Please write. Write to me. I wait for your letters that never come.

The chest toppled from its perch on Cassie's lap and fell to the floor, spilling its contents every which way. She got out of bed and knelt to gather them up. One of the envelopes had skittered partly under the dresser. It was different from the rest, clean and unrumpled with no return address and no stamp, as though it had never traveled anywhere outside its wooden confines. A single name was written in front, with the loopy penmanship Cassie would have recognized anywhere. It read simply, *Daddy.* Inside was a folded sheet of lined paper, torn at the left as if ripped from a notebook. There was no date. *Dear Daddy,* it began.

Cassie sat on the floor with her back against the bed, momentarily unable to continue. She glanced at the blue stone ring her own father had given her on the day he had disappeared long ago, hanging by its ribbon on the picture frame of Lillian and Mimi and the grandfather she had never known, and for a fleeting second was pierced by a profound sense of loss. Taking a deep breath, she began again:

Dear Daddy,

Why did you leave Mama and me? They're bringing you home nailed up in a wooden box with all your stuff and will bury you under dirt out in the woods with the other dead people. I got so mad I burned up all your letters to Mama and me, every single one. Mama cried and cried and now is making me write you and apologize, which is stupid because you won't ever read it. Mama says you will be looking over my shoulder when I write this and will know. That's spooky. I look around and don't see you there at all, but sometimes I think I feel you breathing on my hair so maybe it's true. Are you a ghost, Daddy? I don't want to think of you as a ghost drifting invisible around the house. I would rather think of you as a bird flying high above everything and not lying dead under mounds of stinking dirt.

Mama never smiles or sings anymore, she is so sad. I swear I will never, ever marry unless I know he will stay with me forever, even when I am old and ugly with wrinkles.

Your loving daughter,
Lillian

Cassie refolded the letter, slipped it inside the envelope, and put it in the chest. She lowered the lid gently, waiting for the sound of its closing before withdrawing her hand. A terrible melancholy pressed down on her limbs until she felt heavy with it, as though her body had swollen and grown too large for the bed.

ဢတ

"Merry Christmas, Mother." Cassie held the phone with one hand and her coffee with the other, sipping between words.

"Same to you, *mien* little *freulein*."

"Oh, Lordy. Don't tell me you're in Germany now?"

A high giggle, girlish and off-key. "Germany is too pedestrian for the holidays. I'm in Austria, skiing in the mountains. Well, *he's* skiing. *I'm* sipping some lovely bourbon-laced coffee and chatting to a perfectly charming man who has the good sense to stay inside instead of tramp around in cold mush like a barbarian." Lillian then must have turned her head aside, for her next words were distant: "What's your name, dear...? Arnold? How can such an ordinary name belong to such a handsome face?"

Cassie groaned. "Stop it, Mother. You sound ridiculous."

"And you sound like a prude. You've been living in the sticks too long, that's what it is. How you can stand it beats me."

"A few more months, that's all. I'm thinking of putting it on the market for bids soon."

"I told you to do that ages ago," Lillian snapped. "But you refused to listen."

"I didn't call to argue, Mother. I just wanted to wish you a Merry Christmas." She wanted to say more but kept the words to herself: *I love and miss you.*

"That's nice. Merry Christmas to you, too." A male voice murmured in the background. Lillian laughed brightly and said, "I have to go now. Arnold wants to show me the spectacular view from his room."

"You're asking for trouble, you know."

"Who, me? Don't be silly. Bye-bye now."

The line disconnected and hummed in Cassie's ear. She hung up and sat quietly in the dawning light as Christmas morning awakened.

New Year's Eve came softly, announced by a slow settling of the sun into clouds stacked like great, billowy pillows. The sky blushed scarlet and purple, throwing a quilt of color across the land before slipping into a bed of stars. Cassie sat on the porch swing, a shawl draped around her shoulders. The frosty Norther had been followed by a warmer western front, and the two extremes were now playing a game of tag. Luckily tonight the western winds had the upper hand.

She was taking a moment to relax before dressing for the evening. Everything was ready; the house festive, a buffet prepared, drinks and champagne nestled in ice, confetti at hand, and quirky hats for those daring or tipsy enough to wear them. Pete's oil drum grill stood beside the arbor. He had driven up one afternoon, placed it there, and announced that he wanted to "help with this here shindig." Sitting next to it was an ice chest filled with chicken and spare ribs – that, too, from Pete. Cassie chuckled, remembering his bewhiskered grin and the cigar trailing ashes in his wake as he trundled to and fro, chatting a blue streak along the way. "Lookin' forward to it all," he beamed. "Ain't been no New Year's party around here in a long time."

A buck stepped from behind a cypress across the meadow, antlers held high and proud. Cassie watched, entranced, as it lowered its magnificent head and drank from the stream. It looked at her before gracefully loping away, the hooves tap-dancing along the bank and into the woods.

Excitement shot through her, as if the deer had been a magical creature, as if it had offered a blessing.

It's going to be a great evening, she thought, and hurried inside.

She was halfway through the parlor before she noticed Tatty's nest of twigs beside the clock on the mantle rather than on the Christmas tree as she had planned. "Getting forgetful," she murmured, and rushed to fetch it. The nest would be perfect in the spruce, the dried berries woven among the twigs a festive red, the intertwining crystals glittering like bits of ice.

Cassie almost had the nest in hand when she realized the clock sat cockeyed, knocked off of the penny Mimi had put there long ago to prop a broken foot. Careful not to damage the intricate carvings, Cassie tilted it to the side, intending to slide the penny back in place. The clock was heavier than expected and toppled over with a clatter, the pendulum swinging and bonging against the glass.

"Careful, careful!" she whispered to herself, her heart racing with the frantic *tick-tick-whang* of the clock. Mimi had loved this antiquated, eccentric wreck, and so, Cassie realized, did she. Slowly, she righted it and began to inspect every inch, hoping nothing had chipped.

All was as it should be – almost.

Old German lettering was scrawled along the back, the ink still legible.

She had never before looked at the back of the clock. In fact, she rarely looked closely at the front. It was simply an old part of the house she had taken for granted, something that had always been there, something that never changed. Like Mimi's blue porcelain dishes, or the pipes that gurgled in the walls.

She leaned in close, trying to decipher the writing. Extravagant penmanship, composed at an angle so it read from the bottom left to the top right:

Liebe heute und für immer,

Underneath was the name, *Viktor.*

"Viktor!" Cassie yelped. Rosine's father, the one who died at sea during their journey to Texas! She rushed into the bedroom, opened the family Bible, and found the letter. Yes, there it was! Addressed to Viktor in Germany, signed by his brother Gustav. And there, too, at the bottom, directly above Gustav's signature, a word she remembered from Berta's translation:

Liebe

"Love! It means love!" Cassie laughed aloud and whirled around the room. She'd ask Berta to translate the entire inscription later, but for now it was enough.

The clock carried a message of love from her ancestors. What a wonderful way to welcome the New Year!

༄༅

Billy put aside the guitar for a while, resting between Christmas carols. He had a blast playing them with Ed. Ed was good with the banjo, and the two of them strolled around the place like troubadours in the middle ages. Ed had a huge grin on his skinny face, especially when Darla was around. It was neat to see how Ed and Pete's sister got all mushy, what with Darla's watermelon bosoms and wildcat hair and Ed's puny bald self. He got all puffy in the chest and strutted around like a rooster in the middle of a hen coop, and Darla batted her eyes like she was about to faint with how handsome he was. Love sure was funny.

Mr. Grumm was there, too, sitting in a wheelchair with Mrs. Grumm beside him. The nurse Ima Twerpe stood nearby in a starched uniform with dogs in party hats painted all over it, and clunky white shoes big as footballs. A tiny champagne bottle with pink rhinestone bubbles was pinned to her nametag. Justin pointed to her, moved his lips as if testing how they functioned, and finally managed to say, "My… warden."

Mrs. Grumm clicked with her tongue, *tsk-tsk*, and said, "Stop acting like a cranky old frog." But she sounded happy like she was teasing him, so Billy knew she wasn't really mad.

Billy knelt beside Justin. "You having a good time?"

"Kumquat." He patted Berta's hand. "So beautiful my Schnapps."

"A toast to our lovely hostess!" Pete hopped up on a chair and hopped down again when it wobbled and fell over. "Look what I done here!" he said as Nan glided to him. She always glided. Billy never knew anybody who could look like they sort of floated along instead of walk like normal people, but Nan did. Pete righted the chair and lifted Nan up and put her on it instead. The two of them lifted their glasses. "To Cassie!" they said together. "To Cassie!" everybody hollered and smiled and clapped.

Cassie glowed like a lamp had been switched on inside her. *She's so pretty,* Billy thought, and for some reason felt really proud. She wore a shiny green dress that rippled when she walked, and dangly gold earrings and a sparkly something in her hair. *Hawk thinks she's pretty, too.* Billy could tell by the way he circled the room, looking at her while pretending he wasn't. Wherever Hawk went, Rebecca followed like she was attached by an invisible leash. She was attractive, too, but in a way different than Cassie, with sharp angles and bones and a haughty tilt to the head that made him feel as though he should bow and call her *Madam.*

"Play something saucy, Billy. Let's welcome the new year with a bit of hoo-ha." Tatty smiled at him from under an amazing hat she must have made herself, with sprigs of juniper and berries and mistletoe and a little pottery redbird nesting on top of it all. She looked like an illustration out of a fairytale book.

"Like what, Tatty?"

"You'll think of something." She nodded, the redbird flopping, and turned to sit on the couch. She almost missed it and caught herself on the way down. "Too much of that delicious punch," she said, and laughed.

"Can I get you another?"

"Better not. I'll wait `til Cassandra pops the champagne."

Billy thought about his gift for Cassie tucked inside his backpack, a tape of the song he had written. The wrapping paper was bought special and the ribbon too, although he was all thumbs when it came to making bows. His heart flip-flopped when he thought about singing it for her in front of everyone right before midnight, about two hours from now. He knew it so well he could likely sing it backwards, but it wouldn't hurt to rehearse one more time.

He started to fetch the guitar when he glanced through the open door. Guy was leaning against the arbor outside, alone and pensive with a cigarette in his mouth. He looked real nice, all fancied up in his good cowboy boots and silver scorpion belt buckle and the blue shirt his mom always said went well with his red hair. "Hey, Dad," Billy called as he approached, and Guy's face lit up with a grin.

"Hi, son. You havin' fun?"

Billy nodded. "How about you?"

"Best part was hearin' you sing them carols."

Guy wasn't always expressive, but there were times Billy knew without a doubt that his father loved him. This was such a moment, and it gave Billy courage to grasp his hand and pull him toward the barn. "Dad," he said. "I want to show you the Studebaker."

Guy tagged along, half-listening to Billy's chatter. They opened the barn door and lit the kerosene lantern and there that car was, flickering in the light like a showroom model in need of a paint job. Guy looked wherever Billy pointed and followed wherever he went, too dazed to say anything. The Studebaker was reborn into something better than the original, yet with the same spirit and design. Billy's eyes were bright and happy as he closed the hood and spread out drawings on it. Impressive, detailed sketches that looked like they came right out of an engineer's head. Guy leaned close in the dim light and studied them hard, admiration and amazement and fear churning inside his stomach.

Billy's smarter than I ever was.

"You done good, son. Real good." The barn walls closed in on him, the yellow lamplight dug inside his eyeballs, and he wanted to get out of there.

Without another word he turned and hurried outside near the yawning doorway as Billy put things in order. He could see the house across the meadow, lit up and shining like a Christmas card. Pete was by the grill, looking like Santa in his butcher apron and beard, smoke encircling him as he cooked and joked with people standing around. He had a big laugh and it carried clear and strong. Others were laughing, too, and some were singing. The fast-plunking notes of Ed's banjo clipped the air and a harmonica joined in, and Guy could see people dancing through the windows and doorway. Not ballroom dancing, but a madcap *something*. There was the nurse wheeling Justin around in circles while he whooped and Berta clapped, and Tatty doing a jig, lifting her full skirt and kicking her heels like a gypsy in big boots and a crazy hat.

"Welcome!" Cassie's voice, so sweet and joyful in greeting that Guy wanted to rush over there and take the place of the two newcomers on the front porch. Why couldn't it be *him* she was greeting with open arms, *him* she was so happy to see?

"Let's close up, Dad."

The barn door was unwieldy, spitting out a couple of bats and shaking the walls as they shut it. Like as not one day the whole thing was going to fall down. The timber was old and dry and about to splinter into a mass of oversized toothpicks. "You be careful inside there," Guy said. "Watch your head."

Billy looked up at him with eyes so full of hope that Guy couldn't look back at him. He knew what Billy wanted him to say. He knew, but he couldn't say it.

He gazed instead at the happy people at the happy party and felt decidedly unhappy, like a lonely outsider peering through the windows of a stranger's house. "Think I'm going to the Knot, greet the New Year over a game of pool. You stay and enjoy yourself."

"But I wanted you to hear me sing for Cassie."

Billy's voice was so laden with disappointment Guy almost gave in. "You been rehearsing for weeks, so I heard it already."

"But not the whole thing, just bits and pieces."

Guy patted Billy roughly on the cheek. "You'll do fine," he said, and trotted to the truck, eager to escape.

Billy stood in the shadow of the barn and watched him drive away.

New Year's Eve

GUY DROVE WITH THE WINDOW OPEN, HOPING THE NIGHT AIR WOULD COOL THE burning in his head. The bright lights of Cassie's party faded behind him but the laughter still rang in his ears. Billy was still in his thoughts too, standing by the barn, slumped with sadness and disappointment. Guy couldn't get the picture out of his mind: laughter and lights and Billy alone in the dark, watching his father drive away.

The headlights swept over the cutoff to his house, and he made a quick turn onto the rutted road. Sickness curdled his stomach. He wasn't used to rum punch, but a sandwich at the Knot would take care of things, as would some beers and a few games of pool with his pals. Hell, he'd treat them all to a round or two and greet the New Year proper. All he needed was cash. Problem was, he didn't have enough on hand at the moment. But he knew where some extra cash was hidden – in that shoebox under Billy's bed.

It wouldn't hurt to borrow some. Billy would never know, just like he never knew when Guy had discovered the secret box some years ago and borrowed a couple of bucks then. What with his summer gig at Pete's grocery and odd jobs for Cassie, there should be eight, maybe nine hundred stashed away by now.

He left the motor idling as he shoved the front door open that always stuck and made his way through the darkened hall to Billy's room. The bed was a lump in the shadows, but Guy could see clear enough. He dropped to his knees and swept his hand underneath, pushing aside a pair of sneakers, and grasped the box. He pulled it into the moonlight, opened the lid, and dipped his hand into a handful of nothing.

Six dollars. That was all. Six lousy dollars. What happened to the rest?

Guy dumped the contents onto the braided rug. A notebook and slips of paper fell out, then college catalogues. He gaped at the pile strewn around him and picked up what looked like receipts. What the hell were these for?

Light pale as milk fell through the window. He held a receipt, then another and another, before leaping up and turning on the ceiling light. Glare flashed into the room, harsh and sudden; the papers that had fallen from the overturned box lay scattered on the floor like dead leaves. He knelt amid them, a slow rage building from the pit of his stomach.

Bank receipts. Monthly statements. For Mr. Bill Randall Wilkins, co-signed by Mrs. Cassandra Brighton.

The sound of his breathing filled the room and pressed against his eardrums. He looked down at his hands moving like they had a brain separate from his own as the fingers opened the notebook and traced the inked record of every penny earned, every penny taken, every penny Cassie had given Billy and put into the bank.

Seven thousand dollars. Seven. Thousand.

The steering wheel was cold against his palms and the chill wind hissed through the window as Guy raced along the pitted drive. He slammed the gas pedal to the floorboard and the truck fish-tailed onto the main road, spewing gravel like buckshot. The muscles in his arms hunched up and his cheek twitched and his eyes squinted as if he stared into sunlight.

He couldn't think right. He could only feel, and what he felt he couldn't define.

Fragments drifted through the fog of his thoughts: *Losing my boy... Cassie turned him against me... Like she can buy him, like he's for sale... Charity, that's what it is, god-awful charity like I'm a nobody or a nothing and can't provide for my own.*

He's MY son. Mine! Mine!

Got to put a stop to this.

He flipped open the glove compartment. The gun was still there, in case the wolf-thing decided to make another appearance.

No more Cassie. No more handouts. We stand on our own feet and walk our own path.

Damn her to hell.

Guy turned onto Spring Creek. A pain radiated from his jaw to his ear, and his grinding teeth screeched behind his eyes. The box, the lid haphazardly attached, slid to the edge of the passenger seat. He slapped it back in place.

Not much longer now.

The clock chiming the quarter hour before midnight was barely audible to the laughing, chattering crowd preparing to hear Billy sing. A joyous tumult bounced off the limestone walls and echoed around the spacious room as chairs were moved from here to there, facing the great stone fireplace. Billy waited on a stool beside the tree, flushed with expectation, holding his guitar as everyone jostled to find a seat.

Cassie smiled to herself, a quiet happiness warm inside her. These were her friends, people she cared about, people who had wound a way into her heart. She hurried from one to the other, making sure all were comfortable. Berta and Darla ended up on the couch with Ed squeezed between them, his bony arm stretched up to wrap protectively over Darla's shoulders, which were wider than his entire self. Justin dozed alongside as Nurse Ima, her eyes glazed and her mouth tilted in a lopsided grin, cried for the umpteenth time, "Cheers!" and tipped her glass. Pete claimed an oversized stuffed chair and pulled Nan into his ample lap while she pretended to scold him. "Careful he doesn't bite!" Tatty teased. She had long ago positioned herself on the floor, her colorful skirt spread outward like the petals of an exotic flower.

Cassie couldn't help it; her eyes sought Hawk. His back was to her, and although she couldn't see his face, the protective stance of his body reflected his concern as he helped Rebecca onto the only remaining chair, the patched-together grapevine, and stood sentry beside it. Rebecca gazed up at him, her long auburn hair falling back to reveal the pale slimness of her neck, and smiled.

Hawk didn't seem to notice. As if pulled by an invisible thread, he slowly turned his head and looked over his shoulder directly at Cassie. For a brief second, desire lay naked and exposed upon his face.

Before Cassie could think about it, before she could question whether her imagination had painted the picture her heart wanted to see, Pete got to hollering.

"Let's get this show going, Billy!" he roared as everyone whistled and clapped. "New Year's gonna be here before you know it!"

"Okay." Billy played a few cords as the hullabaloo quieted. "I wrote this special for Miss Cassie."

"Good for you, boy!" Pete cried. "Get her up there with you!"

"Cassie, Cassie!" Voices chanted as heads turned toward her, faces alight, the affection of her friends enfolding her as she walked among them. A tender happiness carried her in its arms. She couldn't feel the floor beneath her feet, as though she floated above it. She wanted to embrace each person she passed, to touch each smiling face, to say or do something to let them know how precious they were, how important and loved.

Billy rose from his stool and scooted it toward Cassie, motioning for her to sit. With the shy, wide grin so familiar and lovable to her, he began playing a jazzy, foot-stompin' mixture of crazy chords and interlocking melodies. He threw his head back, hair glinting copper in the flickering holiday lights, pond-water eyes sparkling as his fingers blurred over the strings. Then he began to sing, his voice sweet and bluesy, curling around the notes. He sang of pain soothed and dreams born, of the pleasures of simple things when shared, of goodness and hope. He sang of friendship, rare and treasured and true.

Cassie knew she would never forget this evening, Billy's song, her friends gathered in this glorious old room filled with memories of Mimi and of lives lived long before, the ghosts of times past lingering and listening. The lights from the tree, the fire burning, the stars peering through the window. Beautiful. Oh, beautiful!

By the time Guy arrived at Cassie's he had calmed down some. It was like Sara had squeezed into his head, whispering for him to be careful, to take things slow, to be in control. He parked and stared at nothing in particular, forcing his breath to come regular. He turned off the ignition, his fingers fumbling and stiff like they had been broken and glued back together funny. The engine grumbled and coughed as he stepped into the cold and leaned against the fender for a moment. A dark shape skulked near the woods, deliberate and stealthy. He eyed the far shadows for the wolf thing, silently daring it to reveal those yellow eyes.

Come on, he thought. *Tonight I won't run. Tonight I'll shoot.*

The seconds passed. Nothing happened. Maybe it had only been the wind tossing the trees, playing tricks. Or maybe the beast was wary of venturing into the light. Cassie's house was lit up bright as a carnival for the blind. It could probably be seen from the moon. He hurried between cars and pick-ups parked every which way in the meadow like they had been tossed there in a storm, and paused by the porch steps. His skin was clammy and his heart rose into his mouth and beat against his tongue. A part of him wanted to crash through the walls of the house, ripping stone and wood to shreds in his wake, and tear his boy away from Cassie and this cursed place. Another part whispered, *Wait. Listen.*

The notes of a guitar. Billy's voice, singing. Guy hesitated, then turned toward the sound. He ducked under the oak and moved alongside the house to the back. It was brighter inside than out from this vantage point, and so he figured if he stood back far enough he could look through the window and not be noticed. He'd see what was happening and then make his move.

He crept slow and careful in the shadows, and peered inside. Christ Almighty, everybody was staring at him! Right at him! Guy jerked backward, startled, before realizing it wasn't him they were looking at. It was Billy, sitting with his back to the window.

Guy waited for his heart to beat normal. The window reminded him of a television screen, with him watching unseen as the action unfolded within a square of light. Here were the faces of people he knew. He had lived among most of them for years, some for almost a lifetime. And there they all sat, entranced, eyes on Billy.

A fierce pride roared through Guy, terrible and wonderful. It filled his chest and rose up into his mouth and burned behind his eyes. *He's mine!* his soul cried. *My son! Mine! Mine!*

The boy's voice carried through the opened doorway. Guy hadn't paid much attention when Billy had practiced at home. Now he listened hard. This wasn't the boy he knew. This was someone else, someone who had grown in ways he hadn't noticed, someone who yearned for things Guy hadn't thought about much. Someone who was now singing about Cassie like she was some sort of perfect angel goddess dropped from the sky.

Where the hell was she? He stepped to the side, angling for a view. Cassie sat on a stool, gazing at Billy with an expression of… of… Sweet Jesus, there was no mistaking the pride and joy shining plain as day on her face.

Then everybody cheered and clapped and whistled. Billy stood and did a fancy bow, like he was in a grand concert hall for God's sake. "Encore! Encore!" they shouted. Cassie leaped up, arms outstretched, laughing.

When Billy moved into her embrace, love ablaze in every feature, the ground tilted under Guy's feet.

"Billy!"

The back door swung wide, letting in a gust of wind as Guy's voice shot through the commotion. He stepped into the room, hat shoved low on his forehead. Only his mouth was clearly visible to Cassie, a thin-lipped slash cut into his flesh.

"Get your things, boy. We're goin' home."

Billy's smile faltered. "Not yet, Dad. They want me to sing again."

"You sang enough."

"Oh, come on, Guy," Cassie interrupted, keeping her tone light and teasing. "Don't be such a grump. Sit with the rest of us and listen to Billy play. He's written this wonderful song and..."

Guy raised the palm of his hand, stopping her short.

"But why?" Billy's voice cracked. "I want to see the new year come on and everything."

"Can't be any harm in it," Hawk said. Others joined in, clamoring, "Grab a drink and set yerself down," and "I don't mind driving him home," and "It's on my way," and "Go if you got to, we'll take care of him."

"Keep your nose on your own face. This ain't nobody's business but mine."

In the abrupt silence that followed everyone and everything seemed rooted in place, as if poised for the camera to flash or the painter to sketch. A hand in mid-air here, a head tilted there, a mouth partially opened as if caught in the act of speaking.

"Oh, Dad." Billy flushed and seemed to shrink inside his clothes, his shoes and hands too big for the rest of him.

"Why not let him stay here with me until morning?" Cassie persisted. "I promise not to keep him up past midnight."

Guy's mouth worked as if words were piling up behind his teeth. He bit them back and snatched the guitar case leaning against the wall. "Take it!" he hissed, and shoved it into Billy's chest.

Cassie reached for Billy without thinking. Guy yanked him away from her touch, pulling him past shocked eyes and gaping mouths toward the door.

Billy put the guitar into the case, fumbling with the clasps. "Wait! I need my backpack."

"Christ! Be quick about it."

Billy turned into the room, his movements uncertain.

"Here." Cassie lifted his backpack from the floor where Billy had tossed it earlier and handed it to him, clasping his hands briefly with her own. He didn't speak. The expression on his face said it all. "It's okay," Cassie murmured. "I'll see you soon."

Guy grabbed him by the shoulder and pushed him out the door. They disappeared into the night as Cassie hurried after, not knowing what to say or do. Billy pleaded with his father, voice ragged and high-pitched. Cassie couldn't see him clearly; Guy was between them, hat bobbing, elbows bent, the muscles in his neck coiling.

"Please, Dad."

"Shut up!" Guy's arm lashed out and whacked Billy on the back.

A hidden part of Cassie split open like an earthen dam, spewing words. "What the hell are you doing, Guy? Think! Stop and think! Why can't he stay? Why not?" Guy grunted and shoved Billy around the corner of the house; the boy tripped, almost losing his footing as he barreled into the meadow. Cassie ran after them, yelling as Guy marched through the festive holiday-lit brightness toward his pickup. "Why are you being such a jackass? Billy's done nothing wrong and you're treating him like dirt!"

The front door opened, and a crowd spilled onto the porch as others gathered behind Cassie. They moved in silence as if words had been shocked out of them. The clock chimed from the opened door, resonating as if from a deep well, *Bong... Bong... Bong....*

Billy's tears glimmered like pearls of ice. "I'm sorry, Miss Cassie," he called.

"It's not your fault, Billy. None of it."

"I'm still sorry."

Bong... Bong... The seconds gathering, collecting, the year's end fast approaching.

"Come by tomorrow. I'll bake peanut butter cookies. Okay?"

"Sure. Okay. "

"I can't wait to hear your song again."

Bong...

A flicker of a smile tugged at Billy's lips, but before he could respond Guy yanked the truck door open, slamming it against the metal in a sickening crunch. "Get in!" he barked.

Billy glanced once more at Cassie then climbed into the truck. He sat, head lowered and turned away from the window.

Guy pulled a shoebox out of the cab and brandished it in the air. "Won't be no more singin'!" he shouted. "No more cookies and no more Studebaker and no more of you, Miz Brighton." He moved toward her in hard-hipped strides, the force of his anger radiating outward and pushing the air aside like stagnant water.

"Here's what I think of your goddamned charity!" He threw the box above Cassie's head. It flew high into the air, tumbling end over end. The lid slipped away and the wind snatched papers from inside, whirling and spinning them in the air like oddly shaped snow.

"Stay away from my boy!" Guy snarled. "He ain't comin' here no more!" He leaped into the pickup, ground the motor, and roared over the bridge. The rear bumper clipped a railing; the splintered wood spun out and away, falling into the creek.

The box landed in the arms of the Emperor Tree. Catalogues scattered on the ground. Dozens of receipts and a few dollar bills drifted around Cassie, settling on her head and shoulders and lap as she sank to the ground.

The clock struck one final note before dying.

The Tempest

Cassie slumped at the kitchen table, a cup of tepid coffee at her elbow half-empty and forgotten. She gazed out the window at the morning fog. Mist hovered above the creek, sheer and fragile as the skirts of ghosts. It trailed across the meadow and brushed against the glass, leaving drops like tears.

She knew she should get up and start the day, should finish straightening the party clutter from the night before. But she hadn't the energy. Nor did she have the heart to walk into a silent room that had, for such a brief time, echoed with music and laughter. She turned slowly and looked at the pile of dishes stacked on the counter. Everyone had been insufferably kind after Billy left. They smiled too broadly and spoke too softly and sat her on the horsehair chair, insisting she relax. They carried dishes from there to here and put leftovers in the refrigerator and all but tiptoed out the door afterward, with instructions for her to get a good night's sleep.

Sighing, she pushed aside the muddy remains of her coffee. What was it Rebecca had whispered, leaning close so no one else could hear? Her breath had been warm against Cassie's cheek. Something murmured, something... Cassie shook her head. She had nodded politely at the time, half-listening, and now only word fragments remained. "Friend" was one of them.

"I could stand that," Cassie mumbled. Time to put jealousies aside. Life was short and full of painful surprises, and needed friendships to keep it glued together.

"Friends keep the world a-turning." She sang quietly, trying to remember Billy's lyrics and melody. "World a-turning... Damn!" Was that all she could remember, a half dozen words? Why, oh why, hadn't she listened more carefully? Billy's promise to give her a copy of the song was kidnapped with him, hijacked in a rotting pickup truck. "It's written down," Cassie murmured. "Not lost, not forgotten. Probably still in his backpack." He'd find a way to get it to her. Maybe Guy would come to his senses in a day or two. Maybe Billy would soon knock on her door as always, calling, "It's me, Miss Cassie!" Maybe she'd glance out the window above the sink and see his bicycle leaning against the barn. She'd bake his favorite cookies and watch as he tinkered with the Studebaker. They'd talk about his future. All would be as it was before.

Fat chance, Cassie thought. *Big fat chance.*

The telephone rang. Startled, Cassie jostled the cup. Coffee splashed onto the checkered yellow tablecloth as she hurried to answer.

"Hello?"

"Happy New Year, daughter mine."

Cassie sank onto the sofa. "You too, Mother."

"You'll never guess where I am!"

"I give up. Where?"

"Oh, come on. Don't be such a spoil sport."

Cassie sighed. "I'm sorry, Mother. I'm feeling down right now, and not in the mood for guessing games."

"Oh? Man trouble?"

"No. Well, yes, in a way."

"I knew it! Men and trouble go hand in hand. Can't find one without the other."

"You've got it wrong. It's about a boy I've grown fond of. His..."

"Good for you! A woman needs a younger man. Keeps the juices flowing."

"Good lord, Mother, you've got a one-track mind. Would you listen?"

"I *am* listening. So talk."

"His name is Billy. He's special, like a son to me. But his father..."

A blare of noise burst over the telephone wires. Lillian laughed, brittle and shrill. "Oh look out the window, darling! They're dancing in the street!"

Another voice, definitely male, cut in. "Hi, Lillian's daughter. This is your future step-dad, if I can convince a certain lovely lady that my charms are irresistible. Ha ha. Say goodbye 'cause I'm taking her to the balcony to see proper. What a sight! Everybody's drunk. Must be a wedding."

Lord help me, what has Mother gone and done this time?

"Don't keep your mother too long or we'll miss the show. Once she starts yappin' she keeps at it, doesn't she? Ha ha."

"Silly man," Lillian giggled. Cassie wanted to whack some sense into her. "Have a happy. Although I don't know if that's possible in the boondunk hollows you're living in. Have you found a buyer yet?"

"Mother, who the hell is that guy? And where are you?"

"Now don't get nasty. Remember Arnold, the lovely man who kept me company in the chalet while you-know-who sloshed around in the snow? Well, I heard wrong, naughty me! He's not from Austria like I thought, but Australia! And look where we are now – in a delightful hotel in Sydney."

"You're insane!"

"Insane in love. Aren't I, sugar buns?" Kissy sounds followed, *mmm-smack, mmm-smack.* Cassie wanted to puke.

"What happened to *you-know-who*? The poor schmuck once called you his snow queen."

A derogatory snort. "His heart's frozen solid and his pocketbook frozen shut. I'm still young enough to need some warmth in my life, don't you think?"

"It's not 'warmth' you need, Mother. It's professional help."

Lillian's reply was swallowed in the rumbling of Arnold's voice calling her away, followed by a droning hum. It took Cassie a moment to realize that her mother had hung up.

Cassie had to admit Lillian was lost to her and had been for a long while. She felt like weeping as though she were an orphaned child, and it suddenly occurred to her that her entire life had been a series of losses: people vanishing, dreams discarded. Yet still she stood, and loved, and dreamed. Life went on as best it could, and so would she.

As long as she didn't lose Billy, too.

She wandered through the day, and the next, and for days after that, feeling as though a stone had lodged in her heart. She did what she promised herself she wouldn't: listened for his voice, looked for his bicycle, peered in the darkness for light glowing from open barn doors. At night she tossed in bed, restless, besieged with dreams she couldn't remember except in pieces: Billy's face, shimmering with tears as the truck carried him away. She ran after him, struggling and getting nowhere, her feet mired in mud, her legs snagged in weeds thick as snakes. Things fell from the sky: dead birds, Billy's drawings, dollar bills that transformed into dung beetles and scurried underground.

It was during one of these dreams that he phoned. Cassie stood in the light of a cold winter moon shining through the parlor windows. It was so clear she could read the face of the clock. It was almost three fifteen.

"Miss Cassie, it's me," Billy whispered. "Dad's asleep and if he wakes up and hears me he'll be madder than ever, so I have to be quick."

"Billy, I've been so worried! Are you okay?"

"I'm okay but Dad's maxed out. He's real crabby and won't let me out of his sight like he's afraid I'll do something sneaky if he isn't looking. I have to go right from school to the shop every day. I can't come see you or call or write or anything. I can't even say your name."

"Oh, God, Billy." Cassie moaned. "What a mess this has turned out to be. I'm so sorry." A long moment of silence followed. "Billy? Is something wrong?"

"He stopped snoring."

"You'd better hang up, then."

"I'll make things right again. I promise. I just don't know how or when."

Billy hung up the phone gentle as he could and paused, his hand still on the receiver. Everything was quiet. The refrigerator hummed and the kitchen clock ticked as always, but the surrounding silence felt wrong and scary, as if someone was hiding in the shadows. Maybe it was his dad. Maybe he had awakened and heard everything, and now gripped the leather belt with the silver scorpion buckle. Billy hated that belt. Guy had walloped him with it more than once, hitting especially hard when Billy disobeyed big-time. And this was definitely big-time.

An owl screeched right outside the window. Billy jerked, knocking the receiver off the hook. It dangled from the cord and slapped the wall.

"What you up to, boy?" Guy called from the bedroom, his voice slurry.

"Nothing." Billy righted the phone, grabbed a glass off the counter, and stuck it under the faucet. "Just getting a drink." He clanked the glass against the metal and turned the water on until it gushed. "Thirsty, real thirsty," he babbled.

"Christ, get back to bed. It's too late to be knockin' around."

Billy turned the water off, hurried to his room, and shut the door. His bed looked silvery in the moonlight, the covers strewn about. He wrapped himself in the blanket and stared out the window at the stars, billions of them, like a sea of crushed glass. He wasn't cold but shivered anyway while he waited and watched the clouds sail by, graceful as phantom ships. Finally the grumble of his father's snores penetrated the walls; only then did Billy close his eyes.

I'll make things right. Somehow I'll make things right.

February rushed in with a bone-chilling blue Norther. Trees flailed their limbs in a frenzied dance, and dry leaves leaped from the ground and whirled across the meadow. Dark, pregnant clouds loomed over the hills as Cassie, bundled in a sweater and gloves, hurried toward the barn. The doors were wide open and the roof leaked more than not, so everything inside was bound to get soaked. None of it mattered, except Billy's things. Those she had to protect.

The windmill groaned and clanked when she passed. The dry timber frame had rotted and skewed to the left. *It's a wonder that monstrosity is still upright, like a stack of kindling ready to topple over.* The barn was just as bad. A gray-weathered slapdash of splintered lumber, it creaked in the wind and the large doors swayed, thumping against the walls. She stepped inside, pausing for her eyes to adjust. Light filtered through splayed cracks, shining on sheets of drawing paper strewn everywhere. A gust played with one, skittering it over the floor. Cassie caught it, dismayed that dirt had smeared Billy's rendering. She collected each sheet, blowing away specks of dust, then stacked them on the front seat of the Studebaker and shut the car door. Billy's sketches would be well protected until – or if – he needed them again. Everything else would be, too. She gathered his tools from the floor, placing them neatly beside the kerosene lantern on the wooden crate. When she reached to lower the hood, it slipped from her grasp and slammed into place with an angry snap as if trying to bite off her hand. "Sorry," she muttered. "I don't like this, either." The tarp was next, age-cracked and heavy. She dragged it from the corner and struggled to drape it over the car before securing the edges with rocks. She had intended to surprise Billy by giving him the Studebaker for his very own when his work was done. Now a large gray hump arose like a shroud over a tomb. Cassie couldn't bear to look at it.

Tugging the heavy barn doors closed, she wound a rope through the hasp and tied a loose knot that would be easy to undo, in case Billy should come when she wasn't home. Everything was ready for him. Just in case.

Her fingers faltered. *This isn't the end. It isn't.*

She pressed her palm on the rough wood, as if in a blessing, then walked away.

࿐

Hawk stood at the studio windows as the dark curtain of rain swept toward him. It swallowed the earth as it moved, pushed by the screaming wind, black clouds rolling.

Thunder growled and rain hit hard, pounding on the roof and walls, water streaming down the eaves.

He looked at the howling night, the churning darkness, the sky shattered by lightning. The storm's anger beat at him. The walls shuddered with it. The ground thrummed under his feet. Old Yeller whined and pressed against him, trembling.

He turned around, only to face Cassie's incomplete portrait. The accusing eyes stabbed him with every lightning flash. He couldn't finish it and didn't know why. Inspiration eluded him. He had left it on the easel, thinking maybe today would be the day he'd find the answer, or maybe tomorrow. Now her image glared at him in the darkness. He grabbed the canvas and put it on the floor in the corner.

Old Yeller followed him into the living room, toenails clicking on the wooden floor. Hawk sank into the leather recliner and closed his eyes, thinking of when Cassie had sat there, long legs resting on the ottoman, her forehead bruised and hair windblown. A bolt of lightning cracked overhead, and he groaned and pressed his hands to his head. Memories raged at him. Another storm, another night, another time that had forever changed his life:

The streets had been slick that night in Fredericksburg five years ago. He was driving an old sedan, his wife Lea in the front seat and her best friend Rebecca in the back. He couldn't remember their destination – a restaurant, perhaps. Or a movie. It didn't matter. Lea said something, laughing, and he looked away from the road to glance at her. A moment, a second, that's all it took. A metal monster leaped from the darkness and rain, windshield gleaming like the eye of a Cyclops, wheels like mountains. The huge truck hit them broadside. Spinning, spinning, the car tumbling end-over-end like a toy tossed down a flight of stairs, a terrible roar, and silence.

He awoke in a hospital with a broken nose and minor concussion. Rebecca was in intensive care with a shattered hip, and Lea in the morgue.

A few weeks later he ran away. He got in the pickup and drove as one day led into the next, heading to wherever his truck decided to take him. He ate little, drank less, and finally stopped somewhere in Sedona. A secluded place, made of orange rock and an eternity of sky. He got out of the truck and dropped to the ground. He must have slept, for when he opened his eyes to daylight an old man was hovering over him. Wrinkled skin dry as corn shuck, eyes dug deep into his head, body hard and sinewy as the scrub trees sprouting from rocky crags.

"Come," the man said. He led Hawk up a trail to a battered trailer with a rocking chair and table under a tin canopy. "Sit. Eat."

And there he stayed, a shell of a man, his soul ripped away.

He never discovered the old Hopi's real name during his two-month stay. It kept changing. One day it was Owl, the next maybe Stone or Mouse or Snake, depending upon the man's whims. Hawk called him Cham, short for Chameleon.

Cham wasn't a man of words, but he taught Hawk how to listen. How to hear the voices of the sun and rock, of the bird and lizard, of the dust. In the silence of Sedona, in the shimmering heat and wind and space, Hawk came to terms with himself.

When he finally returned home, it was Rebecca who cared for him. It was Rebecca who forgave him more than he could forgive himself. It was Rebecca who thrust the brush into his hands and encouraged him to paint again. Once he began painting, he couldn't stop. His days in the spacious wilds of Sedona under the watchful eye of Cham influenced his vision of the world around him. The voices of the land spoke through his hands. Figures changing, figures revealing, figures never quite what they seem on the surface.

The first canvas to emerge was that of a memory: his family as it had been in the beginning. He titled it *Spirit Song*. Lea floating in the water of a pond, their daughter Susan enfolded in her arms. His own spirit watching above, calling to them with his flute. And all about, the souls of the land and air and earth, forever embracing them.

Would he have painted again without Rebecca's forgiveness? Without her encouragement and love?

The storm battered the door as Hawk searched his heart for the answer.

ℵ𝒞

Purple-black clouds rushed from different directions, colliding in a thunderous roar. The sky ripped open in a deluge of hail big as golf balls. It battered the windows and clanged on the tin carport and leapfrogged across the roof. Cassie hurried from one window to another, checking the fragile old glass, fearful it would shatter. She rushed up the narrow stairs to the attic bedroom, pursued by the eerie moans of Firewind as gusts pushed through cracks in the stone fireplace. When she stepped into the little room with its wrap-around windows, she felt as though she had stepped into the midst of the storm. It threw itself at her, impossible, frightening, beautiful. Lightning rippled through the clouds and stabbed the horizon. Mount Bubba was scarred with white; rivulets of hail and loosened rock streamed down the side as water gushed from the heavens. White on the barn roof, white on the field, white flowing in the creek.

Mesmerized, Cassie sat on the cot, heedless of the springs sagging under her weight. She couldn't understand why she wasn't frightened, why exhilaration pounded in her blood as the tempest pounded outside. She closed her eyes, imagining that she was the storm, that her spirit self slipped out of her body and raged with the winds, free and furious. In her imaginings, she opened her mouth and roared thunder, spread her arms and stirred the winds, clapped her hands and ignited streams of fire

The tumult lessened until only rain remained, drumming on the roof. When she opened her eyes, she realized she had fallen asleep. She was lying across the springs, her feet on the floor. The night was pitch dark; no lightning sparked, no moon or stars lit the sky. She felt her way down the stairs into the olden part of the house. The stone fireplace was silent now, masked by the shadows. She turned on a lamp switch but the electricity was out. Holding her hands in front like a sleepwalker, she made her way down the hall to the kitchen, trying to remember where she stashed the flashlight. Until her memory kicked in, candles would have to do.

Candles in the cupboard, matches in the drawer. Her fingers found what she needed. The match flared in the darkness. As she lifted it to the wick, a face appeared in the window. Cassie gasped and froze; the face seemed to do the same, mouth parting, light flickering from staring eyes. *Good lord, I'm spooked by my own reflection!* She lifted the candle in a mock toast. "Salud," she murmured, then affixed it to a tin holder that had belonged to Mimi's grandmother or the grandmother before that. Rain pattered against the walls as Cassie worked. She should check the house for leaks, but would have to wait for tomorrow's sunlight. Not that she was worried; the place was probably tight as a submarine. She walked into the parlor, candlelight leading the way, remembering how irritated she had been at Guy when he climbed all over the house for days on end, repairing it by the inch. Now she was damned grateful.

He's got his good side, if I can just appeal to it.

She opened the front door, hoping the storm hadn't caused any damage. The screen wouldn't budge more than an inch or two. She shoved until it gave way, scraping and crackling against piles of hail fused together in mounds. Rainwater streamed down the porch eaves, glittering in the darkness. She could see little else.

She picked up a piece of rock-solid hail. What harm could hundreds of these things do to Tatty's glass walls and roof? Her studio could be ruined. At this very moment Tatty might be knee-deep in balls of ice and broken shards and torrents of water! Cassie rushed to the phone but heard only static. *Damn!* The stupid thing had a habit of conking out every time it rained. She'd try again tomorrow. By then everything should be back to normal.

The house seemed to sigh, as if settling in for the night. The darkness was soft and mysterious beyond the candle's glow, inviting her to sleep. Lifting the candle high, she walked to the bedroom, her image glimmering from each window she passed, as if her ghost walked with her.

The voices came to her in dreams. Murmuring, whispering, singing – a chorus amid the sound of rain. She opened her dream eyes to shapes surrounding her bed, there but not there, as if imprinted upon a gauze curtain: a fine-boned woman in a bonnet and gown with soft balloon sleeves, braided hair wound around her head; a hulk of a man, muscular and thick-necked, smiling like a kindly giant. A girl emerged from between them, fair skin and hair glowing as if woven from golden threads. Her lips moved, her voice a whisper of leaves in the wind. "It's here, hidden."

Rosine! Cassie thought, her heart racing. *Her diary!* She struggled to speak but her mouth wouldn't obey. *Where? Where else can I look?* The child answered, her words whisked away by the blare of a horn.

Cassie awoke to a room awash in early morning sunlight. It was silent except for the insistent, repetitive blasts of an auto horn. Cassie grabbed her robe and slippers, flung open the door and stumbled onto the porch, hail remnants crunching underfoot.

She stood on an island surrounded by gushing water. The creek had flooded, tumbling over the bridge until the wooden planks vanished from sight. Waves surged over the meadow, pushed by muddy streams that rushed down Mount Bubba. Broken limbs and scattered debris floated past, yards from where she stood, but the house had been built on a rise so she was safe and more or less dry. It reminded her of an enchanted castle surrounded by a moat.

A red pickup had stopped at flood's edge on the far side of the creek. Water lapped at the hubcaps. Hawk stood half-in, half-out of the cab. "Are you okay?" he hollered, hand cupping his mouth. "The phone's out."

"Fine!" she shouted. "How's Tatty?"

"A bit wet, nothing that can't be fixed."

"I'm so glad!" She was glad for herself, too. Hawk had come, valiant as a charging knight, to check up on her! How perfectly, wonderfully lovely.

A motor rumbled, drawing closer. Hawk leaped from his truck, waving as a van appeared in tentative jerks, as if the driver feared that at any moment the car would sink into mud. It parked so far away Cassie couldn't see who was inside. Hawk leaned into the window, talking. He turned and looked in Cassie's direction, then directed the van in a safe turn-around. As it drove away, Hawk came as close to the water as he probably dared. "That was Nan," he yelled. "Tried to phone."

"Thank her for me, would you?" she cried, feeling blessed to have such caring friends.

"Bad news, Cassie."

She took a deep breath and waited.

"Justin's dying."

In My Heart Abide

Justin's dying!

Cassie stumbled and gripped the porch railing. "I've got to go see him!" she yelled across the turbulent flood to Hawk.

"Water's too high."

"I'll wade. Or swim."

"Not in this current! You'll be swept away."

"How about there?" She pointed to Mount Bubba, her voice cracking. Rubble and mud had oozed down the hillside, gouging slimy, glittery trails. "I'll climb over if you meet me on the other side."

"Too dangerous!"

"What else can I do?"

"Wait."

"I don't *want* to wait!"

"I'll be back tomorrow. Creek should be down then." He stepped into the pickup, leaning out to shout, "Don't do anything stupid in the meantime."

"No need to be rude!" Cassie spun around and flung open the screen door.

"Justin's still alive, Cassie. There's still time."

"Promise me!"

Hawk maneuvered a cautious turn-around and sped away, water spewing up on both sides of the truck like Moses parting the Red Sea. Cassie rushed to the edge of the porch, crying, "Promise me! Promise!" until he was gone.

Justin was dying, yet the day blazed with sunlight. Birds flitted among storm-drenched trees and soared in a cloudless sky. The breeze was gentle but cold, and her warm breath puffed from her mouth like smoke.

It wasn't fair. The earth should mourn, the heavens darken, the waters still.

Cassie's knees gave way and she sat on the top step. A piece of hail crunched underneath, soaking her robe. Clumps of ice, melting into odd shapes, lay strewn about the porch and dripped from the swing. She pulled her robe tighter as a shadow moved in the upland shallows of the wood, near the cemetery gate. The wolf paused, looking in her direction.

"Hey, Wolf," she muttered. "It's a sad day." She imagined she could see the sun glinting from its golden eyes, even from this distance. "Justin's been like a grandfather to me. What will I do when he's gone?"

What will Berta do?

The question occurred to Cassie in a voice other than her own, ancient and familiar. The wolf ambled into the shadows as Berta's image appeared in Cassie's mind, the features softened as if viewed through rippled glass: the plump-cheeked face, hazel eyes swimming behind thick lenses like those of a myopic owl, gray hair piled up on her head willy-nilly. *What would I do in an empty house all by myself?* Berta had once asked. *Flap around in circles like a headless chicken, that's what.*

She remembered Justin and Berta holding hands, sitting at their table and saying grace while clocks bonged and chimed in concert. It was the first meal Cassie had eaten with them. They held her hands too, the three of them at that pretty table with a yellowed lace cloth Berta placed there just for her. Justin's bald pate shone while he prayed, and when he raised his head he winked at her, as if she belonged there. Cassie had never before felt so embraced. *This is what a real family is like,* she had thought.

She realized she was chilly and stood, turning toward the door. Something caught her eye and she hesitated, studying the Emperor Tree. The gnarled, bare branches looked no different than before – except for Justin's metal cherub. It hung upside down, barely secured by one little leg wrapped around a narrow limb.

If it falls, Justin will die.

The thought was silly, she knew. An absurd manifestation of her fears. Yet she rushed into the house, tugged on Mimi's galoshes, and hurried to the rescue. She climbed up the trunk, scrabbling for a foothold, her robe catching and pulling on the bark, her palms slick with rain. The limb the cherub rode stretched out and out, creaking under Cassie's weight. She lay on her stomach and crawled toward the dangling figure, gasping when the branch sagged downward. The cherub slid downward, too, the metal hand raised as if in farewell. It bounced against a twig, slipped, and swung to and fro. The only thing keeping it aloft was the heel of its foot. Afraid even to breathe, Cassie inched forward, stretching out as far as she could reach. *Careful,* she whispered, *careful,* until she touched the tip of the heel; she could feel the surprising warmth of it in her fingertips, as though blood pulsed within the metal skin. She almost had the foot in her grasp before the cherub fell. It seemed to happen in slow motion: her fingers reaching, the cherub separating from the branch and floating toward earth. The wings resembled those of a butterfly. Somehow her hand appeared above it, somehow a single finger looped through the wing's design, somehow she pulled it up to safety. The wood pricked her inner thighs as she sat upright, hugging the cherub to her chest. "There, now," she murmured, as if to comfort a child. "There, there." Its legs were molded to encircle the bough. Cassie slipped them over a narrow section and scooted backward, sliding the cherub toward her. She forced it along the tree's ever-widening girth until it wedged on good and tight, exactly as Justin had once placed it. Sighing, she leaned against the trunk and looked up through the branches at a cloudless sky the color of ice water.

I've done what I could.

The cherub was safe, as hopefully Justin would be safe for least another day.

Cassie wandered around the house, restless. She had to *do* something or else go crazy with worry. But what? Mimi's belongings had already been organized and the worst of the lot discarded. The rest would be displayed in an estate sale sometime in the near future. Whatever didn't sell she'd give away, although she planned on keeping a few things – especially the mantle clock, the grapevine chair, the keepsake chest. She felt attached to them and to their time-worn scars, as though evidence of life, hard-lived and long, held clues to her family's past.

Fragments of last night's dream trailed into her thoughts. Maybe she should look for Rosine's diary after all. But there wasn't a single inch in this rambling house that Cassie hadn't already searched time and time again. She had even skimmed her hands over the cellar walls and floor, hoping to find a secret nook hidden behind a loose stone.

There was something about the dream that kept tugging at her mind. Cassie lay on the sofa and closed her eyes, trying to remember: The young girl with golden hair coming to the bedside, gazing down at her. Other figures milling around in clothing from different times. *Like a reunion of ghosts,* Cassie thought, not quite laughing at the idea. The girl was the most vivid, a Technicolor character mingling amid shadowy ones. Lurking behind her, still as the night, was the silhouette of a man in a wide-brimmed black hat.

A wide-brimmed hat! Cassie's eyes snapped open. She leaped up, spurred by memories of the night she had arrived. The thunderstorm, the darkness split by lightning. She had trembled in the kitchen chair, arms wrapped around herself. A flash, and there it stood: the shape of a man straddling the doorway. Dark, featureless. The hat wide, tilted at a cocky angle.

It was just an illusion, she reminded herself. An outline of the parlor floor lamp with its cockeyed shade.

Hurrying to the bedroom, she snatched the keepsake chest and dumped the contents on the bed, rummaging until she found the photo she wanted: her great-grandfather, Jedediah Stowe, long hair curled to perfection, riding outfit crisped and pressed, grandly posed beside his horse. He looked costumed for an old-time Western movie, prepared to ride off into the sunset with a sixty-piece orchestra heralding his triumphant exit. The perfect hero, except for the black hat cocked to the side, the brim almost touching one shoulder.

Was it Jedediah she had sometimes seen out of the corner of her eye, in the night darkness of the house? She fumbled through Mimi's letters, pulling them from the envelopes. She had started to read one of the letters several days ago, but something called her away and she'd not returned to it since. A singular name had jumped from the pages before she put them aside; it was this name she now sought.

She skimmed through the letters, catching bits and pieces as she sped from one to the other, the dates jumbled:

> *The mare got out again and it took me most of the afternoon to track her down.... I bought a dress in your favorite blue to wear when you come home. You will come home. You must come home.... Lillian is blowing you kisses and I have promised to tuck them safely between the pages.... I read terrible things about the war and can't bear to look at photographs of soldiers lying in the fields like broken dolls....*

And there, finally the name she hoped to find:

> *I confess to abiding in loneliness, and my imagination conjures ghosts to fill the empty rooms. One bothers me in particular. I can't see it clear, but fear it to be Jed. If it's Jed come to haunt, I'd be tempted to burn the place down to be rid of him. Maybe he's hanging around because we didn't bury*

him proper. When the weather warms up some I'll look for his bones and cover them up right. Maybe then he'd be satisfied and stay in hell where he belongs.

The idea that her gentle grandmother harbored such consuming hate for her own father was a notion Cassie couldn't absorb, as though she were reading something penned by a stranger. She sat on the edge of the bed and stared out the window with unseeing eyes. Her mind seethed with questions that in all likelihood might never be answered. Mimi loathed her father, even wishing him to hell. Why? And what did Mimi have to do with his burial, proper or otherwise? She would have been only a little girl of four or five when Jedediah died, according to the dates on the back of his photograph. Where was he buried? Was it done in such haste that dirt barely covered his bones?

When the flood's dried up, I'll go to the family cemetery and take a look. I don't remember seeing a stone for Jed, but maybe it's small or flat and embedded in weeds.

And if Jed's grave wasn't there?

I'll search for it and bury him proper, as Mimi wanted.

Cassie snorted. What a simpleton she was! Rooting around for some misplaced skeleton, God! What would she think of next, bringing it to life? Breeding zombies?

The phone rang with erratic hiccups. Working, at last! Cassie put Mimi's box aside and hurried to answer. "Hello?"

"Hi, *Cass-aie*."

There was no mistaking that lovely voice. "Nan, I'm so glad to hear from you! How's Justin?"

"He sleeps mostly. Sometimes he talks in whispers. I told him you wanted to visit but couldn't because you were isolated by the flood, and he seemed to understand."

"I'll be there tomorrow even if I have to sprout wings and fly."

"Berta wants him to die in his own house and own bed, with family by his side." Nan sighed. "She looks so… dazed, like a sleepwalker. She held his hand the whole time I was there, singing to him and asking if he was hungry and wanted something to eat. Oh, *Cass-aie*, it's all so sad."

"They've loved each other since childhood."

"Really? That long? I didn't know."

"In Austria. He threw a dead fish in her lap, and when she whacked him with it he pushed her in the river. She decided at that moment to marry him when they grew up."

"Imagine loving someone for more than seventy years," Nan said quietly. "What will Berta do without him?"

"I don't know. I honestly don't know."

ꙮ

Morning dawned upon the wrecked bridge. Planks had been ripped away, leaving ragged, yawning gaps. Thick fog boiled over the shattered structure as though it had fallen into a witch's caldron. Cassie stepped upon the edge and recoiled when the flooring swayed.

"I think it's off the foundation," she called.

"Could be." Hawk waited on the other end, partly hidden in the heavy mist. "Stay there. I'm coming over."

"Careful!"

She heard his footsteps, the wood creaking under his weight, something splashing into the creek. His figure gradually emerged from the haze, hand outstretched. "It's not too bad, Cassie. Watch my feet and step where I step."

She followed, wary, peering down. Hawk's boots were more mud than leather and tread lightly, testing the area ahead before continuing on. The creek gushed directly below, dangerously high and clogged with debris. "I don't remember Mimi ever talking about a flood as bad as this."

"Comes with the territory. Although this one might've broke the record."

Taking his lead, Cassie jumped over a missing board. The timber was slick and she slipped, landing hard against Hawk. He lost his balance and stumbled backwards, gripping her around the waist and crying, "Easy now, easy!" as she held on. The momentum carried them along, the bridge shuddering. Hawk staggered backward and she forward, arms clasped around one another when the lyrics of an old movie suddenly popped into her head, *Dancing, oh yes I'm dancing...* She pictured Hawk and herself waltzing across the bridge as it crumbled beneath them, she dressed in feathers and fluff and he in a tux like Fred Astaire and Ginger Rogers, and couldn't help it. She simply had to laugh.

Hawk pulled her onto shore, hat askew and face flushed. "I take it you find this amusing."

"Sorry," she gasped. "I got tickled."

"Next time you can rescue yourself," Hawk grumbled as he led her to his truck. She stepped inside and he slammed her door, marched around to the driver's side, slid behind the wheel, turned and kissed her full on the mouth. Then he thrust the key into the ignition and stomped the gas pedal until the truck seesawed in the mud like a thrashing whale.

Cassie braced herself against the dashboard, biting her tongue. She wanted to laugh again, wanted to grab him and dance in the slushy meadow like a crazed woman, wanted to kiss him once more. How could she feel like this when she was so worried about Justin? Her feelings were all mixed up. She studied his profile, remembering the taste of him on her lips.

"You're staring." Hawk flicked his eyes at her and grinned.

Blood rushed to her cheeks and she looked out the window. Mist hung like a gossamer veil, parting to expose broken limbs dangling from trees or strewn along the road. Piles of rubble and debris. A drowned skunk hanging from a tangle of brush. Water everywhere, ponds of it, lakes of it, entire oceans. The sun's rays barely penetrated.

"Everything's gray," she mumbled, and closed her eyes to the storm's destruction.

"Victoria's here," Hawk said as he turned into the Grumm driveway.

"Who?"

"Their daughter. She's a professor at Rice. Teaches German."

He parked behind a white car covered in mire. Cassie scarcely gave it a glance. Her eyes were riveted elsewhere. She got out of the pickup and squinted through the shifting fog.

"Do you see that?" She pointed to the rooftop where an angel sculpture had once posed with wings outspread, ready to leap into the air. Now it lay crumpled in death on the shingled roof.

"Wind must of toppled it."

Something crackled under Cassie's foot. She picked up a feather made out of metal and walked slowly toward the house, eyes on the ground. Pieces lay strewn about – a foot here, a winged helmet there, an arm beside the porch, as if the angel had struggled with an enemy and been brutally dismembered.

The front door swung open and a woman stood waiting. She was tall and thin and made of sharp angles, with Justin's furrowed brow. Her hand was Justin's too, with long knobby fingers that engulfed Cassie's own. "Welcome," she said, her voice husky, perhaps roughened by sorrow. "I'm

Victoria Hubbert, their daughter. You must be Cassandra. Hawk said he was bringing you today. Mother talks about you a lot. Dad, too."

Victoria seemed so familiar, so Justin-like, that Cassie wanted to fling her arms around the woman's shoulders and hug her. "I'm sorry I couldn't come sooner."

"How is he this morning?" Hawk asked.

"Still with us," Victoria replied, "but saying goodbye."

She looked so bereft Cassie's heart lurched. She fumbled for words of comfort but found she couldn't speak them. They caught up in her mouth, banal, inadequate.

"May I see him?"

"Of course. Shall I come with you?"

"No, I'm fine."

"Mother's there, too. I can't get her to step away even for a minute. Whenever she leaves she hurries back again. I think she's afraid he'll die as soon as her back is turned."

She walked toward the hallway, Hawk and Victoria's voices mumbling behind her. The bedroom door was open at the hall's end, and she faltered. Everything around her seemed sharply defined in the half-light – the faded hall rug, the wallpaper of cabbage roses, the framed Austrian landscapes. One of them was crooked, and she righted it. On her left was a plant stand, topped by a porcelain vase with a quaint shepherdess painted on the side. The girl wore a white bonnet and held a staff flowing with pink ribbons. Cassie lingered there, eyeing the girl's impossibly rosy cheeks, before taking a deep breath and stepping through the door.

The brightness startled her. Perhaps in the depths of her imagination she had visualized drawn drapery and gloom, shadows playing around the bed of death. But the curtains were opened and the four-poster was encased in a corona of light, as if preparing to welcome the spirit of the man it embraced. Berta slumped in a chair beside him, chin resting on her chest, asleep. Her silver-gray hair tumbled in unkempt disarray over her shoulders, and her cheeks sagged like wattles. She looked tired and fragile and vulnerable, and Cassie ached with sadness for her.

She tiptoed to the bed. Justin lay with his arms over the covers. He, too, slept. His mouth parted and his lips moved, as if dreaming. He was thin and frail, a skeletal image swallowed by the expanse of bed. She had expected to see that. What she hadn't expected was the look of contentment on his face. She reached toward him, caressing his wispy hair. It felt light, insubstantial, about to puff into dust. His eyelids, thin as tissue paper, fluttered and opened.

"Hi," Cassie said softly. "It's me, Cassie, come to pay a visit."

"Castle," he breathed, lifting his hand toward her.

Berta started, her head jerking upright. Her eyes flew to Justin. "*Schatz*, you're awake? Did you call me?" She tucked the blanket up to his chin before following his gaze to Cassie. "Oh, my! You're here!" She pushed herself out of the chair, then fell back down again. "Old legs," she muttered apologetically, "sometimes don't work as they should."

"You're just over-tired." Cassie rushed to help her up. They stood, arms intertwined, looking down at Justin. He had closed his eyes but his hand was still raised and moved slightly, as if responding to the call of a distant voice.

"Oh, Cassandra," Berta sighed, "oh."

Cassie took her by the shoulders and urged her toward the door. "Why don't you eat something then lie on the sofa and rest? I'll keep Justin company."

"Oh, no, I couldn't."

"Just for a little while."

Berta allowed Cassie to lead her into the hall, then refused to go further. "He might need me. He might want something."

"Berta, please," Cassie said gently. "You need to take care of yourself, too."

Berta peered at Cassie through smudged lenses, then nodded and walked toward the kitchen. She moved in odd, jerky steps and bumped into the plant stand, never noticing that the porcelain vase teetered and would have crashed to the floor had Cassie not hurried to catch it.

The bedside chair still carried Berta's warmth and creaked when Cassie sat in it. She reached for Justin's hand. "Hey there," she said quietly. "I've missed you." His eyes flickered open and a slow grin, shadow of the original but a grin nonetheless, creased his face. Encouraged, she leaned in closer. "Are you comfortable? Do you need anything?"

He didn't move or utter a sound, but life spoke from his eyes. *I'm here. I'm listening. Please talk to me.*

What could she say that would interest him? Her mind was blank. She wished for the impossible, for a magic spell that could lift this dear old man from his bed and make him whole again. The silence stretched long. The multitude of clocks tick-ticked, *talk-now, talk-now.*

And so, fumbling, awkward under his scrutiny, she began. She started with the morning's weather, and that segued into the flooded creek and dancing with Hawk across the bridge. She told him about searching for Rosine's missing diary, and about the recent dream and Mimi's letters and Jed with the large-brimmed hat. She went back into time and reminisced about her father and when she had lost him, and of how her mother was forever changed because of it. She spoke of her husband's fall from the mountain top, and her hiking boots touching the rocky edge as she looked down at the splash of red below, and the sound of the helicopter as it carried him away. She talked of the rosebush and the ashes of lost hopes it carried, and how her life had transformed since she moved here. She spoke of Willow City and the house her ancestors built and the spirits inhabiting it, and of Billy and the friends she held dear to her heart. She spoke of them all, every one: names fell from her tongue, and with them stories of love lost and love found and love yet to be fulfilled, of fears yet to be conquered and of dreams reborn. She talked and talked and talked, careening from one topic to another, until she ran out of words.

And underneath it all, unspoken but perhaps heard nonetheless: *I love you.*

Justin hadn't moved throughout. He simply listened, eyes upon her even in the silence. Cassie patted his arm, now so scrawny she could probably wrap her fingers around the whole of it. She yearned to bundle him up like a cocoon and carry him away, to protect him from the waiting inevitable. Grief gnawed her heart although he was lying right there in front of her, alive and breathing, gentle and kind as always.

How is it life can change in an instant? A wandering blood clot, a minuscule globule, an invisible, tiny villain was all it took. No army of angels could save him. No words, no prayers, no magic incantations. A life gone, *poof!* The soul blown away from the body like the seeds of a dandelion, scattering to the winds.

"Are you being good, *Schatz*?" Berta teased as she entered. Her face glistened from a recent scrubbing, and her flyaway hair was now tamed and pinned. "Not making a nuisance of yourself?"

"I almost talked the ears off his head."

"I know he enjoyed your company." Berta fussed with the comforter at Justin's feet, straightening what didn't need to be straightened. Cassie rose and hugged her. She smelled of lemon soap and sweat and fear.

"I'd best be going." Cassie lingered by the doorway. "Bye, Justin. I'll see you tomorrow." Berta leaned over him, murmuring softly and caressing his forehead. Cassie averted her eyes and stepped into the hallway, pausing as Berta began to sing in a thin, quivery voice:

You are my sweetheart, now and evermore,
Till we walk together along that distant shore
Even then, forever, with you by my side
Now and always you'll in my heart abide
My sweetheart evermore.

Justin's voice joined hers in a wordless, droning moan while Berta sang and Cassie wept:

Now and always you'll in my heart abide
My sweetheart evermore.

Truly Gone

THE SMALL COUNTRY CHURCH NEAR FREDERICKSBURG REMINDED CASSIE OF AN earlier, gentler age: a white steeple atop a simple white building, ancient double doors hanging a bit off-plumb, a narrow porch with steps worn by generations of footfalls, a multitude of beautiful stained glass windows. All it needed to complete the impression was a horse and buggy in the cobbled courtyard, rather than the collection of pickup trucks and cars and Tatty's motorcycle.

Cassie was late. Perhaps unconsciously she didn't want to be there, didn't want to gaze down at a mummified Justin posed stiff and glossy in his coffin. She hurried up the steps toward the mellow, wheezy voice of a pump-organ, and paused at the interior. Soft beams of green and gold and blue poured through the windows and fell upon the crowded pews. The only other light came from a spotlight illuminating the front dais and Pete. Although he played the organ with his back to the congregation, there was no mistaking his boxcar girth – or his enthusiasm. His feet pumped and his hands pounded and his head swayed to and fro, moving with the music.

Cassie swept her eyes around the room, pausing at the sight of Berta in the front pew. She wore a little black hat with a veil, and was cushioned between Victoria and a plump fellow dabbing his eyes with a large floral handkerchief. He had the same round face as Berta, the same flyaway hair. Cassie was certain that if she could look him square in the face he'd have the same myopic gaze. If she was right, Frederick had finally come home. Berta had sometimes mentioned their son with pride and despair – an actor and, to Justin's horror, a homosexual.

A deep chasm had opened between father and son, and Frederick disappeared among the throngs of New York, vowing never to return.

But vows forged in anger could be broken by sorrow.

"*Pssst, Cass-aie!*" Nan appeared out of nowhere, whispering. "We saved a place for you."

Tatty was waiting for them, patting the empty seat beside her in welcome. A voluminous woolen shawl fell from her shoulders to the floor. She must have noticed Cassie eyeing it curiously, because she leaned closer and muttered, "A blanket, really, but I took a fancy to it."

Nan slipped a program into Cassie's hands. It was a single sheet of ivory parchment inked in brown calligraphy, the original of which must have been painstakingly rendered by hand. A wood-block print of Justin was imprinted on the back, the face as Cassie wished to always remember it: kind, intelligent, mischievous. "Beautiful," she murmured, and then noticed a signature sketch at the bottom, so small she almost missed it, of a hawk gazing upward. Trying not to be obvious, she twisted in her seat and searched for Hawk among the throng, but there were too many to catch at a glance.

Tatty smiled and squeezed her hand as the music built to a crescendo, the final notes hovering in the air as a man stepped to the front. He reminded Cassie of an old lion with his thick mane of silver hair and strong, big-jowled face. Cassie glanced at her program: Reverend Joseph Maxwell. "Friends," the reverend intoned, "I am honored to be with you today as we bid farewell to Justin Grumm, a singular person dear to all our hearts. But in our grief we must remember it is also a time of joy, for Justin is now in a far better world, reborn in the holy light of his Creator." With a theatrical gesture he indicated the coffin in its place of honor before the altar. "Justin is not there, as if asleep. We see only the outward shell that once housed the man we knew. That house is empty. He has moved to new real estate as it were, to a heavenly abode of many rooms and healing waters."

Cassie stopped listening. She had heard enough about empty rooms and heavenly abodes. The problem with loving was what lay at that road's end – loss. Her lifetime had been filled with too much of it. She closed her mind to hearing anything more about Justin drifting around in ethereal dimensions, and allowed her eyes to wander to the front row. Berta listened intently, her chin bravely lifted. The man who might be Frederick placed his arm around her and patted her shoulder. Next to Victoria was a slender gent with prominent ears and a young couple trying to hush two restless children, one of whom stood on the pew and gazed up at the ceiling. The Grumm clan, rallying around Berta. The "togetherness" generated among them was so strong Cassie imagined she could feel the impact, a jolt of tenderness and grief aimed straight for the heart.

"Rejoice, because he will always be with us in our thoughts. Rejoice, because he will be our guardian angel, pointing the way if we but listen. Rejoice, because our loss is felt only upon this earthly plane; in good time we will all meet again, gathered into the folds of our heavenly Father." The voice droned on and on, rising and falling like an ocean tide, occasionally breaking and crashing in impressive waves.

"A birdie, a birdie!" the pew-standing child squealed, pointing to a sparrow flitting about in the rafters. "It got losted!" Soft laughter rippled through the room as Cassie watched the bird dart to and fro, and wished it would deposit a memento upon the good reverend's pontificating head.

Then she saw Billy. There was no mistaking him from the back, the shape of his shoulders, the curly red hair. Guy sat with his arm around the boy, drawing him close. Billy leaned into the embrace until their two heads almost touched, red against red, father and son. Cassie looked away, eyes burning. She couldn't describe the ache she felt, nor the reason she felt it. It was simply there, a part of her as much as breath and blood.

Reverend Maxwell finally ran out of steam and offered the podium to others. Frederick rose, fumbling with his notes. He laid the papers on the stand, slipped a pair of round spectacles on his round face, and gripped the podium with both hands as if it were a shield. He reminded Cassie of a teddy bear wearing a jacket too snug for its broad tummy.

"My father liked birds."

His voice was vibrant, expressive. The room's stillness quickened.

"He didn't like ceremonies like this one, or what he called fancy-frilled speaking. He had a roguish side to him, one that looked for the bright, funny side of things. I think he'd get a kick out of that sparrow being in here, bringing a bit of laughter with it." He paused and looked down at his notes, then cleared his throat. "Forgive me. This is difficult."

Victoria rose and stood beside her brother. He loosened his grip on the podium and held her hand. Something seemed to release inside of him and he spoke as if in the circle of his family, unnoticed by the multitude of eyes upon him. "There's so much to say, so much I should have said and didn't. Now it's too late, isn't it? I hope he knew how much I love him. And although he was too stubborn to admit it, I know he loved me in spite of… everything."

"Yes, he did. He did. He loved us all," Victoria said, and led him back to the pew.

Too late, too late, Cassie thought. Now Frederick would never hear the words he probably always sought and Justin probably always thought but never could bring himself to say: *I love you, even if I don't understand you.*

Silence followed, a trembling expectation. Pete slowly turned around, his broad face serious. "I'm not too good with words," he said, "but it came to me that maybe I could say something special." He glanced down at the open coffin, then quickly upward, as if Justin had flown that narrow entrapment and now sat freely on the rafters next to the sparrow. "You listening, good buddy? I wrote this for you." It was strange hearing his voice, usually rather wild and nasal with bluegrass and country, sing so sweetly:

Goodbye dear friend, farewell
Goodbye, auf wiedersehen
May God hold you in the cup of his hand
Until we meet again

Until we meet again, dear friend
Until we meet again
May God hold you in the cup of his hand
Until we meet again

When Pete began to repeat the first stanza, Berta started singing, too, then Victoria, followed by the entire Grumm clan. Soon everyone joined in:

Goodbye dear friend, farewell
Goodbye, auf wiedersehen
May God hold you in the cup of his hand
Until we meet again

Finally the last word was spoken, the last prayer given. Berta, supported by her two children, closed the lid on Justin and caressed the wood as if tucking him in for the night. Pallbearers, led by Frederick, hoisted it upon their shoulders and began the slow, stately journey down the aisle. Hawk was among them, somber and handsome, his white-white hair glinting against the dark suit jacket. *There you are,* she thought. His leaf-green eyes, heavy with sadness, found her. She smiled, wanting to stand and walk beside him, to lift Justin upon her own shoulders, to help carry the precious burden through the doors into sunlight.

The burial was for family only, and for that Cassie was grateful. Standing by an open gash in the earth created to receive someone you loved was barbaric. She had feared peering down the waiting, yawning hole of crumbling moist earth and dark crawling things, had feared the moment she'd have to turn her back and walk away while Justin remained behind. But now she stood in the shadows of the porch as the quaint horse-drawn hearse clomp-clomped toward the cemetery a mile or so away, followed by a small caravan of cars. Tatty led the way on her motorcycle, offering to serve as an escort in lieu of a policeman. People shielded their eyes from the sun and waved goodbye until the procession rounded the bend and disappeared from view.

Gone. Justin's truly gone.

Frederick's words reverberated in her memory: *It's too late, isn't it?* Too late to make amends, too late to tighten cords that had long ago been loosened or severed altogether.

What if Mother were to die today, tomorrow? Would I be forever haunted with the words, too late?

"Miss Cassie!" Billy was suddenly there, clasping her hand and whispering, "I don't care what Dad says or how mad he gets. I'm coming to see you and work on the car like always. Someday soon, I promise." He slipped away and vanished among the crowd.

The Ides of March arrived with the dawning of spring. The afternoon glittered bright and clear, and a breeze carried the fragrance of earth and wild grasses. A beautiful day, a day that should lift Cassie's heart. Yet her heart felt heavy and huge in her chest, squeezing out the air in her lungs.

She leaned on Berta's fence and gazed at the deserted house. It had taken only two weeks to empty. Two weeks, and at the end of it Berta was no longer there. All that remained was a pile of scraps stacked near the barn. No metal angels posed on the roof or stood sentry in the yard or straddled the fence posts. The windows were bare of curtains, the porch empty of rocking chairs, the front door locked against echoes and barren rooms.

Was it just yesterday the U-Haul trailer had driven away, Frederick at the wheel? Berta had lingered by Victoria's car, her face gray as dust, for a final look at the place she had once called home. Now she would begin a new life in Houston with her daughter. "In the Mother-in-law suite, a real nice place," she said lightly, trying to smile.

Cassie couldn't remember how she had replied, the words that scattered from her mouth. "Miss you." "Stay well." "Write to me." The hug was rushed. Berta's skin was dry; her hair smelled of paste and stuck to her cheeks. Cassie helped her into the car and shut the door. Berta placed her palm against the window briefly, fingers spread open, as Victoria drove down the driveway. Cassie followed on foot, waving. The car turned and began the final journey, Berta's chin held high, her gaze straight ahead. Cassie ran to the road, hand lifted in farewell. The car wound down the hillside, growing smaller in the distance. Even then she stood, hand raised, until the car slid among the shadows.

Sighing now, Cassie noticed the gate had yawned open and so she closed it. It clanged shut, a loud reproach. Had she done that just a few days ago, the dogs in the back yard would have barked-barked-barked. But all the animals were gone, too. The dogs went with Berta. The rooster and chickens to Pete and Nan. She didn't know who ended up with the goat. As for Strudel, Victoria's husband was allergic to cats and in a fit of sneezing had threatened to drown it in the toilet. Shortly thereafter, Berta, without a word of warning, thrust Strudel into Cassie's arms. "Please, for me."

Startled, Cassie had blurted, "She's gorgeous, but I don't know a darn thing about cats."

"*Him*. A fat, spoiled *him*. For treats he likes sardines and crackers and milk. If he pats the refrigerator door and yowls he's asking for ice cream. Vanilla. Just give him a dollop." She gathered Strudel's dishes and sundry items, put them into a cloth bag and tied it with a ribbon, her hands trembling. "He should be brushed often, maybe twice, three times a week. And don't forget to take him to the vet for checkups."

"Anything else I should know?"

"I can't remember exactly. My mind's gone all foggy."

Strudel had begun to purr, a contented growl that vibrated against Cassie's arms. Berta turned away quickly, saying, "See? He's loved you from the start. So go. Now take him and go."

Not once afterward had Berta mentioned Strudel's name, as if purposely erasing the cat from memory, as if the pain of losing husband and cat and home and all she had known up to this point was beyond conscious thought, and the only steps she knew to take followed those of her daughter. But she stepped firmly, with eyes focused upon what lay ahead rather than behind.

Courage, Cassie thought, *makes its home in the hearts of the old.*

Imaginings

"SHIT!" GUY SWIPED HIS THUMB ON HIS JEANS, LEAVING A SMEAR OF BLOOD AND motor oil. This was the second time today he'd been careless with his hands.

He kicked a can and sent it flying across the shop. It landed against a pile of discarded tires and junk. Christ, the place was a wreck. He poured another cup of coffee. It smelled like hot piss and tasted about as foul, but he sat on the metal chair and drank it anyway. Got to clear his mind and reason things out. Got to free himself of worries about Billy.

The coffee soured in his stomach as he remembered the day of Justin's funeral. He had waited unseen behind a church pillar as Billy rushed over to Cassie in a big sneaky hurry and whispered something in her ear. She nodded and Billy squeezed her hand quick and rushed away, then turned and glanced back. The look on his face scared Guy plenty. It was like Cassie had an invisible rope tied to the boy, and wherever she went Billy felt the pull of it.

I'll watch him good. If he so much as lifts the phone to give her a call or even thinks about going over there, I'll put an end to it once and for all.

But the truth was he couldn't watch Billy every second of the day. It drove him crazy, not being able to keep tabs on that boy, not knowing if Billy was finding ways to call Cassie or steal over there to see her and fiddle around with that beat-up car. Billy had promised not to, but Guy didn't trust him to keep his word when it came to Cassie or the Studebaker. The lure was too strong.

An idea popped into Guy's head and he jumped from the metal chair, tipping it over in excitement. It clattered to the cement floor as he tossed the foam coffee cup into the trash heap, hurried to the hell-hole closet he called his office, and yanked at the desk drawer. The ledger was buried underneath a confusion of bills, receipts, and invoices. Jesus, when had things gotten so disorganized? Seemed like just yesterday he had everything orderly and neat. He opened the ledger, flipped through the pages, and ran a finger down the columned figures. This was the answer! So simple, so right! He whooped. "Wave goodbye, Cassie. You're toast, baby!"

The Studebaker wasn't the problem, but the answer! If that car was stored in his own garage at home, wouldn't Billy be thrilled? Wouldn't he work on it day and night and every minute in between? There'd be no time and no reason to think about Cassie.

All Guy had to do was buy the damned thing outright and haul it home.

Jesus, what a great idea! Billy would be right there under his nose most of the time. They could even work on the car together, like pals. Hell, in no time at all Billy would see that his father knew more than the airy stuff in college books, practical knowledge gained over years of hands-on experience. He'd see how good working as a team could be, how perfect for the future with the two of them partnered, father and son. *Guy and Billy's Auto Repair.* Or better yet, *Wilson and Son.* Oh, sweet Mary, how beautiful that sounded.

He turned the final page and stared at the totals penciled on the bottom.

Not enough. Not nearly enough. God, he was a jerk-ass dreamer for even thinking he might have enough.

The ledger dropped from his fingers.

ཀ ཁ

Cassie plumped the pillow and sat upright in bed, delighting in the feel of Strudel curled beside her. Reaching for the yellowed photograph on the dresser, she studied the image of Jed Stowe, wondering anew what there was about this man – her great-grandfather, a man whose blood she shared – that Mimi loathed. She studied the face smiling at the camera from under the cocked hat. Where was Mimi reflected in the face of her father? Where was Lillian, or herself? Not in the blonde hair, the delicate features, the lanky frame. Jed looked like a dandified stranger come to visit the family, instead of being a member of it. Perhaps it was possible to resemble ancestors from long ago, from times past memory. Perhaps familial likenesses popped up indiscriminately for generations, for centuries. If she could go back in time, perhaps she'd find scattered images of herself traversing the eons into the distant future.

She placed the photograph on the dresser, turned off the lamp, and snuggled down into the covers. She might never have the answers. She might never know anything more about Jed or why Mimi hated him so. As she closed her eyes, the last thought lingering in her mind was that the man was long dead and past harm. She felt protected and embraced by the spirit of the house and the memories it held. Every creak in the night, every pop of the boards or rattle of the pipes, every shifting shadow or fleeting fragrance, was familiar now, somehow *right* and welcoming.

Perhaps it was best she didn't know the why of things. Maybe the truth was too awful, and best forgotten.

She slept, falling into dreams. Her heartbeat pulsed in her ears, throbbing like a drum from afar. A figure stirred in the corner, approaching in the moonlit darkness. A man in a large-brimmed black hat, coming closer. More daring now, Jed stood at the foot of the bed and, with a hint of mockery, doffed his hat and bowed. Handsome, so very handsome, the stance cocky, the grin sensual, the gaze inviting. Then the shoulders cracked and split open, as if hacked by an ax, and from the bloody cavern a twin burst forth, forming two heads growing side-by-side from the same source. This twin was malformed, twisted and diseased, with blond hair curling around a pair of stubby horns. The twin-headed Jed leaned over the foot of the bed, reached for her, and opened his mouths to speak.

Cassie gasped. *Go away!*

A shadowy form blossomed behind Jed, unfolding like the petals of a lethal flower. It entrapped him in an embrace, wrenched him from the ground, and threw him against the wall. He exploded into fragments of ash, the bits crumbling like sparks of a dying fire. A man stood where Jed once had been, his bare chest glimmering in the dark, his ebony hair bound with a white-tipped feather. Those eyes, oh, those eyes! Midnight deep, piercing, branded with a slash of red paint. He slowly lifted his hand, and Cassie felt the brush of his fingers upon her cheek.

Cassie jerked awake. It took a moment to realize she was alone, except for Strudel asleep beside her. She stroked his fur, calmed by its softness. Her heart was wild in her chest, but she wasn't afraid. "Just dreams," she murmured.

She lay still, quieting her spirit. The faint pulse of the drum continued. *That* was no dream; she was awake, alert. She slipped from the bed, tiptoed down the hall to the parlor, then cautiously opened the door and stepped onto the porch.

The meadow was awash in moonlight, magical, glowing, the new-sprouted leaves glittering silver. The wooden steps were cool against her bare feet, the ground rough underfoot. A breeze teased her hair as she walked beneath the stars, pausing to listen. The entire meadow filled with a breath of sound, a faint throbbing as if the earth's heart were beating. It floated in the wind, sighing, sighing, and slipped away.

"Who you talkin' to on that phone, boy?" Billy's father opened the refrigerator and reached for a beer.

Billy spoke into the receiver, "Just a sec," and turned to Guy. "Chuck Dawson."

"Don't recall you mentioning no Chuck before."

"Sure you have. In the band. He plays the drums."

"That so?" Guy pulled a chair from the table and sat, eyes on Billy.

It wasn't right, his father drinking a beer with breakfast hardly done. The table was still cluttered with dirty dishes gummed by egg bits and toast crumbs. Guy shoved a coffee cup aside as Chuck's voice rang in Billy's ear: "Pete said we could jam at his place tonight. Around seven okay with you?"

"Yeah. I'll be there."

He was about to add that he'd need a ride when Guy stood and ripped the phone out of his hand. "You plan on goin' someplace?" His voice was flat and his eyes like gray stones.

Billy's stomach clenched and his skin got clammy. He used to feel this way as a kid when he had done something bad and was about to be punished. Except now he was almost as tall as his dad and hadn't done anything bad at all. "We're going to practice at Pete's place. For the spring dance."

"Hello there," Guy said into the phone, phony and friendly-like. "Who the hell is this?"

"Dad!" Billy hissed, mortified. He grabbed the phone, trying to wrestle it out of his father's grasp. Guy pushed him with his free hand and Billy stumbled backward, bumping into the sink. A jelly jar wobbled on the counter and crashed into the basin. It broke, oozing grape jelly like purple blood.

"Um hum. Um hum," Guy mumbled as he listened to Chuck and stared at Billy. "All right then." He tossed the receiver and walked from the kitchen without another word, his footsteps following him down the hall.

"Hey, Chuck, I'm sorry." Billy tried to sound casual, but didn't succeed very well.

"What's wrong with your old man?"

"He gets weird sometimes."

Chuck laughed. "Yeah. Mine, too. So we're still on for tonight?"

"I'll need a ride. Hard to carry the guitar on my bike."

"How about your dad's pickup?"

"Can't. He's using it." That was a damned lie, but no way was Billy going to let anyone know how flaky his dad had become. How Guy kept the truck key in his pocket during the day and under his pillow at night and freaked out if Billy so much as looked at the blasted pickup. All because he was afraid Billy would sneak off to Cassie's. Hell, he didn't need wheels to get there. He could ride his bike. Or walk. Or crawl if he had to. He just had to wait for the right time.

"Tough luck, Billy. I'll swing by before seven."

"Thanks."

He hung up, careful and quiet. No sound came from his father's bedroom. Billy mopped up the mess of grape jelly. He cleared the table, stacked dishes in the sink. The kitchen clock ticked the seconds, and moment by moment his anger grew. It boiled in his guts and rose up in his throat and wanted to explode out of his mouth in a vomit of words.

He bit them back. He bit them back so hard his lips bled.

"I promise you'll be among the first to know." Cassie forced a smile in her voice, although she felt like flinging the phone across the room.

"We could arrange a preliminary walk-through," the realtor insisted, "nothing official."

"As soon as I'm ready, I'll call."

"I'd appreciate a quick look at the house and land proper to get a general idea. Early bird gets the worm, right?" His chuckle grated in Cassie's ear. "Best way to give you the best offer."

"Thanks. I'll be in touch."

The caller sputtered his farewells as Cassie hung up, glad to be rid of him. Yet time was running short. She needed to stop procrastinating and make a decision. Ever since the For Sale sign had been posted in Berta's yard, word of her own plans to sell had gotten around. Real estate developers began contacting her: a smarmy big-name somebody with a well-oiled selling pitch, two reps from smaller companies spewing words in a nervous rush, and one good ol' country boy trying to charm with lots of *ain'ts* and *y'alls* thrown in for good measure. Then this persistent fellow. She told them all the same thing: they were welcome to inspect the land as soon as she was ready.

She should be ready, no excuses – especially after receiving a surprising letter last week from Diane, her ex-boutique partner in Houston and current marketer of tacky chicken feather war bonnets. The letter held good news – wonderful news, really. She pulled it from the side table drawer to read for the umpteenth time, shaking her head at the funky stationery border printed with glittery faux turquois:

> *Hi! Thought you might want to know Spirit of the Southwest is struggling along, in spite of the ridiculous rent that keeps going up and up; wouldn't be surprised one day if it hit the moon. Anyway, miss you, even your fussy nit-picky insistence upon selling only "the good stuff." With that in mind, I thought you'd be interested in this news I clipped from an arts mag – can't remember which, sorry. Anyway, it seems a couple of nifty spaces just your size will be opening up next year in La Villita, a historic art village right off the River Walk in San Antonio. Now that's the sort of place where you'd fit right in, surrounded by everything artsy-fartsy.*
>
> *Well, gotta go. Just wanted to touch base.*
>
> *Hugs,*
>
> *Diane*

She tucked the letter back into the drawer, remembering the good things about Diane, her quirky smile and kindness. The anger that Cassie had felt, the frustration with Diane's quest for touristy junk, the hurried sale and frantic desire to leave town, no longer mattered. Now she could look back and think of Diane with fondness and of the boutique without regret. Things had worked out for the best, Cassie knew. Hanging onto that shop would have been, in a sad and twisted way, hanging onto her past.

Now an opportunity presented itself, a terrific opportunity. Realtors were knocking on her door, and the perfect place to open a classy new boutique in San Antonio – the kind she had always wanted – suddenly was there for the taking.

So what's keeping me? Why am I lagging?

She picked up her canvas bag and stepped outside. A rake leaned against the porch and she picked that up, too. *Tomorrow,* she vowed. *I'll contact the realtors tomorrow after this last task is done.*

She looked across the creek and up the high bank into the woods and smiled at the figure standing there. At least one of Justin's angels had been saved from the scrap heap. Until a few weeks ago it had posed in his front yard, larger than any mortal. Now the archangel guarded Cassie's family cemetery, shield raised in perpetual readiness under the shade of a cypress tree. It lifted her spirits to see it, proud and grand, protecting Mimi and the ancestors that were part of them both.

The morning sun bathed the field and splashed into the creek, dazzling Cassie's eyes. She walked across the bridge toward the cemetery, her hand skimming along the new rails. The bridge had been repaired, but the floorboards still groaned as though a troll lurked beneath, gnashing its teeth. She held the rake and the canvas bag swung from her shoulders. Inside were work gloves, gardening shears, clippers. Today was as good a day as any to tidy up the cemetery. She'd search for Jed's stone, too, although she'd not seen it in all the years she played there as a child. Mimi's letter about him had aroused Cassie's curiosity, as had the unsettling dreams. Or visions, if that's what they were. Or hauntings. Or imaginings. Or a crazy mixture of them all.

The cemetery gate dug into the ground, squealing and dragging debris in its wake as Cassie forced it open. A ramshackle wooden fence the color of dried moss enclosed the small graveyard. Vines curled around the posts, the stems thick as fingers, the foliage a chaotic tangle. A clutter of gravestones sprouted from the earth, some so old they sagged as if melting into the ground. Others lay flat as stepping stones in a neglected garden, partially hidden among weeds and undergrowth. She had played here as a child, hopping from one stone to another, chanting the words carved on the engravings as if they were limericks for a game: *Liesbeth Grund, Gone With God; Edwin Dorst, Fell From His Horse; Matty Liest, Beloved Wife Too Soon Departed*. One simple engraving interested her most: *Etta Anne Dorst, February 12th - March 4th, 1849*. The idea of little baby bones lying cold and crumbling in the dirt made her sad, and so she had swept the gravestone clean whenever she played there, and never stepped upon it.

Cassie put the bag aside and set to work with the rake, unearthing years of accumulated undergrowth. The debris was dry on top and moist underneath, like a layered cake embedded with worms and blue-backed beetles and gigantic tree roaches. A garter snake tangled in the prongs of the rake, and she tossed it over the fence. She worked without thinking as the sun traveled its path and morning shadows came and went, sensing only the stretch of her muscles, the song of leaves, the scent of loam clinging to her clothes and hair. The parcel of land was silent; the gravestones grayed hulks, the ruins of a forgotten time. No voices here, no whispers or half-glimpsed shapes, no other-presence. Whatever bodies lay buried clasped no spirits to their graying bones. Those spirits had long departed to the comfort of the house.

She felt at peace, embraced by shadows and memories. There was beauty among the stones, and sorrow, too. So many different lives, breathing for only a flicker of time. If they could speak from their earthen beds, what stories would they tell? "Dust to dust," Cassie murmured, caressing her grandmother's headstone. It was cold and rough under her fingertips.

Jed was not among them. Perhaps he'd been an outcast in the family and buried outside of the enclosed cemetery. Cassie imagined him lying alone, forever longing for his kin on the other side of the fence. She searched there, too, relieved when she couldn't find anything. Being abandoned for all eternity would be too cruel a punishment, no matter how terrible the crime.

She grew tired and took a moment to sit beside Justin's archangel. The meadow sloped down from where she sat, spreading before her like something from a picture postcard: the wandering creek and wooden bridge, the gentle meadow, the looming hills. And in their midst the weathered barn with the windmill beside it, the rambling house protected by the old live oak.

Cassie realized that she loved this place. It was a part of her as much as Mimi was a part of her, as much as her ancestors were a part of her.

Yet here she was, planning to sell it all.

The Remembering

CASSIE LEANED AGAINST JUSTIN'S GUARDIAN ANGEL AND TRAILED HER FINGERS through a drift of fallen leaves, her thoughts troubled. What would happen to the cemetery once she sold? To the spirits? If the house was torn down, would they fade away like smoke or wander around, homeless?

She thought of Rosine, the hasty note scribbled in the Bible, the initials carved inside the lid of the little wooden chest. And, of course, the missing diary. What was she like, this young ancestor? Closing her eyes, Cassie let her imagination roam: *a girl sits among the wild grasses of a field, head bent as she writes in her diary. Sunlight shines upon her long blonde hair and skin so fair it seems made from ivory. She glances up, eyes a startling blue, and smiles.*

"Pensive today?" Tatty stomped into view, her feet in combat boots, her legs encased in baggy cargo pants with twigs sticking out of multiple pockets. She carried a basket overflowing with ball moss, and dropped it beside Cassie.

"Yes, a little."

Tatty slowly lowered herself to the ground. "Rusty joints acting up," she grumbled. Leaves and berry stems tangled in her long gray hair spattered onto her lap.

"Where's your wolf or dog or whatever it is?" Cassie asked. "I haven't seen him lately."

"Over there." Tatty pointed into the woods. "He's likely been watching you all morning."

Cassie saw nothing unusual until she realized the wolf was lying under a cedar, so still she had mistaken him for part of the tree.

"He's not mine, you know," Tatty said.

"Then who owns him?"

"Nobody. He goes where he will."

"There's something special about him, almost eerie."

Tatty shrugged. "He is what he is."

The wolf rose, glancing at Cassie before slipping through the trees. "He's like a magician, isn't he? Appearing and disappearing, blending into the surroundings."

"A magician, eh?" Tatty chuckled. "Rightly put."

"What's his name?"

"It changes, depending. What would you like to call him?"

"I just think of him as Wolf."

"Then that's his name. Wolf."

Cassie shook her head. "You are the most cryptic and amazing creature, Tatty. Sometimes I think you can't possibly be real, that I've made you up."

Tatty sat with her arms wrapped around her knees, gazing at the field below. Something in her posture suggested that she, too, found splendor there. Cassie felt comfortable in her presence, as though they had known one another for eons. She studied Tatty's profile, searching for traces of Hawk in the strong jaw and generous mouth. "Does Hawk play the drums, too?" she asked.

"No. Why?"

"I heard drums last night. I couldn't pinpoint the direction exactly; the sound came from everywhere, throbbing like beating hearts."

"Hawk calls them *memory echoes."*

"He hears drums, too?"

"That, and more."

"*More?* Like a flute?"

Tatty nodded. "Flutes. Plural."

"Oh my God," Cassie breathed. "All this time I thought it was Hawk roaming around the hills at night, playing."

"Sometimes. But not always."

"Memory echoes," Cassie whispered, liking the sound of it.

"Every natural thing upon this earth – including plants, trees, rocks, the hills – has a spirit, a soul if you will," Tatty said. "They listen. They remember. And when our own listening is keen and when the wind blows true, we hear their songs and their sorrows, the remembering."

"You mean I'm hearing flutes and drums that were played years, maybe centuries, ago?"

"You got it."

"What's true for the hills is true for the house, isn't it?" she blurted. "I… hear things. Voices, stirrings. See things, too. In dreams sometimes. Sometimes in the shadows or from the corner of my eyes. Or just… there."

A curious expression flickered across Tatty's face. "Do 'things' include people?"

"Sometimes. Like Jedediah, my great-grandfather. There's a secret about him, a wickedness. Something terrible."

"Anyone else?"

"One especially. A girl. A remarkable girl. Not just in a dream, but in my mind. As if I know her. As if I've seen a portrait or photograph, or as if she knocked on the door and walked into the house. A girl from a different, earlier time."

"Interesting. Any idea what she looks like?"

Cassie shrugged. "No telling, really. Just my imagining."

"Does she have fair skin and yellow hair?"

"How could you know that?" Cassie gasped. "See, I was right! I did make you up. I fell down the rabbit hole with Alice and am conversing with the mad Queen."

"I didn't know. I guessed."

"Well, it's a suspiciously damned good guess. What made you think of it?"

"A story. Want to hear it?"

"Only if it begins with 'Once upon a time.' Seems fitting, don't you think?"

"All right then," Tatty laughed, "since you're in such a fine temper." She crossed her legs, the clunky combat boots giving her some difficulty:

> Once upon a time, a little girl and her great-great grandmother would sit under a cypress tree and tell stories. One of the little girl's favorite was about a woman who fell from the moon. The woman was beautiful, with pale, glowing skin and long golden hair.

Tatty paused, glancing at Cassie. "So far so good?"

"I'm listening, that's for sure."

"Interrupt me if you get bored."

"C'mon, stop dawdling and get on with it. Please!"

"The story began not far from this very place, beyond the western plateaus, in a camp of the Comanche." As Tatty spoke, her voice became rhythmic and melodic, and her gaze distant:

> The woman first appeared among them one autumn night, when the moonlight was so bright it cast shadows upon the land. She was young then, not yet a woman when she walked into their midst. She wore no clothes and did not speak, but stood shining in silence. The holy man prayed to the spirits and learned that she was formed from the skin

> of the moon, and that they would be blessed by her presence. That proved to be true. She grew into womanhood among them, and as she grew she developed healing powers so strong her fame spread throughout the land. People from all the Nations traveled from afar to seek her help, or to wonder at her strange beauty.
>
> She did not live with them always, but came and went as she wished. One night when the winds grew chill she left and never returned. No one knew what happened to her. Some said the moon called her home.
>
> It was always at this point in the story that the little girl would cry, "I don't like that ending! Make up another one!" But the old woman would reply, "I cannot change what is true."

Tatty uncrossed her legs and pulled the basket to her side. "Hungry?" she asked, rummaging under the ball moss. "I've got an apple or two in here someplace."

"Is it?" Cassie asked.

"Is what?"

"You're impossible!" Cassie exclaimed. "Is the story really true, perhaps taken from something that actually happened, or made up?"

"Want one?" Tatty offered an apple to Cassie.

"No! What I want is for you to keep on talking. There's more you haven't told me yet. I can see it in your eyes."

Tatty bit into the fruit, squirting juice down her chin. "You're right," she said, wiping her chin with the back of her hand. "One day, when the little girl demanded that the great-great grandmother make up another ending, she did so. It went like this, in the old woman's words:

> I knew the Moon Woman and loved her and missed her when she was not there. So I decided to follow her when she left again. I packed food and a knife and blanket and waited. I waited for a long time, many days and many nights. Then before dawn in the spring, I saw her slip away. I followed her along the plains and creeks, and followed as the land rose upward to a field surrounded by hills, all

> of it sacred ground. There was a house made of stone. She walked to the house and through the doors with no fear and no hesitation. I knew then that she had two peoples: ours, and whoever else lived behind the stones.
>
> I kept her secret. No one else knows. Except you.

Cassie was so stunned it took a moment before she trusted herself to speak. She motioned to the view before them. "This meadow. This house."

Tatty nodded. "Yes."

"A fair-skinned girl with yellow hair lived here. And grew into a beauty. And lived among the Comanche as a healer from time to time."

"That's how the story goes."

"Rosine!" Cassie cried, delighted. "It must be Rosine!" She fell backward onto the ground, arms outstretched, laughing up at the sky glimpsed through boughs.

"Rosine? How do you know her name?"

"She scribbled a note in the family Bible, in German. Berta translated it for me. The girl I told you about and saw in a dream." A gauzy strip of cloud wafted through the blue; Cassie watched it pass, her mind reeling. "She mentioned a diary. God, I wish I could find it. Just imagine the story she could tell."

Tatty finished the apple and neatly tucked the core into the basket. "It was me, you know," she said. "The little girl was me. And the great-great grandmother was mine."

"You're kidding!" Cassie jerked upright. "Someday I'd love to hear *your* story."

"It's not much; grew up, married a scoundrel, felt like killing him but divorced him instead. The only good thing that came from that union was Hawk."

"Why did you decide to live here, isolated in the woods?"

Tatty stood, absently brushing debris from the seat of her pants. "I need to work in a peaceful place, a place that hears the voice of my ancestors, a place that houses their bones."

"You mean to tell me that Comanche were buried here?"

"Yes, upon the hills."

"Mimi never mentioned it. I wonder if she knew." Cassie looked up at Mount Bubba, wondering who or what might lie there.

"Holy men sang and danced on the ground where your house now sits."

Cassie imagined the dancing, the drums and flutes and rattles, the flash of color in sunlight and the glow of a fire at night. "Tatty," she ventured, "ever since I was a child I've loved anything Indian, bought a zillion books about them and read every word, chased artifacts and artwork, created a business, even. And all along, Comanche history was right here, under my feet." She shivered, as if expecting warrior ghosts to rise from the grass, angry to see her trespass.

"Tatty," she moaned, "oh, Tatty, how could I possibly sell sacred ground?"

Whistling ducks sang along the creek that night. Cassie rocked in the swing and listened to their calls, to the rusty groan of the windmill, the rhythmic squeal of the swing, the jingle of angel chimes. A glow from the bay window fell upon the Emperor Tree and the cherub riding its limb. A shape moved beneath, and two amber eyes caught the light. Wolf was keeping watch.

The woods were obscured by shadows, although moonlight glinted upon the guardian angel. Cassie tucked her legs beneath her, reflecting upon her day at the cemetery. Being around gravestones made her even more aware of the passage of time and those she had loved and lost: her husband Thomas and their almost-child. Mimi. Justin, and now Berta, too. Her father. Cassie absently touched his blue-stoned heart ring on a ribbon around her neck, wondering whether he was alive or dead. As for her mother, Lillian had left long ago, and in her place was a cardboard copy of the woman she once had been, running from a shattered heart.

If I sell and leave, I'll lose even more who are dear to me: Tatty, Nan, Pete, Billy.

And Hawk?

Hawk was forever soaring but never landing. She didn't expect anything from him other than this maddening, erratic, occasionally tender friendship. But Hawk had awakened something inside of her, something she thought had died at the bottom of a cliff and would remain forever buried among the roots of her rosebush. Because of him, she could love again.

Hawk, why can't it be you? It could be you.

The Portrait

Hawk dropped the boulder into place and stood back to study the overall effect. The landscaping was evolving as he had hoped. Soon bluebonnets and red and purple lantana would sprout among the hilltop rocks and prickly pear, along with Texas yellow bells and scarlet butterfly weed and whatever wildflower seeds he'd tossed earlier, allowing the winds to scatter them. He wanted an explosion of color to spring up in unexpected places.

The day was warm; he had been working hard and his shirt clung to his skin. He took it off and tied it around his waist, then stood quietly to gaze at a nearby hill. Mount Bubba, Cassie had called it. He grinned, thinking it did, indeed, resemble a good-old-boy paunch overhanging a low-slung belt.

He wondered what Cassie was doing today, if she, too, was outside and warm under the same brilliant sky. He thought of when he'd seen her last, at Justin's funeral. She had turned in her pew to look at him as he walked past, the casket cutting into his shoulder as the lifeless burden cut into his heart. Her eyes had seemed unusually large and dark, and spoken to him with empathy and sorrow.

She drew close in his mind, lovely, enigmatic. There was an intangible essence about Cassie, one he couldn't capture in his portrait of her. Not that he hadn't tried. Time and time again he'd return to the canvas, his frustration growing as he stood, brush in hand, studying his unfinished work: her face lifting into a beam of light, her hands cupped to receive… what?

A blessing, perhaps. A promise. A gift from the spirit. Winds blew all around her, yet she remained calm amid the storm, eyes raised. A fair enough painting, he supposed. But something vital was missing, something at the tip of his consciousness. The answer wouldn't come, and he eventually thrust the canvas aside, face to the wall.

In his imagination, he stood at the top of Mount Bubba and once again gazed down at Cassie as he had months ago. The sun had been as bright then as it was today, the sky as clear. She was skidding down the hillside, arms outstretched, her big shirt flapping in the wind like wings as if she were trying to lift off the ground and fly. She landed hard on her knees and remained so still he feared she was hurt. He began to climb down, but she looked up at him and shook her head, dark hair tumbling a *No.* The distance between them was too great for him to see the color of her eyes or the shape of her face. She raised her hand in farewell, graceful even on her knees, and he knew she must be beautiful.

In retrospect, she had seemed to be a natural part of the hillside and surroundings, belonging there as surely as did the earth she knelt upon, or the old oak beside the house, or the creek waters. As though she had been born by the elements. Hawk gasped. He hadn't realized that the idea had crept into his mind and hidden there, waiting to make itself known.

That's what's missing!

Hawk rushed to the studio, the familiar room awash in light from tall windows all around. He felt the excitement stirring, a sense of fear and exhilaration, as if he were about to leap from a high cliff into the unknown. Kicking the stool aside, he lifted the portrait and placed it on the easel, grabbed the brushes, grabbed the paints, and began. He worked without sitting, without stopping, intent, focused, lost in the moment. Time had little meaning. The light changed as the sun moved ever westward, yet he barely acknowledged it, shifting his easel as needed.

His concentration was so complete that at first he didn't hear Old Yeller barking, the car coming near. Startled, Hawk turned to the window and saw Rebecca's van rumbling up the drive.

Damn! Sometimes she knew exactly the most inopportune time to visit, as if radar were implanted in her forehead. *Why now, for God's sake?* He put the brush down with a sigh and went to the back porch to meet her.

The van rounded the corner and barely stopped before Rebecca flung open the door and cried, "I have glorious news!"

"Lousy timing, Rebecca. I'm..."

"This can't wait." She hopped down awkwardly, clinging to the doorframe for balance. "Thornwood Gallery in Houston practically begged me for an extensive exhibit of your work! One that reveals the depth of your – and I quote – mystical vision." She grinned, evidently delighted at Hawk's expression. "Wowed you, didn't I?"

"Thornwood is one of the finest galleries in the country. What did you do, promise my eternal soul?"

"Only thirty paintings."

"*What?*"

"Don't panic. It's not `til October." Rebecca slid her cane from the car seat and leaned upon it with both hands, as if she were pausing in the midst of a tap dance routine.

"October? How the hell can I have thirty pieces by October?"

"You have dozens stacked and filed away in your studio, gathering dust like forgotten treasures in an attic. The rest you can paint from scratch. And for heaven's sake, put your shirt on. It's weird talking business when you're half-naked."

Hawk yanked the shirt from around his waist and slipped it on while her eyes followed every movement of his fingers, lingering as he tucked the hem into his jeans. It made him damn uncomfortable. "Take an inventory of what's available, and I'll think about it."

"What's to think about? It's a no-brainer." She came toward him, careful of pebbles along the walkway. "Serious art collectors will be coming, and you'll be busy with television talk shows and reporters and art critics and so on. You can walk away from this thing with great publicity and a nice bank account."

"You know how I hate crowds and all the fuss and bother. And I don't like being rushed."

"I swear, Hawk, you try my patience!" Rebecca snapped. "Getting you out of this hilltop retreat of yours and into the world is like dragging a mule to the water trough!"

"That bad?" Hawk chuckled. "Maybe I can pull it together in time and paint a few more. The rest I'll cull from galleries scattered around the country."

"Can't. I promised new works exclusive to Thornwood."

"My God, Rebecca, you must think I'm a magician, snatching paintings out of a hat like so many rabbits!"

"Might not be as many new works as you think, depending upon what you already have hidden in cupboards for the enlightenment of spiders. Stop being such a grouch."

"Sorry," he grumbled. "I plead artistic temperament."

"Insanity is more like it. Oh – let's ask Cassie if we can use *Spirit Song* for promotional purposes. The title reflects the totality of your work and is perfect for the theme, but in plural: *Spirit Songs*."

"Why ask Cassie?"

Rebecca paused, an odd expression flickering in her eyes. "She bought it. You didn't know?"

Hawk gawked at her, his mind a startled blank.

"Good Lord, Hawk, sometimes you're dense as a mole. Didn't you see it at New Year's, hanging over that pathetic sagging old sofa in the parlor?" She sniffed, "Not the best spot, I might add. Spoiled the effect."

"I didn't go in there."

"Well, now you know. Come on then, let's go see what you've got stored away in that studio of yours."

With uncharacteristic alacrity, she was up the steps and through the door before Hawk thought to stop her. He remained rooted beside the porch, stunned, his memory returning him into the darkened room of Smithy's Barbeque. He had been playing the flute, improvising as he liked to do, when a woman appeared in a shaft of light as if by magic, as if his music had conjured her. She stood before him in beauty so vivid he caught his breath and the notes wavered. She clutched a package wrapped in brown paper bound with red twine, a gold and red stamp on the back. Had he stopped to think at that moment, had his attention not riveted upon her face, he would have recognized the signature wrapping of Whistle Pic Gallery.

Was that the day she bought *Spirit Song*?

"Hawk, stop dawdling!" Rebecca gestured at him through the window, impatient and imperial as always.

Queen Rebecca, he thought with a stab of guilt, *can be a royal pain in the ass.*

The easel beckoned as Hawk entered the studio. It faced in the opposite direction, the back edges of the canvas extending beyond the easel frame. It seemed to expand in his eyes, take up space and air in the room, demand attention. Rebecca didn't notice. She was busy going through the paintings stacked on the shelving or lined up against the wall, exclaiming about this or that, separating them. And all the while Hawk felt the lure of the easel pulling him to the portrait awaiting there.

He didn't want Rebecca to see it, not yet. It wasn't ready. *He* wasn't ready. Damn, he wanted her gone. He positioned his body to block it from her view, determined to keep her attention elsewhere until she finally left. Impatience gnawed at his heels. He needed to get her out of the room and out of the house and out of his driveway. He needed to be alone with his paints.

"Rebecca, enough rummaging." Hawk stifled his irritation and made an effort to be engaging. "I really need to get back to work, especially since you've pledged my every waking hour to Thornwood." Guiding her by the elbow, he escorted her toward the door. "You've been amazing. My career would be in tatters without you." She beamed at his compliment as he had intended, and he hated himself for it.

"What's that?" She asked, twisting around to look at the easel.

Hawk urged her onward, opening the door. "Something I'm working on."

"Well, then, let me see!" She pulled from his grasp, her cane tapping the floor. Remarkable, how fast that woman could walk once the notion got into her.

"It's not ready yet, Rebecca."

"So what? No need to be modest with me." She glanced at him over her shoulder, teasing. "I know it will be wonderful, however unfinished." And with that she turned to the portrait.

Hawk felt her abrupt stillness, as though she had stepped inside herself and shut the door. Her smile grew pinched. She barely moved, save for a subtle shift of the head or the slow traveling of the eyes. "I'm right," she finally said, her voice brittle. "It's wonderful."

"You think so?" God Almighty, why did he feel so damned guilty?

"Yes." She moved away and tap-tapped with her cane to the door. "I simply must be going. When shall we get together next? It should be soon. So much for us to do, so little time to do it in. You're right about that." The words rushed through stiff lips. "Tomorrow, perhaps, or the day after, don't you think? Got to get a grip on things."

"Rebecca, I..."

She spun abruptly, the cane whacking him on the ankle. "Why?" she cried, her voice breaking. "Why Cassie?"

Hawk didn't know how to respond. He followed her outside, offering to help her into the van. She pushed his hand away, the strange smile still plastered on her face. "I can manage just fine," she said. "See you soon." She hoisted herself up, her movements jerking in ways that broke his heart. The pain in her hip was his fault. The cane his fault. He watched, feeling helpless, as she backed up the van and, as always, waved goodbye before heading down the drive. And, as always, Old Yeller chased after, barking until she disappeared.

He wished he could figure out the mixed feelings simmering inside him. He was like a makeshift stew, a mish-mash of emotional odds and ends all stirred together, the taste of one blending with the other until it was impossible to identify the individual ingredients.

Old Yeller came bounding back down the road. He followed Hawk into the studio and flopped into the corner, panting. The room was cast in a golden glow, the edges softened. Hawk paused, thinking he could almost believe the moment magical, the transformation of day into night. A subtle shift, a turning of the world. He approached the easel and gazed at his handiwork as if seeing it anew: Cassie turned partly toward him, her face and shoulders and the swell of her breasts glistening in the surrounding dark. Swirling clouds parted to reveal a great oak arching overhead, roots winding deep and crawling up the border, encircling her. A sliver of sun and moon. The golden eyes of a wolf in the shadows. Wild vines in her hair streamed behind her, curling around the tree trunk, following the path of the roots. A touch of sadness haunted her eyes, and yet she welcomed the approaching storm and lifted her head into the light. And her cupped hands, ones he had thought were open to receive a gift, were instead releasing sparks: handfuls of tiny bright embers, winged as dragonflies, spiraling upward to the heavens.

He had painted a goddess of earth and air, of light and shadow, bound to the elements.

"Why Cassie?" Rebecca had asked. Yet she must have known. The answer was there, on canvas. His hands had formed the words his voice had never dared speak.

Hawk cleaned his brushes and capped the paint tubes. There was nothing more he could add or change. The portrait was finished. He turned slowly away and walked into the living room. His gaze focused on the photographs arranged on the side table, one in particular: Rebecca standing close beside him, smiling up into his face, his arm around her shoulders. She smiled from a multitude of photos: Rebecca with Tatty, Rebecca with his daughter Susan, Rebecca with Old Yeller, Rebecca Rebecca Rebecca. All in matching gold frames. A neat set, thanks to Rebecca. He flipped each one over face downward.

He found an old bottle of Crown Royal in a dusty purple sleeve in the back of the kitchen cabinet, filled half a glass, added a dash of water, and headed for the front porch. The sunset was dazzling, the sky ablaze with color, as if the heavens were burning. He leaned back in the rocking chair, his throat warmed by the whiskey as the night fell upon him.

The Silver Scorpion

CASSIE STEPPED INTO THE COOL DARKNESS OF THE CELLAR, BRACED HERSELF against the wall, and tugged the light cord. The bulb swung to and fro, throwing odd shapes and shadows into the gloom. The space was almost empty; gone were the dozens of jars on the wooden shelves, covered with dust and cobwebs. Gone were the piles of clothing and junk Mimi had tossed from the top step. Cassie had stripped the cellar clean. Only the battered wooden trunk remained. It too, was empty. Cassie hadn't the heart to throw away a single item packed inside so had stored everything in a box printed with the label, *Memory Echoes.*

Careful of the uneven stones underfoot, she walked down the stairs and ran her hand over the trunk lid, dust coating her fingers. It must have been a beauty once, with green leather straps, brass hinges and handles, and painted trim. Now all that remained was a faded, crumbling shell.

"Time for the dumpster, old girl," Cassie murmured, and began to haul it up the steps. It was heavy and bumped against her legs as she dragged it behind her. She turned around and pulled backward, yanking the trunk up the first step.

Something shifted inside, a whisper of sound, a muffled thump. Puzzled, she pushed the trunk back into the circle of light and lifted the lid, expecting to see a forgotten item inside.

Empty. Nothing was there, save for the faint scent of lavender.

She reached for a side handle and tilted the trunk upward until it rested on one end, listening. All was silent except for the moldering wood that creaked against the strain. She dropped it onto the flagstone floor, reached for the opposite handle, and tilted it up onto the other end.

Once again, a soft rustle, a sensation of something sliding from one side to the other.

Something was in there. Something hidden.

She ran her fingers along the inside, searching – and discovered something else, too: the floor of the trunk was pulling away from the decaying frame. It also seemed higher than it should be, by almost three inches.

A false bottom!

Her hands trembled. She had found it. Surely she had found it. What else would be entombed, other than Rosine's diary?

She forced her fingers into the narrow gap between the walls and bottom, in hopes she could wrench away the wood. A few slender pieces split, minute splinters. One of them pierced her thumb, leaving tiny beads of blood. Frustrated, she stood and was about to hop inside the trunk and stomp on it, shatter it with her feet, until she realized she might damage whatever lay hidden within. A screwdriver ought to do the trick. She dashed up the stone steps two at a time, mumbling, "Where the hell did I put it?" before she lost patience and grabbed a claw hammer, then hurried down the steps so fast she stumbled and ended up sprawled over the trunk with a scraped knee. Laughing at her foolish haste and ignoring her inner warning to slow down, to take her time, she ripped into the rotted wood. The trunk groaned and shrieked as she tore its floor and walls apart, as though dying at the moment of giving birth.

A small bundle lay in the hidden womb, swaddled by a lace-trimmed handkerchief musty and fragile with age. She unwound the cloth and discovered a book, the cover tarnished by time into the color of rust. The title was stamped into the leather in faded gold: *Tagebuch.*

She turned to the first page and gaped at the writing in the center, done in grand loops and swirls she recognized as Old German.

Dieses Tagebuch gehört Rosine Dorst.

"Here it is," she whispered, hardly able to believe the treasure she had at last found.

Rosine's diary!

Billy was so excited he thought for sure he would explode.

One single page. One wonderful, miraculous page that might change the course of his life. He read it again, lingering over the words:

> *Dear Mr. Wilkins,*
>
> *Thank you for your interest in California Institute of Technology. We are impressed with your letter and drawings, and encourage you to compile a portfolio of projects and design concepts to include upon application during your senior year. Admission is highly competitive, but the addition of a portfolio of this nature could be advantageous. We look forward to hearing from you at that time.*
>
> *Sincerely,*
>
> *Dale Fitch, Director of Undergraduate Admissions.*

The very best part was a note scribbled at the bottom:

> *Billy, Mr. Fitch asked for my recommendation. He has it in spades. If you are interested in a scholarship, please contact me upon acceptance by Caltech. Your work shows great promise.*
>
> *Dr. Daniel Andrews, Chair, Mechanical Engineering*

Laughter threatened to bubble out of him and ricochet off the kitchen walls. He had written to the university in a frantic, secret rebellion against his father, adding schematics of a futuristic automobile without believing that anything would ever come of it. And look what happened! Never in a million years had he really, truly believed Caltech was anything other than a dream. It was too far away, too expensive, and too prestigious for someone like himself, a poor nobody kid from a dinky nowhere town.

"Oh my God," he whispered, "this is seriously cool."

He had to phone Cassie. No way could he keep this news from her. He glanced at the clock: seven-thirty, past dinner-time. Maybe he could sneak a call before his dad got home. He reached for the wall phone, knowing Guy would go ballistic if he found out.

The phone rang two, three, four times. *Answer, answer!* Five, six.

Guy's pickup rumbled up the driveway, coughing as it came to a stop. Billy slammed the receiver into place, rushed into the bedroom, and hid the letter under his pillow.

"You get the mail, boy?" Guy called from the front door.

"On the coffee table."

Billy returned to the kitchen, appalled to see that he had left the Caltech envelope lying in plain sight on the counter. He tucked it under his shirt the moment Guy entered the kitchen.

"Nothing but bills," Guy grumbled. "You start dinner?"

"Sorry, Dad. I've been busy."

"You don't know busy." Guy opened the refrigerator and pulled out a Coors, flicking the cap with his thumb. "There's nothing in this damned fridge. Just eggs, milk, and something moldy."

"We've got canned beans in the cupboard. How about eggs and beans on toast?"

"Fix some for yourself. I ain't hungry." Guy twirled the chair around, straddling it. "That shit coffee about turned my gut to acid."

"You have a stomach ache?"

"Yeah. That and my head." He drank down the beer, wiping his mouth with the back of his hand. "This'll be my dinner tonight. A hell of a lot more satisfying."

"You should eat."

Maybe Guy didn't hear. He stood up, got another Coors, and sat down again. The cap flicked up and over the table, rolling across the floor as he leaned on his elbows and looked out the window.

Billy warmed the beans and fried the eggs, worried about his dad. Guy hadn't taken care of himself lately. He looked scruffy, his cheeks stubby and hair uncombed and overalls splotched with grease.

"Sky sure is pretty," Guy blurted. "Your mother always liked the sunset."

Billy filled his plate and sat at the table. He began to eat, the food tasteless in his mouth.

"You got to have milk," Guy said.

"I'm okay."

"Don't argue. Get me a beer while you're at it."

"You've already had two."

Guy shrugged and turned again to the window. Billy did as he was told. He sat down again, drinking his milk as Guy watched the sky darken. The envelope scratched Billy's chest. The joy it had brought rose up and just about spilled over. He wished he could tell his father. The words were there, right behind his lips, wanting to be spoken.

"Dad?"

"You finished?"

Billy glanced down at his empty plate. "I guess."

"Clean up then, and do your homework. I'm going to lie down a while." He rose, stumbling, and walked herky-jerky down the hallway.

Billy waited until he heard the bedroom door shut before he withdrew the envelope tucked inside his shirt and smoothed the wrinkles. He rose from the table, stepped outside, and thrust the envelope up at the fading red and gold sky. "Look, Ma," he whispered. "Caltech!"

Guy sat on the edge of his bed. He wanted to close his eyes but was afraid Sarah would be there, waiting in the darkness of sleep.

It had started with a dream that gripped him and wouldn't let go. Every moment was so real it was like living the terror all over again: Sarah heavy in his arms, her soft hair falling over his hands onto the blood-soaked ground. His knees bit into the gravel as he held her, as he tried to will the breath back into her lungs. Pale, her face pale, paler than ever it was in life. A scarlet ribbon spooled from her lips and down her chin and onto his fingers. But it was her eyes that captivated him: wide, open, staring directly into his. Her mouth moved, trying to speak, although no words came out.

Why? the lips had asked. *Why?* silent, silent.

Exhaustion pulled him down onto the bed. He could hear Billy washing the dinner dishes in the kitchen. The sounds bit into his head, traveling down the nerves in the back of his neck. He looked up at the ceiling, eyes traveling the yellow stains where the roof leaked during that bad storm some months back. The stains were in odd shapes, like clouds, and he let his mind conjure up pictures: a wrench, a flying horse, a face.

Oh, God, *her* face. Sarah up there, gazing down at him. Her lips, moving. *Why?*

Christ, I'm sorry. I'm so sorry! Guy tried to speak, but his own mouth wouldn't work proper.

If only I had been more careful that morning. If only I had looked before backing up the truck. If only I had waited just one more second. If, if…

Guy pressed his hands against his skull as guilt ate his soul.

Cassie was lowering the cellar door when the phone rang. She let the door fall shut and hurried to answer, but was too late. "No matter," she murmured, and sank into the stuffed chair, the diary in her lap. It must have been a deep red when new, the leather soft, the gold letters gleaming. Now creases marred the surface like the mottled skin of a beautiful old woman, and gray threads unraveled from the binding. The pages were stippled with brown flecks. She turned them slowly, relishing the texture of the yellowed paper, the thin fusty scent, the hand-scrawled lettering. It was written in ink, sharp-pointed and pressed into the paper amid splotches as if composed with a dip pen and passion. And all, of course, in German.

Such a wonderful find, so many pages to read and so much to discover – in a language she didn't know! Cassie clasped the diary to her chest. Whatever story Rosine had to tell, wherever her bones might lie, her spirit was here, in these time-worn pages and in Cassie's heart.

Rosine. Moon Woman. Sister ancestor who visits me in dreams.

She leaned back, the horsehair cushions prickling her neck, remembering the moment before the telephone rang. She had stood at the top of the cellar steps with the diary in her hands, gazing down into the shadows. It had felt as though something unseen hovered in the quiet nothingness, a benevolent presence. Why else would the scent of lavender have wafted from the trunk? It normally smelled of cedar and mold.

"Thank you," she whispered.

She wondered whether it was her imagination, or whether the cool breeze that touched her cheek truly was an embrace.

Billy hunched over his desk, doing his homework. He glanced up, the lamp casting a glow upon the walls and on the bed. The spread was rumpled, but otherwise the room was neat. Billy prided himself on keeping it that way, with everything in its proper place. His dad would sometimes stand in the doorway and look around with his eyebrows raised and say stuff like, "Neatnick Bill's been at it again." At least he used to. Now Guy hardly noticed anything much. Billy could wear the same stinky old shirt to school every day if he wanted, and still Guy would probably look right through him and not see a thing out of the ordinary.

Billy sharpened a pencil over the trash basket, listening as Guy made yet another trip down the hallway to the kitchen: the click of the nearby bedroom door, footsteps passing, the squeal of the refrigerator as it opened and closed, more footsteps, and the final click of the bedroom door once again, very quiet, as if he didn't want Billy to know what he was doing.

Good God, how could he *not* know? Guy had hidden away in his room like a troll all night, venturing out for beer trips. Back and forth, back and forth. And here he was, doing it again.

Maybe his headache is so bad he can't sleep.

His father always got cranky when he felt bad or couldn't sleep, but nonetheless Billy crossed the hall and knocked on the door. "Dad? Are you okay?"

A muffled response, like a grunt.

Billy hunkered down and peeked through the old keyhole. A stranger slumped on Guy's bed, the sheets and blanket in disarray, the room lit by a single lamp. A stranger in the dimness, staring at empty beer bottles lined up in rows. A stranger who almost looked like his dad, but for the terrible sadness on his face. Billy blinked, and the man turned slowly with bloodshot eyes and looked right at him.

Billy gasped and turned aside. After a moment, he returned to his own room and closed the door behind him.

He couldn't concentrate on homework that night. His mind kept jumping around, first going to his father hiding away like a sick animal, and then to the letter from Caltech and the future it might promise. His feelings followed his thoughts, happy and sad and happy again.

He pulled the letter from under his pillow and read it over and over, savoring each word until the sadness melted away.

Caltech! It could happen, it could really happen.

He picked up the pencil and began a list of things he needed to do:

(1) Study hard for A's, even in boring subjects

(2) Work as much as possible and save every penny

(3) Begin portfolio

Billy tapped the pencil on the desk, thinking of the Studebaker. He had begun a major undertaking that should be a key part of the portfolio. Yet all of his careful paperwork was in the barn and the car not close to being complete. He hadn't even taken photographs.

I've got to go over there and finish what I started.

Antsy, Billy paced the room. He felt strong, as if anything were possible, as if he could lift from the floor and fly into the future. Cassie would be excited too; he was sure of it. He wanted to talk to her so badly he carried on imaginary conversations in his head, dreaming of what she'd say and how glad her voice would sound.

The house settled and grew quiet, and Billy realized that Guy had stopped trolling the hallway. Maybe he was finally asleep. He tiptoed to Guy's door. Usually his father snored when asleep, a rattling, heaving growl. But now there was only silence.

"Dad?" After a moment, Billy stooped to the keyhole.

Guy was lying sideways across the bed in his jeans and socks, feet dangling off the end, arm flung across his brow. His eyes were closed. Billy couldn't tell if he was asleep and so kept watch, scarcely daring to breathe. Waiting, waiting, until he was sure.

Go! Go! Do it now!

He shuffled backwards, then turned and hurried to the kitchen, his bare feet whispering on the cold linoleum floor. His heart thudded as he lifted the receiver and began to dial. The first number. The second. The third.

It was an old-fashioned phone with two brass mouse-ear ringers that had hung in the same place on the wall since before he was born. The loudness had never bothered him until now; each number he touched echoed in the kitchen and down the hall: *brrr-ching! brrr-ching!* It seemed to Billy that it had never been more deafening, *BRRR-CHING!* traveling to every room and likely out the open windows to the neighbor's house a half-mile distant.

Guy's door remained shut. Billy pressed the receiver to his ear and the mouthpiece close to his lips as Cassie's line began to ring.

Answer! Please answer!

"Hello?"

"Hi, Miss Cassie. It's me, Billy."

"Billy! How wonderful to hear your voice!"

She sounded so delighted that for a moment he couldn't say anything more. He started to, but it came out weird.

"Is everything okay?" Cassie asked. "I've missed you!"

"I've missed you, too." He grinned. Everything was fine. Cassie was there, talking to him. He leaned into the telephone, wrapping himself around it, whispering so Guy wouldn't hear. "I've got really great news!" He spoke in a rush, telling her everything. The letter from Caltech. The portfolio. The list of things he needed to accomplish. It all came tumbling out, a waterfall of hushed words. Cassie interrupted with cries of "Wow!" and "Fantastic!" and "I'm so proud of you!" Billy laughed with pleasure, trying to smother the sound with his hand, feeling as though he could accomplish whatever he set his mind to, open any door, walk any path.

"I've got to come and finish the Studebaker. It would be great for the portfolio, the main project, really."

"What about your father? You know how he feels about you coming over here."

"He doesn't know. Not about the letter or anything. I tried to tell him, but couldn't."

"Maybe he's calmed down some and I could talk to him."

"That would just make it worse." Billy sighed, "I don't want to make him mad, but I can't let this opportunity slip through my fingers. I'm coming over. I've got to."

"Listen to me." Cassie's voice turned somber. He imagined her dark eyes looking deep into him like they sometimes did. "The Studebaker is yours. It always has been. You just never knew it."

"Mine?"

"If Guy won't let you come here, then take the car home and work on it there."

"You'd just *give* it to me?"

"With pleasure."

Billy felt a deep flush rise all the way up to his forehead, so emotion-struck he couldn't think of what else to say. It wasn't just the car, which was the most unbelievable gift anyone had ever given him, it was that Cassie cared for him so much she wanted him to have it. *That* was why his eyes misted and his throat closed up and his cheeks turned red.

"What's she's giving you, boy?"

Billy spun around, almost dropping the phone.

Guy leaned against the doorframe, arms crossed. "It's Cassie, ain't it?"

Billy nodded, not trusting himself to speak.

"You going to tell me what's going on, or is it a precious secret between the two of you?" He spit out *precious secret,* as if the words tasted bad.

Billy had the odd sensation of air leaving his body, as if he were disintegrating into molecules and sinking through the floor. He lifted the receiver to his mouth. "Dad's here. I've got to go."

"Bye-bye for now. Take care." Cassie's words rang from the phone before he could hang up. *Take care.* Rebounding against the kitchen walls, bouncing back and forth like a rubber ball. *Take care.*

"You best take care, boy, that's a fact. She's a goddamn witch who got her claws around your heart, squeezing me out of it."

Billy gasped. "That's not true and you know it." Guy just looked at him, a little smile hovering on his lips. It was strange seeing him like that, leaning on the doorway and pretending to be so casual while those awful words spewed out of his mouth.

"Cassie's my friend," Billy said, "the very best friend I ever had."

"So you going to tell me what this very best friend witch gave you, that you was so excited about on the phone?"

"The Studebaker. She gave me the Studebaker, Dad!"

An odd expression flickered in the depths of his father's eyes. "You think she gave you a good-for-nothing beat-up old junk car because she loves you. Ain't that right?" When Billy didn't answer, Guy stabbed his finger at him and demanded, "Ain't that right?"

"Yes."

"Shit, that ain't love." Guy began to unfasten his belt buckle. It was a silver scorpion, large and mean-looking as the real thing. "Love is me working hard every day to make a living for the two of us. Love is me building a business from scratch so you could one day have it for your own. Love is me putting groceries on the table and a roof over your head and clothes on your back. And love is like now, keeping you close to me when she's trying to steal you away." He pulled the belt from around his waist and ran it through his fingers. "What love *ain't* is turning you against your own father and filling your head with nonsense about the future."

"It isn't nonsense, Dad!" He tried to keep his eyes away from the belt. His heart beat so hard he could hear it thrumming in his head. "I got a letter from Caltech and it said my work was promising and for me to apply in my senior year and maybe I'll be accepted and even get a scholarship! I want to show them what I can do, that I have a talent for design and mechanics. One way to do that is with the Studebaker. I could… "

"Shut up about that damn car!" Guy wasn't leaning against the wall now, but had stepped into the kitchen. "You ain't taking nothing that wasn't rightfully bought. And you ain't touching anything or going anywhere that gets you all fired up about leaving home."

"Dad," Billy asked quietly, "aren't you even a little bit proud of me?"

Guy blinked, as if taken aback by the question. "When you give me cause," he said.

"I have given you cause! If you loved me like you said, wouldn't you see it? Wouldn't you say, 'I'm proud of you, Billy?' "

"What kind of dumb ass question is that?"

"You've never said it. Never. Not once."

"All right then. Forget Cassie. Forget that rattletrap car. Forget this nonsense about leaving. Then you'll give me cause enough."

Everything inside of Billy seemed to freeze: his heart, his lungs, the blood pulsing in his veins. He forced his lips to frame the answer:

"No."

"What?" Guy reared up, as if he had been struck.

"I'll work on the Studebaker and apply to Caltech and maybe someday be designing cars." He barely dared breathe, but rushed on. "And Cassie will always be my friend."

The buckle snaked out, grazing Billy on the thigh. "Don't you ever disobey me!" Guy raised his arm and whipped again, wild, erratic. Billy ducked and ran to the other side of the kitchen. The belt missed, striking the cat clock; bits of black and white plastic showered the floor. Guy crunched over the pieces, lurching toward Billy, the leather thrashing.

Although everything was happening fast, for a moment it seemed to go in slow motion: the grimace crawling up Guy's face, the leather belt writhing like a dying snake, the silver buckle floating toward Billy's cheek. The buckle was there, in front of him; Billy reached out, caught it in his fist, and yanked. Guy stumbled into a chair and fell, dragging it down with him, his mouth opened in a howl.

Billy stared at the silver scorpion in his hand, wondering why he had never before noticed the tiny red stone embedded in each eye. The belt slipped from his fingers, landing on the floor as he opened the door and walked into the yard. It was a beautiful night, the sky studded with stars, the moon low on the horizon. He climbed the fence and leaped to the other side, the ground harsh under his bare feet.

"Billy!" Guy hollered behind him. "Billy!"

He hurried deep into the field, where the wild grasses sometimes grew waist-high, and sat hidden in the shadow of a mesquite tree. He could see the fence, the back yard, the house, glimmering in the moonlight. His father staggered in the yard, flailing his belt, yowling. He seemed small in the distance, small and insignificant.

Silken Threads

THE MEADOW BLAZED WITH THOUSANDS OF BLUEBONNETS. BLUE ON THE FIELDS, along the creek, and creeping up the hills as if the morning sky had fallen onto the earth. Sprinkled among them were red Indian paintbrush and snowy blackfoot daisies with yellow hearts and lavender foxglove Mimi had called *fairy thimbles.* Cassie packed lunch in a wicker basket, remembering how she used to sit in the middle of all that blue when she was young, the wildflowers prickling the backs of her legs. Their scent was loamy and mysterious, as if they had seeded in dark, moldy caverns underground.

The bluebonnets were calling! She grabbed the diary, tucked it into her basket, and hurried outside. Perhaps she might walk among the same explosion of color that had met Rosine's eyes long years ago. Perhaps she might even sit in the place where Rosine had once lingered, enjoying the day, eating lunch. She strolled along the meadow, the flowers so thick she couldn't help but crush them with each step. The windmill groaned as she passed, rusty blades fighting with the wind. She averted her eyes from the closed barn door and the rope dangling from the clasp, wishing that Billy were there inside. She missed him. *If wishes had wings, beggars would fly,* Lillian used to say, her voice tart as sour apples.

If wishes had wings and the impossible made possible, Billy would be my son.

Her rational self snorted, *What about Guy?* The dreamer replied, *He vanishes in a puff of smoke and we all live happily ever after. End of fairytale.*

She followed the curve of the creek into the woods. It led her through a canopy of light and shadow before opening into a wildflower-strewn pasture partly encircled by craggy hills, as if enclosed in a broken bowl. She had played here when she was a child, where the peach trees and strawberry patch had grown riotous with neglect. She had shimmied up branches or plucked fruit from vines warmed by the sun. To her right was the slab of rock in the creek where she had sat with her toes in the water. Beyond, the prickly pear cactus shaped like a jackrabbit. She had sewn orange buttons on it for eyes; one still remained, embedded in cactus flesh.

Farther on, nestled in the shade of a small hill, was a pool fed by the creek. A weeping willow grew on the opposite shore, delicate limbs trailing in the water. Something about the way the clouds reflected in the shimmering depths made her pause. She looked down to the pebbled bottom, the mirrored sky and trees and hills seeming to form another, topsy-turvy world. Her face looked back at her, dark hair ruffled by the wind and rippling in the current like sea grass. As if she were a creature of the water, like the woman in the painting hanging on the parlor wall.

That's it! Cassie gasped and spun around to face the hill rising behind her. This must have been the very place Hawk chose for *Spirit Song*! He painted it high up there, looking down. She studied the landscape with new eyes. Hawk had transformed it, revealing the hidden soul, the memory echoes. Through his eyes, horses raced within the clouds, Indians wound among the trees, the wolf – *her* wolf – emerged from the boulder. And the woman became the water, her hair the current protecting a child. Cassie had loved *Spirit Song* since the moment she had seen it in the window at Whistle Pic Gallery, and now here she was, as if she had leaped through the cedar frame and become part of it!

A fierce urgency hit her, a need to stand where Hawk had stood, to look down and see the land as he had seen it. She didn't give herself time to hesitate. If she could drive Tatty's ancient, belching motorcycle up a hill higher and steeper than any around here, she could climb up this small one without the old fear holding her back.

Or so she told herself.

She lasted maybe three minutes before the hill seemed to swell in size and the air grow thick and oily and clog in her lungs. She tried to go on, but it was like pushing against a powerful wind. The last straw was the image of a jagged, blood-spattered cliff rising out of the earth. It slid toward her, a grotesque mirage ripped from memory, and she turned back, sliding and scrambling to level ground.

She paused, gasping, under the shade of a mountain laurel heavy with purple blossoms. A sheen of perspiration dampened her upper lip.

I won't think about that. I won't!

She pulled the yellow checkered tablecloth from the basket, spread it under the mountain laurel, and sat with her back against the trunk, willing her heart to still and spirits settle as dragonflies skipped across the pond and a gray heron posed along the shore. Blue, blue everywhere; she was awash in hues of blue: sky, flowers, pond, mountain laurel. Too beautiful, too perfect a day to berate herself for faults and fears.

At first she put Rosine's diary in her lap, content with the closeness of it. After a time, she opened it and turned the pages, running her fingers lightly over the letters. She fancied that she could sense the girl who had formed those German words: the fair-skinned face, the wheat-gold hair, the eyes blue as the flowers all about. Rosine would have been strong-willed, even passionate; some of the writing was strewn across the paper as if scrawled in a hurried rage, and some splotched with what may have been tears.

When she came to the last entry, she absently riffled through the few remaining blank pages. And stopped short. Something more was there, something much different. She gaped for a moment before the reality of it hit her.

The handwriting was wrong, wide and precise and sloping to the left. The date was wrong, too. And not a word of it Old German.

English! It was written in English!

She read it all the way through without stopping:

> *15 August, 1907*
>
> *My sin is so terrible even God can't forgive me. But it was worth it, what I did. I'd do it again many times over with no regrets.*
>
> *I'll go mad if I don't confess, yet I can't speak of it to anyone, not aloud. So here, hidden among these pages from my grandmother Rosine, I'll whisper the secret. Let the dead hear me. Maybe they will understand and love me still.*
>
> *I killed my husband. God help me, I abandoned his body to the buzzards and his bones to the elements and was glad to be rid of him.*
>
> *I loved Jed when we first wed. He was handsome and greatly proud and could charm a smile on just about anyone. Yet as the first year eased past, and then another, he began to change with the turns of the moon. A fever burned in his soul and a rage consumed him like a wildfire until the air trembled with the heat of it.*
>
> *At first he vented his anger by throwing or smashing things. When he tired of that and turned upon me with his fists, I hid in the cellar. He followed me there, sniffing me out like a hound after a rabbit. He left the house afterward, galloping away on his white horse like a grand hero with my blood smeared on his hands.*

He returned days later vowing never to hurt me again, but I saw the devil's tail flickering in his eyes and so knew he lied. I grew ever watchful, never at peace in my own house. When a stillness swept over him like the calm before the storm, I learned to drop whatever I was doing and make a run for it. Sometimes I hid in the woods, but the safest place was always on the great hill behind the house. It was the one place Jed feared. He heard drums thundering there and the wails of ghosts. I would sit on the crest and watch in safety as he cowered below, cursing and beating his fists at the empty air. Eventually he would leave. I could see his horse growing smaller in the distance, dust kicking up behind the hooves. After a week or two he would return with gifts and empty words, smelling of whiskey and cigars and whores.

The hills became my refuge. Oftentimes I would spend a good part of the day or night upon them, looking at the sky or at the stretch of earth spread so beautiful before me. I heard the flutes, I heard the songs and voices carried in the winds, and wasn't afraid. Maybe the hills spoke differently to me than to Jed, for I always found comfort among them.

Jed's absences grew longer. Weeks grew into months until he never showed up at all. Eventually he wrote to me from jail in New Orleans, where he was to be hanged for killing a man in a brawl over a mulatto woman. He begged my pity and asked me to pray for him. I could not. I would not. I rejoiced! I danced in the field, arms flung wide and the wind in my face, shouting, Free, free, free! *so filled with happiness I thought I would die of it!*

An urgent need to wash away the dark memories sticking to my soul made me step from my clothes and bathe in the pond by the weeping willow. It was there a stranger appeared from the shadows of the woods. He knelt at the shore and looked at me, the sun glittering on his long black hair. He didn't smile or speak, but I felt the voice of his spirit call across the water. To this day I don't know what overcame me, for I stood up slowly, the water dripping from my naked breasts, and waited for him. Like a beast of the field, like a wanton creature of the earth, I waited for him.

His name was Gray Wolf, and I loved him with my whole heart and body.

We lived together for five years as man and wife under the sight of God if not the law of man. I closed my ears against the nasty grumblings of neighbors who sneered at me for loving a Comanche, whom they believed in their stupidity to be akin to a flea-ridden dog. I pretended not to notice when they turned and walked away from me as if I were diseased. I had no need of them. My peace was in Gray Wolf.

When I grew big with child he wove a chair out of grapevines. He carved roses among the vines, as if the chair had sprouted from the earth and been plucked in full blossom. I suckled our daughter in that chair. And now, even though rudely patched from the ruin caused by Jed's hands, it's still beautiful to me.

Jed escaped from jail or was released, I don't know and don't care. He simply showed up on a hot summer afternoon, as handsome as ever and as twisted in the bowels of his soul. I don't remember much except the heat and the blazing anger and him leaping around the room with the crazy grace of a dancer as he smashed my vine chair against the walls. He hollered about the gossip he had heard all the way from New Orleans, and demanded to know if it was true. "Did you cuckold me with a filthy Injun? Am I made a fool by a white squaw?" He drew his pistol, daring me to answer. I didn't know what to say or do, afraid for my daughter sleeping upstairs.

Gray Wolf had been in the woods hunting deer. He must have seen Jed's horse or heard the commotion, for he was suddenly in the doorway with a rifle aimed at Jed's heart. I heard the click as the safety was released. It was then little Wilhelmina awakened from her nap and walked into the room. "Papa?" she said, and opened her arms to Gray Wolf.

I won't ever forget the look on Jed's face when he saw the truth of my betrayal in the shape of a little child. A split second, frozen in time. His face flattened like the head of a deadly snake.

"Papa?"

Gray Wolf's eyes darted to Wilhelmina, and at that moment Jed shot him. Gray Wolf crumpled to the floor, his rifle clattering on the stones, a red hole gaping in the middle of his forehead. I cried out, oh, I cried out, the howl clawing my throat. I wanted to rush by his side, to cradle his head in my arms, to kiss whatever life breath may still linger on his lips, but my feet could not move.

Jed lifted the pistol to my breasts and swung it lazily from side to side, drawling, "Later, don't you think? After I finish the business here." Then he turned to Wilhelmina.

An awful roar filled my head. Without thinking, as if a demon inhabited my body and directed my limbs to move, I grabbed a cast iron skillet from the stove and with every ounce of strength in my body smashed the back of Jed's skull. I heard a muffled crack like a split watermelon. He staggered and fell, landing on his side as the pistol skittered across the floor. He was still breathing; his chest rose, his eyelids fluttered. Not dead yet, not dead! I straddled him, standing with his legs caught between mine as I gripped the skillet and raised it high, ready to bash him into a bloody pulp. My vision shrunk into a dark tunnel, the light at the end piercing Jed's face, the sharp nose, the blond curls. Every beat of my pulse shouted Kill him Kill him Kill him like the beast I was, a non-thinking beast.

Wilhelmina pulled my skirt. "Go to your room! Now!" I shouted. Her footsteps pattered away and up the stairwell, her sobs echoing like the night cry of a screech owl.

Jed grabbed my ankle, his hands squeezing my bones. He bared his teeth and yanked hard. I fell on top of him and we struggled. I remember strange sounds erupting from my mouth, grunts wild as a feral pig, and a rage so consuming that I hit him with the skillet again and again and again, until I realized his neck had snapped. He couldn't move. His one eye rolled with fright. The other dangled on a slick cord lying on the bloody mess that had once been his handsome face.

I grabbed him by the arms and dragged him outside and up the hill. It was difficult. His hands and arms were slippery with blood. He was on his back, the single eye staring up at me, mouth gibbering. Up the hill I pulled as his blood left a trail behind him. I yanked his body over cactus and jagged rocks and crumbling debris, watching as the realization grew in Jed's fading eye that he would die on the mountain he feared, among the ghosts who haunted him. When we reached the top, I ripped off his clothes and left him to the vultures.

The wind was strong that day, whipping my hair and moaning in my ear as I stumbled down the hillside. I stopped halfway, gasping for breath, and looked at the house below. Wilhelmina's ashen face, framed by the upstairs window, gazed at me and then upward to Jed lying helpless and discarded like forgotten trash. She pressed her opened palms on the window pane, as if to push out the glass and fly to my side.

I doubled over in grief; the cries soared with the winds, carrying my sorrow to the ends of the earth.

Yesterday I found pieces of Jed's skeleton scattered hither and yon by coyotes and other wild creatures, and was glad. Let the sun bleach them white. Let the winds fling them farther. I curse you, Jedediah! I hope your spirit is doomed to wander the hills you hated, searching for your bones and yearning for a final resting place.

I buried Gray Wolf in the family cemetery. There is no headstone. Wilhelmina knows where the grave is, and will remember. Later, when she is older, I will tell her to bury me with him when death calls, my body lying on top of his, so my own bones will crumble and intermingle with his as the ages pass.

I will love him throughout the rags of time.

Emilie Anne Stowe

Cassie was numb. She could not think nor feel as she stood, as she folded the tablecloth and returned the diary to the basket and retraced her steps toward the meadow. It was almost as if she had just awakened from a deep sleep and was still in thrall to the dream world, stepping and moving in a body that wasn't yet earthbound. The creek slid past, the rabbit-eared cactus, the peach trees and strawberry patch. The barn doors rattled in the wind and the windmill groaned, yet she didn't glance at them. Her thoughts were blinded by the images that had leaped from the pages of Emilie's letter, and now swirled behind her eyes.

The basket bumped against her hip as she walked across the creek bridge and past the looming angel to the cemetery. The gate squealed under her touch, like the cry of a seagull. She knew where to find Emilie's simple grave, and knelt beside the stone.

Emilie Anne Stowe
1876 – 1938 Beloved Forever

She brushed away the few leaves cluttered at the base, and leaned in to look more closely at the effigy carved there. She had noticed it before, a figure that seemed at odds with the cherubs and angels usually associated with graveyards. And there it was, dimly lit in the shadow of overhanging oaks: the face of a wolf.

Turning to her grandmother's headstone nearby, she rose and ran her hand over the cool surface, lingering for a moment. "Oh, Mimi," she whispered, "Why didn't you tell me?"

She looked out toward the meadow. The land sloped down toward the creek and then up again. From where she stood, she could see the house and the Emperor Tree and the small figure of Strudel sunning on the porch. Light glittered above the steps, and she knew the breeze had stirred the angel chimes hanging from the eaves. Her eyes rose to Mount Bubba; clouds cast shadow patterns gliding like silent phantoms along the crest and across the hills winding out of sight.

My home.

Joy surged through her with such intensity she wept, tears glistening on her cheeks as she ran-danced back over the bridge and threw herself down amid the bluebonnets. She lay on her back, drawing the scent of earth deep into her lungs, gazing up at the blazing sky. A hawk circled overhead, wings outspread. Her spirit lifted up to his and she spread her arms wide, buried among the flowers.

My home.

The diary had opened a gateway and revealed two worlds, Indian and white, mingling in her blood. The songs, the drums, the ghosts, the echoes were her heritage, and the land an inheritance spanning centuries. She closed her eyes, feeling the connection to her ancestors spinning through time like the silken threads of a quilt, sewing them and their stories together.

Her body seemed to grow heavy and sink into the earth, deeper and deeper, roots sprouting from her heels and buttocks and shoulder blades, roots shooting from her fingertips and each strand of hair, binding her there. Roots clasped the Emperor Tree and crawled up the limestone walls of the house and burrowed into the hills. Roots, fine as spun silver, embraced ancestral bones and spread like an underground web until they touched the far hills.

My home!

The following morning, Cassie took her rosebush out of the clay pot and planted it in the cemetery. She chose a spot in the corner of the weathered fence, where the sun was always brightest through the sheltering trees. Digging into the fecund dirt with bare hands, she added the potted soil and the ashes and memories it held. Perhaps in time roses might intertwine with the ancient vines winding there. Perhaps, ages from now, blood-red blooms would embrace this small enclosure, feral and fragrant and vibrant with life.

When she was done, she removed her father's ring from the ribbon around her neck and threw it into the creek. It settled to the bottom, the blue heart glinting among a scattering of stones. She stood, silent, gazing at the sky reflected in the shimmering water.

Secrets

HAWK USUALLY ENJOYED THIS TIME OF DAY: FIVE O'CLOCK IN THE AFTERNOON, the sunlight golden. The air was so clear he could see the horizon sweep around him like the edges of a celestial bowl. Normally he would have strolled along his hilltop with Old Yeller, convinced he stood upon a universe more beautiful and complex than he could ever reproduce in paint.

But not today. Today the sky might as well have been hidden behind a bank of clouds for all the notice he took of it, or the view fogged by curtains of rain. The wooden rocker chafed his shoulders and the lemonade caked his tongue with a tart sour-sweetness. And it was too damned hot for May. The headband of his Stetson was stained with sweat. He took it off and dropped it on the porch floor.

"How's the lemonade?" Rebecca asked from the other rocker close by.

"Fine."

"Not too sweet?"

"Nope." Hawk took a swallow to prove his point. The taste clung to his lips as he closed his eyes and pretended to enjoy a peace he didn't feel.

"You're awfully quiet," Rebecca said.

"Don't feel like talking much."

"What's on your mind?"

"Nothing."

"My, aren't we a man of words?"

Her voice was light, but even in his funk Hawk could tell her feelings were hurt. He turned toward her, smiling, wanting to make amends. She smiled in return, her eyes full of questions. Intelligent eyes. Sensitive eyes. Eyes that were as familiar to him as his own. "Becka," he said. Her face softened at the sound of his nickname for her. "What's the latest with the gallery showing?"

"Lots," she said, and began a recitation of all she had done, the people contacted, the publication notices to be printed, the radio and television appearances and newspaper interviews planned. Excitement animated her: cheeks flushed, long fingers danced. She leaned forward, adjusting her hip as a brief spasm flashed over her features.

It hurts her, Hawk thought. *After all this time, it still hurts her.* His mind wandered and Rebecca's voice faded into the background. How long had they known one another? It had been five years since his wife Lea died, and

Rebecca had been her best friend for as many before that. Maybe six, maybe seven or eight; he couldn't remember. So if he figured correctly, this woman had been in his life for a minimum of ten years. Ten years! Longer than some marriages.

He watched her as if from a distance: the animation, the brightness. And, underneath it all, the desperation. Christ Almighty, he'd dragged his feet too long! What a wimp he'd been, hanging onto the past, drifting along with the status quo until Cassie walked into his life and changed everything. He had thought the crack in his heart would never mend, that he could never truly love again – until Cassie. Cassie, Cassie, Cassie! Not a day went by, not an hour or a minute, in which he didn't yearn to be with her.

The trouble was his long relationship with Rebecca. He couldn't just mumble thanks and wave goodbye. After she had spent years dedicating almost every waking hour of her life to his benefit, after the accident crippled and condemned her to a lifetime of pain, how could he turn away?

"Hawk? You're staring. You haven't even blinked. What's on your mind?"

Startled, Hawk realized that she had stopped talking moments ago. "Sorry," he mumbled. "I was thinking how lovely you are."

He spoke the truth, in a fashion. She *was* lovely, in an uncommon way. Perhaps *striking* would be a better word: auburn hair, a sculptured face, luminous skin so fair the faint blue of her veins traced along the temples and eyelids. Her nose may have been sharp or her lips thin, but they suited her. And in spite of her handicap she carried herself well. Sometimes he even forgot that she struggled, so adept was she at hiding it. Not once had she reprimanded him or said a single word about what he had done to her. Not once, even in passing.

"We've been friends for a long time, haven't we?" he mused.

"Through thick and thin, as the saying goes."

He hesitated, trying to figure how to say what needed to be said. "I owe you a lot, Becka. More than I can put into words. I couldn't find a better business manager or a truer friend."

"You don't *owe* me a damned thing. I don't want anything from you that reeks of gratitude!" She spit out the word *gratitude* as if it were a poisoned toad that had leaped into her mouth.

"Simmer down. I'm just trying to let you know how much I appreciate you."

"Appreciate? What sort of word is that? Just send me a thank-you card and all debts will be settled."

"Christ almighty, but you're prickly! Lea was right. She used to say that you had the face of a Modigliani and the temperament of a water buffalo."

"Really?" Rebecca chuckled. "That sounds like something she'd come up with. I can almost hear her voice with that long, southern twang, *wahta buff-ah-low.*"

"That's her alright."

They grinned at one another, Lea's memory floating between them. Rebecca's smile trembled and she looked away. A surge of fondness for her swept through Hawk, and with it a smothering sadness. He took a sip of the dreadful lemonade and cleared his throat.

"Becka, I've been meaning to talk to you for a while now. It's something that I should have said long ago, well before Cassie came."

"I don't want to hear it."

"What?"

"If it's about Cassie I don't want to hear it."

"Can't you at least listen before you jump to conclusions? Jesus, you're impatient."

"Not now. Not yet." She stood up abruptly. "I've got to run. So much to do."

Hawk sighed. "Please. Just sit."

"It'll have to wait."

"Not this time. Stay. Please."

Rebecca sank back down, gripped the arms of the rocker, and sat rigid as stone.

Do it! Hawk told himself. *Say what you have to say!* He tried to smile but his lips wouldn't follow his command, nor did the words come readily. They stuck in his mouth as if made of paste. What to say? How to say it? He looked at her directly and hoped his face showed the tenderness he felt – and the resolve. "We've been living in the shadow of the past, I think. It's become a kind of habit, something comfortable and familiar. But life changes, people change, and..."

"I love you, Hawk."

"Oh, Becka. Don't. Let's no..."

"And you love me."

"I haven't... I'm fond of you, yes. But..."

"You do love me! You do! You just don't know it." She was crying now, sitting rock-solid still and crying.

"Rebecca, stop. Please stop." He rose and knelt beside her. "You know how dear you are to me, as dear as a sister."

"A *sister*? Good God, Hawk. Is that all you can come up with?"

"You've known my feelings about Cassie. You said as much yourself when you looked at the portrait."

"Shut up! Shut up!" She howled and beat him on the chest with her fists. "You've got to love me. You've got to! That's what Lea wanted."

Hawk staggered backward. "What?"

"It was a secret. She made me promise."

"Promise what?"

"She knew how much I loved you. She knew all along. Weeks before the accident, she asked me to take care of you if anything should ever happen to her. Right out of the blue, she asked. And I promised. With all my heart, I promised.

"Her last breath on that awful day of the accident, her last words to me, were, 'Remember your promise!' And I have. I've kept true to her. And to you, Hawk."

"God. Oh dear God." Hawk gasped and staggered down the steps as though he had been punched in the stomach. He walked into the afternoon sunlight, his shadow stretching behind him.

Rebecca followed, her shadow touching his.

"Hi, Mother." Cassie leaned back on the sofa cushion, the telephone in her lap.

"Buenos dias, muchacha. I haven't heard from you in a while."

"Don't tell me you're in Mexico."

A bright little laugh. "Si! A charming bed and breakfast facing the ocean. The most glorious sandy beach, and mountains all around like a jungle. You'd love it."

"Sounds beautiful. What are you doing there?"

"A vacation with Roberto something. I can never remember his last name, it's too peculiar. So I call him El Grande."

"What happened to your Australian friend?"

"Oh, *him*. He wanted me to live at his ranch with nobody and nothing around except hundreds of smelly *sheep!* Nasty, bleating things. Not exactly my idea of the grand life, is it?" Another tinkle of a laugh. "You never call except to ask for something or to scold. Which is it today?"

Cassie rolled her eyes, torn between the desire to hug her mother or strangle her. "Probably both."

"Hurry it up, then. I'm getting ready to have lunch at the cutest cafe right on the beach. The margaritas are divine."

"Okay, okay. I won't try competing with a divine margarita."

"No need trying, you wouldn't win. So?"

"Good news. I found Rosine's diary." She heard Lillian's sharp intake of breath, the shaky sigh that followed. "It's in German with her name on the front page. A lovely thing, mottled and faded like a rare book you might see behind glass in a museum somewhere."

"Where was it?"

"In that old trunk moldering away in the basement."

"The *trunk*?" Lillian practically shrieked. "I must have looked in that ratty crate a dozen times and found nothing."

"There's a hidden compartment at the bottom. The diary was tucked inside, wrapped in a fancy handkerchief with lace trim. Very old, like it's been around forever."

"I know that hankie. I grew up seeing it almost every day. Mimi said it had belonged to her mother and her mother's mother, and who knows how many before that. After Grandma died Mimi carried it around like a talisman that could magically bring her mama back." She took a deep breath, muttered, "Oh sweet Jesus, what a nightmare."

It took a moment before Cassie realized what Lillian was telling her. "Are you implying that *Mimi* wrapped the diary and hid it?"

"Destroy it, Cassie. Burn it. Tear it to shreds. Bury it six feet under. I don't care how, but that foul book needs to be exterminated once and for all."

"Mother, what's bugging you? This diary is a treasure."

"It's a curse."

"Why would you think..." And then it hit her, the truth behind Lillian's distress. "It's those last few pages you're worried about, right? The ones written by your grandmother Emilie."

"Oh God. Tell me you didn't read them."

"Of course I read them. Why wouldn't I? Do you know what happened to her, the things she did?"

"Yes! I know, I know! I know all the dark, filthy secrets! I had hoped Mimi would take them with her to the grave."

"Mimi told you?"

"Everything. It made me sick. When she showed me Emilie's confession, I grabbed the diary and tried to throw it in the fire. She ripped it from my hands, yelling that I had a heart the size of a gnat. I would have destroyed that diary if I could, or anything even touching those last pages. I looked at every inch of that damned house, trying to find it." She stifled a groan and murmured, "Oh God oh God, right there in front of my eyes the whole time and I had no clue."

"Why didn't Mimi tell *me*? Why did she keep it all a secret? Why did you?"

"I warned Mimi to never say a word to you about it, not a single word, or I'd never speak to her again."

"Why?"

"It's all so… sordid. What we are, who we came from, the horrible things that happened. It's been hard for me to live with that knowledge hanging over me like a stinking dark cloud. I wanted to spare you."

Cassie shook her head, mystified. Sometimes she couldn't believe that this woman was her mother, so different were the two of them. "Listen to me." She spoke carefully, trying to keep the impatient edge out of her voice. "There's no shame. None, except for the evil Jed inflicted. All the rest – the story of Mimi and Emilie and Gray Wolf – is a testament to courage and love. Can't you see that?"

"Romantic twaddle," Lillian snorted. Cassie grimaced, hating the sound. It reminded her of a rooting pig. "You can't glorify the past. That place is haunted with memories of it. The house, the land. The stench of fear still reeking in that stone crypt of a room. I could hardly wait to get away."

"And so you run. How many more miles, how many more years before you stop?"

In the abrupt silence that followed, Cassie could hear the birds chirping in the meadow, the old oak tapping the kitchen window.

"He's still in that house, you know," Lillian said, her voice strangely quiet. "Jed. His spirit seeped into those walls, waiting for revenge. It's in the very air. I can't breathe when I'm there. How can you?"

"Oh, for heaven's sake, Mother…"

"Your great-grandmother didn't just kill Jed. She reveled in it! Rejoiced in it! Left him to the vultures like raw steak rotting in the sun." Words exploded from Lillian's mouth as if she had squeezed them tightly in a box and just now opened the lid. "That vile confession made me look at myself. It made me wonder if I could kill with the same brute violence, wallowing in blood and vengeance, rejoicing afterward. And I'm afraid of the answer! It's there, burning in my veins as it burns in yours. Our genes, our inheritance, our curse. You bet I'm running. I'm running like hell."

"Mother," Cassie said slowly, "what is a curse to you is a blessing to me."

"Jesus, you sound just like Mimi. You've got your head stuck so high in the clouds you can't see the shit at your feet."

"Oh, Mama," Cassie sighed, reverting to the fond name she hadn't used in ages, "are you listening to yourself? Grumbling like a miserable, cranky old grouch at odds with the world."

"*Old?*" Lillian screeched. "*I'm* the one with a zest for adventure. *I'm* the one who's out and about, traveling the world, meeting people, experiencing life. If anyone's old, it's *you*. Stuck away in the backwoods of nowhere, watching the world pass by from the porch swing. God Almighty! How you can tolerate living in such a boondock town escapes me. I hated it! I hated every tiny particle of air I breathed in that house, every second wasted. I hated the stories it held, the sadness and the anger and the fear. I couldn't even stand to go into the upstairs bedroom you love so much, remembering the ugliness that Mimi witnessed, afraid to look out those windows and see Jed's battered ghost rummaging around on the hilltop, searching for a proper grave."

The mantle clock clanged the half-hour before Lillian spoke again. "You should get off your butt and get rid of that house. Sell and never look back."

"I like it here. It feels like home."

"Damnation! If you won't listen to me then why bother calling?" Lillian snapped. "I'm going for that drink. Tequila with a touch of salt and gulls swooping around is more appealing at the moment than talking to the brick wall you call your head."

Cassie laughed. She couldn't help it. Her mother would never change. "Goodbye, then. I love you, even if you are a basket case."

"It takes one to know one," Lillian said gruffly. "Adios, mi muchacha." She hung up, the dial tone buzzing over the tired old wires like a swarm of angry bees.

Hawk hesitated on Cassie's doorstep, the package under his arms. He took a deep breath and knocked. The screen door rattled under his fist.

"Coming!" Cassie called from somewhere in the recesses of the old house.

Oh God. He wanted to turn and run before his resolve melted. But his feet stayed put and his lips stretched in a grin that felt so stiff and fake he stopped trying.

"Hi!" Cassie's face appeared behind the screen. "What a nice surprise!" She opened the door, her welcoming smile so sincere he could hardly bear to look at her.

"Hi yourself." He hesitated in the parlor, awkward as a kid on his first date.

"Go ahead, sit." Cassie gestured to a saggy stuffed chair. "No need to be formal."

The springs squealed under his weight as he sat, cradling the package in his lap.

"Can I get you something?" she asked. "Coffee? Iced tea? A beer?"

"No. Yes. A beer maybe."

"Coming right up."

He heard her in the kitchen behind him: the squeak of the refrigerator door, the *spfft!* of the tab as she opened the can, her footsteps whispering on the wooden floor as she came to him.

"Here you go." She handed him a chilled glass tipped with beer foam, and sat on the couch. Elegant even in jeans and bare feet, her dark hair tucked behind her ears. She tilted her head and after a moment said, "If you're not going to drink it, just put it on the table there."

Jesus, where had his mind and manners gone? He must have been staring like a fool. He took a sip, and then another and another, which kept him from having to talk. She sure didn't help any. The silence grew, heavy with unspoken words. He drank the beer down and set the empty glass on the side table.

"Now what?" Cassie asked, her voice teasing.

"I brought you something." He handed her the package; the brown paper wrapping crackled as she took it from his grasp.

"A present?" She plucked at the string.

"Wait. Don't open it yet. I want to say something first."

She stilled, her smile faltering.

"It's about Rebecca. Me and Rebecca."

Her face paled. She nodded, slowly put the package aside, and looked straight at him. Waiting to hear what she probably already knew but had to be said nonetheless.

"It started years ago, when my wife Lea died." He gestured to the painting on the wall behind her. "That's her there, in *Spirit Song*. And our daughter Susan, when she was little. I painted it afterward."

Cassie's eyes darkened with compassion, and he looked away. "It was an accident. We were in the pickup, Lea and I and Rebecca. I was driving. A sixteen-wheeler came barreling around the corner in front of us. I couldn't stop in time. Lea died instantly, they told me."

"I'm so sorry, Hawk."

He saw her hand reach for him. Her touch would be too much to bear, and so he gently pulled away. "The doctors said Rebecca would never walk again. She proved them wrong, although she's never been the same. She'll always be crippled. She'll always suffer." He looked at Cassie then. He had to say it. She had to understand. "I was an emotional wreck for a long, dark time. Rebecca pulled me out of it, never once throwing my guilt into my face. She's dedicated her life to me. I owe her, Cassie. I owe her."

"Yes." Cassie spoke quietly. "I can see how you would feel that way."

Hawk sighed. It was done. He stood , feeling as though his knees would buckle with the weight of what had been said, with what it meant. "My heart's wrapped in that package." The words burst out of his mouth before he could contain them. "Unfortunately, that's where it ends."

He hugged her quickly and hurried out the door, the screen banging shut. He leaped into the pickup, turned the key, stomped on the gas. Not once did he glance away from the rearview mirror and the image of Cassie's face, framed by the parlor window, watching silent and still as he drove over the bridge and out of her life.

The brown paper lay crumpled on the sofa. Cassie gazed at her portrait, the play of light and dark, the transcendent grace. She propped it against a cushion and sat on the floor close by and studied it for a long, long time. She remembered when she had first glimpsed it on the easel in Hawk's studio. It had been unfinished, but she had caught her breath even then.

Was this how Hawk saw her, as a divine creature of earth and air? This image of oil and brush was too perfect, too primal, too much a creation of imagination and myth. Cassie wanted to weep, it was so beautiful. She ran her fingers over the wild vines, the swirling storm, the winding roots, the winged and glowing embers. The hopeful joy on the uplifted face, like that of an angel.

She couldn't understand the anger that erupted from within, that shot into her fingertips as she grabbed the crisp paper and wrapped it around the frame and bound it with twine that broke in her haste. She carried the portrait into the bedroom and shoved it into the deep recesses of the closet. Maybe she'd never age, and after a hundred years she'd unwrap the portrait again and find it distorted with weaknesses and soul disease, like the portrait of Dorian Gray. Or maybe she'd look at it before then, when her heart had settled. When she no longer thought about Hawk, or missed his presence.

He had made his choice. Now she made hers.

She slammed the closet door shut and left the room.

The Keening

SEVERAL DAYS HAD PASSED SINCE BILLY STOOD UP TO HIS FATHER'S WRATH, YANKED the belt from his hands, and hid in the field while Guy wept in the moonlit yard. Ever since that night, they were polite as strangers tiptoeing around each other. *May-I-this* and *Thank-you-that* and *If you'd be so kind*. Billy hated the sadness in the house, the stiff cordiality, the permeating stench of stale beer and cigarettes. Guy looked awful. His shoulders drooped and his clothes hung on him and deep lines etched the corners of his mouth down to his chin, as if the years had slipped by and suddenly his dad was old.

Billy shoved the front door open. It stuck as usual and then gave way, banging against the wall. He kicked it shut and went into the kitchen. Sunlight peered through the smudgy windows and lit the dirty table cluttered with cigarette ashes and a coffee mug and a plate with scummy sunny-side-up eggs that looked like squashed eyes. Guy had been eating breakfast when Billy left for school this morning and hadn't cleaned up after himself. A saltshaker sat on top of a wrinkled piece of paper. Billy recognized his father's handwriting:

Call me at Knot in the Loop when you get home from school. I might be there a while.

Billy tossed the dishes in the sink, grinning. Classes had been cut short early today for a faculty meeting, and he had the afternoon all to himself. A whole, entire afternoon. It was the perfect opportunity to go see Cassie. He could be there and back before dinner and Guy would never be the wiser. He looked at the cat-clock. The pendulum tail had cracked when it got hit by the belt buckle, and ever since the time had been off-kilter. It was one fifteen, give or take ten minutes. He normally got home from school around four. He could call his father from Cassie's house at that time, pretending to be at home. A great plan. A terrific plan. He could hardly wait to begin.

He reached for the phone, intending to call Cassie first, but changed his mind. He would surprise her! Ride his bike right up to the porch and knock on the door and see her face light up with a big smile when she saw him standing there. He laughed aloud when he thought of it.

A few minutes later he was on his bicycle, the wind urging him along. He felt happy and free and powerful, as though he could lift off the road and fly, bicycle and all, like a metal-winged bird.

ഗ്ര

"Bye, now. Come again, y'hear?" Darla waved from behind the counter at Gas `n Grub, her shortened bright red fingernails flashing – as did the engagement ring. She looked toward the group of domino players at the rear of the store and sang out, "Ed, darlin', would you mind helping Cassie carry this here watermelon to the car? She's got her hands full, what with groceries and all."

"Sure thing, sugar lumps," he replied, his voice carrying over the *whump-whump* of the ceiling fan.

"Thanks, but it won't be necessary." Cassie lifted her loaded sack with the watermelon wobbling on top as Pete moseyed down the aisle, his heavy tread vibrating the floorboards before he swung open the screen door.

"Seen Billy lately?" he asked, a cigar clamped between his teeth.

"No," she sighed. "I wish."

"Guy's an idiot," Pete grumbled, ashes spattering his beard. "You're the best thing that's happened to that boy since his ma died. A shame Guy can't see it."

"Maybe he does and it scares him."

"Seems to me Guy ain't never been scared of nothing much. But angry, that's different. Guy gets riled up faster'n anybody I ever seen. Maybe if he *is* scared the feeling's so dreadful and strange he don't know what to do with it."

Cassie stood on tiptoe, leaned over the paunch of Pete's belly, and kissed him on the cheek. "You're a dear old soul, you know that?"

"Hey, who you callin' old?" he joshed.

The hound Pooh-bah, stretched out on the top step, blinked at Cassie with baleful eyes as she nudged him with her foot. "C'mon, move your lazy self!" He complied, none too politely.

"Maybe Guy will come around and be more sensible," Pete hollered as she walked across the dusty parking lot. "Don't ever know what tomorrow might bring." The screen door thumped shut and Pooh-bah once again settled down for his nap.

Cassie slid the sack onto the rear seat of her car, pushed aside the mail she had picked up at the post office earlier, and headed home along the meandering road, bouncing over cattle guards, passing grazing cows and goats and a startled deer. The dirt driveway that lead to Billy's house appeared and she stopped for a moment, scowling at the riot of brush and trash alongside. If she hadn't known better, she would have assumed the drive and the house it led to were abandoned. "Billy deserves better!" she groused and sped away, so engrossed with thoughts of him it came as a surprise when the weathered sign *Spring Creek* came into view, dangling from the giant mesquite.

She turned onto the rutted roadway, her mind going back to almost a year ago when she had crash-landed in the jagged ravine on her left and ruined a tire, all because of an armadillo. And the wild black cherry farther up the hill, where she had placed the rosebush in the shade while she walked for help at the Grumms. She slowed in front of their house, the windows dark and empty, the angels tossed in a pile beside the barn. One metal hand stuck up from the heap, as if an angel lay buried underneath and was begging for help. Sighing, she drove on, the front yard receding in her rearview mirror, when she suddenly braked and backed up to get a better look.

The grass had been recently mowed and the *For Sale* sign was missing.

It made her sadder still, this final proof that Berta was gone and someone else would claim the house. She stepped on the gas until she rounded the bend and arrived at the gray-weathered fence surrounding her property. *Life goes on*, she told herself. *That's the way it is.* She got out of the car and pushed the wooden gate, careful of splinters. It opened reluctantly, squealing, *Everythinggg chaaanges.* "Oh, shut up," she grumbled, and whacked it with her fist.

So it was with a melancholy spirit that she clattered over the bridge toward home. Then she saw it: a bicycle propped near the porch. *Billy's* bicycle! Stomping on the brake, she hopped from the car and rushed toward the house, thinking he might be waiting for her inside. She was halfway up the steps before she noticed the opened barn doors.

She hurried over the meadow and peered inside the barn. Light from the kerosene lantern fell upon the ground and surrounding timbers, and sunlight streamed through cracks in the roof and walls. Billy had taken the tarp off of the Studebaker and now leaned into the open hood, fiddling with something. A fragment from a long-forgotten poem swam up from the depths of her memory, words that spoke so truly about how she felt at this moment that they could have been written by her own heart:

Child of my heart,
a wildflower vine climbing toward the sun.

"Hey, Billy," she said.

He jerked upward, smacking his head on the hood. "Miss Cassie! I wanted to surprise you but you weren't home so I came to the barn and worked on the car and I've missed you." The words spilled out as Cassie opened her arms. He came directly into them, hugging her so awkwardly she stumbled backward, laughing along with him, convinced that she couldn't have loved a child of her own more than she loved this boy.

Cassie puttered about in the kitchen while glancing through the narrow window above the sink, thrilled at the sight of the opened barn doors. Billy was there again, even if for a little while, even if just for now, and she was happy. She hadn't asked whether Guy had given permission. She figured she knew the answer already, and didn't want it confirmed. Now, this moment, this lovely afternoon, was all that mattered. She'd worry about tomorrow... tomorrow.

The kitchen filled with the aroma of brown sugar and vanilla and peanut butter. One batch of cookies cooled on the counter while another cooked in the oven. She sat at the table, the Emperor Tree tapping the bay window beside her and the wrought-iron angel swaying in the breeze. The cherubic face seemed to giggle at her through the glass. Cassie reached for the mail and absently flipped through it. Bills, ads, junk mail – and a pink envelope with no return address. She opened it and a photograph slipped out, landing upside down on the tablecloth. A note scrawled on the back read: *Dolly's third birthday.* Puzzled, Cassie flipped it over.

Berta Grumm, wearing a silly party hat with crepe paper ribbons streaming from the crown, smiled into the camera from behind a picnic table festooned with balloons. A little girl dressed in a sparkly tiara and pink tutu – the same little girl who had pointed to a sparrow in the church during Justin's funeral and squealed, "A birdie! It got losted!" – sat on one side, and a boy not much older sat on the other, sandwiching Berta between the two. A woman, tall and angular as Justin had been, stood close by, brow furrowed in concentration as she cut a double-layer cake with a ballerina figurine perched on top.

Of course! Cassie thought. *It's Berta's family!* She looked inside the envelope and found a letter:

> *My Dear Cassandra,*
>
> *I am doing well, although Victoria treats me as if I'm so decrepit I can't lift a finger for myself without dying on the*

spot. But it's a rather nice change being treated like a grand old dame, I must admit, chauffeured here and there, and not having to cook unless I twist an arm to do so. She won't even let me dust or sweep the floors, so I do it on the sly (Ha ha). It's quite nice here, with my own room and bathroom and even my own porch. I've started a vegetable garden and planted flowers alongside the house, helped by my spoiled darlings, great-grandchildren Dolly and Johnny. They beg me to plant in practically every space available, so I reckon in a few years we'll be living in a flowering jungle, the house hidden among it all.

Dolly and Johnny love it when I read stories to them. I never realized there were so many delightful children's books! When I was a young mother, we were lucky to find a few tucked away in the corners of the village library. Did you know that libraries nowadays have entire rooms dedicated to children? The one in our neighborhood has books by the hundreds, tiny tables and stuffed chairs, even plush carpets and cushions for them to sit on. Mercy! One day I began reading aloud to Dolly there, and before I knew it a handful of children had gathered around, clamoring for more. The librarian got so excited she talked me into doing it every Saturday. One small fellow took it in his head to call me Mrs. Owl, probably because of my big glasses, and it caught on. Now there's a nice sign by the door announcing the reading hours of Mrs. Owl, the Storybook Lady!

Needless to say, I'm quite content, although I miss you and Strudel and, of course, life as it was. But, as my Schatz would say, We should live each day fully, else we end our time on this earth with nothing to show for the years except a pile of forgotten moments.

So live fully, my dear girl, and I will, too.

With affection always,

Berta

Cassie propped the photograph against the salt shaker on the table and gazed at the fondly remembered face, imagining Berta surrounded by a gaggle of children, the plump cheeks, flyaway gray hair, and huge magnified eyes making her look very much indeed like a benevolent owl. *A happy one,* Cassie thought. *And that's what really matters.*

The oven timer dinged, and as she hurried to take out the sheet of cookies the screen door opened. "Miss Cassie!" Billy called. "Can I use the phone? I've got to call Dad at the Loop."

"Sure!" She hesitated, then asked what she must. "Does he know you're here?"

"No."

"Are you going to tell him?"

"No."

Still holding the baking sheet, Cassie watched Billy dial. He glanced at her quickly then turned aside, as if ashamed of the lie he was about to tell but determined to do it anyway.

Cassie set the cookies to cool and leaned against the counter, wondering if she should intervene yet knowing she wouldn't.

"Knot in the Loop Saloon," a disembodied voice in Billy's ear shouted over the thump and twang of a western band.

"Is Guy Wilkins there?"

"Hell, just a minute." *Shuffle-shuffle clunk,* as if the phone had been dropped on something. It sounded as though a party was in full swing: howls, rowdy laughter, the whack of pool balls. "Hey, asshole, tell Guy some kid's on the phone." "Who you calling asshole, you dumb dip shit?" Hoots and more hilarity, a voice yelling over it all, "Hurry it up, we're waiting on you here."

"Billy?"

"Hi, Dad. You playing pool?"

"My luck sucks. Can't win for nothin." He slurred his words, running them together, *canwinfernothin.'* "Not seein' straight."

"Maybe you're drunk."

"A few beers never hurt nobody," *neverhurdnobod.* "I won't be home by dinner so fix yourself something."

"Okay."

"What you got to keep busy?"

"Homework." Well he did, in a way. The Studebaker was a kind of homework.

"Don't get no stupid ideas in your head because I ain't around. Check in with me every couple hours."

"Sure."

Background jeers: "Must be gabbin' to a woman." "Nah, he likes cows better."

"Christ, I'm playin' with a bunch of turds," Guy grumbled, and hung up.

Billy could hardly believe his good luck. "Good news, Miss Cassie! Dad's going to keep playing pool until sometime after dinner, so I don't have to leave for a while yet."

"Guess that means you'll be stuck eating with me tonight." Her dark eyes sparkled, and Billy knew she was as glad about the turn of events as he was.

Cassie made spaghetti with her special slow-cooked sauce, tossed a salad, slathered garlic butter on crusty French bread, and set the table with Mimi's prettiest china that had bluebirds painted along the rim. Billy added a collection of wildflowers – yellow, purple, red – in a jelly jar. He couldn't stop smiling. He smiled as he ate, smiled as he drank, smiled as he talked about whatever came to mind. The clock chimed the passing hour once, twice, yet they lingered at the table until dusk shadows stretched long upon the ground. They washed the dishes afterward – she washing and he drying – then wrapped fistfuls of cookies in a napkin and ate them outside by the creek. Their two images, sitting side by side, reflected in the water.

"I hope Dad stays at the Loop until it closes," Billy muttered.

"When's that?"

"Around midnight, I think." Picking up a pebble, he threw it into the creek. It skipped across the surface, ripples shattering their reflections. "It's time for me to call him again but I don't want to."

"I know."

They looked at one another, then slowly rose and walked back toward the house.

Guy hung up the phone and stared at it for a moment, as if the thing could talk. Billy had called but something didn't feel right. He headed for the bar, bumping into a chair on the way.

"What time is it?" he asked the bartender, a big tub of a man with jowls, like one of those sad-looking dogs with flappy cheeks.

"Hell, just look at the clock there on the wall."

"Numbers fuzz up."

"It's five after eight. Time to go home. If you can't see clear you can't hit the balls neither. Just throwin' your money to the hogs."

"I ain't no quitter."

The bartender shrugged. "Suit yourself."

"Gimme another Coors." Guy wiped his mouth with the back of his hand. Something nagged him, nibbling at his brain. Something…

"Your poison." The beer was set in front of him. He took a swig. What all had Billy said? He couldn't remember exactly. Homework. Dinner. Everything okay.

"Hey Guy!" a pal called from across the room, holding a pool cue. "You playin'?"

Guy raised his bottle in a salute and walked in that direction, mildly surprised to discover the floor swaying, as if he had been sailing and went ashore with landlubber knees. A door opened from somewhere, a creak and slam, then creaked open again. People coming and going, coming and going, like clockwork almost.

Clockwork.

Guy stopped dead in his tracks. *That's* what had been eating at him. The sound of a clock coming over the phone, *ticka-tick, ticka-tick,* with a kind of grinding noise like rusty gears. Maybe it was the kitchen clock, although he never knew it to grind like that.

"Gotta call Billy," he muttered in the general direction of the pool table. The phone was on the wall in an alcove. He fumbled with the dial, leaning in close, mouthing each number. Bracing himself against the wall, he listened as the line rang. One, two, three times, his heart beating harder with each ring. "Answer, answer!" Four, five, six. He hung up on the tenth.

Billy wasn't there. Damn it to heaven, Billy wasn't there.

I know where you are, boy. I know where you are and I'm coming to get you.

"Dad told me not to wait up. That means he's going to stay real late, maybe until closing!" Billy plopped down on the overstuffed chair, laughing as Strudel jumped into his lap.

"You should still be home by dark or soon after. I don't want you to get in trouble with Guy. You know how he feels about me."

"Yeah, I know. And I hate it!"

"Maybe he'll change his mind someday," Cassie said, not believing a word of it.

"You think so? Mom used to call him a bull-headed softie, that he gets mad and screams to hide tenderness inside."

"A smart woman, your mother." She glanced at the clock. "It'll be dark soon. What would you like to do until then? Work on the car?"

"Let's watch the sunset!" He leaped up, Strudel in his arms. "From upstairs! I bet the view is terrific with all those windows." He hurried down the hallway and through the flagstone great room and up the narrow stairwell, Cassie behind him. "I'll pretend it's my room, and after it gets dark I could lie there on my bed if I wanted and look out at all the stars."

She climbed upward, following Billy's eager footsteps. *If wishes had wings...*

Guy knew he was drunk but figured he could handle it well enough. He gunned the motor and rushed hell-bent down the road. Another ten minutes or so and he'd be at Spring Creek. He rolled the windows down, welcoming the rush of air. He was too damned hot. He glanced in the rearview mirror and saw his flushed face glaring back at him through bloodshot eyes. Hell, his whole torso was on fire, his palms sweating, his hands slick on the wheel.

Billy lied to me. Right-out lied. Snuck around like a thief behind my back.

The sky blazed red, rays streaking across the horizon like spilled blood. Everything was tinged red: sky, plateaus, hills, road. His gut ached and bile rose up and burned his throat, but he clenched his jaws and kept on driving, the taste of beer sour in his mouth.

A liar and a sneak.

What had happened to the soft-spoken, shy boy, the one who would obey without question or sass-back and never lied about nothing?

Cassie's got Billy spell-bound. Guy snorted, disgusted with himself having been caught in that same spell, thinking she was beautiful and that maybe he even loved her.

"I wish she was dead," he spat, "and rotting in hell."

A nightmare image crawled into his brain. He knew it was a dream-thought, but he couldn't get rid of it: Billy, walking on the road ahead, his back turned. Walking, walking, each step taking him farther and farther away, until he was swallowed by the sun. All that was left was an empty stretch of loneliness.

Jesus, oh Jesus, had he lost his boy to that stupid, selfish woman who didn't care about any damage she caused, who fed Billy ideas of moving hundreds of miles from home, who acted like she owned him? Guy howled, "Billy belongs to me! He's *mine! My* son! *Mine!*" He pounded the steering wheel, the horn blaring, *blat! blat! blat!*

"Hush now." Sarah whispered from the back seat, her voice soft, caressing.

Guy yelled and swerved, the truck clipping a fence post before he stopped. Afraid to turn around and look, he stared straight ahead with sweat trickling into his eyes.

Shhhhh! Sarah sighed, her breath against the nape of his neck.

"Jesus!" Guy cried. "Oh sweet Jesus!" Shuddering, he risked a quick glance over his shoulder. Nothing was there. Nothing, nothing, nothing. Just empty seats and the usual trash.

Guy took a long, shaky breath and combed his hair with his hands. Got to pull himself together. Got to think straight. He would drive up to Cassie's, get Billy, and take him home. No nonsense. No arguing. If the wolf-dog made trouble, he'd make short work of it.

He pulled the gun from the glove compartment, just in case.

"That was the best sunset ever." Billy leaned against the upstairs windowsill, Strudel purring in his arms as the final rays slipped into darkness. "The sky lit up from one end to the other."

A glow caught Cassie's eye and she glanced down at the barn. "Looks like somebody forgot to turn off the lantern."

"Oh wow. I'm sorry."

"Don't worry. I'll do it."

"No. It's my responsibility." Billy moved from window to window, lingering as if to memorize the view. "I don't know when I can come back. Maybe not for a long while." He spoke without looking at her, his voice wistful.

Cassie nodded, his words sticking pins into her heart. "Don't get into trouble with your father for my sake, Billy. Maybe things will work out."

"I left kind of a mess behind. I should clean up. Get stuff organized. Lock up until..." He shrugged and said no more.

"You can do that before you leave, if you like."

"Time for me to go, isn't it?" He sighed. "It gets dark quick after the sun goes down. You blink your eyes and the stars are there."

Cassie started to reply, but was cut off by the grinding blast of a motor.

"Oh my God." She looked down at Guy's pickup roaring over the bridge. By now it was a deep twilight, the earth shadowed, the sky purple-black. The truck tore through the pale moonlight, bounced over the meadow, and screeched to a stop beside the barn.

"It's Dad." Billy groaned. "I'm in serious trouble."

Guy jumped from the truck, stumbling as he hit the ground, and looked into the barn. He lingered at the open doors, the light from inside shining on his face.

"What's he staring at? He's seen the car already."

"Maybe thinking of you in there, working on it."

Guy turned and lurched toward the house, head thrust forward and arms swinging, as if he would barrel though anyone or anything in his path.

"He's flat-out drunk," Billy said quietly.

"I'll go down and talk to him."

"What's that in his hand?"

Cassie peered into the growing darkness. "I can't tell."

"A gun! He's got a gun!"

"God, what is the matter with him?" she cried, pushing Billy into the middle of the room. "Don't stand near the windows!"

Guy glanced up at them and stopped dead in his tracks, swaying. "Billy!" he shouted. "Get your ass down here!"

"I've got to go," Billy whispered.

"Not with that gun in his hand."

"Billyyy!" Guy howled. "Come on down before I go up there and drag you down. We're goin' home."

"It's no good. I got to do what he says!" Billy dropped Strudel and ran for the stairs.

"Wait!" Cassie grabbed him by the arm. "Let me talk with him first."

"He's too angry to talk. I know him, I know what he's like when he gets like this." Billy tried to pull away, but Cassie yanked him back.

"Let go of my boy!" Guy jerked forward, lost his balance, and toppled over. *Crack!* A window shattered, spewing glass shards. The spent bullet pinged against the metal bed and rolled across the floor.

"Go!" Cassie yelled, shoving Billy toward the stairs. "Go! Stay out of sight!"

"He didn't mean it!" Billy cried, running down the steps. "It was an accident!"

"The man's an idiot," Cassie muttered. "A dangerous stinking-drunk idiot." Anger exploded inside her, anger and fear so strong she could have taken that spent bullet and rammed it up his rear end. Her heart was wild in her chest, beating against her ribs. *Keep your cool,* she warned herself. *He could have killed both of us.*

Billy stood in the unlit parlor, a shadow among shadows. Cassie put her arm around him as Guy reeled into view, the gun still in his hand.

"Billyyy!"

Cassie squeezed Billy's shoulder. "This isn't good. I'm going to call the police."

"No! Don't! Please don't. I'll go. That's all he wants."

"Stay here," she whispered, her mouth dry. He nodded, and she walked to the opened door, hesitating behind the screen. "Guy!" she called. "Put the gun down."

"Hell, I ain't gonna shoot nobody."

"Then put it down." She tried to speak calmly and keep her voice from shaking. "Billy's not coming out until it's safe."

"*Safe*? Christ, he's my son!"

Cassie cautiously opened the screen door. "Of course you love him," she said. "I do, too."

"And that's the problem, ain't it?"

Cassie risked stepping onto the porch. "Just hand me the gun." She tried to smile, but her trembling lips wouldn't cooperate. "Billy shouldn't see you like this."

"He's seen worse." Guy seemed to deflate, to sink into himself, and began to pocket the gun when something caught his eye at the corner of the house. "Jesus!" he muttered, staring past the old oak. "That thing ain't natural!"

The porch light flicked on, the illumination capturing Guy standing hunched and tense, glaring at the shadows. "It's okay," Billy said as he stepped from the house. "I'm coming with you."

Guy whirled toward them, the gun swinging wildly. Billy gasped and Cassie darted in front of him. "Drop the damned gun!" she shouted, walking backward and forcing Billy toward the door.

Guy bolted for the steps, "Get your hands off him!"

A deep growl rumbled from beneath the Emperor Tree. Guy spun around the moment the wolf leaped, fangs bared in a snarl, yellow eyes afire. It seemed to suspend, to hang in the air the moment Guy shot it. The wolf landed hard on Guy's chest, knocking him to the ground. Guy fell with the wolf on top of him, as if animal and man were joined at the ribs.

"Dad!" Billy yelled, and rushed down the steps.

"Ain't dead yet! Ain't dead!" Guy hollered, crawling out from underneath. "Devil's still got breath in it!" The wolf's blood slicked his chest and chin, gleaming like tainted oil. His hands were slippery with it as he grappled with the gun and took aim.

"Aieeeee!" Tatty burst into the moonlight, shrieking. She ran like a woman possessed, lifting a branch large and sturdy as a baseball bat over her head, and brought it down with a fury on Guy's hand. The gun flew from his grasp, landing some feet away. Guy yelped in pain as she kicked the fallen gun with her combat boot. It arched over the creek bank and splashed into the water.

"It's broke," Guy whimpered, cradling his injured hand.

Tatty turned her back to him and crouched beside the wolf. She stroked his forehead, crooning softly.

"Why? Why?" Billy cried, hurrying to Guy. "Why did you shoot him?"

"It was me or it."

Fearful of what she was sure to see, Cassie's approached the wolf. Her shoulder brushed against Tatty as she sat, the earthy scent of wildflowers mingling with that of the animal lying still before them, his blood staining the ground, the firelight in his eyes crumbling away.

"You killed him!" Billy yelled at Guy. "You didn't have to kill him!"

Cassie caressed the dense fur, wishing her own life force could stream from her into him. A final gasp quivering under her touch. A breath warm against her cheek. Then there was nothing, save an empty shell that had once housed the spirit of Wolf.

"He's gone," Tatty murmured.

"Come home." Guy pleaded, his voice strangely quiet. He stood, holding his injured hand to his chest, and would have wobbled had Billy not grabbed him.

I've got to clean up the barn first," Billy said. "I promised."

"I don't give a damn what you promised."

Tatty raised her face and palms to the sky and began to keen a death song, her sinewy body rocking to and fro. The lament pulsed over the meadow and traveled among the hills, perhaps joining the memory echoes of other songs keened in centuries past.

"What the hell?" Guy muttered, his face ashen. "C'mon, Billy. Forget the barn and the damned car." He slumped in Billy's embrace, as if he were old and frail and sick.

Billy's face betrayed his anguish. Cassie yearned to comfort him but didn't dare approach. "Go on," she said. "I'll take care of the barn." When he hesitated, she urged, "It's okay. Go."

Billy nodded and the two began walking. As they passed, Guy came to an abrupt halt and looked directly Cassie. He was so close Cassie could smell the cold sweat clinging to his skin. "You've ruined my life." He spoke without the usual swagger, as if the words were ripped from his heart. "You've destroyed what was left of my family. Leave us alone. You've done enough damage. Just leave us alone."

"Dad," Billy whispered, pulling him onward. After a few steps he glanced back at Cassie, his eyes glistening with tears.

He loaded the bike into the pickup and got behind the wheel as Guy slumped in the passenger seat, and drove away so slowly that Cassie could have easily trotted alongside, reached through the truck window and taken Billy's hand, murmured some word of comfort. But she was rooted to the ground, her knees locked, her throat shuttered.

The wolf was heavy in her arms. She and Tatty wrapped him in a quilt shroud, laid him in the wheelbarrow, and carted him to the pond under the light of a Comanche moon. Night creatures fell silent all around them as if grieving for what had been lost. Even their footfalls were hushed, cushioned by prairie grass and wildflowers. The only sound was the squeal of the wheelbarrow, mournful as the wail of ghosts.

They buried him beside the large boulder, placing juniper boughs over his body and filling the cavity with earth. Then they gathered rocks scattered about and piled them over the grave like a cairn.

"Now the spirit of Wolf lives within the stone," Tatty murmured.

Cassie was comforted, knowing that whenever she glanced at Hawk's *Spirit Song* she would see Wolf emerge from that same boulder, golden eyes alight.

The Sundering

YOU'VE DESTROYED WHAT WAS LEFT OF MY FAMILY. *LEAVE US ALONE.*

Awake, asleep, Guy's parting words droned on and on in Cassie's mind like the unwanted lyrics of a horrid song.

Destroyed my family. Leave us alone. Leave us. Leave.

And always: Billy's face, awash with tears. Guy leaning upon him as they walked away. Father and son, stumbling across the meadow. The dead wolf at Cassie's feet.

On the third morning the voices stopped, the images vanished. She awoke to a clear day, knowing what she had to do.

It was a warm afternoon and the air smelled like summer already, pungent with ragweed and cedar. Billy stood in his father's bedroom doorway, trying to look more relaxed than he felt.

"I'm sorry, Dad. I shouldn't have lied."

Guy was sitting on the edge of the bed, smoking. He didn't say anything, just jabbed the stub in an ashtray and sat there, quiet and strange. Billy waited for him to explode and carry on about Cassie and the car as he normally did. The silence was worse. The silence was scary.

"I didn't want to lie. I don't want to lie to you now, either." His lips were dry. He licked them and continued. "I can't quit working on the Studebaker."

Guy nodded, his face expressionless. His eerie calm gave Billy the jitters.

"I've got diagrams and sketches just half-finished. Important stuff. I've got to go back."

"Only if Cassie ain't around."

Billy could hardly believe he had heard right and he felt like laughing for the surprise of it all. But there was a trick demand behind it. "How can I do that? She comes and goes a lot."

"You're a smart boy. Figure it out."

"Okay."

"Promise."

"I promise to try and do like you said."

"Fair enough." Guy sighed and lay back on the bed with an arm over his eyes, like he was exhausted and ready for sleep even though it wasn't yet three in the afternoon.

Billy stood on one foot and then the other, wary. His father had been way too agreeable. "Thanks, Dad."

Guy spoke so soft Billy hardly heard it. "Got a mind of your own, like your mother."

Billy waited a while, in case Guy had more to say. But his father lay like he was already asleep, not a muscle twitching. Just the ready rise and fall of his chest. Billy tiptoed down the hall, feeling as though he had been dropped into a dream, so unreal had this conversation been. His father had given him permission to work on the car! Unbelievable!

Guilt dampened his relief. He had sort of promised to be there when Cassie wasn't. Well, he would. Kind of. Maybe. Figure it out, that is.

Who was he kidding? He wanted to be with her more than anything. If he had to choose between her and the car, there wouldn't be a moment's hesitation.

The problem was that it had come down to a bigger choice: Cassie or his own father.

I don't give a damn what you promised. That's what Guy had said a few nights ago, after he'd shot the wolf. So what the hell? If a promise to Cassie could be broken, a promise to Guy could, too.

He went outside, closing the back door quietly behind him, and began to pull weeds from alongside the house. He could think better working in the sunshine. Feel better, too. With each weed he snatched from the stubborn ground, dirt clinging to the roots, his spirits grew lighter, as if he were pulling out weeds from inside himself.

Guy wasn't fooled. There was no way that boy was going to avoid Cassie. He'd probably go running to her first thing and lie about it afterward.

He could see the top of Billy's head through the window, the red curls shining in the sunlight as the boy bent down to dig in the flowerbed. The red-shining head gradually traveled from one side of the window to the other and disappeared from view. Guy watched all the while, aching with grief and love so strong it squeezed the breath from his lungs.

The pain in his head was worse than ever. He looked up at the ceiling, absently wondering if Sarah's face would swim into view, too exhausted to feel anything more except heavy emptiness, like his heart had dried up and left crumbs behind.

"Don't you worry, sweetheart." His mouth moved the words, although he wasn't sure if he said them aloud. "I've got a plan."

Cassie knew it was time to sell and leave Willow City. What was left for her here but heartbreak? Love for a man, love for a child – each brought its own grief. Perhaps distance would help her stop yearning for the impossible.

La Villita awaited her in San Antonio, a new boutique, a new beginning, a new life. All she had to do was leave here and go there, with no more excuses for lingering.

She hurried past the windmill and barn, trying to keep in stride with the long-legged Phil Jameson of Jameson Homes. He didn't say much as the minutes passed, but quietly studied the land as if already planning how to make use of it. They entered the valley, stopping beside the rugged knoll near the pond, and she waited below while he climbed the slope and stood for a while to look at the view. She followed his gaze, her eyes sweeping over the pasture sparkling from a recent shower, and when she glanced up again he was talking on a cell phone. She caught snatches of his conversation: *Potential. Investment. You gotta see.*

Mr. Jameson was the third real estate developer she'd seen this week and the most likable of the lot. The most handsome, too, his craggy, strong-jawed face right out of an old-time Western. She hoped this land spoke to him in ways far different from the other two developers. The first had wanted to build homes squeezed on half-acre lots terraced into the hills and on ground stripped of what he called "trash trees." Number Two had envisioned a family resort. "I could design a hell of a water slide down that mountain yonder," he had enthused while pointing at Mount Bubba, "and a tamer one on the slope by that gate and rusty statue thing."

"That's the family cemetery."

"Dead folks won't mind getting a little wet. Ha ha!" When Cassie frowned, he shrugged and added, "I can dig `em up, bury `em someplace else."

Cassie had thanked them both and shoved their business cards into the far recesses of the silverware drawer.

She began to doubt that Mr. Jameson's card would join the others. She liked him. She liked his serious manner and easy smile and the way he stood, Stetson pushed back from his forehead, intent upon the valley below.

Hopefully he imagined something better than bulldozed hills and waterslides.

Cassie sat alone at the kitchen table. The sun was low in the horizon, and the old oak cast a long shadow across the yellow checkered cloth and the papers strewn about: a contract from Jameson Homes. She picked up a pen, hesitated, put it down again.

Mr. Jameson – Phil, he had asked to be called – wanted the property for himself, fulfilling a dream of breeding thoroughbreds. Stables could be built without felling the woods. The hills and family cemetery would remain unscathed. The house was another matter, however. He couldn't promise to leave it intact. In fact, he couldn't promise to leave anything, not even the foundation.

Gone. Not a trace left, as if it had never existed.

Nothing was permanent. She couldn't expect the house to last forever, years upon years. It was only wood and stone.

Wood and stone and lifetimes echoing within the walls.

She shut out the thought and leaned back in the chair, imagining horses galloping over the meadow and in the valley beyond, tails and manes streaming in the wind as they had in the days of the Comanche. Sighing, she fingered a page and again looked at the purchase price offered: One million two hundred fifty thousand. She probably couldn't get a better proposition, nor find someone so well suited for this place. So why hesitate?

It had been a long day, and she was tired. "Later," she murmured, gathering the pages together. "I'll sign later, after I've thought about it awhile."

The mantle clock bonged twice. Cassie moved through the house shadows, the pine floor cool under her bare feet. Moonlight glimmered through the parlor windows, touching the coffee table and the contract waiting there. She sat on the sofa and reached for the pen. Her fingers moved rapidly over the paper; the pen clattered to the floor when she was done.

She rose quickly. The amber eyes of the wolf in the painting seemed to follow as she stood by the opened doorway, arms braced on either side, gazing into the dark.

After a time, she moved aimlessly through the rooms, as if to prove to herself that the house was still intact, that she had not yet left.

Hawk climbed up the hill, his flute case slung by a strap over his shoulder, his steps confident. Shale crumbled from beneath his boots, spilling down the incline and falling into night shadows. The full moon hung low in the sky, lighting his way past cactus and juniper and sage. He crested the hill, walked to the far side, and looked down at the house below shaded by the outstretched limbs of an old oak. Light glowed from the kitchen window; he could glimpse part of a yellow tablecloth. A figure moved to and fro, appearing and disappearing from sight. He was too far away to see it clearly, but his memory and imagination filled in the details: a lovely face, a haunting face, a face that pierced his heart.

He turned toward the voice of the wind, letting it speak to him. When his spirit was ready, he took off his shirt, boots, and socks, and laid them aside. He sat on the ground, his legs crossed and chest bared as his ancestors had done before him, and opened the case.

The wooden flute was smooth and warm to his touch. He held it to his lips and the music began from deep inside him, the notes carrying fragments of his soul. He played for Cassie, for her midnight eyes and tempting mouth and hair like silk between his fingers. He played for her laughter and impossible temper and touch of her hand upon his skin. He played of his desire and fear and things he could not name.

She came to the window once, and then turned out the lights and reappeared in the meadow. She gazed at the sky as if the music emanated from the stars. Still, so still, still as a creature of the woods, she became part of the landscape: a sapling, a shadow, a deer.

Hawk's spirit flew down the hillside, calling to her. Lifting her arms, she swayed across the grass. His music wound around her, caressing her, loving her as she danced in the moonlight.

Then he could play no more.

The hills would not be silent; memory echoes of flutes and drums from times long past would come as always, when the wind was right. But no longer from him. He was done.

He would finish the paintings promised to Thornwood Gallery and leave for Sedona. Perhaps he could live like old Cham for a while and find peace among the quiet, the rocks and sky, the earth voices. Perhaps the ache in his heart could be stilled, and he could turn toward Rebecca without regret.

"Cassandra," he whispered, "Cassandra, my love, goodbye."

❧

The music came to her on the wind. It drifted from the hills, wound among the trees, wandered over the creek. It came as if sprung from the earth and air, whispering of love and sorrow. And so Cassie danced in the night, face lifted to the moon, her heart breaking.

Farewell hills. Farewell meadow and pasture and pond. Farewell cemetery and house and the memories living there.

Farewell those I've grown to love.

She danced until the wind died and took the music with it. She walked slowly up the steps and through the parlor. The floorboards creaked under her footsteps and the contract on the coffee table glimmered pale in the moonlight. Shadows followed her to the bedroom; she lay down, the pillow soft, the quilt fragrant with lavender, and fell asleep.

Hawk appeared in dream fragments, as if she were flitting through a scrapbook of moments and living them once again: He's playing the flute at Smithy's Barbeque, his face half-shadowed until he lifts his oak-leaf eyes. He stands on the other side of the bridge, hand reaching out to help her across the flooding creek. They kiss in his pickup, his touch burning her lips. He walks down the aisle with Justin's coffin on his shoulder, his stricken eyes seeking hers. He turns and looks at her from across the room on New Year's Eve, his expression yearning, his hand on Rebecca's shoulder. And more, more, more moments flee past, until images overlap like a tumbling deck of cards.

She awoke suddenly, certain that Hawk loved her, and equally certain that he had bound himself in a cage of his own making, then tossed the key to Rebecca.

Dawn was breaking. A new day, a new beginning. She walked to the kitchen, pausing in front of the small painting she had purchased at Pete's months ago, and studied it anew: the stark, empty landscape. The gnarled tree with bare, twisted limbs. The tortured face of a man peering from the bark, mouth open in a silent plea. The trunk enclosing his legs, the branches his outstretched arms, the twigs his fingers. And there, at the bottom right, a hawk. It perched on a knobby root, wings folded, facing the distant horizon as if waiting for something to appear.

She took it off the wall and lay it face down in a drawer. If this was his self-portrait she wanted none of it.

I'll forget him.

I'll forget him.

I must forget him.

Farewell

Cassie felt her teeth vibrate as Nan's van rattled and bounced along the road like a crippled old horse out for a good run. Boxes filled with canned food, fresh peaches, packaged goods, cooking utensils and who knows what else slid around in the back, adding to the racket.

"Thanks for picking me up," Cassie said with a smile. "Fredericksburg isn't exactly around the corner."

"When will your car be ready?" Nan asked.

"Not for a few days. The mechanic had to order a part. Routine stuff."

"Consider me your personal chauffeur until then."

The seat had been pushed forward and Cassie's long legs had nowhere to go, her knees dangerously close to colliding with the dashboard. She glanced at Nan, the dainty limbs and little feet and perfect nose. "Sometimes I feel like a gangly giant in your presence."

"Sometimes I feel like an elf in yours."

"The giant and the elf." Cassie laughed. "What an improbable pair."

The minutes and miles flew by until Nan passed a building in the center of a dry, barren yard, as if the owner had rooted out every living thing within reach. "It's closed."

Strange how a closed-up building could seem dead and colorless, the faults glaring: the faded sign, *Guy's Auto Repair*, the cracked window, the ramshackle feel to it all. "It looks like a dump," Cassie said.

"People would come even if Guy worked in a slime pit."

"He's that good?"

"He used to be. Nowadays the place is closed more often than it's open. I don't think he has the heart for it like he once did."

"It's my fault." The shop receded in Cassie's side view mirror, abandoned and desolate from this perspective, like a tattered photograph of times gone by. "I've caused nothing but trouble between him and Billy, and really messed things up."

"Don't you believe that! Billy was a lost waif after Sarah died and hardly ever smiled. Look at him now! Like a new boy, thanks to you."

"Guy says I've come between them."

"Maybe you have. And maybe that's a good thing."

"How so?"

"Think about it." Nan turned sharply onto Spring Creek, sending the boxes into a sliding frenzy. One of them whacked the back of Cassie's seat.

"I have thought about it! Why else have I been seeing the realtors? For entertainment? Billy will be better off without me around."

They rode in silence until they stopped by Cassie's gate. A flock of mourning doves perched on the rickety fence, their feathers iridescent in the sunlight.

"I'm sorry," Cassie said. "I didn't mean to bark at you."

"It's okay. You've been worried."

"That's no excuse."

"Guy chose the wrong way to love. That's the problem."

Cassie groaned. "If this is along the line of 'think about it,' enough said."

"An old proverb from my childhood says it best: Hold a bird in your fist, and it will struggle to escape. Hold it with open fingers, and it will sing in the palm of your hand."

Cassie gazed at the woods as her memory vaulted her into the sheltering arms of a man whose face she had forgotten. "Some people throw the bird in the bushes and never look back. Like my father."

Nan was silent for so long Cassie was about to ask what was wrong, but before she could speak Nan murmured. "I threw my two babies in the plane and never looked back."

"Oh, my God." Cassie reached for her friend's hand. "I didn't mean it the way it sounded. I'm so sorry."

"Do you think I'm heartless?"

"Of course not! You did what you had to do, and saved their lives."

"Was your father any different?"

"I... I never thought of it that way."

"Maybe he did what he had to do. Maybe he sacrificed himself for your happiness."

"I'll never know, will I?" Cassie opened the door, startling the doves into a whir of wings as they scattered into the trees. "Thanks for the ride. And thanks for listening. So much has happened I'm not thinking straight. My mind goes one way and my heart the other. It's a battle between the two."

"Which one is winning?"

Cassie paused, releasing her grip on the handle. "I signed the contract last night."

"So it's done then."

"Not officially. The papers are still on my coffee table."

"Oh, Cass-*aie.* I don't want to think about you gone."

Cassie's eyes misted, and she was tempted to dash into the house and rip the contract into shreds. "I'll miss you, too."

"Where will you go?"

"San Antonio. There's an art village right off the River Walk called La Villita, a quaint hodge-podge of old building turned into galleries and so on. The perfect place to open a boutique of Native American art. Quality stuff, like Tatty's weavings and pottery."

"And Hawk?"

"Yes, his paintings, too."

"I wasn't asking about his paintings. I've seen you light up whenever his name is mentioned."

"God, why do you have to be so dammed perceptive?"

"Tell me this," Nan challenged. "If Hawk asked, would you stay?"

Cassie pushed the door and stepped out before Nan could say anything more.

Billy waited by the front door, itching to get going as Chuck drove up the driveway in a funky Volkswagen bug that looked like it had been assembled from a pile of rusty junk. Chuck stuck his head out the window. "C'mon!"

"One minute." Billy picked up his guitar and hurried to the kitchen. "Bye, Dad."

Guy slouched over the table, a cigarette dangling from his lips. "What you gonna do at Chuck's house you can't do here?"

"Play around some. He's got a mean new setup in the garage."

"Be home by six." The cigarette jiggled as he spoke, spattering ashes.

Bleeep! Bleeep! Chuck tapped the horn.

"See you later." Billy tried to keep the excitement from his voice. It was hard to lie to his dad, but he was getting better at it.

The Volkswagen door was jammed so Billy clambered through the window. He was used to that by now and had a pretty good idea of how to go about it: grip the roof, arm-lift torso up, aim the legs, and sort of slide in real loose.

"You got that down to a science, man." Chuck grinned. "Must be your skinny butt."

"My amazing athletic prowess."

They laughed as the bug sped along. When they came to the main road, Chuck asked, "You sure you want to do this?"

Billy nodded, and Chuck made a right-hand turn instead of a left. If Guy had seen it, he would've known they were up to something, but this part of the drive was blocked from view by trees and brush. The bug shot along like a growling racecar, the landscape whizzing by under a lake-blue sky. Billy wanted to shout or pound the dashboard, he felt so good.

"Too much coffee this morning?" Chuck tapped a drumbeat on the steering wheel. "You're sure antsy."

"I know. It's like I popped out of a cage or something."

"My friend, the nut case." Chuck shook his head. "Your dad said you could work on the car, so why sneak around?"

"Because Miss Cassie's there and he hates the sight of her. If he knows I've spoken to her or got close enough to see the color of her eyes he'll get crazy mad."

Chuck turned into Spring Creek. "What time do you want me to pick you up?"

"Five-thirty okay?"

"Sure."

They stopped at Cassie's fence. Chuck stepped out of the car and Billy slid over and out, leaving the guitar in the back seat. "Thanks," Billy said. "I owe you one."

"Later, man." Chuck waved goodbye and drove off, the muffler growling.

Billy jumped over the gate, jogged along the rutted drive toward the bridge, and saw Cassie on the porch swing. From this distance she looked like part of the house. Roots from the big old oak spread clear across the front and branches reached up and leaned over, as if the tree encircled her. Like the house and the tree and Cassie all belonged together.

"Hey, Miss Cassie!"

She smiled and hurried down the steps to welcome him.

It was maybe eleven in the morning when Guy got to the shop. He shut the door and locked it. The place smelled like oil and rubber and rot. Christ, when had he cleaned it last?

Funny how his hands shook when his mind was so calm. He stepped around a pile of tires, a jingle replaying in his head as it sometimes did, one he had heard a lot on the radio when he was growing up. *Brylcream, a little dab'll do ya. Brylcream, you'll look so debonair.* He hummed along, turning this way and that, trying to remember where he had put the gas cans.

He found them in a corner, partially buried under coffee-blackened foam cups and greasy rags. Two should be enough. He shook them to make sure; the weight and slosh indicated they were almost full. Satisfied, he put the cans in the bed of his pickup and drove toward Cassie's.

Two cans. Enough gasoline to ignite the entire Eiffel Tower if he wanted.

Brylcream, a little dab'll do ya.

Cassie glanced out the kitchen window at the wind tugging the barn doors and torturing the windmill blades until they screeched. She was about to return to the cookie dough when sheets of paper flew out of the barn and lifted into the air like white kites. Billy burst from the doors, leaping and grabbing as the kites dipped and swirled in a game of tag. He corralled a handful but the wind snatched a few more, until eight or ten soared around the meadow.

Cassie dropped what she was doing and ran to help. They splashed in the creek and hopped every which way, laughing at the chase. "Hey, look at that!" Billy shoved his catch in her hands and began to climb up the windmill, reaching for a paper caught half-way. The wood frame groaned, and a good-sized piece fell away.

"Careful!" Cassie gasped.

Billy got what he was after and scurried down. "Ought to get rid of that thing in a year or two. Chop it up for firewood."

He grinned at her, bright and happy, his cheeks flushed. Cassie's smile faltered. She hadn't told him she was leaving. He'd see the contract in the parlor. She'd tell him then.

He took the papers from her hands. "Thanks. I'll shut those doors to keep the wind out." Trotting to the barn, he called over his shoulder, "Cookie break coming up?"

"Sure thing." Her voice sounded odd, like the croak of a sick bird.

Guy drove off the road and parked behind a bushy mesquite, squeezing between it and the fence. The hood got scratched up, but that didn't matter. He got out and looked around. Everything was quiet, except for the wind in the trees.

He dropped the cans on the other side of the fence, jumped over, and with a can in each hand stepped into the woods. The sun was huge, a glaring yellow ball. He felt exposed under its eye, and crept from shadow to shadow, sometimes pressing flat against a tree trunk.

He made his way behind the old graveyard. Some headstones leaned over like they wanted to sink into the ground with whatever bones lay down there. He shuddered at the sight and moved away, not really believing in ghosts but not disbelieving, either. Especially since Sarah had come to visit so often, whispering like she did.

He stooped behind a thicket and peeked through the prickly stems. He was on a knoll, with the creek and house and barn below. The carport was empty. Sweet Jesus, empty, and her car nowhere in sight. Maybe luck was with him and Cassie wasn't home! Sunlight bounced off the front windows, so there was no telling if she was walking around inside. He hunkered down, taking a moment or two to think things out. It wouldn't be smart to go rushing in without proper caution.

It was somewhere around noon. He had forgotten his watch so was forced to guess by the position of the sun. The barn was pretty much in broad daylight, with skimpy shadows from the hills behind. There were a couple of trees near it, but still he'd be out in the open. Anybody with a pair of eyes could see him coming down the knoll and splashing through the creek to get there. He moved inside the edge of the woods, keeping low to the ground until he faced the barn. The doors were closed. The whole thing looked old as God, the timber gray and dried up, the roof sagging like it was going to collapse in on itself any moment.

Perfect.

He steeled himself for action. Once the Studebaker was destroyed, Billy wouldn't have any reason to come here. He'd forget it soon enough, forget college, forget Cassie. Everything would go back to the way it was.

Do it. Do it now, for Billy. He leaped up, hurtled down the slope, jumped into the creek and waded across, water up to his thighs, his mind blaring, *hurry, hurry, hurry,* the weight of the cans pulling his shoulders. The creek bottom was slippery, and he had to go easy and careful with sunlight glittering in his eyes. A turtle popped up out of nowhere and tangled with his legs. *Shit!* He wobbled, almost losing his balance, and staggered onto the shore with mud sucking at his feet.

He probably looked like a madman rising from the water, drenched and lurching across the meadow. *Move! Move!* A dozen or so steps more and he was on the far side of the barn. Dropping the cans, he leaned over, gasping. His pulse drummed in his head and his heart careened in his chest and his hands had the palsy.

Now! Now! Now! He unscrewed the lids with clumsy fingers and splashed the contents along the back and side and doors. By the time he was finished, he reeked of gasoline and his jeans were spattered with it. He replaced the lids and put the cans close by, where he could pick them up quickly when he made his escape.

He had a pocket full of matches, although one was all he needed. It flared in his fingers the moment before he tossed it. *Whoosh!* A giant snake of fire gobbled the wood and began to climb. He reeled back with a startled cry. Jesus, it happened fast! Before he could breathe the whole wall writhed and shrieked in the wind. God Almighty, who knew fire could *shriek*? Thick black smoke curled up and glowing embers rained all around, burning his scalp and arms and eating holes in his shirt.

God, it was beautiful! A glorious, roaring, red-blooming monster.

Cassie tugged at the baking sheet wedged behind a large pot in the bottom cabinet and the entire contents came tumbling out; pots, muffin tins, a sieve and a couple of lids clattered onto the linoleum floor. She rescued the baking sheet and shoved everything else back in willy-nilly. She planned to pack it all tomorrow, so why worry about neatness?

Bowls of dough waited on the counter – oatmeal raisin, peanut butter, chocolate chip – enough for dozens instead of one single boy. This was likely the last time she'd cook for him. The last time he'd sit at her table. The last time he'd work in the barn. Her days here were quickly coming to an end.

She reached for a bowl and glanced out the window.

The world stopped. She couldn't move, couldn't think, couldn't breathe.

Great clouds of smoke rose from the barn. Flames whipped by the wind licked the walls and doors and slithered over the roof.

"Billyyy!" The scream tore from the core of her being, lifting her off her feet and pushing her out the door. *"Billyyy!"* Oh God oh God oh God. She stumbled down the steps and fell on her knees, eyes riveted on the blazing horror. Up again, wailing, she ran. She ran. She ran. *"Billyyy!"* Her legs couldn't move fast enough. Her cries sucked into the fire, unheard.

"Billyyy!"

Guy appeared from the red-tinged air like a devil emerging from the bowels of hell. Red hair, red eyebrows, red reflected off of the scorpion belt buckle and the two gas cans he held.

Cassie didn't stop to wonder why he was here or what he carried. "It's Billy! Billy's in there!"

He gawked as if she had spouted gibberish.

She rushed toward the doors, the terrible heat pushing against her. "Oh, Jesus, how am I going to get around the flames?"

"Aaaaaaaa!" Guy dropped the cans and howled, shoving her aside. *"Aaaaaaaa!"* His howl went on and on and on as he hammered on the doors, as he kicked, as he found a handle through the smoke and pulled. Fire ate his sleeves and the hem of his jeans and ignited in his hair as the door swung open. "I'm coming, Billy!" he cried, "I'm coming!"

Cassie caught a glimpse of smoldering rafters, of embers swirling down to the car below, of the lantern beside it. Frantic bats, some with flaming wings, spewed from the blaze and scattered. Guy charged inside, his cries muffled, his arms reaching into the thickening haze like a player in a game of blind man's bluff.

"Miss Cassie!"

Cassie whirled toward Billy's voice. There he was, bounding off the porch. *Alive! Dear God, alive!* Her legs gave way and she sank onto the ground.

Billy knelt beside her. "Are you okay? What happened?"

"We... We thought..." She held onto him, struggling to speak. "Where were you?"

"In the bathroom."

"Your father..." She pointed to the barn.

"He's in there?" Billy jerked upright, his face ashen. "Dad! Dad!"

Whoomph! A huge glowing plume exploded from the opened door. Billy staggered backward and fell, landing on Cassie's legs. She caught him by the shoulders as the roof groaned and shuddered. "Don't look," she demanded, turning his face away. It wasn't the fire she hoped to spare him from seeing. It was Guy, bathed in flames and twitching a grotesque dying dance, sprawled over the hood of the Studebaker.

"No!" Billy wailed as the roof caved in, burying the car in an avalanche of sizzling rubble. "No! No!" He wrenched from her grasp and lunged toward the inferno. Cassie threw herself on his back, knocking him to the ground. He gasped, hands scrabbling at the dirt.

"It's too late! Too late!"

"Let me go!"

She wrapped her arms around him and held on for all she was worth. Sparks shot into the sky, spiraling in the air like poisonous hissing insects before spattering on the ground. Small flares erupted at their feet as Billy pressed his fists against his cheeks, sobbing with his mouth wide open.

A grinding crack ripped the air above them; the windmill quivered and grumbled as blazing fingers crawled up the legs of the rickety frame and slapped at the blades.

"Move! Move!" Cassie yelled, urging Billy to his feet and pulling him along, the blistering light reflected in his eyes. "Hurry!"

He stopped abruptly. "Those are gas cans on the ground over there. I don't remember you having any gas cans."

"C'mon!"

"Dad keeps cans like those in the shop."

"Billy!" she tugged at his hand.

"It was him, wasn't it? He wanted to burn the barn down, didn't he? Oh, Jesus! Stupid! Stupid! How could he be so stupid? Why did he go inside? What was he thinking?"

"Let's go and talk later!"

"Why aren't the firemen here? They should be here! Did you call them?"

"Not yet. Now move, damn it!"

"I got to do something. I got to do something. I got..." He paused in mid-sentence, then turned and ran for the hose, coiled beside the garden fence like a snake basking in the sun.

By the time she caught up he was already attaching it to the spigot.

"I'll do this." She grabbed the hose, wanting him safe inside. "You go make that call."

He pushed her hand away and turned on the water. Pipes rattled and mist spurted from green-encrusted joints and water arched from his grasp, pitiful against such an enemy. He looked straight at her, his jaws clenched, his expression fierce, and she realized that this beloved boy was, for this moment at least, a boy no longer. And so she left him there, shoulders squared, freckled face seared by the heat, battling the firestorm with nothing but a garden hose.

She rushed into the house, stumbled over Strudel, grabbed the phone. Static hissed in her ear. Damn it to heaven, static! She would have to use the cell.

The only place she could get reception was the one she dreaded beyond any other.

Thank God she had thought to charge the phone before her trip to Fredericksburg! She tucked it in her pocket and hurried through the rooms and out the back door, hesitating at the base of Mount Bubba. It loomed above her, jagged and steep, reaching into a gray-smudged sky. The contractor Phil Jameson had used his phone from the knoll by the pond, so she knew a connection was possible if she climbed high enough. She only had to put one foot in front of the other. And. Climb. Up.

Smoke curled and slithered along the crest like a malevolent fog. Rubble crunched under her shoes as she began the ascent. She kept low to the ground, grasping onto boulders or brush to keep from slipping. The air felt thick as mud oozing down her throat, the taste of ash on her tongue. Up she climbed, and up, the wind hot on her cheeks and tearing at her hair, the fire raging and bellowing from below. One more step. Another. Another.

The hillside wavered, undulating like a scab-crusted ocean. She closed her eyes and pressed flat against the earth, feeling it solid beneath her. The old fear hovered beside her like an incubus lover, cold fingers caressing her limbs and crushing her lungs and sucking her breath. The images awaited: the yawning cliff, the figure splayed helplessly below, her red hiking boots teetering over the edge, the *whap-whap-whap* of the helicopter blades. All waiting in the darkness behind her eyes, waiting in the haze curling toward her, waiting for her next step up Mount Bubba.

Billy screamed. Cassie's eyes flew open as the windmill shrieked and toppled, flames trailing in its wake. It crashed to the ground and shattered, throwing thousands of sparks into a whirlwind of exploding stars. Billy pranced around the meadow with the hose, yelling and dousing erupting fires that blossomed like exotic wildflowers. He didn't see the cinders bursting into life in the Emperor Tree behind him or multiplying on the rooftop.

"Billy, the tree! The roof!"

He didn't hear. Cassie glanced at the phone, hands shaking, the world tipping to its side. Still no reception. She'd have to go higher, and so dared a quick look upward. The crest was obliterated, as if the mount had thrust into a bank of storm clouds.

I can do this. I have to do this.

She took a shuddering breath and began, walking half-upright, grabbing whatever was at hand for balance. Her breath grated in her ears, a rapid, panicked rasp. She fell to her knees but kept on going, grasping fistfuls of earth to pull herself forward, stones scraping her legs and elbows. *If I made it up Hawk's hill, I can make it up this one.* It became a mantra, whispered over and over: *If I made it up Hawk's hill, I can make it up this one. If I made it up Hawk's hill, I can make it up this one.* The passing of time had no meaning. It could have been seconds or minutes or an eon until the phone signaled a reception. She dialed, crying, "Fire! Fire! Fire!" until she realized a remote voice was telling her to speak calmly. She fumbled over words as if they were strange to her, as if she rarely spoke English. The voice asked questions and she tried to make her lips and tongue respond, her gaze riveted to the mayhem erupting in what had been her home.

"Fire! Fire! The barn, the windmill, the house! Everything, everything!"

Hawk sat on a stool in front of a blank canvas, his back to the windows. Light played upon the glaring nakedness of a rectangular piece of white nothingness. Inspiration had taken a holiday and left him high and dry, which seemed to be the norm lately.

Yeller was unusually restless and paced from room to room, toenails clicking on the wood floor. Hawk sighed. Maybe what he needed was some peace and quiet. "Alright, that's enough. Out you go." He opened the back door, shooing Yeller into the yard, and smelled an acrid bitterness that usually came with autumn. "Odd time of the year to burn leaves," he muttered, and stepped outside.

Yeller scampered around the side of the house, nose twitching. Hawk followed, eyes sweeping the view, expecting to see a puff of gray somewhere. What he found was something else entirely: a churning dark cloud rising from the hill he had walked upon only hours ago.

"Cassie!"

The moment he cried her name, he heard the distant siren. Seconds later he was in the pickup and roaring down the hillside through a tunnel of overhanging limbs, craning to glimpse a piece of the hidden sky. When he shot from the shadows onto the road, there it was: billowing smoke. The wind grabbed it and threw it around like a torn curtain.

Dear God, Cassie! Cassie!

ꙮ

She had only a vague recollection of sliding down Mount Bubba, of her panic when she couldn't see Billy, of rushing through the side door calling his name. "Here! The bedroom!" he yelled, his voice muffled. She clasped a hand over her mouth and nose; the air was hot and viscous and seared her lungs. The fire crackled as it ate the porch and roof. The hallway was still untouched; through the parlor door at the end she could see flames latch onto the velvet drapes. In the choking dark she found Billy partly under the bed, reaching for Strudel. She threw a quilt over his head and, with the cat safe in his arms, they stumbled into the great room and outdoors.

"The diary!" she turned and ran back. The smoke was denser now, creeping along the ceiling, pushing her down. Coughing, she felt her way along the walls and furniture like a blind woman: the doorway, the footboard, the dresser. The diary. The framed photo of Mimi and Lillian and the grandfather Cassie never knew. Mimi's letterbox. She snatched them all and crawled toward daylight and safety.

Hawk found her holding Billy, her cheeks smeared with ashes, her hair wild around her face. She turned to him and he tried to speak but the words wouldn't come. He opened his arms and embraced them both, drawing them to his heart as the siren grew closer.

Home Among the Hills

Spring, 2002

THE FIELD RIPPLED WITH BLUEBONNETS EXCEPT FOR A RAGGED PATCH WHERE THE barn had once stood. Cassie let her mind wander, picturing again the gray-weathered walls and sagging roof, the Studebaker inside, the windmill nearby. She sighed and looked away, reminded of a fragment from the Book of Psalms: *For the wind passeth over it, and it is gone; and the place thereof shall know it no more.*

The patch had a larger twin in the meadow, a rambling affair that marked the former boundaries of the house. The fire had destroyed every scrap of wood from the front steps to the rear hall. The porch, parlor, kitchen, bedroom and bath were gone. The Emperor Tree was gone, too, although the big knotty roots, too deeply burrowed into the earth to remove, still reached for the creek. A sapling grew amid them, slender limbs lifting toward the sun.

But the original stone house remained. It had risen from the ashes, standing now as it had stood more than a hundred sixty-odd years ago: the wide stone porch, the iron heart-shaped lock on a carved pecan door much like the original, the flagstone floors and limestone walls and rambling fireplace that still moaned in the wind, the shadowed basement. And the many-windowed bedroom on top of it all, new glass sparkling in the afternoon light.

Cassie paused under the sapling, proud of all that had been accomplished in the two years since that fateful day. What Hawk called "good structural bones" had made it possible. The stone foundation and walls were solid, and the ceiling beams singed but strong at the core. Although a kitchen and bath were added in the back, the new construction blended in so well Cassie felt as though she had stepped into the past and gazed at the house through the eyes of her ancestors.

"Cassiemom!" Billy hugged her around the waist, his cheeks flushed. "Isn't this a great day for a housewarming? So many people!" After another hug, he ran toward a rowdy game of tag football, the taunts and laughter ringing in the air.

Cassiemom. His name for her since the moment of his adoption. She watched as he jumped into the melee, her heart going with him.

Billy was right. It *was* a great day, a late afternoon made perfect for the celebration of a restored home by the scent of honeysuckle and gauzy clouds drifting toward a westward sun. An assortment of vehicles were parked on the far side of the creek under the protection of Justin's archangel or spilled past the gate onto the road. Friends streamed over the bridge, piled food on the picnic tables, set up lawn chairs, chatted with Pete as he worked his barbeque magic on the oil drum grill.

"Hi there!" Tatty ambled toward her. A headpiece of ivy, flowers and ribbons bobbed on her tousled hair like the nest of a crazy bird, and her bright flowing skirt dragged on the bluebonnets.

"Look at you, Tatty. I swear, you must have been a gypsy in a former life."

"And you a magician for bringing this house back to life. It's so welcoming I want to move right in."

"Then pack up and do it! Except for Billy's room upstairs. He's already painted his name on the door in big red letters."

"Thanks, but my own place suits me, tumbledown as it is with creepers over it all. I like feeling as if I'm part of the woods, maybe a quaint sort of plant. When I die you'll probably find I've taken root and sprouted tiny flowers."

"You're half-way there, what with that concoction on your head."

"For you." Tatty took it off and handed it to Cassie. "Something festive to celebrate the occasion."

Pleased, Cassie put it on; the long streamers fluttered against her cheeks and the back of her neck. "I must look like a maypole."

"What's a maypole without dancers?" Tatty's face creased in a mischievous grin as she gripped Cassie by the hands and whirled her around, the ribbons flying and the gypsy skirt swaying with the motion. "Hang on!"

Cassie laughed, breathless while the world reeled past – the house, the lawn chairs and tables and friends mingled on the meadow, the woods beyond, Billy. From the corner of her eye she glimpsed Hawk and the familiar lope of his stride as he neared, and for a fleeting moment she was glad for the fire. It had reshaped and renewed her life.

He wrapped them both in an embrace, then lightly kissed Cassie, his lips tasting of beer and salt. "Took me aback for a moment when I saw you dancing around with that crown of wildflowers in your hair, as if your portrait had come back to haunt me."

"No such luck. You're stuck with the real thing." She was about to say more but heard Billy shout, and looked toward his voice.

"Our boy's doing well, isn't he?" Hawk murmured.

Cassie nodded. There he was, cutting up with his pals in that helter-skelter game, sun glinting in his copper hair. You'd never know by the looks of him the grief he had gone through, or the guilt he had tried to shoulder for his father's death.

"It's not come easy. But he's happy, I think. And growing more so as the days pass."

"Must be contagious." Tatty's dark eyes glittered. "You two carry on like somebody slipped a grinning potion in that wedding cake."

"It's your fault," Cassie teased, "for waving sprigs of sage over us as a blessing. That did the trick."

"Powerful stuff, sage. We've been hoodwinked." Hawk brushed his lips against Cassie's forehead. "I've got to help set up the band. Billy wrote a song for today, and he and Pete have been practicing on the sly. They want me to jump in with the flute after a verse or two."

"Can it wait a bit? I want to show you something first. Both of you." Tatty lifted her skirt and scurried up the rocky porch steps, then pushed the heavy door and disappeared inside.

Cassie lingered on the porch. It felt strange to stand there, as if she were once again in the back hall of the house as it used to be, and should she turn around she'd see the wooden walls behind her, the old hall and doorways leading to Mimi's bedroom and the parlor. On the far right would be a side door, the corner cluttered with mismatched rubber galoshes.

"Daydreaming?" Hawk asked.

She smiled and followed him into the great room, bare except for a table and bench from an antique shop in Fredericksburg. Light from the window glittered upon the floor, as if flecks of silver were embedded in the stone. It was a peaceful place, no longer burdened by the specter of Jed with his wide-brimmed hat and vengeful spirit. The fire seemed to have consumed those, too – as well as her fear of heights.

"There," Tatty said, pointing to a fabric-covered hump on the table. "It was too big for me to wrap so I hid it under a serape." Hawk pulled the cloth aside, revealing what at first glance resembled the crystal-laden nest of an eagle.

"It's gorgeous," Cassie said. "A wreath?"

"A housewarming gift for your front door." Tatty stroked the entwined stems. "These sturdier twigs are from your old oak. The random splintery ones are fragments from the house."

"Oh, Tatty. It's wonderful."

"Memories are interwoven inside." Tatty's gnarled fingers explored each item she mentioned. "Blue and white pottery chips…"

"Mimi's favorite cookie jar!"

"…. A spoon angel from your porch chimes. A piece of wing from Justin's cherub in the oak tree."

"And the sparkly crystal pieces. Shards of glass?"

"Yes, from the windows. I was careful to smooth the edges."

"They look like tears," Cassie whispered.

"And this?" Hawk fingered a flat piece of wood the size of his palm. A vine was carved on one edge, and the petal of a flower. "There's writing on the back."

"It's from the mantle clock!" Cassie exclaimed, her eyes misting. "See the Old German lettering? *Liebe heute und für immer.*"

"Sure would like to know what it means," Hawk murmured.

"*Love now and forever.* Berta translated it for me once."

"Couldn't be more perfect!" Hawk hurried outside, saying, "I'll find a nail and hang it this very minute."

"Dear Tatty!" Cassie embraced her, the woman's bony shoulders sharp against her own. "You must have spent ages sifting through the rubble and lacing it all together."

"Sometimes things weave themselves. I just follow their voices." Tatty pointed to the clock fragment. "Something told me to pick up this piece, although I didn't know what it was or what the writing meant. *Love now and forever.* That's your blessing, yours and Hawk's, a gift from the spirits of this place."

"*Cass-aie*!" Nan's elfin face peered through the doorway. "Someone's asking for you."

"Who?"

"She didn't say."

A sharp voice snapped, "For heaven's sake, *move.* You're blocking the doorway." Nan stepped aside for a slender woman in stiletto sandals and a linen outfit that screamed *couture*. She carried a huge bouquet of silk flowers dyed in hues that nature never imagined, artfully arranged in an oriental cloisonné vase.

"My God," she moaned, "it's the same wretched place."

"Mother! I didn't think you'd come!"

"Me either. Where can I put this thing? It's damned heavy."

"Here on the table." Tatty picked up the wreath and left without another word, nodding at Lillian as she passed.

Cassie helped set the vase down gently. It really was damned heavy – and, Cassie had to admit, damned beautiful in an arty, artificial way better suited to a fashionable uptown penthouse.

"Why didn't you ask someone to carry this for you?"

"Can't trust these yokels to handle a floral arrangement or vase that wasn't bought at the local food mart. And who was that woman? My God, the way she was dressed, you'd think we were at a costume party."

"You should know. You saw her at my wedding, remember? She's my mother-in-law, Tatty."

"How awful."

"She's a marvelous, caring person and a talented artist."

"Oh. Well, that explains it. Artists are notoriously eccentric. As you probably know, since you married one."

"Good Lord, Mother! Why did you come? You could have insulted me, my family and friends on the phone just as readily."

Lillian paled and stilled for a moment. "Old habits, I guess."

"Seriously, why are you here? You hate this house and everything for miles around."

"But I don't hate *you*. I came for you."

"You'll probably get antsy and leave, like you did at my wedding. So why bother?"

"I wanted to see you. Just to see you." Her voice faltered, and she sat abruptly on the bench. "It really is ugly, isn't it, that bouquet? Those gaudy flowers don't belong here. No more than I do."

She sagged, as if air had leaked from her body like a punctured balloon. *She looks tired,* Cassie thought with a start, *and lots older.* Cracks appeared under the skillfully applied makeup, the skin crinkling like thin wrapping paper.

"I tried to stay at your wedding," Lillian blurted. "I wanted to. I tried. But I couldn't."

"Another man, another place calling you elsewhere?"

"Just let me say this and be over with it!" Lillian snapped. "I sat on that hard wooden pew in that plain little church and saw your joy. Yours and his, so strong it hit me in the stomach." She gulped and quieted, clenching her fists in her lap. "You found it, didn't you? A second chance at love. The kind that's true. The kind I've wanted for myself and can't find and likely never will. And I guess I couldn't face the loss. So I ran." Lillian tried to laugh, but it wavered and faded away. "Selfish, I know. But the truth."

Cassie gaped at her mother, this impossible, soul-crumpled woman, and the anger hidden in the corners of her heart slipped away. She sat beside Lillian and reached for her hand.

"I'm glad you're here, Mom."

Lillian straightened, lifted her chin, and looked around. "So when are you going to move in?"

"Never. We'll stay where we are now, in the house Hawk built before we met. I can hardly wait to show it to you, so high up on a hill you can see the horizon all around. It's lovely there, and peaceful."

"Then why the hell are you hanging onto this dump? You could make a good mint selling it. The land is probably worth a fortune."

"Because I love this so-called dump. It'll be here for Billy whenever he wants to use it."

"So it will just sit here until then?"

"I'm thinking of turning it into a retreat for artists, writers, and such. Or a bed and breakfast. Something special."

"My daughter, the innkeeper," Lillian grumbled. "You could do better."

Cassie laughed. She couldn't help it. Her mother was beyond redemption. "Yes, and in another few months the owner of a boutique specializing in Southwestern Indian art. I've found the perfect spot in Fredericksburg."

"Well, I hope it works out for you." Lillian pursed her lips and gazed through the opened doorway. "Look at those people milling about. You know them all?"

"Of course. They're my friends. Why?"

"There are... so many."

"I've been lucky."

"It's not just luck!" Lillian blurted. "You're smart and kind and loving, and deserve every good thing life has to offer. You are everything I admire, everything I wish I could be." Her eyes reddened, and she rushed on, her fingers gripping Cassie's hand. "If Hawk looks half as good close up as he did from that pew, he's handsome as sin. Women must be drawn to him like starving ants at a picnic. Have there been... other women? Adversaries, so to speak?"

"Only one I know of, before we married. Rebecca Stanch. I liked her."

"Never trust a woman with a Biblical name. All pure on the surface and a devil underneath. Does she live here?"

"Not any more. She works in an art gallery in Greenwich Village."

"Good for her, stepping out into the world. I've always liked New York. Maybe I'll move there myself. Find a little apartment, enjoy the theatres and shopping, and forget men. I've had enough of them."

"Forget men? *You*? That'll be the day."

Lillian laughed. "You're right, as always." She stood and brushed her skirt. "Now take me to that husband of yours. And Billy, too. It's time I met your family."

"*Our* family," Cassie said, putting her arm around her mother's shoulders. "*Our* family."

"What a wonderful surprise!" Cassie rushed to meet Berta as the old woman walked over the bridge. She was plump as always, with wispy gray hair wound into a knot on the top of her head and magnified hazel eyes huge and smiling behind thick round glasses.

"Berta! I'm so glad to see you!"

A younger woman followed, holding a large tray of pastries smothered in plastic wrap. Cassie recognized her immediately, the sharp-boned face and upturned grin a duplicate of Justin's. "Mother couldn't stay away," Victoria said with a chuckle. "If I hadn't been around, she would have hopped in the car and driven here herself."

"I wish I had," Berta said. "You drive too fast."

"Sixty-five miles an hour is hardly warp speed, Mother. Now why not go sit down? It's been a long trip and you're probably tired."

"See how she bosses me around?" Berta grumbled as Cassie walked with her to a chair. "How's my Strudel? I miss him sometimes."

"He's happy and fat and lazy, and likes to sit on the windowsill and intimidate the birds. I spoil him terribly."

"And you? Are you happy? Although I don't need to ask. It's there, in your eyes. You glow like a candle in a darkened room."

"Sometimes I feel as though I'm living in a fairytale."

"Happily ever after really is possible, you know." She reached up and patted Cassie's cheek. "Like me and Justin. I treasure every moment we spent together. I wish that for you, too."

"Thank you." Cassie wanted to say something more, but couldn't find the words to explain the fullness of her heart.

"Hi, Mrs. Grumm!" Billy waved both hands from across the meadow, scissoring them in the air like a referee.

"Oh my, but he looks grand!" Berta exclaimed and waved back. "You wrote that he has enough put away for college?"

"More than enough, thanks to Guy."

"How so?"

"Guy willed everything he owned to Billy – house, shop, truck, you name it. The profits from their sale guarantee that he can go to school wherever he wants for as long as he wants."

"I'm glad. I wish Justin were here to see it." Berta smiled, her expression wistful. "He would have loved the way things turned out with you and Hawk and Billy together, and how beautiful the house is, like it's reborn."

Shadows crept across the land, silent companions to the deepening sky. The meadow rang with laughter and the babble of conversation as folk mingled among cluttered picnic tables and scattered lawn chairs, the air redolent with the pungent tang of barbeque sauce and a smorgasbord of foods. The empty space that had once housed the parlor now served as the stage of the bluegrass band, Razorbacks. Everything was set up, ready and waiting: Pete's keyboard, Ed's banjo, various fiddles and guitars, a bass, a drum set, and Hawk's flute, there on a tall stool.

Pete tossed his spattered cooking apron aside, walked through the crowd to the keyboard, and banged out some notes along the line of *Ta daaaa! Ta daaaa!* "Draw up and gather 'round!" he hollered, grinning through his beard. "Time for some celebratin'!"

And gather around they did, some arranging chairs in rows and others reclining on the ground in front. Members of the band settled in for a good-time gig, the sky behind them ablaze in pink and purple rays as the golden sun melted into the horizon. Hawk perched on the stool and hooked his boot heels on the bottom rail as he had done when Cassie first saw him playing the flute at Smithy's Barbeque. His eyes were hidden then as they were now, by the tilt of his head and brim of his hat. And now, like then, she felt his spirit reaching for her.

"Hit it, boys!" Pete pounded the keys. The music exploded, bright and sparkling, bursting with joy and echoing among the hills. Cassie couldn't help but laugh, it was so good. Everything, everything, everything was so good she felt as though she would lift off the ground and soar, drifting overhead like a leaf carried by the wind.

Then she noticed a single guitar propped against an empty stool. Billy should be there, playing along with everyone else. A hunch made her look upward, at the bedroom. His face hovered behind an opened window, his melancholy gaze lingering at the bare patch that had once held the barn.

She hurried up the porch and through the house, familiar with that inward look of his. Her footsteps pattered along the narrow winding staircase and through the door with his name emblazoned on it in red paint. And there he was, leaning on a window sill, lit by the setting sun. She put an arm around him, amazed at how tall he'd grown, how sweet and precious he was, this boy, her son.

She didn't speak, understanding the sorrow that came and went in his heart for love of his father, for regrets and loss. She understood, too, the inner strength of him, and his resilient spirit. So she hugged him lightly, glad when he smiled and turned toward the sunset.

"It's pretty, isn't it?" he said, as the sky blushed a fierce rose-red.

"Got a surprise for y'all!" Pete cried. "Somethin' special for today and for that little lady standin' by the window." He jerked his thumb at Cassie. "Right beside her is the talented young man who wrote it. Billy, come on down and strut your stuff! Let's get that song of yours on the road!"

Billy laughed suddenly, a bright, quick splash of sound. "I got to go, Cassiemom! You stay here where I can see you, and listen real good." Then he was gone, his feet clattering down the steps.

She leaned through the window, a warm breeze lifting her hair as Billy burst into view. He glanced up, grinned, and grabbed his guitar.

"Let's do it!" Pete's fingers ran up and down the keys, then lit into a bouncing, gospel-tender rhythm as Billy sang:

This here ol' house
Sprang up renewed
Walls and timbers holdin' love inside.
Angels watchin',
Spirits movin',
As years go by, as seasons change.

This here ol' house
Sprang up renewed,
Walls and timbers holdin' love inside.
Give it blessings
Give it grace,
Give it memories of lives well lived.

"Hoo-yah!" Pete leaped up from his chair. "Everybody join in! Sing along with us, c'mon! Play it, boys!"

Hawk looked up at Cassie and smiled, his oak-green eyes reflecting the soft glow of twilight. She smiled in return, every inch of her smiled, every molecule of her soul. His eyes caressed her across the distance while he played and she sang, her voice joining all the others:

This here ol' house
Sprang up renewed,
Walls and timbers holdin' love inside.
Angels watchin',
Spirits movin',
As years go by, as seasons change.

Cassie felt something inside herself expand, as if she were enveloping every heart that beat nearby, every breath exhaled, every smile given, every hand extended. Her love opened to them all, sweeping over the field and creek and woods and hills, flying over the distant plateaus, and joining the sun as it transformed day into a star-jeweled night.

THE END

Author's Note

Willow City Loop is a private Ranch Road near Fredericksburg, Texas, that wanders for thirteen miles through a spectacular landscape of steep hills, deep canyons, and low-lying meadows. In spring, if it rains, the fields are ablaze with wildflowers, especially bluebonnets. Any description of Willow City or the Loop in *Hidden Shadows* that may seem at odds with fact is the fault of my muse, which allowed inspiration to lead the way.

Pete's Gas 'n Grub came from my imagination, but Knot in the Loop Saloon did not. It's located in Eckert, only minutes from the Loop. Described as "part Saloon and part Wild West Museum," the bar is even more colorful and welcoming than described in *Hidden Shadows*. I want to thank the wait staff for graciously allowing me to wander around, take photographs, and absorb the unique ambiance.

The "olden" part of Cassie's house, made of stone and wood, was loosely fashioned after the Kammlah Home and Store displayed at the Pioneer Museum Complex in Fredericksburg. Other buildings in this amazing museum dedicated to the history of German Texas life brought Cassie's barn and windmill to life, and birthed the cottage of Justin and Berta Grumm.

Fredericksburg is a unique, delightful town with a variety of restaurants and shops – but Smithy's Barbeque rests entirely in my mind, as does Grady's Goods and Betters. However, the Whistle Pic Gallery is really there, a lovely and charming place. Rebecca Stanch, of course, never truly walked those rooms or wandered among the exhibits, except in my imagination.

Thornwood Gallery in Houston, Texas, is exactly the sort of gallery in which Hawk would be proud to have his paintings exhibited. I want to thank Zelma Legendre for allowing him to do so within these pages.

A heart-felt thank you to Daedalus, my writer's critique group par excellence, for perceptive insights and suggestions: Florence Weinberg, Ned Bailey, Bill Stephens, Cindy Massey, Jim Peyton, and Diana Lopez. Many thanks to my sister, Suzi Harkey, for unwavering support, to brother Ed Shuler for computer wizardry throughout the years, and to brother John Shuler for loving books and saying good things about mine.

And a special thanks to my mother, Linda Lay Shuler. I found among her many writings the poem, *Wishes*, which is in this book.

About the author

Linda Lucretia Shuler wrote her first story when she was six, *Koko the Monkey,* which she still has tucked into a drawer. Her first published work was a poem she composed while in the third grade. Since then her stories and poems have appeared in anthologies and literary journals, and a handful of her plays have been produced in schools and community theatres.

Linda received a BFA in theatre from the University of Texas, and an MA in theatre from Trinity University while in residence at the Dallas Theatre Center. She taught theatre arts in college and high school for three decades, loving every moment and directing nearly a hundred plays in the process. She also wrote theatre arts curriculum K-12 for Houston ISD, conducted numerous workshops, and performed in community theatres.

Hidden Shadows takes place in Willow City, a small community snuggled in the ruggedly beautiful Texas Hill Country less than two hours from her home in San Antonio. Several other manuscripts are in the works, reaching across the genres. These include a prequel to *Hidden Shadows,* plays, and a collection of poems and a half-dozen different story ideas demanding attention.

Linda enjoys participating in Toastmasters International, writer organizations, critique groups, and book clubs. She continues her love of theatre, delights in watching the birds flocking outside her office window, and is an enthusiastic fan of San Antonio's championship basketball team, the Spurs.